Out to Canaan

Other Mitford Books by Jan Karon

AT HOME IN MITFORD

A LIGHT IN THE WINDOW

THESE HIGH, GREEN HILLS

The Mitford Years

Out to Canaan

JAN KARON

Viking

VIKING
Published by the Penguin Group
Penguin Books USA Inc., 375 Hudson Street,
New York, New York 10014, U.S.A.
Penguin Books Ltd, 27 Wrights Lane, London W8 5TZ, England
Penguin Books Australia Ltd, Ringwood, Victoria, Australia
Penguin Books Canada Ltd, 10 Alcorn Avenue,
Toronto, Ontario, Canada M4V 3B2
Penguin Books (N.Z.) Ltd, 182–190 Wairau Road,
Auckland 10, New Zealand

Penguin Books Ltd, Registered Offices:
Harmondsworth, Middlesex, England

First published in 1997 by Viking Penguin,
a division of Penguin Books USA Inc.

1 3 5 7 9 10 8 6 4 2

Publisher's Note
This is a work of fiction. Names, characters, places, and incidents
either are the product of the author's imagination or are used fictitiously,
and any resemblance to actual persons, living or dead, events, or
locales is entirely coincidental.

LIBRARY OF CONGRESS CATALOGING IN PUBLICATION DATA
Karon, Jan, date.
Out to Canaan / Jan Karon.
p.   cm.—(The Mitford years)
ISBN 0-670-87485-X
I. Title.   II. Series: Karon, Jan, date.   Mitford years.
PS3561.A678O78   1997
813'.54—dc21   97-5867

This book is printed on acid-free paper.
∞

Printed in the United States of America
Set in Adobe Garamond   ·   Designed by Francesca Belanger

Illustrations by Hal Just

For all families
who struggle to forgive
and be forgiven

❧

*"I will restore unto you
the days the locusts
have eaten . . ."*

Joel 2:25

ACKNOWLEDGMENTS

My warmest thanks to:

Candace Freeland; Barry Setzer; Joe Edmisten; Carolyn McNeely; Dr. Margaret Federhart; Fr. Scott Oxford; Jerry Walsh; Blowing Rock BP; Crystal Coffey; Mary Lentz; Jane Hodges; Jim Atkinson; Derald West; Loonis McGlohan; Laura Watts; David Watts; Rev. Gale Cooper and my friends at St. John's; Rev. Jim Trollinger and my friends at Jamestown United Methodist; Fr. Russell Johnson and my friends at St. Paul's; Roald and Marjorie Carlson; W. David Holden; Alex Gabbard; Kay O'Neill; Dr. Richard Chestnutt; Everett Barrineau and all my friends on the Viking Penguin sales force; Aunt Wilma Argo; The Fellowship of Christ, The Saviour; Charles Davant, III; Posie Dauphine; Chuck Meltsner; Kenny Johnson; Fr. Richard Bass; Rev. Richard Holshouser; Christine Hillis; Danilo Ragogna; Dr. Rosemary Horowitz; Helen Horowitz; Susan Weinberg; Sarah Cole; and Tim Knight.

Special thanks to Judy Burns; Jerry Torchia; Dan Blair, a national umpire staff member of the Amateur Softball Association; Flyin' George Ronan of Free Spirit Aviation; Dr. Bunky Davant, Mitford's attending physician; Tony diSanti, Mitford's legal counsel; Alex Hallmark, Mitford's tireless realtor; and all the wonderful readers and booksellers who are helping put the little town with the big heart on the map.

Contents

Out to Canaan

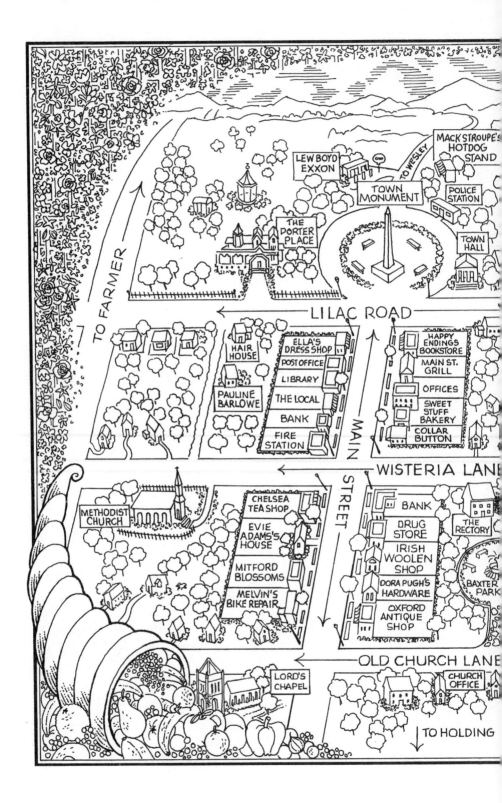

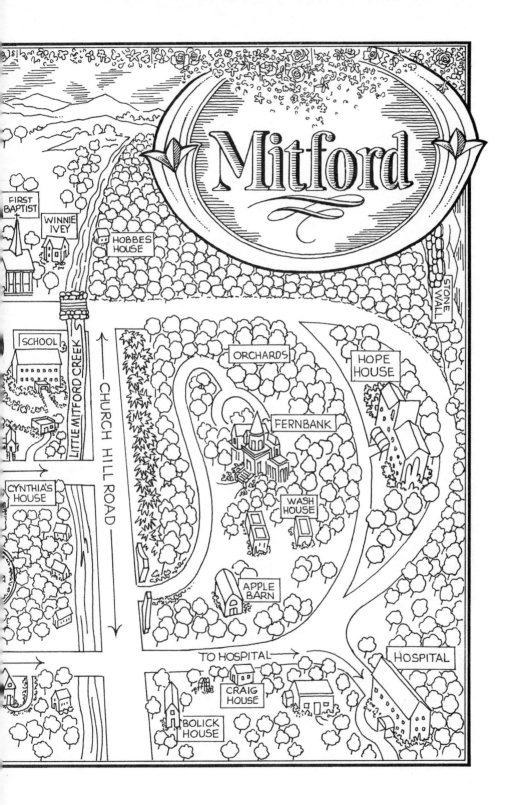

A Tea and a Half

The indoor plants were among the first to venture outside and breathe the fresh, cold air of Mitford's early spring.

Eager for a dapple of sunlight, starved for the revival of mountain breezes, dozens of begonias and ferns, Easter lilies and Wandering Jews were set out, pot-bound and listless, on porches throughout the village.

As the temperature soared into the low fifties, Winnie Ivey thumped three begonias, a sullen gloxinia, and a Boston fern onto the back steps of the house on Lilac Road, where she was now living. Remembering the shamrock, which was covered with aphids, she fetched it from the kitchen and set it on the railing.

"There!" she said, collecting a lungful of the sharp, pure air. "That ought to fix th' lot of you."

When she opened the back door the following morning, she was stricken at the sight. The carefully wintered plants had been turned to mush by a stark raving freeze and minor snow that also wrenched any notion of early bloom from the lilac bushes.

It was that blasted puzzle she'd worked until one o'clock in the morning, which caused her to forget last night's weather news. There she'd sat like a moron, her feet turning to ice as the temperature plummeted, trying to figure out five letters across for a grove of trees.

Racked with guilt, she consoled herself with the fact that it had, at least, been a chemical-free way to get rid of aphids.

At the hardware, Dora Pugh shook her head and sighed. Betrayed by yesterday's dazzling sunshine, she had done display windows with live baby chicks, wire garden fencing, seeds, and watering cans. Now she might as well haul the snow shovels back and do a final clearance on salt for driveways.

Coot Hendrick collected his bet of five dollars and an RC Cola from Lew Boyd. "Ain't th' first time and won't be th' last you'll see snow in May," he said, grinning. Lew Boyd hated it when Coot grinned, showing his stubs for teeth. He mostly hated it that, concerning weather in Mitford, the skeptics, cynics, and pessimists were usually right.

"Rats!" said Cynthia Kavanagh, who had left a wet scatter rug hanging over the rectory porch rail. Lifting it off the rail, she found it frozen as a popsicle and able to stand perfectly upright.

Father Timothy Kavanagh, rector at the Chapel of our Lord and Savior, had never heard such moaning and groaning about spring's tedious delay, and encountered it even in Happy Endings Bookstore, where, on yet another cold, overcast morning, he picked up a volume entitled *Hummingbirds in the Garden*.

"Hummingbirds?" wailed young Hope Winchester, ringing the sale. "*What* hummingbirds? I suppose you think a hummingbird would dare stick its beak into this arctic tundra, this endless twilight, this . . . this *villatic barbican?*"

"Villatic barbican" was a phrase she had learned only yesterday from a book, and wanted to use it before she forgot it. She knew the rector from Lord's Chapel was somebody she could use such words with—he hadn't flinched when she said "empirical" only last week, and seemed to know exactly what she was talking about.

While everyone else offered lamentations exceeding those of the prophet Jeremiah, the rector felt smugly indifferent to complaints that spring would never come. He had to admit, however, that last

Sunday was one of the few times he'd conducted an Easter service in long johns and ski socks.

Turning up his collar, he leaned into a driving wind and headed toward the office.

Hadn't winter dumped ice, snow, sleet, hail, and rainstorms on the village since late October? Hadn't they been blanketed by fog so thick you could cut it with a dull knife, time and time again?

With all that moisture seeping into the ground for so many long months, didn't this foretell the most glorious springtime in years? And wasn't that, after all, worth the endless assault?

"Absolutely!" he proclaimed aloud, trucking past the Irish Woolen Shop. "No doubt about it!"

"See there?" said Hessie Mayhew, peering out the store window. "It's got Father Tim talking to himself, it's that bad." She sighed. "They say if sunlight doesn't get to your pineal glands for months on end, your sex drive quits."

Minnie Lomax, who was writing sale tags for boiled wool sweaters, looked up and blinked. "What do you know about pineal glands?" She was afraid to ask what Hessie might know about sex drive.

"What does anybody know about pineal glands?" asked Hessie, looking gloomy.

Uncle Billy Watson opened his back door and, without leaving the threshold, lifted the hanging basket off the nail and hauled it inside.

"Look what you've gone and done to that geranium!" snapped his wife of nearly fifty years. "I've petted that thing the winter long, and now it's dead as a doornail."

The old man looked guilt-stricken. "B'fore I hung it out there, hit was already gone south!"

"Shut my mouth? Did you say shut my mouth?" Miss Rose, who refused to wear hearing aids, glared at him.

"I said *gone south*! Dead! Yeller leaves!"

He went to the kitchen radiator and thumped the hanging basket on top. "There!" he said, disgusted with trying to have a garden in a climate like this. "That'll fire it up again."

The rector noted the spears of hosta that had congregated in beds outside the church office. Now, there, as far as spring was concerned, was something you could count on. Hosta was as sturdy a plant as you could put in the ground. Like the postman, neither sleet nor snow could drive it back. Once out of the ground, up it came, fiercely defiant—only, of course, to have its broad leaves shredded like so much Swiss cheese by Mitford's summer hail.

"It's a jungle out there," he sighed, unlocking his office door.

§

After the snow flurry and freeze came a day of rain followed by a sudden storm of sleet that pecked against the windows like a flock of house sparrows.

His wife, he noted, looked pale. She was sitting at the study window, staring at the infernal weather and chewing her bottom lip. She was also biting the cuticle of her thumb, wrapping a strand of hair around one finger, tapping her foot, and generally amusing herself. He, meanwhile, was reading yet another new book and doing something productive.

A low fire crackled on the hearth.

"Amazing!" he said. "You'd never guess one of the things that attracts butterflies."

"I don't have a clue," said Cynthia, appearing not to want one, either. The sleet gusted against the windowpanes.

"Birdbaths!" he exclaimed. No response. "Ditto with honeysuckle!"

He tried again. "Thinking about the Primrose Tea, are you?"

The second edition of his wife's famous parish-wide tea was coming in less than two weeks. Last year at this time, she was living on a stepladder, frantically repainting the kitchen and dining room, removing his octogenarian drapes, and knocking holes in the plaster to affect an "old Italian villa" look. Now here she was, staring out the window without any visible concern for the countless lemon squares, miniature quiches, vegetable sandwiches, and other items she'd need to feed a hundred and twenty-five women, nearly all of whom would look upon the tea as lunch.

His dog, Barnabas, ambled in and crashed by the hearth, as if drugged.

Cynthia tapped her foot and drummed her fingers on the chair arm. "Hmmm," she said.

"Hmmm what?"

She looked at him. "T.D.A."

"T.D.A.?"

"The Dreaded Armoire, dearest."

His heart pounded. Please, no. Not the armoire. "What about it?" he asked, fearing the answer.

"It's time to move it into our bedroom from the guest room. Remember? We said we were going to do it in the spring!" She smiled at him suddenly, as she was wont to do, and her sapphire-colored eyes gleamed. After a year and a half of marriage, how was it that a certain look from her still made him weak in the knees?

"Aha."

"So!" she said, lifting her hands and looking earnest.

"So? So, it's not spring!" He got up from the sofa and pointed toward the window. "See that? You call that spring? This, Kavanagh, is as far from spring as . . . as . . ."

"As Trieste is from Wesley," she said, helping out, "or the Red Sea from Mitford Creek." He could never get over the way her mind worked. "But do not look at the weather, Timothy, look at the calendar! May third!"

Last fall, they had hauled the enormous armoire down her stairs, down her back steps, through the hedge, up his back steps, along the hall, and finally up the staircase to the guest room, where he had wanted nothing more than to fall prostrate on the rug.

Had she liked it in the guest room, after all that? No, indeed. She had despised the very sight of it sitting there, and instantly came up with a further plan, to be executed in the spring—all of which meant more unloading of drawers and shelves, more lashing the doors closed with a rope, and more hauling—this time across the landing to their bedroom, where, he was convinced, it would tower over them in the night like a five-story parking garage.

"What are you going to do about the tea?" he asked, hoping to distract her.

"Not much at all 'til we get the armoire moved. You know how they are, Timothy, they want to poke into every nook and cranny.

Last year, Hessie Mayhew was down on her very hands and knees, peering into the laundry chute, I saw her with my own eyes. And Georgia Moore opened every cabinet door in the kitchen, she said she was looking for a water glass, when I know for a fact she was seeing if the dishes were stacked to her liking. So, I certainly can't have the armoire standing on that wall in the guest room where it is clearly . . ." she paused and looked at him, "*clearly* out of place."

He was in for it.

§

He had managed to hold off the move for a full week, but in return for the delay was required to make four pans of brownies (a specialty since seminary), clean out the fireplace, black the andirons, and prune the overgrown forsythia at the dining room windows.

Not bad, considering.

On Saturday morning before the big event the following Friday, he rose early, prayed, studied Paul's first letter to the Corinthians, and sat with his sermon notes; then he ran two miles with Barnabas on his red leash, and returned home fit for anything.

His heart still pounding from the final sprint across Baxter Park, he burst into the kitchen, which smelled of lemons, cinnamon, and freshly brewed coffee. "Let's do it!" he cried.

And get it over with, he thought.

§

The drawers were out, the shelves were emptied, the doors were lashed shut with a rope. This time, they were dragging it across the floor on a chenille bedspread, left behind by a former rector.

"*. . . a better way of life!*"

Cynthia looked up. "What did you say, dearest?"

"I didn't say anything."

"*Mack Stroupe will bring improvement, not change . . .*"

They stepped to the open window of the stair landing and looked down to the street. A new blue pickup truck with a public address system was slowly cruising along Wisteria Lane, hauling a sign in the bed. *Mack for Mitford*, it read, *Mitford for Mack*.

"*. . . improvement, not change. So, think about it, friends and neigh-*

bors. And remember—here in Mitford, we already have the good life. With Mack as Mayor, we'll all have a better life!" A loud blast of country music followed: *"If you don't stand for something, you'll fall for anything. . . ."*

She looked at her husband. "Mack Stroupe! Please, no."

He wrinkled his brow and frowned. "This is May. Elections aren't 'til November."

"Starting a mite early."

"I'll say," he agreed, feeling distinctly uneasy.

§

"He's done broke th' noise ordinance," said Chief Rodney Underwood, hitching up his gun belt.

Rodney had stepped to the back of the Main Street Grill to say hello to the early morning regulars in the rear booth. "Chapter five, section five-two in the Mitford Code of Ordinance lays it out. No PA systems for such a thing as political campaigns."

"Startin' off his public career as a pure criminal," said Mule Skinner.

"Which is th' dadgum law of the land for politicians!" *Mitford Muse* editor J. C. Hogan mopped his brow with a handkerchief.

"Well, no harm done. I slapped a warning on 'im, that ordinance is kind of new. Used to, politicians was haulin' a PA up and down th' street, ever' whichaway."

"What about that truck with the sign?" asked Father Tim.

"He can haul th' sign around all he wants to, but th' truck has to keep movin'. If he parks it on town property, I got 'im. I can run 'im in and he can go to readin' *Southern Livin'*." The local jail was the only detention center the rector ever heard of that kept neat stacks of *Southern Living* magazine in the cells.

"I hate to see a feller make a fool of hisself," said Rodney. "Ain't *no*body can whip Esther Cunningham—an' if you say I said that, I'll say you lied."

"Right," agreed Mule.

"Course, she *has* told it around that one of these days, her an' Ray are takin' off in th' RV and leave th' mayorin' to somebody else."

Mule shook his head. "Fifteen years is a long time to be hog-tied to a thankless job, all right."

"Is that Mack's new truck?" asked Father Tim. As far he knew, Mack never had two cents to rub together, as his hotdog stand across from the gas station didn't seem to rake in much business.

"I don't know whose truck it is, it sure couldn't be Mack's. Well, I ain't got all day to loaf, like you boys." Rodney headed for the register to pick up his breakfast order. "See you in th' funny papers."

J.C. scowled. "I don't know that I'd say nobody can whip Esther. Mack's for improvement, and we're due for a little improvement around here, if you ask me."

"Nobody asked you," said Mule.

§

Father Tim dialed the number from his office. "Mayor!"

"So it's the preacher, is it? I've been lookin' for you."

"What's going on?"

"If that low-down scum thinks he can run me out of office, he's got another think coming."

"Does this mean you're not going to quit and take off with Ray in the RV?"

"Shoot! That's what I say just to hear my head roar. Listen—you don't think the bum has a chance, do you?"

"To tell the truth, Esther, I believe he does have a chance. . . ."

Esther's voice lowered. "You do?"

"About the same chance as a snowball in July."

She laughed uproariously and then sobered. "Of course, there is *one* way that Mack Stroupe could come in here and sit behind th' mayor's desk."

He was alarmed. "Really?"

"But only one. And that's over my dead body."

§

Something new was going on at home nearly every day.

On Tuesday evening, he found a large, framed watercolor hanging in the rectory's once-gloomy hallway. It was of Violet, Cynthia's white cat and the heroine of the award-winning children's books created by his unstoppable wife. Violet sat on a brocade cloth, peering into a vase filled with nasturtiums and a single, wide-eyed goldfish.

"Stunning!" he said. "Quite a change."

"Call it an *improvement*," she said, pleased.

On Wednesday, he found new chintz draperies in the dining room and parlor, which gave the place a dazzling elegance that fairly bowled him over. But—hadn't they agreed that neither would spend more than a hundred bucks without the other's consent?

She read his mind. "So, the draperies cost five hundred, but since the watercolor is worth that and more on the current market, it's a wash."

"Aha."

"I'm also doing one of Barnabas, for your study. Which means," she said, "that the family coffers will respond by allotting new draperies for our bedroom."

"You're a bookkeeping whiz, Kavanagh. But why new draperies when we're retiring in eighteen months?"

"I've had them made so they can go anywhere and fit any kind of windows. If worse comes to worst, I'll remake them into summer dresses, and vestments for my clergyman."

"That's the spirit!"

Why did he feel his wife could get away with anything where he was concerned? Was it because he'd waited sixty-two years, like a stalled ox, to fall in love and marry?

❧

If he and Cynthia had written a detailed petition on a piece of paper and sent it heavenward, the weather couldn't have been more glorious on the day of the talked-about tea.

Much to everyone's relief, the primroses actually bloomed. However, no sooner had the eager blossoms appeared than Hessie Mayhew bore down on them with a vengeance, in yards and hidden nooks everywhere. She knew precisely the location of every cluster of primroses in the village, not to mention the exact whereabouts of each woods violet, lilac bush, and pussy willow.

"It's Hessie!" warned an innocent bystander on Hessie's early morning run the day of the tea. "Stand back!"

Armed with a collection of baskets that she wore on her arms like so many bracelets, Hessie did not allow help from the Episcopal

Church Women, nor any of her own presbyters. She worked alone, she worked fast, and she worked smart.

After going at a trot through neighborhood gardens, huffing up Old Church Lane to a secluded bower of early-blooming shrubs, and combing four miles of country roadside, she showed up at the back door of the rectory at precisely eleven a.m., looking triumphant.

Sodden with morning dew and black dirt, she delivered a vast quantity of flowers, moss, and grapevine into the hands of the rector's house help, Puny Guthrie, then flew home to bathe, dress, and put antibiotic cream on her knees, which were skinned when she leaned over to pick a wild trillium and fell sprawling.

The Episcopal Church Women, who had arrived as one body at ten-thirty, flew into the business of arranging "Hessie's truck," as they called it, while Barnabas snored in the garage and Violet paced in her carrier.

"Are you off?" asked Cynthia, as the rector came at a trot through the hectic kitchen.

"Off and running. I finished polishing the mail slot, tidying the slipcover on the sofa, and trimming the lavender by the front walk. I also beat the sofa pillows for any incipient dust and coughed for a full five minutes."

"Well done!" she said cheerily, giving him a hug.

"I'll be home at one-thirty to help the husbands park cars."

Help the husbands park cars? he thought as he sprinted toward the office. He was a *husband*! After all these months, the thought still occasionally slammed him in the solar plexus and took his breath away.

§

Nine elderly guests, including the Kavanaghs' friend Louella, arrived in the van from Hope House and were personally escorted up the steps of the rectory and into the hands of the Altar Guild.

Up and down Wisteria Lane, men with armbands stitched with primroses and a Jerusalem cross directed traffic, which quickly grew snarled. At one point, the rector leaped into a stalled Chevrolet and managed to roll it to the curb. Women came in car pools, husbands dropped off spouses, daughters delivered mothers, and all in all, the narrow street was as congested as a carnival in Rio.

"This is th' biggest thing to hit Mitford since th' blizzard two years ago," said Mule Skinner, who was a Baptist, but offered to help out, anyway.

The rector laughed. "That's one way to look at it." Didn't anybody ever *walk* in this town?

"Look here!"

It was Mack Stroupe in that blasted pickup truck, carting his sign around in their tea traffic. Mack rolled by, chewing on a toothpick and looking straight ahead.

"You comin' to the Primrose Tea?" snapped Mule. "If not, get this vehicle out of here, we're tryin' to conduct a church function!"

Four choir members, consisting of a lyric soprano, a mezzo soprano, and two altos, arrived in a convertible, looking windblown and holding on to their hats.

"Hats is a big thing this year," observed Uncle Billy Watson, who stood at the curb with Miss Rose and watched the proceedings. Uncle Billy was the only man who showed up at last year's tea, and now considered his presence at the event to be a tradition.

Uncle Billy walked out to the street with the help of his cane and tapped Father Tim on the shoulder. "Hit's like a Chiney puzzle, don't you know. If you 'uns'd move that'n off to th' side and git that'n to th' curb, hit'd be done with."

"No more parking on Wisteria," Ron Malcolm reported to the rector. "We'll direct the rest of the crowd to the church lot and shoot 'em back here in the Hope House van."

A UPS driver, who had clearly made an unwise turn onto Wisteria, sat in his truck in front of the rectory, stunned by the sight of so much traffic on the usually uneventful Holding/Mitford/Wesley run.

"Hit's what you call a standstill," Uncle Billy told J. C. Hogan, who showed up with his Nikon and six rolls of Tri-X.

As traffic started to flow again, the rector saw Mack Stroupe turn onto Wisteria Lane from Church Hill. Clearly, he was circling the block.

"I'd like to whop him upside th' head with a two-by-four," said

Mule. He glared at Mack, who was reared back in the seat with both windows down, listening to a country music station. Mack waved to several women, who immediately turned their heads.

Mule snorted. "Th' dumb so-and-so! How would you like to have that peckerwood for mayor?"

The rector wiped his perspiring forehead. "Watch your blood pressure, buddyroe."

"He says he's goin' to campaign straight through spring and summer, right up to election in November. Kind of like bein' tortured by a drippin' faucet."

As the truck passed, Emma Newland stomped over. "I ought to climb in that truck and slap his jaws. What's he doin', anyway, trying to sway church people to his way of thinkin'?"

"Let him be," Father Tim cautioned his secretary and on-line computer whiz. After all, give Mack enough rope and . . .

❦

Cynthia was lying in bed, moaning, as he came out of the shower. He went into the bedroom, hastily drying off.

"Why are you moaning?" he asked, alarmed.

"Because it helps relieve exhaustion. I hope the windows are closed so the neighbors can't hear."

"The only neighbor close enough to hear is no longer living in the little yellow house next door. She is, in fact, lying right here, doing the moaning."

She moaned again. "Moaning is good," she told him, her face mashed into the pillow. "You should try it."

"I don't think so," he said.

Warm as a steamed clam from the shower, he put on his pajamas and sat on the side of the bed. "I'm proud of you," he said, rubbing her back. "That was a tea-and-a-half! The best! In fact, words fail. You'll have a time topping that one."

"Don't tell me I'm supposed to *top* it!"

"Yes, well, not to worry. Next year, we can have Omer Cunningham and his pilot buddies do a flyover. That'll give the ladies something to talk about." He'd certainly given all of Mitford something to talk about last May when he flew to Virginia with Omer in his rag-wing taildragger. Four hours in Omer's little plane had gained him more credibility than thirty-six years in the pulpit.

"A little farther down," his wife implored. "Ugh. My lower back is killing me from all the standing and baking."

"I got the reviews as your guests left."

"Only tell me the good ones. I don't want to hear about the cheese straws, which were as limp as linguine."

"'Perfect' was a word they bandied around quite a bit, and the lemon squares, of course, got their usual share of raves. Some wanted me to know how charming they think you are, and others made lavish remarks about your youth and beauty."

He leaned down and kissed her shoulder, inhaling the faintest scent of wisteria. "You are beautiful, Kavanagh."

"Thanks."

"I don't suppose there are any special thanks you'd like to offer the poor rube who helped unsnarl four thousand three hundred and seventy-nine cars, trucks, and vans?"

She rolled over and looked at him, smiling. Then she held her head to one side in that way he couldn't resist, and pulled him to her and kissed him tenderly.

"Now you're talking," he said.

The phone rang.

"Hello?"

"Hey."

Dooley! "Hey, yourself, buddy."

"Is Cynthia sending me a box of stuff she made for that tea? I can't talk long."

"Two boxes. Went off today."

"Man! Thanks!"

"You're welcome. How's school?"

"Great."

Great? Dooley Barlowe was not one to use superlatives. "No kidding?"

"You're going to like my grades."

Was this the little guy he'd struggled to raise for nearly three years?

The Dooley who always shot himself in the foot? The self-assured sound of the boy's voice made his hair fairly stand on end.

"We're going to like you coming home, even better. In just six or seven weeks, you'll be here. . . ."

Silence. Was Dooley dreading to tell him he wanted to spend the summer at Meadowgate Farm? The boy's decision to do that last year had nearly broken his heart, not to mention Cynthia's. They had, of course, gotten over it, as they watched the boy doing what he loved best—learning more about veterinary medicine at the country practice of Hal Owen.

"Of course," said the rector, pushing on, "we want you to go out to Meadowgate, if that's what you'd like to do." He swallowed. This year, he was stronger, he could let go.

"OK," said Dooley, "that's what I'd like to do."

"Fine. No problem. I'll call you tomorrow for our usual phone visit. We love you."

"I love you back."

"Here's Cynthia."

"Hey," she said.

"Hey, yourself." It was their family greeting.

"So, you big galoot, we sent a box for you and one to share with your friends."

"What's in it?"

"Lemon squares."

"I like lemon squares."

"Plus raspberry tarts, pecan truffles, and brownies made by the preacher."

"Thanks."

"Are you OK?"

"Yes."

"No kidding?"

"Yep."

"Good!" said Cynthia. "Lace Turner asked about you the other day."

"That dumb girl that dresses like a guy?"

"She doesn't dress like a guy anymore. Oh, and your friend Jenny was asking about you, too."

"How's Tommy?"

"Missing you. Just as we do. So hurry home, even if you are going to spend the summer at Meadowgate, you big creep."

Dooley cackled.

"We love you."

"I love you back."

Cynthia placed the receiver on the hook, smiling happily.

"Now, you poor rube," she said, "where were we?"

§

He sat on the study sofa and took the rubber band off the *Mitford Muse*.

Good grief! There he was on the front page, standing bewildered in front of the UPS truck with his nose looking, as usual, like a turnip or a tulip bulb. Why did J. C. Hogan run this odious picture, when he might have photographed his hardworking, good-looking, and thoroughly deserving wife?

Primrose Tee Draws
Stand-Out Crowd

Clearly, Hessie had not written this story, which on first glance appeared to be about golf, but had given her notes to J.C., who forged ahead without checking his spelling.

Good time had by all . . . same time next year . . . a hundred and thirty guests . . . nine gallons of tea, ten dozen lemon squares, eight dozen raspberry tarts . . . traffic jam . . .

The phone gave a sharp blast.

"Hello?"

"Timothy . . ."

"Hal! I've just been thinking of you and Marge."

"Good. And we of you. I've got some . . . hard news, and wanted you to know."

Hal and Marge Owen were two of his closest, most valued friends. He was afraid to know.

"I've just hired a full-time assistant."

"That's the bad news? It sounds good to me, you work like a Trojan."

"Yes, but . . . we won't be able to have Dooley this summer. My assistant is a young fellow, just starting out, and I'll have to give him a lot of time and attention. Also, we're putting him up in Dooley's room until he gets established." Hal sighed.

"But that's terrific. We know Dooley looked forward to being at Meadowgate—however, circumstances alter cases, as my Mississippi kin used to say."

"There's a large riding stable coming in about a mile down the road, they've asked me to vet the horses. That could be a full-time job right there."

"I understand. Of course. Your practice is growing."

"We'll miss the boy, Tim, you know how we feel about him, how Rebecca Jane loves him. But look, we'll have him out to stay the first two weeks he's home from school—if that works for you."

"Absolutely."

"Oh, and Tim . . ."

"Yes?"

"Will you tell him?"

"I will. I'll talk to him about it, get him thinking of what to do this summer. Be good for him."

"So why don't you and Cynthia plan to spend the day when you bring him out? Bring Barnabas, too. Marge will make your favorite."

Deep-dish chicken pie, with a crust like French pastry. "We'll be there!" he said, meaning it.

§

"Will you tell him?" he asked Cynthia.

"No way," she said.

Nobody wanted to tell Dooley Barlowe that he couldn't spend the summer doing what he loved more than anything on earth.

§

She opened her eyes and rolled over to find him sitting up in bed. "Oh, my dear! Oh, my goodness! What happened?"

He loved the look on his wife's face; he wanted to savor it. "It's already turned a few colors," he said, removing his hand from his right temple.

She peered at him as if he were a butterfly on a pin. "Yes! Black . . . and blue and . . . the tiniest bit of yellow."

"My old school colors," he said.

"But what happened?" He never heard such *tsk*ing and gasping.

"T.D.A.," he replied.

"The Dreaded Armoire? What do you mean?"

"I mean that I got up in the middle of the night, in the dark, and went out to the landing and opened the windows to give Barnabas a cool breeze. As I careened through the bedroom on my way to the bathroom, I slammed into the blasted thing."

"Oh, no! Oh, heavens. What can I do? And tomorrow's Sunday!"

"Spousal abuse," he muttered. "In today's TV news climate, my congregation will pick up on it immediately."

"Timothy, dearest, I'm so sorry. I'll get something for you, I don't know what, but something. Just stay right there and don't move."

She put on her slippers and robe and flew downstairs, Barnabas barking at her heels.

T.D.A. might stand for "The *Dreaded* Armoire" as far as his wife was concerned. As far as he was concerned, it stood for something else entirely.

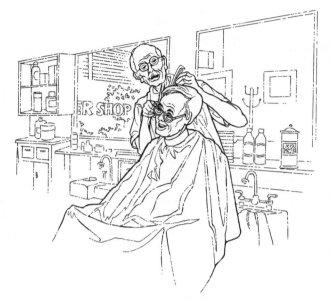

CHAPTER TWO

Step by Step

He was missing her.

How many times had he gone to the phone to call, only to realize she wasn't there to answer?

When Sadie Baxter died last year at the age of ninety, he felt the very rug yanked from under him. She'd been family to him, and a companionable friend; his sister in Christ, and favorite parishioner. In addition, she was Dooley's benefactor and, for more than half a century, the most generous donor in the parish. Not only had she given Hope House, the new five-million-dollar nursing home at the top of Old Church Lane, she had faithfully kept a roof on Lord's Chapel while her own roof went begging.

Sadie Baxter was warbling with the angels, he thought, chuckling at the image. But not because of the money she'd given, no, indeed. Good works, the Scriptures plainly stated, were no passport to heaven. "For by grace are you saved through faith," Paul wrote in his letter to the Ephesians, "and that not of yourselves, it is the gift of God—not of works, lest any man should boast."

The issue of works versus grace was about as popular as the issue of sin. Nonetheless, he was set to preach on Paul's remarks, and soon. The whole works ideology was as insidious as so many termites going after the stairs to the altar.

Emma blew in, literally. As she opened the office door, a gust of cold spring wind snatched it from her hand and sent it crashing against the wall.

"Lord have mercy!" she shouted, trying to snatch it back against a gale that sent his papers flying. She slammed the door and stood panting in front of it, her glasses crooked on her nose.

"Have you *ever*?" she demanded.

"Ever what?"

"Seen a winter that lasted nine months goin' on ten? I said, Harold, why don't we move to Florida? I never thought I'd live to hear such words come out of my mouth."

"And what did Harold say?" he asked, trying to reassemble his papers.

"You know Baptists," she replied, hanging up her coat. "They don't move to Florida; they don't want to be warm! They want to freeze to death on th' way to prayer meetin' and shoot right up to th' pearly gates and get it over with."

The Genghis Khan of church secretaries wagged her finger at him. "It's enough to make me go back to bein' Episcopalian."

"What's Harold done now?"

"Made Snickers sleep in the garage. Can you believe it? Country people don't like dogs in the house, you know."

"I thought Snickers was sleeping in the house."

"He was, 'til he ate a steak off Harold's plate."

"Aha."

"Down th' hatch, neat as a pin. But then, guess what?"

"I can't guess."

"He threw it all up in the closet, on Harold's shoes."

"I can see Harold's point."

"You would," she said stiffly, sitting at her desk.

"I would?"

"Yes. You're a man," she announced, glaring at him. "By the way . . ."

"By the way what?"

"That bump on your head is the worst-lookin' mess I ever saw. Can't you get Cynthia to do somethin' about it?"

Then again, maybe works *could* have an influence. Exercising the patience of a saint while putting up with Emma Newland for fifteen years should be enough to blast him heavenward like a rocket, with no stops along the way.

Emma booted her computer and peered at the screen.

"I nearly ran over Mack Stroupe comin' in this morning, he crossed th' street without lookin'. I didn't know whether to hit th' brakes or the accelerator. You know that hotdog stand of his? He's turnin' it into his campaign headquarters! Campaign headquarters, can you believe it? Who does he think he is, Ross Perot?"

The rector sighed.

"You know that mud slick in front that he called a parkin' lot?" She clicked her mouse. "Well, he's having it paved, the asphalt trucks are all over it like flies. Asphalt!" she muttered. "I hate asphalt. Give me cement, any day."

Yes, indeed. Straight up, right into a personal and highly favorable audience with St. Peter.

§

"Something has to be done," he said.

"Yes, but what?"

"Blast if I know. If we don't get a new roof on it soon, who can guess what the interior damage might be?"

Father Tim and Cynthia sat at the kitchen table, discussing his second most worrisome problem—what to do with the rambling, three-story Victorian mansion known as Fernbank, and its endless, overgrown grounds.

When Miss Sadie died last year, she left Fernbank to the church, "to cover any future needs of Hope House," and there it sat—buffeted by hilltop winds and scoured by driving hailstorms, with no one even to sweep dead bees from the windowsills.

In Miss Sadie's mind, Fernbank had been a gift; to him, it was an albatross. After all, she had clearly made him responsible for doing the best thing by her aging homeplace.

There had been talk of leasing it to a private school or institution, a notion that lay snarled somewhere in diocesan red tape. On the other hand, should they sell it and invest the money? If so, should they sell it as is, or bite the bullet and repair it at horrendous cost to a parish almost certainly unwilling to gamble in real estate?

"We just got an estimate on the roof," he said.

"How much?"

"Thirty, maybe thirty-five thousand."

"Good heavens!"

They sat in silence, reflecting.

"Poor Fernbank," she said. "Who would buy it, anyway? Certainly no one in Mitford can afford it."

He refilled his coffee cup. Even if they were onto a sour subject, he was happy to be hanging out with his wife. Besides, Cynthia Kavanagh was known for stumbling onto serendipitous solutions for all sorts of woes and tribulations.

"Worse than that," she said, "who could afford to fix it up, assuming they could buy it in the first place?"

"There's the rub."

After staring at the tablecloth for a moment, she looked up. "Then again, why worry about it at all? Miss Sadie didn't give it to *you* . . ."

So why had he worn the thing around his neck for more than ten months?

". . . she gave it to the church. Which, in case you've momentarily forgotten, belongs to God. So, let Him handle it, for Pete's sake."

He could feel the grin spreading across his face. Right! Of course! He felt a weight fly off, if only temporarily. "Who's the preacher around here, anyway?"

"Sometimes you go on sabbatical, dearest."

He stood and cranked open the kitchen window. "When are we going up there and pick out the token or two that Miss Sadie offered us in the letter?"

She sighed. "We don't have a nook, much less a cranny that isn't already stuffed with *things*. My house next door is full, the rectory is brimming, and we're retiring."

She was right. It was a time to be subtracting, not adding.

"What have the others taken?" she wondered.

"Louella took the brooch Miss Sadie's mother painted, and Olivia only wanted a walnut chest and the photographs of Miss Sadie's mother and Willard Porter. The place is virtually untouched."

"Did anyone go sneezing through the attic?"

"Not a soul."

"I absolutely love sneezing through attics! Attics are full of mystery and intrigue. So, yes, let's do it! Let's go up! Besides, we don't have to shop, we can *browse*!"

Her eyes suddenly looked bluer, as they always did when she was excited.

"I love it when you talk like this," he said, relieved.

At least one of the obligations surrounding Fernbank would be settled.

§

Fernbank was only his second most nagging worry.

What to do about Dooley's scattered siblings had moved to the head of the line.

Over the last few years, Dooley's mother, Pauline Barlowe, had let her children go like so many kittens scattered from a box.

How could he hope to collect what had been blown upon the wind during Pauline's devastating bouts with alcohol? The last that Pauline had heard, her son Kenny was somewhere in Oregon, little Jessie's whereabouts were unknown, and Sammy . . . he didn't want to think about it.

Last year, the rector had gone with Lace Turner into the drug-infested Creek community and brought Dooley's nine-year-old brother out. Poobaw was now living in Betty Craig's cottage with his recovering mother and disabled grandfather, and doing well in Mitford School.

A miracle. But in this case, miracles, like peanuts, were addictive. One would definitely not be enough.

§

"This news just hit the street," said Mule, sliding into the booth with a cup of coffee. "I got it before J.C."

"Aha," said the rector, trying to decide whether to butter his roll or eat it dry.

"Joe Ivey's hangin' it up."

"No!"

"Goin' to Tennessee to live with his kin, and Winnie Ivey cryin' her eyes out, he's all the family she's got in Mitford."

"Why is he hanging it up?"

"Kidneys."

Velma appeared with her order pad. "We don't have kidneys n'more. We tried kidneys last year and nobody ordered 'em."

"Meat loaf sandwich, then," said Mule. "Wait a minute. What's the Father having?"

"Chicken salad."

"I pass. Make it a BLT on whole wheat."

"Kidneys?" asked the rector as Velma left.

"I don't have to tell you Joe likes a little shooter now and again."

"Umm."

"Lately, he's been drinkin' peach brandy, made fresh weekly in Knox County. The other thing is, varicose veins. Forty-five years of standing on his feet barbering, his legs look like a Georgia road map." Mule blew on his coffee. "He showed 'em to me."

Except for a couple of visits to Fancy Skinner's Hair House, Joe Ivey had been his barber since he came to Mitford. "I hate to hear this."

"We all hate to hear it."

There was a long silence. The rector buttered his roll.

"I despise change," said Mule, looking grim.

"You and me both."

"That's why Mack won't call it change, he calls it improvement. But you and I know exactly what it is. . . ."

"Change," said Father Tim.

"Right. And if Mack has anything to do with it, it won't be change for the better."

What the heck, he opened the container of blackberry jam left from the breakfast crowd and spread that on, too. With diabetes, life may not be long, he thought, but the diet they put you on sure makes it seem that way.

"Have you thought of the bright side of Joe getting out of the business?" asked Father Tim.

"The bright side?"

"All Joe's customers will be running to your wife."

Mule's face lit up. "I'll be dadgum. That's right."

"That ought to amount to, oh, forty people, easy. With haircuts at ten bucks a head these days, you and Fancy can go on that cruise you've been talking about, no problem."

Mule looked grim again. "Yeah, but then Fancy'll be gettin' varicose veins."

"Every calling has an occupational hazard," said the rector. "Look at yours—a real estate market that's traditionally volatile, you never know how much bread you can put on the table, or when."

J.C. threw his bulging briefcase onto the bench and slid into the booth.

"Did you hear what Adele did last night?"

"What?" the realtor and the rector asked in unison.

The editor looked like he'd just won the lottery. "She busted a guy for attempted robbery and probably saved Dot Hamby's life." Adele was not only a Mitford police officer, but J.C.'s wife.

"Your buttons are poppin' off in my coffee," said Mule.

"Where did it happen?"

"Down at the Shoe Barn. She parked her patrol car in back, went in the side door, and was over behind one of the shoe racks, tryin' to find a pair of pumps. Meanwhile, this idiot walks in the front door and asks Dot to change a ten, and when Dot opens the cash register, he whips out a gun and shoves it in her face. Adele heard what was going on, so she slipped up behind the sucker, barefooted, and buried a nine-millimeter in his ribs."

"What did she say?" asked Mule.

"She said what you're supposed to say in a case like that. She said, 'Drop it.'"

Mule raised his eyebrows. "Man!"

J.C. wiped his face with a handkerchief. "His butt is in jail as we speak."

"Readin' casserole recipes out of *Southern Living*," said Mule. "It's too good for th' low-down snake."

"It's nice to see where my recyclin' is ending up," said the editor, staring at Mule.

"What's that supposed to mean?"

"I just read it takes twenty-six plastic soda bottles to make a polyester suit like that."

"Waste not, want not," said Mule.

J.C. looked for Velma. "You see what Mack's doing up the street?"

"We did."

"A real improvement, he says he's throwing a barbecue soon as the parking lot hardens off. Live music, the whole nine yards. I might give that a front page."

Mule appeared frozen.

"What's the deal with you not liking Mack Stroupe?" asked J.C. "The least you can do is listen to what he has to say."

"I don't listen to double-dealin' cheats," snapped Mule. "They don't have anything to say that I want to hear."

"Come on, that incident was years ago."

"He won't get my vote, let me put it that way."

J.C.'s face flushed. "You want to stick your head in the sand like half the people in this town, go ahead. For my money, it's time we had something new and different around here, a few new businesses, a decent housing development.

"When they staffed Hope House, they hired twenty-seven people from outside Mitford, and where do you think they're living? Wesley! Holding! Working here, but pumping up somebody else's economy, building somebody else's town parks, paying somebody else's taxes."

The rector noticed that Mule's hand was shaking when he picked up his coffee cup. "I'd rather see Mitford throw tax money down a rat hole than put a mealymouthed lowlife in Esther's job."

"For one thing," growled J.C., "you'd better get over the idea it's *Esther's* job."

The regulars in the back booth had disagreed before, but this was disturbingly different.

The roll the rector had eaten suddenly became a rock.

❧

"Just a little off the sides," he said.

"Sides? What sides? Since you slipped off and let Fancy Skinner do your barberin', you ain't got any sides."

What could he say? "We'll miss you around here, Joe. I hate like the dickens to see you go."

"I hate like the dickens to go. But I'm too old to be doin' this."

"How old?"

"Sixty-four."

Good Lord! He was hovering around that age himself. He instantly felt depressed. "That's not old!" he said.

"For this callin', it is. I've tore my legs up over it, and that's enough for me."

"Where are you moving in Tennessee?"

"Memphis. Might do a little part-time security at Graceland, with my cousin. I'll be stayin' with my baby sister—Winnie's th' oldest, you know, we want her to move up, too."

Winnie gone from the Sweet Stuff Bakery? Two familiar faces missing from Mitford, all at once? He didn't like the sound of it, not a bit.

"Here," said Joe, handing him a bottle with an aftershave label. "Take you a little pull on this. It might be your last chance."

"What is it?"

"Homemade peach brandy, you'll never taste better. Go on and take you a snort, I won't tell nobody."

For fifteen years, his barber had offered him a nip of this, a shooter of that, and he had always refused. The rector had preached him a sermon a time or two, years ago, but Joe had told him to mind his own business. Without even thinking, he unscrewed the cap, turned the bottle up, and took a swig. *Holy smoke.*

He passed it back, nearly unable to speak. "That'll do it for me."

"I might have a little taste myself." Joe upended the bottle and polished off half the contents.

"Are you sure you poured out the aftershave before you poured in the brandy?"

Joe cackled. "Listen here," he said, brushing his customer's neck, "don't be lettin' Mack Stroupe run Esther off."

"I'll do my best."

"Look after Winnie 'til she can sell her bake shop and get up to Memphis."

"I will. She's a good one."

"And take good care of that boy, keep him in a straight line. I never had nobody to keep me in a straight line."

"You've done all right, Joe. You've been a good friend to us, and you'll be missed." He might have been trying to swallow down a golf ball. He hated goodbyes.

He got out of the chair and reached for his wallet. "I want you to take care of yourself, and let us hear from you."

Tears stood in Joe's eyes. "Put that back in your pocket. I've barbered you for fifteen years, and this one's on me."

He'd never noticed that Joe Ivey seemed so frail-looking and pallid—defenseless, somehow. The rector threw his arms around him in a wordless hug. Then he walked down the stairs to Main Street, his breath smelling like lighter fluid, bawling like a baby.

§

The date for the Bane and Blessing sale was official, and the annual moaning began.

No show of lilacs, no breathtaking display of dogwoods could alleviate the woe.

Three ECW members suddenly developed chronic back trouble, and an Altar Guild member made reservations to visit her sister in Toledo during the week of the sale. Two Sunday School teachers who had, in a weak moment, volunteered to help trooped up the aisle after Wednesday Eucharist to pray at the altar.

After Esther Bolick agreed to chair the historic church event, she went home and asked her husband, Gene, to have her committed. The Bane and Blessing was known, over the years, for having put two women flat on their backs in bed, nearly broken up a marriage, and chased three families to the Lutherans in Wesley.

Besides, hadn't she virtually retired from years and years of churchwork, trying to focus, instead, on cake baking? Wasn't baking a ministry in its own right? And didn't she bake an orange marmalade cake at least twice a week for some poor soul who was down and out?

In the first place, she couldn't remember saying she'd *do* the Bane. She had been totally dumfounded when the meeting ended and everybody rushed over to hug and thank her and tell her how wonderful she was.

In the end, she sighed, determined that it should be done "as unto the Lord and not unto men."

"That's the spirit!" said her rector, doling out a much-needed hug.

He wouldn't have traded places with Esther Bolick for all the tea in China. Esther, however, would do an outstanding job, and no doubt put an unprecedented amount of money in the missions till.

Because it was the most successful fund-raising event in the entire diocese, the women who pulled it off usually got enough local recognition to last a lifetime, or, at the very least, a couple of months.

"October fourth," Esther told Gene.

"Eat your Wheaties," Gene told Esther.

❧

He'd rather be shot. But somebody had to do it.

"Hey," said Dooley, knowing who was on the phone.

"Hey, yourself. What's going on up there?"

"Chorus trip to Washington this weekend. We're singing in a church and a bunch of senators and stuff will be there. I bought a new blazer, my old one got ripped on a nail. How's ol' Barnabas?"

"Sitting right here, licking my shoe, I think I dropped jam on it this morning. There's something I need to talk with you about."

Silence.

"Hal Owen hired an assistant."

He may as well have put a knife in the boy, so keenly could he feel his disappointment.

"That means he'll have help this summer, and the fellow will be . . ."—he especially hated this part—"be staying in your room until he gets situated."

"Fine," said Dooley, his voice cold.

"Hal had to do it, he's been asked to vet a riding stable that's moving in up the road. He's got his hands full and then some."

He couldn't bear Dooley Barlowe's silences; they seemed as deep as wells, as black as mines.

"Hal and Marge want you to come out for two weeks when you get home from school. They'll . . . miss having you for the summer."

"OK."

"You might want to think about a job."

More silence.

"Tommy's going to have a job."

"Where?"

"Pumping gas at Lew's. He'll probably have a uniform with his name on it." It was a weak ploy, but all he could come up with. He pushed on. "Summer will give you time with your brother. Poobaw would like that. And so would your granpaw."

Give him time to think it over. "Listen, buddy. You're going to have a great summer, you'll see. And we love you. Never forget that."

"I don't."

Good! "Good. I'll talk with you Saturday."

"Hey, listen . . ." said Dooley.

"Yes?"

"Nothin'."

"OK. God be with you, son."

He took out his handkerchief and wiped his forehead.

§

"He who is not impatient is not in love," said an old Italian proverb.

Well, that proved it right there, he thought, leaving his office and hurrying up Main Street toward home.

Why did he feel such excitement about seeing his wife, when he had seen her only this morning? She had brought them coffee in bed at an inhuman hour, and they'd sat up, drinking it, laughing and talking as if it were high noon.

A woman who would get up at five o'clock in order to visit with her husband before his prayer and study time was a saint. Of course, he admitted, she didn't make a habit of it. And didn't that make it all the more welcome?

Cynthia, Cynthia! he thought, looking at the pink dogwood in the yard of the tea room across the street. Like great pink canopies, the trees spread their lacy shade over emerald grass and beds of yellow tulips.

Dear Lord! It was nearly more than a man could bear—spring coming on like thunder, and a woman who had kissed him only hours ago, in a way he'd never, in his bachelor days, had the wits to imagine.

It wouldn't take more than a very short memory to recall the women who'd figured in his life.

Peggy Cramer. That had taught him a thing or two. And when the engagement broke off while he was in seminary, he'd known that it was a good thing.

Then there was Becky. How his parish had worked to pull that one off! She was the woman who thought Wordsworth was a Dallas department store. He hoofed it past Dora Pugh's hardware, laughing out loud.

Ah, but he felt an immense gratitude for his wife's spontaneous laughter, her wisdom, and even her infernal stubborness. He snapped a branch of white lilac from the bush at the corner of the rectory yard.

He raced up his front steps, threw open the door, and bounded down the hall.

"Cynthia!"

As if he had punched a button, a clamor went up. Puny Guthrie's red-haired twins, Sissy and Sassy, began squalling as one.

"Now see what you've done!" said Puny, standing at the ironing board in the kitchen.

"I didn't know you'd still be here," he said lamely.

"An' I just rocked 'em off to sleep! Look, girls, here's your granpaw!"

His house help, for whom he would be eternally grateful, was determined that he be a granpaw to her infants, whether he liked it or not.

"So, looky here, you hold Sissy and I'll jiggle Sassy, I've got another hour to finish all this ironin' from th' tea."

He took Sissy and, as instantly as Sissy had started crying, she stopped and gazed up at him.

"Hey, there," he said, gazing back.

"See? She likes you! She loves 'er granpaw, don't she?"

He could not take his eyes off the wonder in his arms. Because Puny was often gone by the time he arrived home, or was next door at the little yellow house, he hadn't seen much of the twins over the winter. And now here they were, nearly a full year old, and one of them reaching up to pull his lower lip down to his collar.

Puny put Sassy on her hip and jiggled her. "If you'd jis' walk Sissy around or somethin', I'd 'preciate it. Lord, look at th' ironin' that come off of that tea, and all of it antique somethin' or other from a bishop or a pope. . . ."

"Where's Cynthia?"

"I've not seen 'er since lunch. She might be over at her house, workin' on a book."

As far as he knew, his industrious wife was not working on a book these days. She'd decided to take a sabbatical since last year's book on bluebirds.

"I'll just take Sissy and go looking," he said.

"If she cries, jiggle 'er!"

Wanting to be proactive, he started jiggling at once.

He walked through the backyard, ignoring the dandelions that lighted his lawn like so many small, yellow fires. No, indeed, he would not get obsessive over the dandelions this spring, he would not dig them out one by one, as he had done in former years. Dandelions come and dandelions go, and there you have it, he thought, jiggling. Wasn't he a man heading into retirement? Wasn't he a man learning to loosen up and live a little?

Sissy gurgled and squirmed in his arms.

"Timothy!"

It was his wife, trotting through the hedge and looking like a girl. "You'll never guess what!"

"I can't guess," he said, leaning over to kiss her. He tucked the branch of lilac in her shirt pocket as Sissy socked him on the chin.

"Thank you, dearest! Mule just called to say someone's interested in Fernbank! He tried to ring you at the office, but you'd left. Can you imagine? It's someone from out of town, he said, a corporation or something. Run and call him, and I'll take Sissy!"

Why didn't he feel joyful as he went to the phone in his study? He didn't feel joyful at all. Instead, he felt a strange sense of foreboding.

§

He lay on his side, propped up on his elbow. "I thought about you today," he said, shy about telling her this simple thing.

She traced his nose and chin with her forefinger. "How very odd! I thought about you today."

"It was the five o'clock coffee that did it," he said, kissing her.

"Is that what it was?" she murmured, kissing him in return.

Perhaps almost anyone could love, he thought; it was the loving back that seemed to count for everything.

§

He tossed the thing onto a growing pile.

A man who had time to dig dandelions was a man with time to waste, he thought.

While he had no time at all to do something so trivial, he found he couldn't help himself. He'd been lured into the yard like a miner lured to veins of gold.

There were, needless to say, a hundred other things that needed doing more:

The visit to Fernbank's attic, and get cracking now that a possible buyer was on the scene.

Fertilize the roses.

Mulch the beds.

Get up to Hope House and talk to Scott Murphy. . . .

Scott was the young, on-fire chaplain that he and Miss Sadie had hired last year. Ever since he'd come last September, they'd tried to find time to run together, but so far, it hadn't worked. Scott was like the tigers in a favorite childhood story—he was racing around the tree so fast, he was turning into butter.

The new chaplain not only held services every morning, but was making personal rounds to every one of the forty residents, every day.

"It's what I was hired to do," he said, grinning.

In addition, he'd gotten the once-controversial kennel program up and running. In this deal, a Hope House resident could "rent" a cat or a dog for up to two hours a day, simply by placing an advance order for Hector, Barney, Muffin, Lucky, etc. As the rector had seen on his visits to Hope House, this program doled out its own kind of medicine.

Evie Adams's mother, Miss Pattie, who had been literally out of her mind for a decade, had taken a shine to Baxter, a cheerful dachshund, and was, on certain days, nearly lucid.

Every afternoon, the pet wagon rolled along the halls at Hope House, and residents who weren't bedridden got to amuse, and be amused by, their four-legged visitors. There were goldfish for those who couldn't handle the responsibility of a cat or dog, and, for everyone in general, Mitford School kept the walls supplied with bright posters.

"I'll be dadgum if I wouldn't like to move in there," said several villagers who were perfectly able-bodied.

He sat back on his heels and dropped the weed-puller. What about the Creek community? Hadn't he and Scott talked last year about doing something, anything, to bring some healing to that place? It was overwhelming even to think about it, and yet, he constantly thought about it.

And Sammy and Kenny and Jessie . . . there was that other overwhelming, and even more urgent issue, and he had no idea where to begin.

He dug out a burdock and tossed it on the pile.

And now this. A corporation? That didn't sound good. Mule hadn't known any details, he had merely talked on the phone with a real estate company who was making general inquiries about Fernbank.

"Take no thought for the morrow . . ." he muttered, quoting Matthew.

"Don't worry about anything . . ." he said aloud, quoting his all-time standby verse in the fourth chapter of Philippians, "but in everything, by prayer and supplication with thanksgiving, make your requests known unto God, and the peace that passes all understanding will fill your hearts and minds through Christ Jesus."

He'd been doing it all wrong. As usual, he was trying to focus on the big picture.

He glanced at the stepping-stones he and Cynthia had laid together last year, making a path through the hedge. There! Right under his nose.

Step by step. That was the answer.

CHAPTER THREE

Eden

"You know how some people think all we have to do in Mitford is watch paint peel?"

"I do."

Emma snorted with disgust. "Mack Stroupe's house could've held us spellbound for th' last fifteen years."

"I haven't driven by there in a while."

"Looked like a shack on th' Creek 'til guess what?"

"I can't guess."

"Four pickups hauled in there this mornin' with men and stepladders. Th' first coat was on by noon, I saw it myself when I went to Hessie's for lunch."

"Aha."

"They painted it blue. I hate blue on a house. Somebody said blue is the color of authority—which is why police officers are th' men in blue. They say it's a color that makes you look like you *are* somebody!"

"Well, well . . ."

"An' take pink. What do you think happened when a sheriff in Texas painted his jail cells pink? The men calmed down, no more violence, can you beat that?"

"Hard to beat," he said, gluing the wooden base back onto the bookend. "And Texas, of all places."

"Where do you think Mack Stroupe gets his money?"

"What money?"

"To buy a new truck, to paint his house. I even heard he had a manicure at Fancy Skinner's place."

"A manicure? Mack?"

"A manicure," she said icily.

"Good heavens." This was serious. "He didn't get a mask, too, did he?"

"A mask? Why would he need a mask when he can lie, cheat, and steal without one?"

"Now, Emma, I don't know about the stealing."

"Maybe you don't, but I do." She looked imperious.

Run from gossip! the Scriptures said. It would be hard to put it more plainly than that.

"I'm going up the street a few minutes. It looks like rain, better close the windows before you leave. Give Harold my congratulations on being moved off the route and into sorting."

"Sorting *and* working the window," she said proudly.

§

"Winnie!" he called, as the bell jingled on the bakeshop door.

Blast if he didn't love the smell of this place. What would happen if the bakery was sold? Anybody could move in here, hawking any manner of goods and wares. Could cards and stationery smell this wonderful, or piece goods, or kitchen wares?

Five years before he arrived on the scene, Winnie had scraped together the money for this storefront, painted it inside and out, installed ovens and secondhand display cases, stenciled *Sweet Stuff Bakery* on the window, and settled into twenty years of unflagging hard work.

Her winning smile and generous spirit had been a hallmark of this street. Hadn't she faithfully fed Miss Rose and Uncle Billy when the old couple tottered by for their daily handout? Yes, and sent something home for the birds, into the bargain.

He found her in the kitchen, sitting on a stool and scribbling on a piece of paper. "Winnie, there you are!"

She beamed at the sight of her visitor. "Have an oatmeal cookie," she said, passing him a tray. "Low-fat."

He was suddenly as happy as a child. "Well, in that case . . ."

He sat on the other stool and munched his cookie. "You know, Winnie, I've been thinking . . ."

Winnie's broad face sobered. She had never known what preachers thought.

"Sweet Stuff isn't a bakery."

"It's not?"

"It's an *institution*! Do you have to go to Tennessee? Can't we keep you?"

"I might be here 'til kingdom come, the way things are lookin'. Not one soul has asked about buyin' it."

"They will, mark my words. God's timing is perfect, even in real estate."

"If I didn't believe that, I'd jump out th' window."

"Wouldn't have far to jump," he said, eyeing the sidewalk through the curtains.

Winnie laughed. He loved it when Winnie laughed. The sound of it had rung in this place far more often than the cash register, but she had done all right, she had come through.

"I'm goin' home in a little bit," she sighed. "I'm not as young as I used to be."

"Who is? I'll be pushing off soon myself, I just came to say hello. How do you like living on Lilac Road?"

"I miss my little cottage by the creek, but that young preacher from Hope House takes good care of it."

"Scott Murphy . . ."

"He washed the windows! Those windows have never been washed! My house sittin' right on th' street and all keeps 'em dirty."

"Well, never much traffic by there to notice."

They sat in silence as he finished his cookie.

"Have another one," she said, wanting him to.

He did. It was soft and chewy, just as he liked cookies to be, and low-fat into the bargain. This was definitely his day. "What do you hear from Joe?"

"Homesick."

"But Tennessee is home."

"Yes, but Mitford's more like home; he's been away from Tennessee fifty years. To tell th' truth, Father, I don't much want to go up there, but here I am with no family left in Mitford, and it seems right for me to go."

Sometimes, what seemed right wasn't so right, after all, but who was he to say?

"Look here," she said, picking up the sheet of paper she'd been scribbling on. "I'm enterin' this contest that's twenty-five words or less. You're educated, would you mind seein' if th' spelling is right?"

He took the paper.

I use Golden Band flour because it's light and easy to work. Also because my mother and grandmother used it. Golden Band! Generation after generation it's the best.

"They sure don't give you much room to rave," he said. "And it looks like you've got twenty-eight words here."

"Oh, law! I counted wrong. What do you think should come out?"

"Let's see. You could take out 'my' and say, 'because Mother and Grandmother used it.'"

"Good! Two to go," she said, sitting on the edge of her stool.

"You could take out 'flour' in the first sentence, since they know it's flour."

"Good! One more to go!"

"This is hard," he said.

"I know it. I been writin' on that thing for four days. But look, they give you a cruise if you win! To the Caribbean! Have you ever been there?"

"Never have."

"Only thing is, it's for two. Who would I go with?"

"Cross that bridge when you get to it," he said. "OK, how about this? 'Generation after generation, Golden Band is best.'"

"How many words?" she asked, holding her breath.

"Twenty-five, right on the money!" He cleared his throat and read aloud. "I use Golden Band because it's light and easy to work. Also because Mother and Grandmother used it. Generation after generation, Golden Band is best."

"Ooh, that sounds good when you read it!" Winnie beamed. "Read it again!"

He read it again, using his pulpit voice. He thought the town's prize baker would fall off the stool with excitement. Why couldn't his congregation be more like Winnie Ivey, for Pete's sake?

As he left the bakery, he saw Mitford's Baptist preacher, Bill Sprouse, coming toward him at a trot.

"Workin' the street, are you?" asked the jovial clergyman, shaking hands.

"And a good day for it!"

"Amen! Wish I could work the south end and we'd meet in the middle for a cup of coffee, but I've got a funeral to preach."

"I, on the other hand, had a baptism this morning."

Bill adjusted the white rose in his lapel. "Coming and going! That's what it's all about in our business!"

"See you at the monument!" said the rector. Since spring arrived, they'd often ended up at the monument at the same time, with their dogs in tow for the evening walk.

He ducked into Happy Endings to see if his order had arrived.

"How do you like your new butterfly book?" asked Hope Winchester, looking fetching, he thought, with her long, chestnut hair pulled back.

"Just the ticket!" he said. "You ought to review it for the *Muse* and first thing you know, half of Mitford would be attracting butterflies."

"That," she said, "is a *very* preponderant idea!"

"Thank you."

"The Butterfly Town! It would bring people from all over."

"I don't think the mayor would much take to that. Unless, of course, they all went home at night."

"Well, Father, progress is going to happen in Mitford, whether our mayor likes it or not. We can't sit here idly, not growing and adapting to the times! And just think. People who like butterflies would be people who like books!"

"Aha. Well, you certainly have a point there."

"Sometimes our mayor can be a bit overweening."

He grinned. "Can't we all? Did my book come in?"

"Let's see," she said, "that was the etymological smorgasbord, I believe."

"'Amo, Amas, Amat,'" he said, nodding.

"I declare!" sniffed Helen Huffman, who owned the place. "Why don't y'all learn to speak English?"

§

"Father, is this a good time?"

He heard the urgency in Olivia Harper's voice when she rang him at the office.

"It's always a good time for you," he said, meaning it.

"Lace went to the Creek to see her friend Harley. I implored her not to go, Father, I know how dangerous it could be. But she went, and now she's home saying that Harley's sick and she's going back to nurse him. Hoppy's in surgery, and I don't . . . Please. She's packing her things. You're so good at this."

"I'll be right there," he said.

Barnabas leapt into the passenger seat of his Buick and they raced up Old Church Lane.

No, he was not good at this. He was not good at this at all. His years with Dooley Barlowe had been some of the hardest of his life; it had all been done with desperate prayer, flying by the seat of his pants. Who was good at knowing the right parameters for wounded kids? Yet, blast it, it was his job to know about parameters. Being a clergyman, being a Christian, had a great deal to do with parameters, which is why the world often mocked and despised both.

He felt the anxiety of this thing. Lace Turner was a passionately determined girl who had suffered unutterable agony in her thirteen years at the Creek—a bedridden mother whom she had faithfully nursed since early childhood, and a brutalizing father suffering the cumulative effects of drugs, alcohol, and regular unemployment.

Through it all, the toothless, kindhearted Harley Welch had looked after Lace Turner's welfare, shielding her whenever he could from harm. It was Harley's truck that Lace had used to transport Dooley's mother, then another Creek resident, to the hospital last summer.

He shuddered at the memory of Pauline Barlowe, who, burned horribly by a man known as LM, had not only endured the agony of skin grafting and the loss of an ear, but had to live with the bitter truth that she'd given away four of her five children.

Though Lace's father and older brother disappeared last year, no one knew when Cate Turner might return to the Creek, nor what he might do if he found his daughter there.

He made a right turn into the nearly hidden driveway of the Harper's rambling mountain lodge. With its weathered shingles, twin stone chimneys, and broad front porch, it was a welcome sight.

Barnabas leapt out, barking with abandon at the sudden alarm of countless squirrels in the overhead network of trees.

Thanks be to God, Lace was now in the care of the Harpers and doing surprisingly well at Mitford School. Naturally, she continued to use her native dialect, but she had dazzled them all with her reading skills and quick intelligence. He was even more taken, however, by the extraordinary depth of her character.

Another Dooley Barlowe, in a sense—with all of Dooley's hard and thorny spirit, and then some.

He put the leash on his dog and left him secured to the porch railing, then opened the screen door and called. Olivia rushed down the hall and gave him a hug.

"Father, you're always there for us."

"And you for us," he said, hugging back.

"She's in her room, packing. I'm sorry to be so . . . so inept. . . ."

"You're not inept. You're trying to raise a teenager and deal with a broken spirit. Let's pray," he said. He looked into her violet eyes, which he always found remarkable, and saw her frantic concern.

He took Olivia's hands. "Father, this is serious business. Give us your wisdom, we pray, to do what is just, what is healing, what is needed. Give us discernment, also, by the power of your Holy Spirit, and soften our hearts toward one another and toward you. In Jesus' name."

"Amen!" she said.

"Shall we talk to her together?"

"I've said it all, she's heard enough from me, I think. Would you . . . ?"

He found Lace in her room, wearing the filthy hat from her days at the Creek, and zipping up a duffel bag.

She turned and glared at him. "I knowed you'd come. You cain't stop me. Harley's sick and I'm goin'."

"What's the matter with Harley?"

"Pukin' blood. Blood in 'is dump. Cain't eat, got bad cramps, and so weak he cain't git up. But they's somethin' worser."

"What?"

"Somebody stoled 'is dogs."

"Why is that worse?" He'd try to stall her until he collected his wits.

"His dogs bein' gone means anybody could go in there and take th' money he's saved back in 'is bed pillers. I've got t' drive 'is truck out, too, or they'll be stealin' that."

"What do you think the sickness might be?"

"I ain't no doctor!" she said, angry.

"It could be something contagious."

"So? Harley done it f'r me time an' again. I was sick nearly t' dyin' an' he waited on me, even went an' fed my mam when my pap was gone workin'."

She picked up the bag and shoved the hat farther down on her head, and walked to the door.

"I'll go with you," he said. Was he crazy? It was broad daylight. He had gone into the drug-infested Creek with her once before, to bring out Poobaw Barlowe—but that had been under cover of darkness and he'd never felt so terrified in his life.

"You ain't goin' in there with me in th' daylight, a preacher wouldn't be nothin' but trouble. Besides, you couldn't hardly git up th' bank that time, you like t' killed y'rself."

She was right about that. He'd taken one step up and two back, all the way to the top. "What kind of medicine have you got?"

She stopped and looked at him.

"Why go in empty-handed? What can you do, not knowing? Come with me to the hospital, we'll talk to a nurse."

"I ain't goin' t' no hospital."

"Lace. Get smart. You can't do this without help. Drive to the hospital with me, I'll get Nurse Kennedy to come out to the car, if necessary. Tell her what you know, see what she thinks."

Lace looked at the floor, then at him. "Don't try t' trick me," she said.

"I don't think you'd be easy to trick."

God in heaven, he didn't have a clue where this was leading.

§

Nurse Kennedy leaned down and talked to Lace through the open car window. Lace sat stoically, clutching the duffel bag in her lap.

"It could be a bleeding ulcer," said Kennedy. "Does Harley drink?"

"Harley was bad to drink f'r a long time, but he's sober now."

"Any diarrhea?"

"An awful lot, an' passin' blood in it."

"How's his color?"

"Real white. White as a sheet."

The nurse looked thoughtful. "Vomiting blood, passing blood, pale, weak, cramps, diarrhea. All symptoms of a bleeding ulcer."

At least whatever it was wasn't contagious, thought the rector, feeling relieved. And it was curable.

"What's the prognosis?" he asked.

"I could be wrong of course, but I don't think so. If it's a bleeding ulcer, it can be treated with antibiotics. Diet plays a part, too. The main thing is, he'll need treatment. His hemoglobin will be low, and that's serious."

"We can't thank you enough."

As they drove down the hill, he still didn't know where he was headed or how this would unfold.

He pulled the car to the curb in front of Andrew Gregory's Oxford Antique Shop. "Let's stop and think this through. If you go to the Creek, there's nothing you can do. You heard the nurse, he's got to have treatment. Let me get Chief Underwood to drive us in there, we'll bring Harley out, money, truck, and all."

"Where would you take 'im to? He ain't goin' t' no hospital."

"I don't know. Let me think." Not Betty Craig's, that was for certain. Betty's little house was stuffed to the gills with Russell Jacks, Dooley's disabled grandfather; Dooley's mother, Pauline Barlowe, who was looking for work; and her son, Poobaw. There wasn't a bed available at Hope House, even if Harley could qualify, and the red tape for the county home would be a yard long.

"Blast!" he said.

"Is that some kind of cussin'?" asked Lace.

"In a manner of speaking," he replied.

§

He was running late for dinner, and he had no idea how he would explain it all to his wife.

Of course, she was vastly understanding about most things, he had to hand her that. So far, she hadn't run him out of the house with a broom or made him sleep in the study.

This, however, could definitely turn the tide in that direction.

She was standing at the back door, looking for him, when he walked up to the stoop with Lace Turner and a weak and failing Harley Welch.

She said only "Good Lord!" and came out to help him.

§

Hoppy Harper was on his way, possibly the last of that sterling breed of doctors who made house calls.

Heaving Harley up the stairs to the guest room was worse than hauling any armoire along the same route. Though shockingly frail, Harley's limp body seemed to have the weight of a small elephant. It took three of them to get Harley on the bed, where the rector undressed him and bathed him with a cloth, which he dipped in a pan of soapy water.

Harley looked comic in the rector's pajamas, which had to be changed immediately, given Harley's inability to make it to the adjoining bathroom on time. "I didn't go t' do that," said Harley, whose flush of embarrassment returned a bit of color to his face.

What had he gotten into? Father Tim wondered. He didn't know. But when Harley Welch looked at him and smiled weakly, the rector felt the absolute wisdom of this impulsive decision, and smiled back.

§

He went to bed, exhausted. Lace had gained permission to stay over, sleeping in Dooley's room next to Harley's, and keeping watch.

He reached for his wife, and she took his hand. "Am I dead meat around here?" he asked.

She rolled toward him and kissed him softly on the nearly bare top of his head.

"I married a preacher," she said. "Not a banker, not an exporter, not an industrialist. A preacher. This is what preachers do—if they do it right."

§

Nobody on the vestry had heard a word from the real estate company that had made inquiries around town.

Oh, well, they'd thrown out the line and there would be another bite at another time. But had they made the bait attractive enough? They couldn't worry about that. They couldn't install additional bathrooms in the hope that Fernbank would lure a bed and breakfast. They couldn't cut up the ground floor into classrooms in the hope it would lure an academy. In the end, they couldn't even afford to paint and roof it, hoping to lure anyone at all.

At eight in the morning he dropped by Town Hall and sat in a Danish modern chair that once occupied the mayor's own family room. He declined the weak coffee in a Styrofoam cup.

"Barbecue?" growled the mayor. "Barbecue? Two can play that game. Ray Cunningham makes the best barbecue in the country—outside the state of Texas, of course."

"I don't know if I'd fight barbecue with barbecue," he said. "I hear Mack's planning to have these things right up 'til election day."

The mayor was just finishing her fast-food sausage biscuit. "Why do anything at all, is what I'd like to know! I don't see how that snake could oust me, even if I was the most triflin' mayor ever put in office."

"Any town in the country would be thrilled to have you running things, Esther. Look at the merchant gardens up and down Main Street, look at our town festival that raised more money than any event in our history. Look at Rose Day, and how you put your shoulder to the wheel and helped turn the old Porter place into a town museum! Look how you rounded up a crew and painted and improved Sophia's little house. . . . The list is endless."

"And look how I don't take any malarkey off the council. You know we've got at least two so-and-sos who'd as soon put a paper plant and a landfill in here as walk up th' street."

"You've never taken your eyes off the target, I'll hand you that."

"So what do you think?" asked Esther, leaning forward. The rector saw that she'd broken out in red splotches, which usually indicated her enthusiasm for a good fight.

"I think I'd wait a while and see how things go in the other camp."

"That's what Ray said."

"In the meantime, I hope you'll have a presence at the town festival. I hear Mack's setting up quite a booth."

"You can count on it! Last year I kissed a pig, this year I'll be kissin' babies. And one of these days, I want to do somethin' for the town, thanking them for their support all these years. Lord, I hope talkin' to you doesn't infringe on any laws of church and state!"

He laughed. "I don't think so. By the way—how about laying off the sausage biscuits for a while? I'd like to see you make it through another couple of terms."

She wadded up the biscuit wrapper and lobbed it into the wastebasket. "You're off duty," she said. "So I'll thank you not to preach."

§

School would be out in two weeks and Dooley would be home.

Where in the dickens would he find the boy a job, or where would Dooley find one for himself? It would have to be in Mitford, which was no employment capital. He'd talk to Lew Boyd when he filled up his tank, or maybe the fellow who was looking after the church grounds could use a helper. . . .

Another thing. Maybe he and Cynthia could do something he'd never done in his life: take a week at the beach, rent a cottage—his wife would know how to do that. As for their mutual dislike of sand and too much sun, weren't there endless compensations—like time to read, the roar of the ocean, and seafood fresh from the boat?

Dooley would like that, and he could take Tommy. They'd load the car and head out right after Dooley's two weeks at Meadowgate Farm.

A vacation! For a man renowned for his stick-in-the-mudness, this was a great advance.

Whistling, he headed toward home.

§

Lace Turner was still wearing the battered hat. But her life with the Harpers had revealed a certain beauty. Her once-tangled hair was neatly pulled away from her face, dramatizing the burning determination in her eyes.

"He ain't doin' too good," she said, indicating the pale, small man who lay in the guest room bed.

For someone devoid of a single tooth, Harley Welch's smile was infectious, the rector thought. "I am, too, Rev'rend, don't listen to 'er. She's makin' me walk a chalk line."

"He ain't eat nothin' but baby puddin'."

"Cain't have no black pepper, no red pepper, no coffee, and no choc'late candy," said Harley. "They say it makes you gastric. Without a little taste of candy, I'd as soon be dead."

"You nearly was dead!" said Lace.

"How's your setup?" asked the rector. "Do you have everything you need?"

"Everything a man could want, plus Lace an' your missus an' Puny to look after me. But I feel it's my bounden duty t' tell you I run liquor most of my early days, and I been worryin' whether th' Lord would want me layin' in this bed."

"Seems to me the Lord put you in this bed," said the rector.

Harley's birdlike hands clutched the blanket. "I've not always lived right," he announced, looking the rector in the eye.

"Who has?" asked Father Tim, looking back.

"I pulled y'r shades down," Lace said, "'cause he cain't have no sunshine, he's on this tetra . . . cyline stuff four times a day f'r three weeks. He's got t' take all that's in this other bottle, too, an' look here—Pepto-Bismol he's got t' swaller twice a day."

"I ain't never lived as bad as all that," said Harley.

Father Tim sat on the side of the bed. "Dr. Harper says you're going to be all right. I want you to know we're glad to have you and want you to get strong."

"He has t' eat six times a day. It ain't easy f'r me'n Cynthia t' figure out six snacks f'r somebody with no teeth."

"Teeth never give me nothin' but trouble," said Harley, grinning weakly. "Some rotted out, some was pulled out, and th' rest was knocked out. I've got used t' things th' way they are. Teeth'd just take up a whole lot of room in there."

"I'm comin' after school an' stayin' nights," Lace announced. "Olivia and Cynthia said I could."

"Good, Lace. Glad to have you around. You've got a fine friend, Harley."

Harley grinned. "She's a good 'un, all right. But awful mean to sick people."

"Well, you're lying on your money and your truck's over at Lew Boyd's getting the oil change you mentioned, so you can rest easy."

"I hate that I've let my oil go, but here lately, I've had t' let ever'thing go. I didn't mean f'r you t' do that, Rev'rend, I'm goin' t' do somethin' for you an' th' missus, soon as I'm up an' about."

"Oh, but I wasn't saying—"

"I know you wasn't, but I'm goin' t' do it, I'm layin' here thinkin' about it. Lace tol' me you got a Buick with some age on it, I might like t' overhaul your engine."

Father Tim laughed heartily. "Overhaul my engine?"

"After my liquor days, I was in car racin'.'"

Was he imagining that good color suddenly returned to Harley Welch's cheeks? "You were a driver?"

"Nossir, I was crew chief f'r Junior Watson."

"Junior Watson! Well, I'll say!"

Harley's grin grew even broader. He didn't think preachers knew about such as that.

That explains it, mused the rector, going downstairs. Yesterday, he had headed Harley's old truck onto Main Street, thinking he'd have to nurse it to Lew Boyd's two blocks away. When he hammered down on the accelerator, he saw he had another think coming. He had roared by Rodney Underwood's patrol car in a blur, as if he'd been shot from a cannon.

He had never gone from Wisteria Lane to the town monument in such record time, except on those occasions when Barnabas felt partial to relieving himself on a favorite monument boxwood.

§

"Landscaping," announced Emma, her mouth set like the closing on a Ziploc bag.

"Landscaping?" he asked.

"Mack Stroupe."

"Mack Stroupe?"

"Hedges. Shrubs. Bushes." In her fury, his secretary had resorted to telegraphic communications. *"Grass,"* she said with loathing.

He didn't recall ever seeing grass in Mack's yard. Dandelions, maybe . . .

"Plus . . ."

"Plus what?"

Emma looked at him over her half-glasses. "Lucy Stroupe is getting her hair dyed today!"

Manicures, landscaping, dyed hair. He didn't know when his mind had been so boggled by political events, local or otherwise.

§

He thought he'd never seen his garden look more beautiful. It filled him with an odd sense of longing and joy, all at once.

Surely there had been other times, now forgotten, when the beauty and mystery of this small place, enclosed by house and hedges, had moved him like this. . . .

The morning mist rose from the warm ground and trailed across the garden like a vapor from the moors. Under the transparent wash of gray lay the vibrant emerald of new-mown grass, and the unfurled leaves of the hosta. Over there, in the bed of exuberant astilbe, crept new tendrils of the strawberry plants whose blossoms glowed in the mist like pink fires.

It was a moment of perfection that he would probably not find again this year, and he sat without moving, almost without breathing. There was the upside of a garden, when one was digging and planting, heaving and hauling, and then the downside, when it was all weeding and grooming and watering and sweating. One had to be fleet to catch the moment in the middle, the mountaintop, when perfection was as brief as the visit of a butterfly to an outstretched palm.

For this one rare moment, their garden was all gardens, the finest of gardens, as the wild blackberry he'd found last year had been the finest of blackberries.

He remembered it distinctly, remembered looking at its unusual elongated form, and putting it in his mouth. The blackberry burst with flavor that transported him instantly to his childhood, to his age of innocence and bare feet and chiggers and freedom. The blackberry that fired his mouth with sweetness and his heart with memory was all the blackberry he would need for a very long time, it had done the work of hundreds of summer blackberries.

He gazed at the canopy of pink dogwoods he had planted years ago, at the rhododendron buds, which were as large as old-fashioned Christmas tree lights, and at the canes of his French roses, which were the circumference of his index finger.

Better still, every bed had been dressed with the richest, blackest compost he could find. He had driven to the country where the classic makers of fertilizer resided, and happened upon a farmer who agreed to deliver a truckload of rotted manure to his very door. He'd rather have it than bricks of gold. . . .

He took a deep draught of the clean mountain air, and shut his eyes. Beauty had its limits with him, he could never gaze upon great beauty for long stretches; he had to take rest stops, as in music.

"Praying, are you, dearest?"

His wife appeared and sat beside him, slipping her arm around his waist.

He nuzzled her hair. "There you are."

"I've never seen it so lovely," she whispered.

A chickadee dived into the bushes. A junco flew out.

"Who loves a garden still his Eden keeps," she said, quoting Bronson Alcott.

He had looked upon this Eden, quite alone, for years. The old adage that having someone to love doubles our joy and divides our sorrow was, like most adages, full of plain truth.

He wanted to say something to her, something to let her know that having her beside him meant the world to him, meant everything.

"I'm going to buy us a new frying pan today," he said.

She drew away and looked at him. Then she burst into laughter, which caused the birds to start from the hedge like cannon shots.

He hadn't meant to say that. He hadn't meant to say that at all!

CHAPTER FOUR

A Full House

He put two pounds of livermush and a pack of Kit Kats in a paper sack, and set out walking to Betty Craig's.

Thank heaven his wife wasn't currently working on a book— they'd sat up talking like teenagers until midnight, feeling conspiratorial behind their closed bedroom door, and coming at last to the issue of Dooley's siblings.

"I don't know, Timothy," she said, looking dejected. "I don't know how to find lost children."

Why did he always think his wife had the answers to tough questions? Even he had the sense to believe that milk cartons, though a noble gesture on someone's part, probably weren't the answer.

"You must press Pauline for details," Cynthia told him. "She says she can't remember certain things, but that's because the memories are so painful—she has shut that part of herself down." His wife leaned her head to one side. "I wouldn't have your job, dearest."

People were always telling him that.

He peered through Betty Craig's screen door and called out.

"It's th' Father!" Betty exclaimed, hurrying to let him in.

He gave her a hug and handed over the bag. "The usual," he said, laughing.

"Little Poobaw's taken after livermush like his granpaw! This won't go far," she said, peering at the contents.

Russell Jacks shuffled into the kitchen with a smiling face. "It's th' Father, Pauline! Come an' see!" The old sexton had run down considerably, but there would never be a finer gardener than this one, thought the rector. A regular Capability Brown. . . .

The two men embraced.

"He's buildin' me a little storage cupboard, go and look!" said Betty Craig, pulling at his sleeve.

"I know you b'lieve if a man can build a cupboard, he can keep th' church gardens," said Russell, "but I've not got th' lung power t' plant an' rake an' dig an' all." He looked abashed.

"I understand, I know. And the leaf mold, that's not good for your lungs."

Russell looked relieved as they walked out to the back porch. "See this here? That was a wood box, I'm turnin' it into a cupboard for waterin' cans an' bird seed an' all. Puttin' some handles on it that we took off th' toolshed doors. If I was stout enough to do it, I'd pull that shed down before it falls down."

"Dooley and I might give you a hand with it this summer. He'll be home in two weeks, you know."

"Yessir, and it'll do his mama a world of good. She's not found a job of work nowhere, it's got to 'er a good bit."

"I understand. But something will come through, mark my words."

"Oh, an' I do mark y'r words, Father. I been markin' y'r words a good while, now. About fifteen year, t' be exact."

Poobaw came to the screen door and peered out shyly, his mother standing behind him. "Father?" she said. Tears sprang to her eyes at once and began coursing down her cheeks.

"Oh, law," sighed Russell, looking at the porch floor.

§

"I don't know," Pauline said. "I don't remember."

Her storm of weeping had passed and she sat quietly with him in the small rear bedroom of Betty Craig's house.

"You've got to remember."

He noticed the patch of skin on the left side of her face, only one of the places where grafting had been done—it was a slightly different color, with a scar running along its boundaries like pale stitching on a quilt. Her long brown hair, tinged with red, covered her missing left ear and hid most of the grafting on her neck. A miracle that she was sitting here. . . .

They sat for a time, wordless. He wouldn't try to chink the cracks of silence with chitchat. He would force her, if he could, to do what she dreaded. But he dreaded it more. He didn't want to force anyone into sorrow. Yet, without this, he couldn't help her do the thing he'd promised when she lay mute and devastated from the horrific burns.

"Holding," she said, turning away from him.

"You were living in Holding?"

"Yes. Mama's second cousin, Rhody, she came and took Jessie. I never told Daddy who done it." She continued to look away from him. "I remember missin' Jessie th' next morning, and there was a note. Rhody said she was taking Jessie for life and for me not to look for her." There was a long silence and Pauline bent her head. "I didn't look. By then, things were so bad . . ."

She was suffering, but without tears.

He waited.

". . . I knew I couldn't take care of her, I might hurt her, I used to lose my temper and throw things. I remember hitting Dooley, it was Christmas. . . ."

She put her head in her hands.

"He'd rode down the mountain on his new bicycle to see me, he was living with you then. I hurt him awful bad when I hit him, and he never said a word back. . . ."

Dooley! He wanted to get in the car and drive to Virginia and find him in his classroom and bring him home and love him, take him fishing, though he didn't have a clue how to fish. He remembered seeing the abandoned boy in overalls for the first time, and his eager, freckled face. . . .

"I remember he rode off on his bicycle and I thought . . . I'll kill myself, I don't deserve to live. And I tried to, Father, I did. I tried to kill myself with drinkin'."

He prayed for her silently.

"I don't know where Rhody is, I wisht I could say she's a good person, but . . . she's not. I think she was glad to see me go down, glad to run off with one of my kids." Pauline took a deep breath. "I've tried to forgive her. Sometimes I can, sometimes I can't. But . . . maybe Jessie was lucky that someone took her."

One thing at a time, his heart seemed to say. This wasn't the day to talk about Sammy and Kenny.

§

They walked around the sagging toolshed, checking it out.

Why beat around the bush? "Russell, tell me about your wife's cousin Rhody."

The old man looked at him somberly.

"Double-talkin' is what I say. Two-faced. I ain't seed much of 'er since Ida passed."

"How can I find her?"

"Be jinged if I know. Her man run out on 'er, he used t' work at th' post office in Holding, but I don't know what come of 'im. Her mama died, I guess they won't much left in Holding to keep 'er. Seems like th' last I heard, she was off in Florida som'ers."

"Any recollection of where in Florida?"

"Law, I cain't recollect. Seem like it started with a *L*. Los Angelees, maybe."

"Aha," he said.

§

When he retired from Lord's Chapel and moved out of the rectory, the yellow house next door would be home. And not enough room inside those four walls to skin a cat.

It was time, and then some, he reasoned, to get an architect to tell them how to add a sunroom and study, enlarge the downstairs bath and Cynthia's garage.

Speaking of expansion projects, it was also time to call the president of Buck Leeper's company, the people who'd done such a shining job of constructing Hope House, and see whether he could get in line for Buck as superintendent of the church attic project.

That, and find Dooley a job. And go through Miss Sadie's attic. And figure out what to do with Fernbank before it ran down so badly there'd be nothing to do with it, period.

It was no surprise that he'd never made it up the ladder to bishop; it was all he could do to say grace over being a country parson.

§

He was hoofing it toward home when Avis Packard stepped out of The Local, wearing his green apron. The screen door slapped shut behind him.

"I don't reckon you'd be havin' a boy who'd like to bag groceries this summer?"

Bingo!

§

It was different having a full house.

Olivia was in and out, helping Cynthia with the responsibility of a man who wasn't yet able to help himself. Lace arrived after school and did her homework in Harley's room, where she was clearly good medicine for what ailed him.

Violet was spending more time at the rectory, since her mistress wasn't often at the little yellow house, and Barnabas lay in wait for the glorious opportunity of finding Violet on the floor instead of the top of the refrigerator, which she had claimed as permanent headquarters with a potted gloxinia.

"Perfect!" said Cynthia, who set Violet's food up there as nonchalantly as if all cats lived on refrigerators.

With the increased workload of the household, Puny was sometimes still there with the twins when he came home.

Five o'clock in the afternoon might have been ten in the morning, for all he could see. It was not unusual for the washing machine to be running, the vacuum cleaner roaring, the blender turning out nutrition for the toothless and infirm, and the twins jiggling in their canvas seats suspended in the kitchen doorway.

During all this, Barnabas sat patiently in front of the refrigerator, blocking traffic and gazing dolefully at Violet, who scorned his every move.

A madhouse! he thought, grinning. Blast if it wouldn't run most men into the piney woods. But after more than sixty years of being an only child and a bachelor into the bargain, the whole thing seemed marvelous, a veritable circus of laughing and slamming and banging and wailing. He wouldn't wish it on his worst enemy, but for himself, he liked the novelty of it.

"Come in, Rev'rend!" Harley was sitting up in bed, having one of his multiple snacks.

"How're you?" Lace asked, without taking her eyes off the patient.

A civil greeting! Olivia was making headway with her indomitable thirteen-year-old charge. "I'm fine. How about you?"

"I'm OK. Harley, if you hide that banana bread an' don't eat it, I'll knock you in th' head."

Harley grinned. "See there? A feller don't have a chance, she's like a revenue agent lookin' f'r liquor cars, got eyes in th' back of 'er head."

"You're stronger today."

"Yessir, I am. I ain't never laid up in such style as this in m' life, we had it hard when I was comin' up in Wilkes County. We was s' poor, all we had t' play with was a rubber ball, an' th' dog eat half of that."

"Kind of hard to judge which way it would bounce," said the rector.

"Shoot, we was s' poor, I went t' school one time, I was wearin' one shoe. Th' teacher said 'Harley, have you lost a shoe?' an' I said, 'No, ma'm, I found one.'"

"Don't lie," said Lace. "It ain't right."

Harley looked doleful. "I ain't lyin'! Another thing, Rev'rend, I'm gittin' out of this bed tomorrow, sure as you're born. I looked out that back winder and seen y'r yard, you need some rakin' around that hedge."

Lace glared at Harley from beneath her hat brim. "You ain't movin' 'til Doc Harper gives you th' green light."

"Lord have mercy! Git that girl a job of work t' do."

The rector laughed. "She's got a job of work to do! And you leave my hedge alone, buddyroe."

"I hate t' be hangin' on you an' th' missus like a calf on a tit."

"I don't want to hear about it. Eat your banana bread."

"Law, now they's two of 'em," said Harley, taking a bite.

"An' drop y'r crumbs on y'r napkin," said Lace.

§

"Lace has real beauty."

"But she hides it with that dreadful hat. We let her wear it in the house, of course, but never to school or church."

"Sounds fair," he said.

Cynthia had gone next door for a cake pan, and Olivia was finishing a cup of tea with him.

"It represents something to her," said Olivia. "It's a defense of who she is, I think, of something she doesn't want us to change."

"You're doing a grand job, you and Hoppy, we're seeing a difference."

"We love her. She's quite extraordinary." Olivia stirred her tea, thoughtful. "Perhaps what we want more than anything . . . is for Lace to be able to cry."

"What I wanted more than anything was for Dooley to be able to laugh."

Olivia smiled. "The two things aren't so different, perhaps. Laughter, tears . . . it's all a way of letting something out, letting something go. Forgiveness . . . somehow, I think that's the answer. Did I tell you she's making straight A's?"

"Amazing!"

"She hasn't had much schooling, really, yet she loves to learn, it comes naturally to her. She keeps her nose in a book, with the radio tuned to a country music station."

They sipped their tea.

"She adores Hoppy, of course," Olivia said.

"I'm sure she cares for you, too."

"I don't know. She . . . fights me."

"Ah, well. I know about that."

"I take her to see her mother twice a week."

"What's her mother like?"

Olivia shook her head slowly. "Hard and unkind. I hoped she'd be different. Lace has taken care of her mother all her life, Lila Turner has been ill since Lace was a toddler. I think the only person who ever really cared about Lace, who loved her, is Harley."

"Was Harley ever married? Any children of his own?"

"His wife died years ago, he loved her deeply and never quite got over her death. There weren't any children." Olivia finished her tea. "Well, on to brighter things," she said, smiling. "Our school is out in two weeks. When is Dooley coming home?"

"Next Friday," he said. "He'll come in with a friend's parents. Avis wants him at The Local for the summer."

"Lovely! How does he feel about Meadowgate not being there for him?"

"He'll tough it out. After a couple of weeks at The Local, and hanging around with Tommy, and a few days at the beach . . ." He shrugged, hopeful.

"All the best," she said, her violet eyes bright with feeling.

"All the best to you," he replied, meaning it.

§

Avis wanted Dooley ASAP, which could mean three days at the farm and four at the beach. Or no days at the beach and a week at the farm. Another thought: Maybe Dooley would like to take Poobaw to the beach and let Tommy fill in for him at The Local before Tommy went to work at Lew Boyd's.

Why did something so simple boggle his mind? Should he call Dooley and tell him he had a job that would place some constraints on the farm? Should he even mention the beach? Should he just wait 'til Dooley came home and deal with it then?

"Lord . . ." he sighed, lifting his hands.

§

"A billboard," said Emma.

"A billboard?"

"Mack Stroupe."

Mack on a billboard? Is that why Mack had gotten a manicure? He didn't know how these things worked.

"On the highway after you pass Hattie Cloer's market. Right in your face. It's enough to make you jump out of your skin, that thing loomin' up on you. You talk about ugly, his nose takes up half th' board. And those bushy eyebrows, and that egg-suckin' grin . . ." Emma shivered.

"What does it say?"

"It says *Mack for Mitford, Mitford for Mack, Vote Stroupe for Mayor.* I told Harold to stop the car while I puked."

"A billboard. Amazing." Who was repackaging Mack Stroupe?

"Have you seen Lucy since she got her hair dyed? Blond! Can you believe it? Her hair's been the color of a church mouse for a hundred years. You know Mack made her do it. Lucy Stroupe would no more think of dyin' her hair blond than I'd think of runnin' a marathon. But—do you think blond hair will keep Mack Stroupe from cheatin' on his wife with that black-headed hussy in Wesley? I don't think so."

Emma glowered at him as if he were personally responsible for the whole affair. "Are you goin' to his barbecue on Saturday?"

"Dooley's coming in Friday, and we'll be spending the day at Meadowgate on Saturday."

"Good! I hope th' whole town stays away in droves."

"Unfortunately, a lot of people love barbecue."

"You can bet your boots that Harold and I won't be staying more than fifteen minutes."

"You're *going?*"

"Of course we're going, I want to see what the lowlife has to say. How can you knock the opposition when you don't know what they stand for?"

"Aha," he said.

§

Dooley was home and Barnabas was wild with excitement. The rector wondered if the joy that people seemed so expert at containing somehow transferred to their dogs, who had nothing at all to hide.

"Hey, Barn! Hey, buddy!"

Barnabas licked Dooley on every exposed area with special attention to his left ear. "Say a Scripture!" he yelled.

The rector laughed. "You say a Scripture!"

"Ah . . . the Lord is my shepherd, I shall not want!" Dooley thundered.

Barnabas crashed to the floor and sighed.

"A miracle, if I ever saw it," said Cynthia, of the only dog anyone had ever known whose behavior could be controlled by Scripture recitation.

"Well, you've had your bath," said the rector, putting his arms around the boy in the navy school blazer. "Welcome home!"

"Welcome home, you big lug!" said Cynthia, giving him a warm embrace. "Good heavens, you're tall! You're positively towering!"

"I'm the same as when you saw me the last time," said Dooley.

"Then I guess I've gotten shorter!"

Father Tim hoisted two duffel bags. "I'll help carry your things up. There's someone we'd like you to meet. We have a guest in the guest room."

"Who?"

"Harley Welch," said Cynthia. "He hasn't been well, so he'll be recuperating with us. Put on some old clothes and get comfortable. Dinner will be ready soon. Are you hungry?"

"I'm starved!" said Dooley, meaning it.

§

Dooley came into the kitchen, glaring at them. "Some girl's stuff is in my room," he said curtly.

Cynthia was taking a roast from the oven. "What kind of stuff?"

"A jacket. A hairbrush. Some . . . hair clips or somethin'."

"Lace Turner has been staying in your room and helping nurse Harley."

He glared at Cynthia. "That's what I thought. My room smells different. She better not come in there again . . . and I mean it!" he said, raising his voice.

Cynthia set the roast on the stove top and took a deep breath. "For the moment, this is a happy, busy, contented household. That is a precious thing for any household to be, and each of us must work to keep it that way.

"It was important for Lace to help with Harley, as I could not do it all myself. She is now out of your room, and you are in it. I will expect you to treat her civilly when you see her, and I expect to be treated civilly, as well. Dinner is nearly ready, it is everything you like best. If your stomach is upset by this incident, which I expect it may be, go to your room and pray about it, then come down and eat like a horse.

"You have," she said, looking at him steadily, "ten minutes."

Dooley stood for a moment, then turned and stomped upstairs.

The rector placed forks, knives, and spoons on the table, trying to be quiet about it. With his wife and Lace Turner running things around here, he and Dooley might be heading for the piney woods, after all.

⚛

Dooley Barlowe was indeed taller and, if possible, thinner. For twenty thousand bucks a year, didn't those people at school put food on the table?

And where were his freckles?

"Waiting for the sun to get to them!" exclaimed Cynthia.

What about his cowlick, then? Would they never see that again?

"Not in this lifetime," his wife said.

And his grades—how about those grades? Not bad! Not bad at all! He owed the boy a small fortune. A couple of twenties, at least.

"Would you tell him?" he asked her after dinner.

"What do you think?"

"I think you won't do it," he said, striding into the study and trying to appear casual.

Dooley was waiting for Tommy to come over and fooling with the electric train they kept in the corner by the windows.

"Buddy, I've got good news!" He sounded as phony as a three-dollar bill. "You've got a job for the summer . . . which means, of course, that—"

"I know," said Dooley, looking up.

"You do?"

"Avis told Tommy and Tommy called me up. Avis is hiring Tommy, too."

"I thought Tommy was going to work for Lew Boyd."

"He was, but Lew's nephew turned up for the job. We start Monday."

"Really?"

"Eight o'clock sharp, Avis said."

"Ah, well. We were going to take you to the beach for a few days with Tommy or Poobaw. Stay in a cottage. Swim. Like that." Swim? He couldn't swim a stroke, but Cynthia was a fish. "Eat seafood." Dooley was fooling with the train again. "Have . . . you know, *fun.*"

Dooley looked up and suddenly grinned at him. "That's OK. You do stuff for me all the time. It'll be fun working. Me'n Tommy will have a blast."

"Right. Well. Congratulations! We can go out to Meadowgate on Saturday, then. For the day. How's that?"

"Great."

"There!" Cynthia said when he came back to the kitchen. "See how easy it was?"

Easy? Except for the relief of Dooley's grin, he hadn't found it easy at all.

There was, of course, an unexpected compensation.

Now they wouldn't have to get in the car and drive five long hours to the beach. He could stay right here in Mitford like the stick-in-the-mud he was known to be.

§

Meadowgate.

The very name soothed him, and was, in fact, an apt description.

A broad, green meadow ran for nearly a mile along the front of the Owens' property, sliced in half by a country lane that led through an open farm gate.

He had found solace in this place time and time again over the years, first as a new priest with a brand-new parish.

It had taken months, perhaps even a couple of years, to come to terms with the fact that he'd followed in the footsteps of a canonized saint. Father Townsend had been tall, dynamic, handsome, and at Lord's Chapel for nearly twenty years. Though the parish had called

Timothy Kavanagh after a tough and discriminating search, it had taken all his resources to wean them, at last, from the charismatic Henry Townsend.

He thought back on the pain he'd felt through much of that time, glad, indeed, that he could now laugh about it.

"Dearest, you're laughing!"

"Darn right!" he said, feeling the happiness of driving along a beckoning lane with a comfortable wife, a happy boy, and a dog the size of a haymow.

"Let me drive the rest of the way." Dooley was suddenly breathing on the back of his neck.

"I don't think so."

"Tommy's dad lets him drive. Jack, this guy at school, his dad lets him drive his four-wheel all the time—"

"You can drive when you're sixteen—and believe me, you won't have long to wait."

"You could just let me drive to the house. I know how."

"Since when?"

"Since I went home with Jack and his dad let me drive."

"Aha."

The house came into view and, failing any more intelligent response, he stepped on the accelerator. He'd completely forgotten about the torrid romance between boys and cars.

§

Marge Owen's French grandmother's chicken pie recipe was a study in contrasts. Its forthright and honest filling, which combined large chunks of white and dark meat, coarsely cut carrots, green peas, celery, and whole shallots, was laced with a dollop of sauterne and crowned by a pastry so light and flaky, it might have won the favor of Louis XIV.

"Bravo!" exclaimed the rector.

"Man!" said Dooley.

"I unashamedly beg you for this recipe," crowed Cynthia.

The new assistant, Blake Eddistoe, scraped his plate with his spoon. "Wonderful, ma'am!"

Hardly anyone ever cooked for diabetes, thought the rector as they trooped out to eat cake in the shade of the pin oak. Apparently it was a disease so innocuous, so bland, and so boring to anyone other than its unwilling victims that it was blithely dismissed by the cooks of the land.

He eyed the chocolate mocha cake that Marge was slicing at the table under the tree. Wasn't that her well-known raspberry filling? From here, it certainly looked like it. . . .

Ah, well. The whole awful business of saying no, which he roundly despised, was left to him. Maybe just a thin slice, however . . . something you could see through. . . .

"He can't have any," said Cynthia.

"I can't believe I forgot!" said Marge, looking stricken. "I'm sorry, Tim! Of course, we have homemade gingersnaps, I know you like those. Rebecca Jane, please fetch the gingersnaps for Father Tim, they're on the bottom shelf."

The four-year-old toddled off, happy with her mission.

Chocolate mocha cake with raspberry filling versus gingersnaps from the bottom shelf. . . .

Clearly, the much-discussed and controversial affliction from which St. Paul had prayed thrice to be delivered had been diabetes.

§

They were sitting on the porch, working up the energy to pile into the Buick and head back to Mitford.

When in Mitford, it seemed only the small, unhurried village that one loved it for being, with a populace of barely more than a thousand. From out here, however, Mitford seemed a regular metropolis, with traffic, political billboards, and barbecue events staged on slabs of asphalt.

Dooley had been to his room and silently carried out a box of his things.

Thump, thump, thump, thump . . . One of the farm dogs scratched himself vigorously, then licked the irritated flesh.

"Oh, dear," said Marge. "Here we go! It's skin allergy season for Bonemeal."

Hal took his pipe from his pocket. "Every year, he has a hot spot on his right rear flank, where he chews and scratches the skin."

"I can give him a shot of Depo-Medrol," said Blake. He turned to the Kavanaghs. "A long-acting steroid. Goes into the system and lasts up to three months. He'll stop scratching in a couple of hours."

Dooley looked up from the box he was holding between his legs. "I wouldn't do that."

There was a brief silence.

Blake looked awkward. "What would you do?"

"Use a short-acting cortisone, which is easier on his system, and follow it up with tablets and a change of diet . . . medicate his shampoos."

"This is a country practice," said Hal Owen, tamping the tobacco in his pipe. "Not much time to fool with new diets and fancy shampoos."

Dooley stood up with his box. "Right," he said.

They were silent on the way home to Mitford. Maybe it was because of the late afternoon meal and the fresh country air.

§

"Is Dooley home from school yet?"

It was Jenny, the girl who lived down the street in the house with the red roof. She had shown up at their door, off and on, for the last couple of years, and he knew for a fact that Dooley had once spent hard-earned money on a coffee-table horse book for this girl.

"He is! Won't you come in?"

She came in, looking only slightly less shy than last year.

Barnabas skidded up, wagging his tail and barking. But there was no need to shout a Scripture verse. Jenny looked his dog in the eye and began scratching behind his ears.

He dashed upstairs to Dooley's bedroom, feeling some odd excitement in the air. "There's someone here to see you."

"Who?"

"Jenny."

Aha. He couldn't help but see Dooley's face turning red.

§

"You missed it," she said archly.

Why did he ever part with fifty cents for a newspaper, when all the news that was fit to print poured unhindered from his secretary?

"Say on."

"You know th' big wooded area behind the Shoe Barn?"

"I do."

"When Mack is elected, that whole sorry-looking scrub pine deal will be a fancy new development called Mitford Woods."

"Mitford Woods?"

"Plus, he said he personally knows of big-money interest in Miss Sadie's old house, which will be revealed shortly."

"Aha." If there was nothing to worry about as far as Mack Stroupe's mayoral win was concerned, why did he feel as if someone had punched him in the solar plexus? "So how was the barbecue?"

"Great. None of that vinegary stuff you sometimes get with politics. Plus, he had a whole raft of country musicians that got half th' crowd to clogging."

He looked at her, but she avoided his eyes. "Hmmm. So what do you think about Mack?"

"Oh . . . time will tell," she said, clicking on her menu. Was this the woman who, barely forty-eight hours ago, had labeled the candidate low-down scum?

"Esther Cunningham has been a great mayor for this town," she said, "but . . ."

He hated to hear it.

". . . but there's always room for improvement."

§

At the light on Main Street, Rodney Underwood yelled from his patrol car.

"What do you think this is? *Talladega?*"

Could he help it if Harley's truck blew past Rodney like he was standing still? Besides, what business did Rodney have being on Main Street every time he tried to do somebody a favor and take care of their vehicle?

Rodney winked at him. "Don't let it happen ag'in, buddyroe."

He felt the heat above his collar as the truck lunged away from the light and roared south on Main Street.

§

"What have you got under the hood of that '72 Ford? You nearly got me nailed twice in a row."

The rector thought Harley's toothless grin might meet at the back of his head.

"Lord, I was hopin' you'd ask. Here's what I done. I got rid of th' Ford engine and transmission, took out th' drive train an' rear end, an' dropped a '64 Jagwar XKE engine and transmission in there. Then I bolted in a Jagwar rear end and hooked it up to a new drive shaft. Three hundred and twenty horses! Course, that's all a man needs on a public highway."

He didn't understand a word Harley said, but he knew one thing: He was leaving that truck alone.

"I messed with flathead V-8s most of my life, 'til one day I looked under th' hood of a Jag and seen a steel crank case, twin alumium valve covers, an' a alumium head. Now, you take Junior, he didn't like nothin' foreign, but t' me, hit was th' prettiest thing I ever seen. Well, Rev'rend, when I left th' business, I fell away from flatheads an' ain't never looked back."

"Aha."

"You got t' handle it gentle or it'll jump over th' moon."

Father Tim laid the keys on the dresser. "Tell me about it. I sucked the awnings off every storefront on Main Street."

Harley hooted and cackled 'til the tears streamed from his eyes. If laughter was the medicine the Bible claimed it to be, Harley Welch was a well man.

The patient wiped his eyes on his pajama sleeve. "I thank you ag'in f'r all you an' th' missus do f'r me. Ain't nobody ever treated me s' good, an' I'm goin' t' make it up to you. Doc Harper lets me up to-morrow, said take it easy a day or two an' first thing you know, I'll be ol' Harley ag'in. I'll git me some new dogs an' go back t' my little setup on th' Creek. But not before I do somethin' t' repay y'uns."

"Don't think about it, my friend. Do you have a job to go back to?"

"I had one, but it give out th' same time as I did. I ain't worked in a good while, what with my stomach s' bad off. But I'll git back, I ain't lazy—I like a good job of work."

"We'll see how it goes," said Father Tim. "Has our boy been around this afternoon'

"Heard 'im come in, heard 'im go out is all."

"This was his first day at the store. Where's Lace?"

"After her school lets out tomorrow, she'll be here t' he'p me git up, take me out in th' fresh air an' all."

"Good! I want you to take it easy."

"Yessir, Rev'rend, I will. I want t' be feelin' strong when I go t' work on y'r car engine."

The rector laughed. "You leave my car engine alone," he said, meaning it.

CHAPTER FIVE

Out to Canaan

He peered into the vegetable crisper and took out three zucchini, a yellow onion, two red potatoes, and a few stalks of celery.

Somewhere in here was a beef bone he'd picked up at The Local. Aha. Wrapped in foil, behind the low-fat mayonnaise which he wouldn't touch with a ten-foot pole . . .

He put it all in a brown paper bag with a can of beef broth and a pound of coffee, and set out to Scott Murphy's house next to the bridge over Little Mitford Creek.

§

They walked along the path by the creek, with Luke and Lizzie straining ahead on their leashes.

It was hot for a June afternoon in the mountains, and he and Scott Murphy were going at a trot. The rector moved the grocery bag to his other arm and took out his handkerchief and wiped his face.

"Father, about your concern for having a Creek ministry . . ."

"Yes?"

"It occurs to me that you have one."

The rector looked at him, puzzled.

"You brought Dooley's kid brother out of there, who's living in the first real home he ever had. You're also providing a home for their mother. . . ."

"But—"

"And look at Lace Turner—last year she was living in the dirt under her house, trying to keep away from an abusive father. Now she's living with one of the most privileged families in town and making straight A's in school."

"Aha."

"And Harley Welch, your race car mechanic . . . you and Mrs. Kavanagh have taken him in, nursed him, maybe even saved his life."

"Yes, well . . ."

Luke stopped to lift his leg at a tree.

"I think we're always looking for the big things," Scott mused. "The big calling, the big challenge. Seems like Bonhoeffer had something to say about that."

"He did," said the rector. "Something like, 'We think we dare not be satisfied with the small measure of spiritual knowledge, experience and love that has been given to us, and that we must constantly be looking forward eagerly for the highest good.'"

"Yes, and I like that he talks about being grateful even where there's no great experience and no discoverable riches, but much weakness, small faith, and difficulty."

The two men pondered this as they walked. It was good to talk shop on a spring day, on a wooded path beside a bold creek.

"Before I came here," said Scott, "I told you I'd go in there and see what can be done. I'm sticking to it."

"Good fellow."

"I've been meaning to tell you we got the garden in at Hope House, fourteen of the residents are able to plant and hoe a little, we have peas coming up."

"You're everything Miss Sadie wanted," said the rector. "You're making Hope House live up to its name."

"Thank you, sir. Mitford is definitely home to me. Maybe I can buy Miss Ivey's little cottage when she sells the bakery and moves to Tennessee—I don't know, I'm praying about it."

They rounded the bend in the footpath and saw Homeless Hobbes sitting on the front step of his small, tidy house, a colorful wash hanging on the line.

"Lord have mercy, if it ain't town people!" Homeless got up and limped toward them on his crutch, laughing his rasping laugh. His mute, brown-and-white spotted dog crouched by the step and snapped its jaws, but no sound escaped. Luke and Lizzie barked furiously.

"Homeless!" The rector was thrilled to see his old friend, the man who'd given up a fast-lane advertising career, returned to his boyhood home, and gone back to "talkin' like he was raised."

"I'm about half wore out lookin' for company! I told Barkless a while ago, I said somebody's comin', my nose is itchin', so I put somethin' extra in th' soup pot!"

The rector embraced Homeless and handed over the bag. "For the pot. And this is Scott Murphy, the chaplain at Hope House. He works sixteen hours a day and still has time to meddle in Creek business."

Homeless looked at the tall, lanky chaplain approvingly. "We need meddlin' in here," he said.

§

"I'd like to see th' dozers push th' whole caboodle off th' bank, and good riddance!"

Homeless had brought out two aluminum folding chairs that had seen better days, and set them up for his guests. He sat on the step, and the dogs lay panting in a patch of grass.

"They say th' whole thing'll be a shoppin' center in a couple of years. Where all them trailers is parked—Wal-Mart! Where all them burned-out houses is settin'—Lowe's Hardware! Where you could once go in and get shot in th' head, you'll be able t' go in an' get you a flush toilet.

"Still an' all, two years is a good bit of time, and you could do a good bit of work on the Creek, if you handle it right. Now, you take ol' Absalom Greer, he come in here and preached up a storm and some folks got saved and a good many lives were turned around, but Absalom was native and he was old, and they let him be.

"They won't take kindly to a young feller like yourself if you don't give 'em plenty of time to warm up.

"What I think you ought to do is come to my place on Wednesday night when I make soup for whoever shows up, and just set an' talk an' be patient, an' let th' good Lord do a work."

"I'll be here," said Scott.

Homeless grinned. "I wouldn't bring them dogs if I was you. Jack Russells are a mite fancy for my crowd."

&

"We lost our dining room manager last week," Scott said on the walk back home. "A family problem. Everybody's been pitching in, it's kind of a scramble."

"I like scrambles," said the rector, who was currently living in one.

&

Sometimes, a thought lodged somewhere in the back of his mind and he couldn't get it out, like a sesame seed stuck between his teeth.

Walking down Old Church Lane the following day, his jacket slung over his shoulder, he tried to focus on the place—was it in his brain?—that had something to tell him, some hidden thing to reveal.

Blast! He hated this. It was like Emma's aggravating game, Three Guesses. He couldn't even begin to guess. . . .

A job. Why did he think it had to do with a job?

We lost our dining room manager last week, Scott had said.

Yes!

Pauline!

Hanging on to his jacket, he started running. He could go to the office and call from there, but no, he'd run across Baxter Park, through his own backyard, and then up the hill and over to Betty Craig's house. Why waste a minute? Jobs were scarce.

He was panting and streaked with sweat when he hit the sidewalk in front of Betty's trim cottage. He stopped for a moment to wipe his face with a handkerchief when Dooley blew by him on his red bicycle.

"Hey!" shouted Dooley.

"Hey, yourself!" he shouted back.

He saw the boy throw the bicycle down by Betty's front steps, fling his helmet in the grass, and race to the door.

"Mama! Mama!" he called through the screen door.

Pauline appeared at the door and let him in as the rector walked up to the porch.

"Mama, there's a job at Hope House! Something in the dining room! I heard it at the store, they need somebody right now."

"Oh." Pauline grew pale and put her hand to the left side of her face. "I . . . don't know."

"You've waited tables, Mama, you can do it! You can do it!"

He saw the look on Dooley's face, and tried to swallow down a knot in his throat. In only a few years, this boy on a bicycle would be worth over a million dollars, maybe two million if the market stayed strong. Dooley wouldn't know this until he was twenty-one, but the rector could see that Sadie Baxter had known exactly what she was doing when she drew up her will.

"Come on, Mama, get dressed and go up there, I've got to get back to The Local or Avis'll kill me, I got five deliveries."

"I'll take you," the rector told Pauline. "I'll go home and get the car, won't be a minute." Hang the meeting in the parish hall at two o'clock.

Pauline looked at him through the screen door, keeping her hand over the left side of her face. "Oh, but . . . I don't have anything to . . . I don't know . . ."

"Don't be afraid," he said.

Tears suddenly filled Pauline's eyes, but she managed to smile. "OK," she said, turning to look at her son. "I can do it."

"Right!" said Dooley. He charged through the door and raced down the steps and was away on his red bicycle, but not before the rector saw the flush of unguarded hope on his face.

"I'll be back," said Father Tim. "Wear that blue skirt and white blouse, why don't you? I thought you looked very . . ."—he wasn't terribly good at this; he searched for a word—"nice . . . in that."

She gazed at him for a long moment, almost smiling, and disappeared down the hall.

An attractive woman, he thought, tall and slender and surprisingly poised, somehow. Her old life was written on her face, as all our lives are written, but something shone through that and transformed it.

❧

In his opinion, Hope House might have done a notch better on their personnel director, Lida Willis.

"How long have you been sober?" asked the stern-looking woman, eyeing Pauline.

"A year and a half."

"What happened to turn you around?"

"I prayed a prayer," said Pauline, looking fully into the director's cool gaze.

"You prayed a prayer?"

Though he sat well across the room, feigning interest in a magazine, Father Tim felt the tension of this encounter. God was calling Pauline Barlowe to come up higher.

"Yes, ma'am."

"Are you in AA?"

"No, ma'am."

"Why not?"

"I don't know. I . . . feel like God has healed me of drinkin'. I don't crave it no more."

"Shoney's fired you for drinking on the job?"

"Yes. But they said that . . . when I was sober, I was the best they ever had."

"Miss Barlowe, what makes you think you might be right for this job?"

"I understand being around food, I get along real well with people, and I'm not afraid of hard work."

The director sat back in her chair and looked at Pauline, but said nothing.

"I need this job and would be really thankful to get it. I know if you call Sam Ward at Sam and Peg's Ham House in Holding, he'll tell you I do good work, I never missed a day at th' Ham House, my station was fourteen tables."

"Were you drinking when you worked there?"

Pauline looked down for a moment, then looked straight at Lida Willis. "Not as bad as . . . later."

"Has your personal injury handicapped you in any way?"

"Sometimes I don't hear as good out of my left ear, but that's all. My arm works wonderful, it's a miracle."

"I appreciate your honesty, Miss Barlowe." She stood up. "Please don't call us. We'll be in touch."

Pauline stood, also. "Yes, ma'am."

Dear God, he wanted this job for Pauline. No, wrong. He wanted this job for Dooley.

He saw Scott Murphy in the hall. "If there's anything you can do," he said under his breath as Pauline drank at the water fountain. "Your dining room manager's job . . ." He never begged anyone for anything, but this was different and he didn't care.

Scott looked at him, knowing.

"She can do it," he told the chaplain.

§

He was looking something up in his study when he heard a noise in the garage. It sounded like his car engine revving.

Surely Harley wasn't already working on . . .

He went through the kitchen, carrying J. W. Stevenson's rare volume on his ministry in the Scottish highlands.

Dooley was sitting in the Buick, gunning the motor. Barnabas sat on the passenger side, looking straight ahead.

"What's going on?" Father Tim asked through the open car window.

"Nothin'."

"Nothing, is it? Looks like you're gunning that motor pretty good."

"I'm checking it out for Harley."

"Really?"

"He didn't ask me to, but I thought it would help him to know how it sounds."

"Right. Well, you're out of there, buddy. Come on."

Dooley gave him an aloof stare. "Jack's dad lets him—"

"Look. What Jack's dad does is beside the point." Was it, really?

He didn't have a clue. Why would people let fourteen-year-old kids drive a car, two years before they could get a license? Or was that the going thing and he was a stick-in-the-mud? "Maybe one day we can drive out to Farmer. . . ."

Dooley turned off the ignition: "Cool," he said. "Your engine's got a knock in it."

§

At six-thirty, Barnabas was finishing up last week's meat loaf, Violet was sneering down from the refrigerator, Cynthia was running a garlic clove around the salad bowl, Dooley was taking one of his endless showers, and Lace was stuffing a snack down a reluctant Harley Welch.

Father Tim still couldn't get over the fact that only three or four years ago, the rectory had been quiet as a tomb. No dog, no boy, no wife in an apron, no red-haired babies, and hardly ever a soul in the guest room, with the agonizing exception, of course, of his phony Irish cousin and an occasional overnight visit by Stuart Cullen, his seminary friend and current bishop.

"Can I talk t' you som'ers?" Lace wanted to know.

Harley was sitting on the side of the bed, fully dressed, but looking weak. He scraped the last bite from a cup of peach yogurt and wiped his mouth with his sleeve.

"Rev'rend, Lace has got a notion I cain't argue 'er out of. Don't pay no attention to 'er if she talks foolish."

"I don't believe I've ever heard Lace talk foolish," he said. "You look a little peaked today, Harley. How're you feeling?"

"Wore out. We was up an' down an' aroun' ever' whichaway, th' doc said I needed exercise. I been eatin' like a boar hog an' layin' up in this bed 'til I was runnin' t' fat."

"We could go down t' y'r basement," said Lace, tugging at her hat brim.

"My basement?"

"I hate like th' dickens I couldn't talk 'er out of this," said Harley. "She's pigheaded as a mule, always has been since I knowed 'er as a baby."

"What's the deal?" he asked as they trooped down the basement stairs.

"You'll see," she said.

The musty smell of earth came to him, and he remembered the cave he and Cynthia had been lost in only last year. They had wandered in circles for fourteen agonizing hours, until the local police, led by Barnabas, brought them out.

He shuddered and flipped the switch that lit the dark hallway.

There was the bathroom that hadn't been used since he moved here fifteen years ago, and the two bedrooms and the little kitchen—which had served, during the tenures of various rectors, as a mother-in-law apartment, a facility for runaways and later for elderly widows, a home office, an adult Sunday School, a church nursery, and storage space for the detritus of nearly a century of clergy families.

Lace folded her arms across her chest. "This is what I think."

"Shoot."

"When me'n Harley was ramblin' around today outside, we seen y'r basement door. F'r somethin' t' do, I tried t' git th' door open and had t' nearly bust it in."

"Really?"

"But it ain't broke, it was just stuck."

"Good!"

"So we seen how this is a place t' live, with a toilet an' kitchen an' all. An' I got to thinkin' how if Harley goes back to th' Creek, how he ain't goin' t' take care of hisself, an' besides, somethin' bad could happen to 'im."

"Aha."

"So I thought if you was to like th' idea, Harley could live down here and go t' work f'r you an' Cynthia."

He pulled at his chin.

"Harley can work, you ain't never seen 'im work, you just seen 'im laid up sick. Harley can rake, he can saw, he can hammer, he can paint."

"I'll be darned."

"An' he wouldn't charge you a cent to keep you an' Cynthia's cars worked on."

She looked at him steadily under the dim glow of the bulb.

"Well, I don't know. I'd have to think about it, talk to Cynthia about it."

"He wouldn't be no trouble. They wouldn't be no cookin' or nothin' to do for 'im, he could take care of hisself. He could paint this place for you, fix it up, I'd help 'im."

She paused, then said: "You ought t' do it, it'd be good for ever'-body."

Lace Turner had made her case, and rested it.

§

"Can he draw cats?" asked Cynthia. "He could do my next book."

Uh-oh. "Your next book?"

"I've been meaning to tell you, dearest. I'm starting a new book. You know how I said I'd never do another Violet book?"

"You definitely said that. Several times."

"I lied."

"Aha."

"You won't believe the advance they'll give me to do another Violet book."

It was true. When she told him, he didn't believe it. "Come on. That's four times what they gave you for the bluebird book."

"Well, you see, I refused so fiercely to do another Violet book, they had to make me an offer I couldn't resist."

"You're tough, Kavanagh."

"So kiss me!" she said, laughing.

He kissed her, inhaling the elusive scent of wisteria. "Congratulations! We can build a boat and retire to the Caribbean and spend our lives cruising and fishing."

"Where did you get an idea like that?"

"From Mike Jones at Incarnation in Highlands. He said that's what he wants to do when he retires—the only problem is, he's never mentioned it to his wife."

"The only problem is," she said, "we'll need gobs of money to enlarge my little yellow house to contain a man, an ocean of books, and a dog the size of Esther Bolick's Westinghouse freezer."

"Well, then. What do you think?"

"I think we should let him have the basement and fix it up. I love Harley. He's funny and good-hearted and earnest. And it would be wonderful to have some more help around here. For openers, your garage could use a cleanup and my Mazda needs a new alternator."

"What do you know about alternators?"

"Absolutely nothing. Which means it would be nice to have Harley living in the basement. We'll buy the paint and I'll make his kitchen curtains."

"Done!" he said.

A new book? He knew what that meant. It meant his wife would be working eight hours a day or more, complaining of a chronically stiff neck, staring out the window without speaking, getting headaches from eye strain, and crashing into bed at night as lifeless as a swamp log.

Oh, well. He sighed, trudging up the stairs with his dog to tell Harley the news.

§

"Goodnight, buddy."

He had left Harley's room and stepped down the hall to sit on the side of Dooley's bed.

"'Night."

"We're praying that your mother gets the job."

"Me, too."

"How about your job? You like it all right?"

"It's neat. But I'm about give out."

When Dooley was tired or angry, Father Tim noted, he often lapsed into the vernacular. He grinned. That prep school varnish hadn't covered the boy's grain entirely. "Are you going to run a booth at the town festival?"

"Yep. Avis wants Tommy and me to do it. Avis'll be the bigwig and take the money."

"Sounds good. What will you do?"

"We'll sell corn and stuff from the valley. Avis has buckets of blackberries and strawberries comin' in from Florida, and peaches from Georgia and syrup from Vermont and all. He's calling it 'A Taste of America.'"

"Great idea! That Avis . . ."

"I'm about half killed."

"Well . . . see you at breakfast."

"What were you doing up at Mama's today? Taking livermush to Granpaw?"

"Just dropped by to say hello, that's all, and check on Poobaw."

"He likes to be called Poo now."

"I'll remember that. I'm glad you heard about the job at Hope House and didn't waste any time."

"Me, too. 'Night."

"Goodnight."

He went downstairs with a heart nearly full to bursting. To borrow a phrase from Dooley's granpaw, blast if he didn't love that boy better than snuff.

§

In less than a week, the bishop would arrive at Lord's Chapel on his annual confirmation pilgrimage. This year, however, he also had a dirty job to do. It had fallen on him to break the news of Timothy Kavanagh's retirement, just eighteen months away.

Stuart Cullen did not look forward to this bitter task. The parish wouldn't like the news, not even a little. In fact, he was prepared to duck after divulging this woe. Unless he and Martha got out of there immediately after the service, he was in for a virtual cantata of moaning and groaning, not to mention wailing and gnashing.

All that, he knew, would be followed by a series of outraged letters and phone calls to diocesan headquarters, and possibly a small, self-appointed group who would show up on his doorstep, begging him to force Father Tim to remain at Lord's Chapel until he was on a walker or, worse yet, senile and unable to commandeer the pulpit.

The rector, in the meantime, was trying to get himself in shape for an occasion that seemed variously akin to a wedding and then a funeral. His feelings rose and plummeted sharply. Bottom line, he couldn't dismiss the fact that once the words left Stuart's mouth, the deed was done, it was writ on a tablet, he was out of there.

His wife had certainly done everything in her power to help, though nothing seemed to calm his nerves. Certainly not the new suit she ordered from New York and which, he was aghast to find, was double-breasted. Would he look like some Mafia don at the parish brunch, as he struggled to give his stunned parish a look of innocent piety?

And so what if he'd managed to lose a full four pounds six ounces and appear positively trim? The downside was, his stomach stayed so infernally upset, he couldn't eat.

For years, he had feared this whole retirement issue. Even Stuart confessed to dreading it, and had once called retirement "a kind of death."

For himself, however, he had made peace with his fear last year in the cave. He had been able, finally, to forgive his father, to find healing and go on.

In some way he would never fully understand, he'd thought that by preaching into infinity, he could make up for having been unable to save his father's soul. Not that he could have saved it, personally— that was God's job. But he had somehow failed to soften his father's heart or give him ears to hear, and had believed he could never make up for that failing, except to preach until he fell.

Now he knew otherwise, and felt a tremulous excitement about stepping out on faith and finding his Canaan, wherever it may be. Indeed, the fear he now wrestled with was the fear of the unfamiliar. Hadn't he been wrapped in a cocoon for the last sixteen years, the very roof over his head provided?

"By faith, Abraham went out," he often quoted to himself from Hebrews, "not knowing where. . . ."

He knew one thing—he didn't want to leave the priesthood. He was willing to supply other pulpits here, there, anywhere, as an interim. Wouldn't that be an adventure, after all? Cynthia Kavanagh certainly thought so. He suspected she had already packed a bag and stashed it in the closet.

There were only a couple of things left to be done prior to Sunday. One, attend the closed vestry meeting on Friday night and tell them the news before it hit the pulpit. He dreaded it like a toothache. As far as he knew, they didn't have a clue what was coming, and they'd be shocked, stunned. He could stay and take it like a man, or duck out the back door while Buddy Benfield gave the closing prayer.

The list was all downhill from there. Two, book Stuart and Martha's lodging in Wesley, and three, get a haircut.

But hadn't he just had a haircut?

His hair was growing fast, Cynthia said, because of the olive oil in his diet.

Emma said he looked shaggy because Joe Ivey had gotten slack toward the end and hadn't given him his money's worth.

Somebody else declared it was the time of year when hair had a growth spurt like everything else, from ragweed to burdock.

He called Fancy Skinner for an appointment. Today, if possible, and get it over with.

"Oh, law, I don't have an openin' 'til kingdom come! Ever' since Joe Ivey went to Tennessee, I've gone like a house afire! The haircuts he's let loose around here gives me th' shivers, you can spot a Joe Ivey cut a mile away, it's always these little pooches of hair over th' ears, it'll take me a year to get rid of that chipmunk look in this town.

"Let's see . . . Ruth Wallace at eleven for acrylic nails, J. C. Hogan at noon, that's a cut, Beth Lawrence for a perm at twelve-thirty, that'll take two hours, you should see her hair, she calls it fine, I say she's goin' bald. Do you know her, she always wears a hat—if you ask me, wearin' a hat will make you bald, and oh, Lord, look here, at three o'clock I've got Helen Nelson, she will gnaw your ear off talkin', you can't get a word in edgewise, on and on and on, about every old thing from her husband growin' a mustache and how it scratches when he kisses, to th' pig they bought to keep as a house pet. Have you ever heard of keepin' a pig as a house pet? They say they trained it to a litter box!

"I'd rather have a dog any day, which reminds me, did you know one of my poodles ran away and Rodney Underwood found her under the bridge and brought her home in the front seat of his patrol car? Mule took a picture, you should ask to see it.

"How's your wife, how come she don't let me highlight her hair sometime? Does she do it herself? It looks like she does it herself. I bet she uses a cap—honey, foil works better, but don't tell her I said so.

"Let's see, four o'clock, oh, Lord, look here. I've got Marge Beatty's three kids, all at the same time, I should get a war medal. Then at five,

I'm doin' a mask—which reminds me, have I told you about my new product line called Fancy's Face Food? What it is, your face desperately needs nourishment just like your body, did you know that? Most people don't know that.

"First, I do th' Vitamin E Deluxe Re-Charge and Hydration Mask, which is the entrée, followed by a Cucumber Apricot Sesame Soother, which is the dessert, and honey, I'm tellin' you, you will walk out of here lookin' ten years younger, some say fifteen, but I try not to stretch the truth.

"The mask I'm doin' at five takes an hour, so the answer is, no, I couldn't take you today if my life depended on it, how about next Wednesday at ten o'clock?"

§

Harley removed two twenty-dollar bills from under the guest room mattress and was on his way to the Shoe Barn for new work shoes.

"Harley, be careful. Rodney Underwood has it in for that truck."

"Don't you worry," said Harley. "I'd never let them horses loose in town."

"I don't want to have to haul you out of jail."

"Nossir, Rev'rend, you won't."

So why did he watch that truck like a hawk, all the way to the end of Wisteria, 'til it turned north on Main?

§

"Miami," said Emma, looking curious.

He lifted the receiver from the phone on his desk.

"Hello?"

"Father, this is Ingrid Swenson with Miami Development Group. I'd like to talk with you about the old Fernbank property, which we understand is owned by your church."

"That's right."

"We're very interested, Father, in viewing this property next week, if that would be convenient."

"Well . . ."

"It is our intention, if everything looks as good as we hope it might, to develop this property as a world-class spa."

"A spa."

"Yes. We've developed similar properties around the country that have gained international clientele."

"Aha."

"How does next Wednesday look to you? Say, around eleven?"

"Ah, well, fine, I think. Yes. I'll have to gather up some of the vestry, and our realtor."

"Good. There'll be two of us."

"We're at the corner of Old Church Lane and Main Street, just as you come into town. Very easy to find."

"You may like to know that Mr. Mack Stroupe has highly recommended this property to us."

"I see."

"We're very grateful for such valued assistance in locating a property as special as Fernbank promises to be. We're told it has seventeen rooms."

"Twenty-one."

"Marvelous!"

"Yes. Well. We'll be looking for you, Miss Swenson."

"Ingrid, Father. And thank you for your time."

He put the phone on the hook.

"You don't look so good," said Emma.

Strange. He didn't feel so good, either. That phone call should have him dancing in the streets, shouting from the rooftops.

If Fernbank was such an albatross, why did he suddenly know he didn't want to lose it?

§

His heart hadn't pounded like this, even on the day of his ordination. It had pounded, yes, when he preached his first sermon to his first parish in his first small church. But he couldn't remember anything like this. He was glad he was sitting down, and glad he'd been able to persuade Cynthia to trim his hair.

He looked for his lifeline, which was the third pew, gospel side, where his wife sat scratching her nose. That was her signal for "Smile!"

Sitting next to her was Pauline Barlowe, then Poobaw, who was gazing at the ceiling, and Dooley. Russell Jacks anchored the pew at the opposite end.

"I have some good news and some bad news," Stuart told the congregation at the eight o'clock.

Did he have to put it that way? The rector shifted in the carved chair. This was the dress rehearsal for the more formal, well-attended eleven o'clock; whatever happened now would also happen then—except worse. Much worse.

"The good news," said Stuart, smiling the smile that had undoubtedly helped him rise in his calling, "is that Timothy Kavanagh, your beloved priest, generous counselor, and trusted friend . . ."

Get it over with, he thought, gripping the chair arms and closing his eyes. This was like flying with Omer Cunningham in his ragwing taildragger. . . .

". . . is getting ready to . . . *go out to Canaan!*"

How odd that Stuart would have had the same thought, found the same analogy! He noted that most of his congregation didn't seem to know anything about Canaan. Where was Canaan? He saw Esther Bolick glance at Gene and shrug her shoulders. Maybe it was overseas. Or maybe somewhere in Wilkes County, where they had that cheese factory.

"We're told in Genesis that Abram took Sarai his wife, and Lot his brother's son, and all their substance that they had gathered, and they went forth into the land of Canaan . . . a strange land, an alien land.

"God was sending Abram, whom He would later call Abraham, on the greatest journey, the grandest mission, of his life. But what would Canaan be like? Some said giants inhabited the land, and I recall what Billy Sunday once said, 'He said if you want milk and honey on your bread, you must be willing to go into the land of giants!'"

Father Tim felt his hair standing up on his head.

"What," asked Stuart, looking resplendent in embroidered brocade, "did Abraham *feel* when he was called by God to go out into this unfamiliar land, hundreds of miles from home?"

The rector believed he clearly heard the thoughts of half the crowd: *Beats me!*

In fact, Abraham hadn't even made an appearance in this morning's Old Testament reading. Oh, well. Bishops could do whatever they darn well pleased.

Stuart leaned over the pulpit and peered at the assembly, most of whom were admiring his satin mitre.

"Did he, like your faithful friend and priest, feel fearful of this journey into the unknown? Of course! Did he feel sorrow for leaving the familiar behind? Almost certainly! But"—and here Stuart drew himself up to his full height of six feet plus—"given what God had in store for him, didn't he also feel hope and excitement and expectation and *joy*?"

None of the above, thought the rector. What he felt was sheer, holy terror.

§

With no small amount of admiration, he observed Stuart Cullen getting exactly what he wanted from the congregation, rather like a conductor extracting a great symphony from an orchestra.

Where Stuart wanted tears, he got unashamed tears.

Where he wanted riotous laughter, there it came, pouring forth like a mighty ocean.

By the end of the service, nearly everyone felt as if they'd been called out to a Canaan of their own; that life itself was a type of Canaan.

The rector left the eleven o'clock on legs that felt like cooked macaroni, clinging to the arm of his wife, who was beaming.

"There, now, dearest, this is not a lynching, after all! Cheer up!"

He couldn't believe that his congregation had kissed him, hugged him, pounded him on the back, congratulated him, and wished him well.

Where he had expected faces streaming with tears, he saw only lively concern for his future. Where he had feared stern looks of indignation, he received smiles and laughter and the assurance they'd always love him.

Didn't they *care*?

"Don't kid yourself," said Stuart, as he and Martha dove into the car after the parish hall brunch. "The backlash is yet to come."

As Stuart gunned the Toyota Camry away from the curb, the rector felt brighter. So, maybe his parishioners really would hate to see him go! Right now they were just having a good time—after all, the bishop's visit was always a festive occasion.

CHAPTER SIX

A Small Boom

Emma was right. The billboard of Mack Stroupe's face seemed to loom over the highway. And whoever was responsible for the photo didn't appear to think much of retouching.

Zooming past it in his Buick, he wondered at his feelings about the new candidate, and determined, once and for all, to think the thing through and come to a conclusion he could live with. He was tired of the whole issue crawling around in the back of his mind like so many ants over a sugar bowl.

Why did he feel queasy and uncomfortable about Mack Stroupe being his mayor? J.C. was right—the mayorship wasn't Esther's job, it was the job of anybody who qualified to make the most of the office. But—did Mack qualify?

He couldn't think of a single reason why he should. Was it mere gossip that Mack had carried on a long-term extramarital relationship with a woman in Wesley? People were notorious for giving clergy all manner of information, and apparently the affair wasn't rumor at all, but fact.

While that sort of behavior may be acceptable to some, for him, it wouldn't fly. The whole business spoke of treachery and betrayal, however admissible it might be in the world's view.

He thought of Esther's plank, so well known by everyone in Mitford that first graders could recite it: Mitford Takes Care of Its Own.

Esther had carried out that philosophy in every particular, never wavering.

Wasn't it true that when you take care of what you have, healthy growth follows? Hadn't his trilliums, planted under all the right conditions, spread until they formed a grove? And the lily of the valley, established in the rich, dark soil behind his study, had become a virtual kingdom from only three small plants.

Actually, there had been growth in Mitford; it was no bucolic backwater. The little tea shop next to Mitford Blossoms was flourishing. They were still limited to cakes, cookies, tea, and coffee, but as everyone agreed, you have to crawl before you walk.

Recently, Jena Ivey, their florist, had been forced to add a room to her shop. And take the Irish Woolen Shop. Now, there was a flexible endeavor. In late spring and summer, when temperatures soared, Minnie Lomax removed the word *Woolen* from the store sign, thereby assuring a brisk, year-round trade.

Avis Packard was another example. Avis was a small-town grocer who had done such a terrific job of providing world-class provender that people came from surrounding counties to fill up his rear parking lot and jam the streets, especially when the Silver Queen corn rolled in.

And Happy Endings. When he first came here, there was no such thing as a bookstore; he'd been forced to drive to Wesley and spend his money in another tax jurisdiction. Last summer, there had actually been a queue in front of Happy Endings—he had seen it with his own eyes—when the newest Grisham book arrived by UPS. The UPS man had been astounded when he pulled to the curb and everybody cheered.

Mitford was making it, and without neon signs and factory smoke. So, yes, maybe some well-planned growth would be good, but face it, they were doing something right, and he didn't want to see that mind-set replaced by a mind-set that was only for development and change, whatever the cost.

Another thing. It boggled his mind that Mack Stroupe knew anyone outside the confines of Wesley and Holding. How had Mack engineered contact with what sounded like a large Florida development firm? And this thing about Mitford Woods, and Mack being the ringleader . . .

In the end, what about Mack's platform?

Was Mack really for Mitford?

Or was Mack for Mack?

§

He found his breakfast cereal tasting exactly like oil-based latex.

Every window was up, three fans were running wide open, and Violet sprawled as if drugged on the top of the refrigerator. Even the gloxinia seemed oppressed by the noxious fumes rising from the basement.

"Let's move!" said Cynthia, meaning it.

"Where?" he asked, liking the idea.

"The little yellow house! I don't even know some of the people I'm meeting in my own hallway!"

"You know Tommy," he said. "He only spent three nights."

"Yes, but—"

"And Harley's friend Cotton, didn't he tell great stories?"

"Of course, but—"

"And certainly Olivia was well meaning when she came down with the women from the hospital auxiliary to bring pots and pans and scatter rugs for Harley's kitchen. I'm sure they didn't mind that you still had curlers in your hair."

"I married a bachelor who led the quietest of lives, and now look!" she exclaimed, eyeing a kitchen sink that contained a roller pan, rollers, and a bevy of brushes.

"The plumbing repairs in the basement," he said lamely, "will be finished tomorrow, and they can wash the brushes down there."

"A likely story!"

"You're beautiful when you're mad," he said.

"I read that line in a pulp novel thirty years ago!"

"So sue me."

She came around the breakfast table and sat in his lap. "I love you, you big lug."

"I love you more," he said, pulling her to him and kissing her hair. "Have you started your book?"

She laughed gaily. "Of course I've started my book! None of this would have happened if I hadn't started my book!"

§

These days, clergy seldom liked living in rectories. Because they generally preferred to own their own homes, and because the upkeep of the rectory had been considerable over the years, the vestry had long ago voted to sell the old house at the end of his tenure. What with the recent improvement below, the rector suspected they'd get a much better price for it.

Who would have dreamed he'd ever see the grim downstairs hallway come alive under a coat of Peach Soufflé, or a kitchen transformed by Piña Colada and his wife's bright curtains fluttering at the window?

Harley Welch would be living high in this basement.

§

Before the Miami contingent arrived the following day, he cleaned up some matters at his desk.

Emil Kettner, head honcho of the construction company that built Hope House, regretted that Buck Leeper would be tied up for two years on a project in Virginia.

Perhaps after that, Kettner said, they could send Buck to Mitford for six months, which ought to be enough time to overhaul the church attic. His company never sent Buck on small jobs, but in this case, they'd try to make an exception. Could they wait?

Their Sunday School wasn't yet overflowing, said the rector, but they were getting there.

The conclusion was, Lord's Chapel was willing to wait, as they really wanted Buck for the job.

"He's doing better, I thought you'd like to know that," said Emil.

"A few weekend benders here and there, but nothing daily like it was for years. What happened in Mitford, Father?"

"Buck got rid of something old, so something new could come in."

"You have my personal thanks."

"No thanks to me," said the rector. "Thanks be to God!"

❧

Lace Turner met him at the foot of the basement steps.

"He's done eat a whole bag of choc'late candy!" she said.

Harley, who was a ghastly color, was sitting on the floor of the hallway, clutching his stomach. "Don't be tattlin' on me like I was some young 'un!"

"You act like a young 'un!" said Lace. "That choc'late'll git your ulcer goin' again, just when you was gettin' better!"

"Rev'rend, hit was all that baby puddin' that made me do it. A man needs somethin' he can get 'is teeth into, you might say. But oh, law, I repent, I do, I'm sorry I ever bought that bag of candy, I'll never take another bite long as I live! Nossir!"

"Forty-two pieces, I counted 'em," said Lace. "He wadded up th' wrappers and stuck ever' one under 'is mattress."

"You cain't git by with a thing around this 'un, she's th' worst ol' *po*lice I ever seen." Harley stood up suddenly, looking distraught. "Oh, law! You 'uns better leave!"

He headed for the bathroom at a trot.

What timing. The basement plumbing had been completed barely an hour ago.

❧

He squirmed in his office chair and looked at his watch.

In thirty minutes, he and Ron Malcolm and several others on the vestry were squiring strangers around Sadie Baxter's homeplace. He hated the thought, but he despised himself more for his wishy-washy attitude about the whole situation.

They needed desperately to sell it, get it off the shoulders of the parish; yet, here was a golden opportunity driving up the mountain in a rented car, and he wanted to run in the opposite direction.

Surely it was as simple as his dread of letting Sadie Baxter go entirely. Surely he was trying to hold on to what was vanished and gone, to another way of life that had been vibrantly preserved in Miss Sadie's engrossing stories.

When Fernbank was sold, all that would be left of the old Mitford was three original storefronts on Main Street, Lord's Chapel and the church office, the town library, and the Porter mansion–cum–town museum where Uncle Billy and Miss Rose lived in the little apartment.

Blast! he exhorted himself. Stop being a hick and move on. This is today, this is now!

He glanced at Emma, who was staring at her computer screen. What did people find to stare at on computer screens, anyway? Nothing moved on the screen, yet she was transfixed, as if hearing voices from a heavenly realm.

"I'll be darned," she muttered, clicking her mouse.

He sighed.

"Look here," she said, not taking her eyes off the screen.

He got up and went to her desk and looked.

"What? It looks like a list."

"It is a list. It's a list of everybody in the whole United States, and their addresses. Our computer man sent it to us. See there?"

She moved her pointer to a name. "Albert Wilcox!" he exclaimed. "Good heavens, do you suppose . . ."

"We've been lookin' for Albert Wilcox for how long?"

"Ten years, anyway! Do you think it's *our* Albert Wilcox?"

"We heard he'd moved to Seattle," she said, "and we tried to find him in the phone book, but we never did. This town is somewhere close to Seattle, it's called Oak Harbor."

"Well done! Let's write this Albert Wilcox and see if he's the one whose grandmother's hand-illuminated prayer book turned up in the parish hall storage closet."

"A miracle!" she said. "I remember the day we found it—right behind the plastic poinsettias that had been there a hundred years. How in th' dickens it ended up *there* . . ."

"That book could be worth a fortune. Every page is done in calligraphy and watercolor illustrations—by his own grandfather. When it disappeared out of the exhibition we did for a Bane and Blessing, it broke Albert's heart."

"It was only Rite One, remember, not th' whole thing!"

"Nonetheless . . ."

"And don't forget he was goin' to sue the church 'til Miss Sadie talked him out of it."

Well, that, too.

§

Ingrid Swenson was fashionably thin, deeply tanned, and expensively dressed.

"Arresting!" she said, as they drove along Fernbank's proud but neglected driveway.

Tendrils of grapevine leapt across the drive and entwined among a row of hemlocks on the other side. To their right, a gigantic mock orange faded from bloom in a tangled thicket of wisteria, star magnolia, and rhododendron.

The house didn't reveal its dilapidation at once, and for that he was relieved. In fact, it stood more grandly than he remembered from his caretaker's visit in March.

He was touched to recall that exactly two years ago there had been the finest of fetes at this house.

On the lawn, young people in tuxedos had served champagne and cups of punch on silver trays, as lively strains of Mozart poured through the tall windows. Inside, the ballroom had been filled with heartfelt joy for Olivia and Hoppy Harper, the glamorous bride and groom, and with awe for the hand-painted ceiling above their heads, which was newly restored to its former glory.

Roberto had flown from Italy to surprise Miss Sadie, and Esther Bolick's orange marmalade cake had stood three tiers high, each tier supported by Corinthian columns of marzipan bedecked with imported calla lilies. It had been, without doubt, the swellest affair since President Woodrow Wilson had attended a ball at Fernbank and given little Sadie Baxter a hard candy wrapped in silver paper.

The man who came with Ingrid Swenson seemed interested only

in biting his nails, speaking in monosyllables, and exploring Fernbank quite on his own. The rector saw him peering into the washhouse and wandering into the orchards, taking notes.

"A little over twelve acres," said Ron Malcolm, a longtime member of Lord's Chapel who kept his broker's license current.

"Excellent," said Ingrid, who took no notes at all. "Twelve acres translates to twenty-four cottages. Town water, I presume?"

"On a well."

"Town sewer, of course. . . ."

"Afraid not," said Ron. "And I must tell you in all fairness that the cost to connect this property to town services will run well above a hundred thousand. The connection is a half mile down the hill and the right-of-ways pose some real problems."

Ingrid looked at him archly. "It could behoove you to make that investment and offer your buyer an upgraded property."

"It behooves us even more," said Ron, "to avoid putting a burden of debt on the parish."

She smiled vaguely. "That is, in any case, a trifle, Mr. Malcolm. But let's consider an issue which is the polar opposite of a trifle, and that's the number of jobs such a facility would bring to your village. An upscale property of twenty-one rooms and twenty-four cottages, including a state-of-the-art health center, would employ well over a hundred people, many of them coming from Europe and the British Isles and requiring satisfactory housing. This, gentlemen, could create a small boom." She paused for effect. "A small boom for a small town!" she said, laughing.

"Yes ma'am," said Ron Malcolm.

"But we'll get to all that later. Now I'd like to start in the attic and work down to the basement."

"Consider it done," said the rector, wanting the whole thing behind them.

§

She would talk it over with her associates, Ingrid told them in the church office. They wouldn't buy an option—they'd take a risk on the property still being available when they returned with an offer in thirty to sixty days.

"Risk," she said, toying with the paperweight on his desk, "has a certain adrenaline, after all."

Their lawyer would begin the title search immediately, and a full topo would be done by a surveyor from Holding. No, they didn't want the window treatments or furnishings, with the possible exception of Miss Sadie's bed, which Ingrid concluded was French, a loveseat and secretary that were almost certainly George II, and a china cabinet that appeared to be made by a native craftsman.

Her people wanted to talk with the town engineer again, and expressed regret that the heating system appeared defunct and the plumbing would have to be completely modernized.

Before leaving, she mentioned the seriousness of the water damage due to years of leakage through a patched roof, and frowned when the subject of the well and sewer emerged again.

He tried to be elated, but was merely thankful that the first phase was over and done with. He made a note to get up to Fernbank with Cynthia and go through the attic, pronto.

§

Pauline Barlowe had the job and was to report to work on Monday morning at six-thirty.

He called Scott Murphy at once.

"Thank you!" he said. "I can't thank you enough."

"What for, sir?"

"Why, for . . . saying anything that might have helped Pauline Barlowe get the job in your dining room."

"I didn't say a word."

"You didn't?"

"Not a peep out of me. That was our personnel director's idea. She said she knew she might be taking a chance, but she wanted to do it and came to talk to me about it. Lida Willis is tough, she'll watch Mrs. Barlowe like a hawk, but Lida has a soft center; she wants this to work."

"We're thrilled around our place. This means a lot to Dooley as well as his mother. When will you come for dinner? We've got a regular corn shucking going at the rectory; it's just the thing to liven up a bachelor."

"Name the time!" said the chaplain.

"I'll call you," said the rector.

§

"We're giving a party," announced his wife, flushed with excitement.

"We are?"

"Friday night. In the basement, a housewarming! I'm baking cookies and making a pudding cake for Harley, and Lace is doing the lemonade. I've invited Olivia, Hoppy has a meeting, and oh, I've asked Dooley, but he's not keen on the idea. Who else?"

"Ummm. Scott Murphy!" he wondered

"Perfect. Who else?"

"Tommy. But wait, I think Dooley mentioned that Tommy has a family thing on Friday, and Dooley's going over there later to watch a video."

"OK, that's seven. Terrific! They finished painting today, the place looks wonderful, and it's all aired out and Harley is excited as anything. He raked tons of leaves from under the back hedge, and in the next couple of days he's replacing my alternator."

"Wonderful!" he said

"Harley's so happy, he can't stop grinning, and Lace—she doesn't say so, but she's thrilled by all this."

"It was her idea, and she was bold enough to step forward and ask for it."

"Let us come *boldly* to the throne of grace . . ." said his wife, quoting one of their favorite verses from Hebrews.

". . . that we may obtain mercy and find grace to help in time of need!" he replied.

"Amen!" they cried in unison, laughing.

He frankly relished it when they burst into a chorus of Scripture together. As a boy in his mother's Baptist church, he'd been thumpingly drilled to memorize Scripture verses, which sprang more quickly to memory than something he'd studied yesterday.

"One of the finest exhortations ever delivered, in my opinion," he said. "Well, now, what may I do to help out with the party?"

"Help me move that old sofa from the garage to Harley's parlor, I don't think he's strong enough, then we'll shift that maple wardrobe from the furnace room to his bedroom."

Was there no balm in Gilead?

"Oh, and another thing," she said, smiling innocently. "We need to haul that huge box of books from his parlor to the furnace room."

For his wife's birthday in July, she was getting a back brace whether she wanted it or not. In fact, he'd get one for himself while he was at it.

❧

On his way to Hope House, he stopped at the Sweet Stuff Bakery to buy a treat for Louella.

Winnie Ivey looked at him and burst into tears.

"Winnie! What is it?"

"I heard you're leaving," she said, wiping her eyes with her apron.

"Yes, but not for a year and a half."

"We'll miss you somethin' awful."

"But you'll probably be gone before I will."

"Oh," she said. "I keep forgetting I'm going."

"Besides, we'll still be living in Mitford, in the house next door to the rectory."

"Good!" she said, sniffing. "That's better. Here, have a napoleon, I know you're not supposed to, but . . . ."

What the heck, he thought, taking it. At least one person was sorry to hear he was retiring. . . .

❧

When he left the bakery, he looked up the street and saw Uncle Billy sitting in a dinette chair on the grounds of the town museum, watching traffic flow around the monument.

He walked up and joined him. "Uncle Billy! I'm half starved for a joke."

"I cain't git a new joke t' save m' life," said the old man, looking forlorn.

"If you can't get a joke, nobody can."

"My jokes ain't workin' too good. I cain't git Rose t' laugh f'r nothin'."

"Aha."

"See, I test m' jokes on Rose, that's how I know what t' tell an' what t' leave off."

"Try one on me and see what happens."

"Well, sir, two ladies was talkin' about what they'd wear to th' Legion Hall dance, don't you know, an' one said, 'We're supposed t' wear somethin' t' match our husband's hair, so I'll wear black, what'll you wear?' an' th' other one sorta turned pale, don't you know, an' said, 'I don't reckon I'll go.'"

"Aha," said Father Tim.

"See, th' feller married t' that woman that won't goin' was *bald,* don't you know."

The rector grinned.

"It don't work too good, does it?" said Uncle Billy. "How about this 'un? Little Sonny's mama hollered at 'im, said, 'Sonny, did you fall down with y'r new pants on?' An' Sonny said, 'Yes 'um, they won't time t' take 'em off.'"

The rector laughed heartily. "Not bad. Not half bad!"

"See, if I can hear a laugh or two, it gits me goin'."

"About like preaching, if you ask me."

"Speakin' of preachin', me 'n Rose ain't a bit glad about th' news on Sunday. We come home feelin' s' low, we could've crawled under a snake's belly with a hat on. It don't seem right f'r you t' go off like that."

"I'll be living right down the street, same as always. We'll be settling in the yellow house next door to the rectory."

"Me 'n Rose'll try t' git over it, but . . ." Uncle Billy sighed.

Father Tim couldn't remember seeing Bill Watson without a big smile on his face and his gold tooth gleaming.

"See, what Rose 'n me don't like is, when you leave they'll send us somebody we don't know."

"That's the way it usually works."

"I figure by th' time we git t' know th' new man, we'll be dead as doornails, so it ain't no use to take th' trouble, we'll just go back to th' Presbyterians."

"Now, Uncle Billy . . ."

"I hate t' say it, Preacher, but me 'n Rose think you could've waited on this."

The rector made his way down Main Street, staring at the sidewalk. It was the only time in his life he hadn't come away from Bill Watson feeling better than when he went.

§

At the corner of Main and Wisteria, he saw Gene Bolick coming toward him, and threw up his hand in greeting. It appeared that Gene saw him, but looked away and jaywalked to the other side.

§

June.

Something about June . . .

What else was happening this month? His birthday!

Dadgum it, he'd just had one.

In fact, the memory of his last birthday rushed back to him with dark force. His wife had brought him coffee in bed and wished him happy birthday, then the phone had rung and he'd raced to the hospital and discovered that a woman who would be irrevocably fixed in his life had been horribly burned by a madman.

He sat back in his swivel chair and closed his eyes. Wrenching, that whole saga of pain and desperation. And days afterward, only doors down the hall from Pauline, Miss Sadie had died.

No wonder he'd come close to forgetting his birthday. When was it, anyway? He looked at the calendar. Blast. Straight ahead.

How old would he be this year? He could never remember.

He called Cynthia at home. "How old will I be this year?"

"Let's see. You're six years older than I am, and I'm fifty-seven. No, fifty-six. So you're sixty-two."

"I can't be sixty-two. I've already been sixty-two, I remember it distinctly."

"Darn!" she said. "Then you're sixty-three?"

"Well, surely I'm not sixty-five, because I'm retiring at sixty-five."

"So you must be sixty-three. Which makes me fifty-seven. Rats."

He realized as he hung up that they could have used their birth years to calculate the answer. What a pair they made! He hoped nobody had tapped his phone line and overheard such nonsense.

§

"I've been thinking," said Emma.

Please, no.

"I might as well retire when you retire."

"Well!" He was relieved. "Sounds good!"

She looked at him over her half-glasses. "But I wasn't expecting you to give up so soon."

"Give up?"

"I guess you can't take it anymore, the pressure and all—two services every Sunday, the sick and dying . . ."

"It has nothing to do with pressure, and certainly not with the sick and dying. As you know, I've committed to supply pulpits from here to the Azores."

"Yes, well, that's vacation stuff, anybody can go supply somewhere and not get involved."

He felt suddenly furious. Thank God he couldn't speak; he couldn't open his mouth. His face burning, he got up from his desk and left the office, closing the door behind him with some force.

There! he thought. Right there is reason enough to retire.

He deserved a medal for putting up with Emma Newland all these years—which, he realized only this morning, would be a full sixteen in September.

Sixteen years in an office the size of a cigar box, with a woman who made Attila the Hun look sensitive and nurturing?

"A medal!" he exclaimed aloud, going at full trot past the Irish Shop.

"There he goes again, talking to himself," said Hessie Mayhew, who had dropped in to share a bag of caramels with Minnie Lomax.

"What do you think it is?" asked Minnie, who hoped the caramels wouldn't stick to her upper plate.

"Age. Diabetes. And *guilt*," she announced darkly.

"Guilt?"

"Yes, for leaving those poor people in the lurch who've looked after him all these years."

"My goodness," said Minnie, "we don't look after our preacher at all. He looks after himself."

"Yes, but you've got a Baptist preacher. They've been *raised* to look after themselves."

"I declare," said Minnie, who had never considered this possibility.

§

At The Local, he saw Sophia Burton, who wasn't even a member of Lord's Chapel, and was flabbergasted when she burst into tears by the butcher case.

"I'm sorry," she told him.

"Don't be sorry!" he implored, not knowing what else to say.

"It's just that . . . it's just that you've been so good to us, and . . . and we're *used* to you!"

Didn't he despise change? Didn't he hate it? And here he was, inflicting it on everyone else. If his wife wasn't so excited about the whole adventure of being free, he'd call Stuart up, and . . . no, he wouldn't do any such thing. Actually, he was excited, himself.

"I'm . . . pretty excited, myself," he muttered weakly.

"That's easy for you to say!" Mona Gragg, a former Lord's Chapel Sunday School teacher, strode up to him, clutching a sack of corn and tomatoes. For some reason, Mona looked ten feet tall; she was also mad as a wet hen.

"When I heard that mess on Sunday, I just boiled. Here we've all gotten along just fine all these years, *plus* . . . you're still plenty young, and no reason in the *world* to retire. Did Grandma Moses quit when *she* was sixty-five? Certainly not! She hadn't even gotten *started*! And Abraham, which Bishop Cullen was so quick to yammer about on Sunday . . . he moved to a whole new *country* when he was way up in his *seventies* and didn't even have that *kid* 'til he was a *hundred*!"

Mona stomped away, furious.

"One of my ah, parishioners," he said, flushing.

Sophia wiped her eyes and smiled. "Father, now I can see why you're retiring."

He checked out, liking the sight of Dooley bagging groceries at one of Avis's two counters.

"How's it going, buddy?"

Dooley grinned. "Great! Except for people raisin' heck about you retiring."

"Ah, well." For some reason he didn't completely understand, Dooley seemed to approve of his plans. It wasn't the first time Dooley had stood up for him. A year or so ago, when Buster Austin had called the rector a nerd, Dooley had proceeded to beat the tar out of him.

As he left The Local, he saw Jenny parking her blue bicycle at the lamppost.

§

He left one end of Main Street feeling like a million bucks, and reached the other end feeling like two cents with a hole in it.

Up and down the street, he was besieged by people who had heard the news and didn't like it, or, on the rarest of occasions, proffered him their sincere best wishes.

Rodney Underwood was shocked and, it seemed, personally insulted.

Lew Boyd shook his head and wouldn't make eye contact. Why in heaven's name his *car mechanic* was piqued was beyond him.

The owner of the Collar Button rushed into the street and extended his deepest regrets. "What a loss!" he muttered darkly, sounding like a delegate from a funeral parlor.

A vestry member called him at the rectory. "This," she announced, "is the worst news since they found somethin' in Lloyd's limp nodes."

He phoned Stuart Cullen.

"Gene Bolick crossed to the other side of the street!" he said, feeling like a ten-year-old whining to a parent.

"Denial! If he doesn't have to talk to you, he doesn't have to acknowledge the truth. He'll get over it. It takes time."

"And some people are mad because I'm retiring so early! I feel like a heel, like I'm running out on them."

"Let them squawk!" Stuart exclaimed. "When people don't express their anger, it turns into depression. So, better this than a parish riddled by resentment and low morale."

"Then," Father Tim said miserably, "there are those who feel it's merely a blasted inconvenience."

"They're right about that," said Stuart. "By the way, your Search Committee is already up and running, but it'll be a long process. So hang in there."

His bishop hadn't been any help at all.

§

The hasty trim he'd gotten from his reluctant wife had carried him through Stuart's visit, but wouldn't carry him a step further. And blast if Fancy Skinner wasn't booked. That was the way with those unisex shops, he thought, darkly. He made an appointment for a month away, and deceived himself that he could talk Cynthia into an interim deal.

"No, a thousand times no. I can't cut hair! Go to Wesley, where they have the kind of barbershop you like, where men talk trout fishing and politics!"

"I know zero about trout fishing, and even less about politics," he said. "Where did you get that idea?"

"Oh, phoo, darling!" she said, waving him away.

"I'll trim you up!" said Harley, who was getting ready for the party in his basement.

"Oh, I don't—"

"Law, Rev'rend, I've cut hair from here t' west Texas, they ain't nothin' to it, it jis' takes a sharp pair of scissors. Now, th' right scissors is ever'thing. I've cut with a razor, I've cut with a pocketknife, but I like scissors th' best. I ain't got a pair, but I got a good rock I use t' sharpen m' knife, so you git me some scissors, an' we're set. What're you lookin' for—mostly t' git it off y'r collar, I reckon."

"I don't know about this, Harley."

Harley looked at him soberly. "You ought t' let me do it f'r you, Rev'rend. I don't want th' Lord sayin' 'What did you do f'r th' Rev'rend?' an' me have t' tell 'im, 'Nothin', he wouldn't let me do nothin'!' I know what th' Lord'll say, he'll say, 'Harley, that ain't no excuse, you jis' git on down them steps over yonder, I know hit's burnin' hot, but . . .'"

"Oh, for Pete's sake," said the rector. "I'll get the scissors."

There went Harley's grin, meeting behind his head again.

§

"Ummm," said Cynthia, looking at him as he dressed for Harley's housewarming party.

"Ummm, what?"

"Your hair . . ."

"What about it?"

"It's sort of scalloped in the back."

"Scalloped?"

"Well, yes, up, down, up, down. What did Harley use—pinking shears?"

"Scissors!"

"Not those scissors I cut up chickens with, I fondly hope."

"Absolutely not. He used the scissors from my chest of drawers, which I keep well sharpened."

"You would," she said, looking at him as if he were a beetle on a pin. "Why don't you sit on the commode seat and let me sort of . . . shape it up? You know I hate doing this, but you can't go around with that scalloped look."

Certainly not. He sat on the commode seat, draped with a bath towel, glad he'd soon have the whole dismal business behind him.

§

Cynthia had done the deed and dashed downstairs. He was putting on a clean shirt when Dooley wandered into the bedroom.

He looked at the boy, fresh from a day's work, and now fresh from the shower. Clean T-shirt, clean jeans; hair combed, shoe laces tied. Upstanding! Getting to look more like a millionaire every day!

The rector might have been a statue in a park, the way Dooley walked around him, staring.

"Man . . ." said Dooley.

"What are you looking at?"

"Your hair."

"What about my hair?" He was beginning to feel positively churlish at any mention of his hair.

"It's cut in a kind of V in the back. I've never seen that before."

"A V? What do you mean, a *V*?"

He stomped to his dresser and, with his wife's hand mirror, looked at the back of his neck in the trifold mirror. It wasn't a V, exactly, it was more like a U. What was the matter with people around here, anyway?

"I'll trim it up for you," said Dooley, "if you'll let me drive your car Saturday."

"Dooley . . ."

"You can drive as far as Farmer, and I can take over at the cutoff."

"This is no time—"

"Anyway, you better let me fix your hair. I know how to do it."

"You're kidding me."

"I'm not kidding you. I've cut Tommy's hair bunches of times."

"A likely story."

"I swear on a stack of Bibles."

"I wouldn't do that. The Bibles you so casually stacked up ask us not to swear."

"That V is hanging down over your collar."

He would drive to Memphis next week, it was only nine or ten hours one way, and see Joe. While he was there, maybe Joe would give him a tour of Graceland. . . .

He sighed deeply. For the third time that day, he got his scissors out of his dresser drawer and handed them over. This time, however, he had the good sense to pray about it.

CHAPTER SEVEN

Housewarming

The showy pudding cake had been reduced to crumbs, the fruit bowl ransacked, the cookies demolished. All that remained in the glass pitcher were two circles of lemon and a few seeds.

In the freshly painted sitting room, Harley opened the last of his housewarming presents.

"Oh, law!" he said, holding up the framed picture of Jesus carrying a sheep. "Hit's th' Lord an' Master, ain't it?"

"Bingo!" said Cynthia, who had given him the print to go over his bed.

"That sheep was lost," Dooley announced. "Tell about it," he said, looking at the rector.

"Why don't you tell about it?"

Dooley scratched his head. "Well, see, it's like . . . if you had a hundred sheep and one of 'em ran off and got lost, you'd go after it, you'd go to the mountains and all, looking for it. And like, when you found it, it would make you feel really good, I mean better than you even feel about the ninety-nine that didn't run off."

"By jing!" said Harley.

Lace sat forward in the chair. "What th' story's about," she said, "is when somebody's lost and Jesus finds 'em an' they give their heart to 'im, it makes 'im feel happier than He feels about all them other'ns that wadn't lost."

Dooley looked at her coldly.

"I reckon that's what th' Lord done with me," said Harley. "Searched through th' mountains lookin' t' find me, an' brought me here." He grinned. "And I ain't lost n'more."

The rector was captivated by an odd confidence—a new maturity, perhaps—in Lace Turner.

"Well, now, I want t' thank ever' one of you'ns," said Harley, tears coming to his eyes. "I ain't never had a Bible with m' name on it, I ain't never had a 'lectric fan that moves to th' left an' right . . ."

He took a paper napkin from his pocket and blew his nose.

". . . I ain't never had a picture t' hang on m' wall 'cept of m' mama as a little young 'un . . . an' Lord *knows,* I ain't never had a . . ." Harley patted Scott's gift, which lay beside him on the sofa. "What d'you call this what you give me?"

"That's an afghan," said the chaplain, grinning. "One of our residents crochets those. They're a big hit on the hill."

"What exactly is it f'r, did you say?"

"It's to keep you warm in winter when you lie on the sofa and watch TV."

"I'll use it, yes, sir, I will, and I thank you, but I ain't goin' t' be layin' on no sofa watchin' TV, I'm goin' t' be workin'."

"Harley's going to change my alternator!" announced Cynthia.

"I'd sure appreciate it if you'd take a look at my brakes," said Scott. "They're sticking."

"Might be y'r calibers."

"I'll pay the going rate."

"Th' only rate goin' for you 'uns is no rate," Harley declared.

Scott Murphy glanced at his watch and stood. "I've got to look in on my folks before they get to sleep. Thanks for inviting me, sir . . . Mrs. Kavanagh—"

"Cynthia!" said Mrs. Kavanagh.

"Cynthia! I had a really good time. Harley, come up and see me at Hope House. And let me know when you can look at my brakes."

Scott left by the basement door, as the rest of the party said their goodbyes to Harley, then trooped up the stairs to the rectory kitchen and along the hall to the front stoop.

"Soon as I get my stuff, I'm going to Tommy's house!" Dooley raced up the steps to his room, Barnabas at his heels. "His dad's waitin' for me, we're going to Wesley to rent a video."

The rector stood on the front walk and talked with Cynthia and Olivia as Lace searched under the bench on the stoop. Then she came down the steps to the yard and peered into the boxwoods near the steps.

"Lace—what is it?" asked Olivia.

"Somebody's stoled my hat," she said. "My hat ain't where I left it at."

"Where did you leave it?" wondered Cynthia.

"I asked her to leave it on the bench," Olivia confessed, looking concerned.

"I'll have a look with you," said the rector, going to the boxwoods. "It probably fell . . ."

"It didn't fall nowhere!" Lace shouted. "It's gone!"

The screen door slammed and Dooley ran down the steps.

"It was you that stoled my hat, won't it? I ought t' bash y'r head in!"

She lunged toward Dooley, and Olivia moved almost as quickly, catching Lace's jumper. There was a ripping sound as the skirt tore from part of the bodice.

"Look what you done t' my new outfit!" Lace struggled to free herself from Olivia. "Let me go, I'm goin' t' knock his head off—"

"Lace! Don't." Cynthia caught her wrist.

"I ought t' kill you, you sorry, redheaded son of a—"

Dooley's face was crimson. "Why would I steal your dirty, stinking, stupid, beat-up hat?"

The rector put his hand on the boy's shoulder. "Easy, son."

"Well, why would I?" he yelled.

"You better give it back and give it back now!" Lace trembled with rage, her own face ashen.

"What would anybody want with your dumb, stupid hat that makes you look so stupid everybody laughs behind your back? Who would even touch your stupid, snotty, dirty hat?"

Lace wrenched away from Cynthia and Olivia and flew at Dooley, who threw his arm in front of his face. She slammed her fist into his left rib, which sent him reeling backward toward the stoop.

Barnabas barked furiously as the rector grabbed Lace by the shoulders. "Stop it *now*," he said.

Dooley regained his balance and stood without a word. He straightened his shirt. "I've got to go," he said, tight-lipped. "Tommy's dad is waiting for me."

"Go," the rector said quietly.

"If you done it," Lace shouted after Dooley, "I'll stomp your butt 'til you're flatter'n a cow dab."

Cynthia and Olivia walked with Lace to the blue Volvo at the curb, as the rector sat wearily on the top step. Barnabas crashed beside him. He felt shaken by the intensity of Lace Turner's sudden and virulent outburst.

If Dooley Barlowe were, indeed, the culprit, he'd do well to hide in the piney woods 'til this thing blew over.

§

He sat in the chair next to Dooley's desk, reading the Thirty-seventh Psalm, the first two words of which he considered an entire sermon.

He looked up as Dooley raced into the room on the stroke of his curfew.

"Did you do it?"

Dooley stood in the doorway, panting. He hesitated for a moment, peering at his shoes, then faced the rector and said, "Yes, sir."

"Why did you lie about it?"

"I didn't lie. I never told her I didn't do it."

That was true. Dooley had responded to her questions with questions. "Where is it?"

"In my closet."

"Take it to her in the morning and apologize. To Lace *and* Olivia." He would also call Olivia in the morning.

"Do I have to?"

"What do you think?"

Dooley went to the closet and opened the door. He lifted the hat off the floor as if it were something Barnabas had deposited in the backyard. "Man, I hate this stupid hat."

"So do I," said the rector.

"You do?"

"I do. But that hat belongs to someone else, and you were wrong to steal it."

"Yeah." Dooley looked at the hat for a moment, then looked the rector in the eye.

"I'm sorry," he said.

A genuine apology! If this is what that fancy prep school had accomplished, he should be forking over an extra twenty thousand a year, out of the mere goodness of his heart.

"You'll also apologize to Cynthia."

"What for?"

"Helping put a bitter end to Harley's party."

"Lace Turner makes me puke. I could've knocked her stupid head off."

"But you didn't, and I commend you for it."

Dooley sat on the bed, holding his left side. "She'll kill me," he said.

"You might want to apologize to Lace while Olivia is in the room—then run for it."

There was a long silence. A moth beat around the lamp bulb.

"Do something like this again," the rector said, "and I'll . . ." What he needed in closing was a good, hair-raising threat, something like taking the car keys away for a couple of weeks—but Dooley didn't drive.

"And I'll . . ." he said.

Blast. He realized he couldn't come up with a decent threat if his life depended on it.

§

The mayor asked him to trot to her office—and be quick about it, according to the tone in her voice.

When Esther Cunningham pulled the string, he, like most people, jumped. He hated that about himself, but why not? Esther had kept an unflagging vigil over Mitford, sacrificing years of her time and even her health to keep things on the up and up. They hadn't even had a tax hike in her long tenure. So yes, he came when she called, and glad to do it.

She leaned across the desk, the splotches on her face and neck looking redder than ever.

"Guess what th' low-down jackleg has done now."

"I can't guess."

"He's throwin' one of his free barbecues next Friday—th' very day of the town festival." She looked at him darkly. "See th' strategy?"

He didn't.

"That'll siphon th' crowd down to his place and leave us sittin' under those shade trees at th' town museum like a bunch of flour sacks."

"Aha." The cheese was getting binding.

"Here's what I want you to do," she said, looking at the door and lowering her voice.

He was in for it.

"Sittin' in a booth draped with th' flag won't cut it this election. Times are changin.' I want you to go home and pray about it and come up with somethin'.'"

"But the town festival is only four days away."

"Somethin'," she said, "that'll blow Mack Stroupe and his barbe-cue deal clear to Holding."

"You want *me* to do that?"

"And be quick about it," she said, scratching a splotch.

§

Hadn't his wife arranged countless retreats to help him relax, and cooked dinner on evenings when he wasn't up to the task?

Hadn't she prayed for him faithfully, and overhauled the rectory, and given him a complete set of Charles Dickens, not to mention a lighted world globe?

And wasn't she working on a book nearly eight hours a day?

He would do what the Russians do. Though it was his very own birthday, he would be the host, he would give the dinner.

It would be just the two of them, and afterward, they would dance. He'd put on the CD of the rhumba—or was it the tango she liked?—and positively whirl her around the study. His blood was getting up for it.

And champagne! That was the ticket. Something expensive, of course, that wouldn't give you a blinding headache even as it went down your gullet. Avis would know which label, and didn't Avis mention that a shipment of fresh lamb was expected any day?

Furthermore, weren't his antique French roses blooming like he'd never seen, drenching the air with their intoxicating scent?

By jing!

He examined the back of his head in the mirror again. He'd been fairly butchered in the privacy of his own home.

Best to nip out and get the matter settled, once and for all.

A decent haircut, the new blue sport coat Cynthia had found on sale, dancing with his wife on his birthday—what else could a man want or imagine?

Suddenly he didn't feel a hundred years old in the shade, he was feeling more like—why not say it?—seventeen.

As he looked up Fancy's number, he had to admit he missed Joe Ivey. So what if Joe had never gone to hair conventions to learn the latest thing? Joe was eminently companionable, and never talked your ear off while he barbered your head.

Another thing—Joe hadn't been shy about slapping on the Sea Breeze, an all-time favorite treat for the way it made the scalp tingle. Fancy Skinner, on the other hand, considered the use of Sea Breeze beneath her station.

Ah, well. He sighed, dialing 555-HAIR. Fancy Skinner was the only game in town, and he hoped she could work him in.

"Th' shop's closed today, I'm here givin' Mama a rinse. Mama, she lives in Spruce Pine, but I'm from Newland. If you get over here quick, I'll trim you up because it's you. You might be th' only one I'd do this for, I'm not sure I'd do it for my own preacher, did you see what his wife did to him, it looked like she put a soup bowl on his head and hacked around it with a steak knife. How he had th' nerve to preach a revival lookin' like that is beyond me.

"Oh, Lord, I just remembered, would you mind stoppin' by Th' Local and gettin' me some sugarless gum, I'll pay you th' minute you get here or take it off your bill, either one, I like to have gum in th' shop, I do my best work if I have somethin' in my mouth, at least it's not a cigarette, law, I used to suck down two packs a day, unfiltered, can you believe it?

"Well, if you're comin', come on, tomorrow'll be a zoo, everybody's gettin' ready for the town festival, why anybody would want highlights to eat barbecue in a parkin' lot is beyond me, and if you could pick up a sack of peppermint while you're at it, that'd be great, I like to have it for people with onion breath, doin' hair is close work."

§

As Fancy draped him with the pink shawl, he sighed resignedly and closed his eyes.

"Prayin', are you? You ought to know by now I won't cut your ear off or poke a hole in your head. Law, I've had too much coffee this mornin', you know I can't drink but two cups or I'm over the moon, how about you, can you still drink caffeine, or are you too old? Course, your wife is young, she probably can do it, I used to drink five or six cups a day . . . and smoke, oh, law, I smoked like a stack! But not anymore, did you know it makes you wrinkle faster? I hate those little lines around my mouth worse than anything, but that wadn't coffee, that was sun, honey, I used to lay out and bake like a chicken.

"Look at this trim! Who did this? I thought Joe Ivey was workin' at Graceland. Mama, come and look at this, this is what I have to put up with. Father, this is Mama, Mama, he's a friend of Mule's, he got married a while back for the first time.

"He preaches at that rock church down the street where they use incense, I declare, Mule and I passed by your church one Sunday, you could smell it comin' out of th' chimney! Lord, my allergies flare up somethin' awful when I smell that stuff, I thought incense was Catholic, anyway, do y'all talk Latin? I had a girlfriend one time, I went to church with her, I couldn't understand a word they said.

"Your hair's growin' like a weed. I hear if you eat a lot of grease, it'll make your hair grow, you shouldn't eat grease, anyway, you've got diabetes.

"Mama! Did you know th' Father has diabetes? My daddy had diabetes. Is that what killed him, Mama, or was it smokin'? Maybe both.

"Look at that! Whoever trimmed your hair, you tell 'em to leave your hair alone. You can call me anytime, I'll work you in. I'm sorry I couldn't take you—when was it?—I think your pope was here, I guess he don't always stay at the Vatican, have you ever been to the Vatican? Law, I haven't even been to Israel, everybody's been to Israel, our preacher is takin' a whole group next year, but I'd rather go on a cruise, do you think that's sacrilegious?

"You ought to let me give you a mask with Fancy's Face Food while we're at it, especially with your wife havin' a birthday, or is it you that's havin' one? Either way, my mask is about as good as a face-lift, not to mention four thousand dollars cheaper. No, I mean it, I'll do it for you, it won't take but an hour. Just *name* a better birthday present than lookin' fifteen years younger, which is more in your *wife's* age group, if I'm not mistaken. OK, lay back, you're stiff as a board, I'm not goin' to claw your eyes out, men are babies, aren't they, Mama? She can't hear for beans, bein' under th' dryer an' all.

"Now, don't try to talk while I'm puttin' this on your face, OK? It'll get hard and you have to lay like this for thirty minutes without sayin' a word or th' whole thing'll crack off and fall on th' floor and that's forty bucks down the tubes. You ought to see this nice green color, it's got mint in it, and cucumber, and I don't know what all, I think there's spinach in here, too, and burdock—my granmaw used to dig burdock for whoopin' cough medicine!

"Don't that feel good, don't you just feel your skin releasin' all those toxins? And those wrinkles on your forehead, I bet you pucker your forehead when you think, you seem like th' type that thinks, well, you can kiss your wrinkles goodbye, honey, 'cause I'm talkin' sayonara, adios, outta here. . . ."

§

Lying in Fancy's chair had given him a headache, not to mention a crick in his neck that seemed to extend to his upper shoulders and into most of his spinal column. Oh, well. A small price to pay for looking forty-eight on his sixty-third birthday.

Fancy had urged him not to look in the mirror at Hair House. "Why look in the mirror," she asked in what he considered a marvelous burst of philosophy, "when you can see th' real difference by lookin' in her eyes?" She winked at him hugely and blew a bubble, which wasn't easy to do with sugarless spearmint gum.

Not wanting to seem ungrateful, he tipped her five dollars, noting that she hadn't offered a discount for clergy on this particular deal.

§

He couldn't help himself. The minute he came in the back door, he turned and looked in the mirror.

Good Lord!

His face was . . . *green.*

Unbelievable! Surely not. Was it the dim natural light in the kitchen? He switched on the overhead fixture, fogged his glasses, and looked again.

It wasn't the light.

He dialed 555-HAIR from the kitchen phone, his heart beating dully. No answer.

He raced up the stairs to the bedroom and looked in the mirror he was accustomed to using.

Green.

His watch said five p.m. He'd invited Cynthia to come over at seven.

The birthday dinner, the champagne, the roses . . . the whole deal dashed. Blown on the wind.

He went to the bathroom and lathered his hands with soap and warm water and scrubbed his face.

Who would want to dance the tango with someone whose face was green? And how could he possibly confess that he'd had a facial, something which no other man in the village of Mitford would ever do in a hundred—no, a million—years?

He splashed his face and dried it and looked in the medicine cabinet mirror, which was topped by a 150-watt bulb that never lied.

Green. No two ways about it.

He stood gazing into the mirror, stunned. That's what he got for being a weak-minded sap, unable to say no to a woman in a pair of Capri pants so tight they looked as if they'd been robbed from a toddler.

He wanted to dig a hole and crawl in it.

§

They had dined, they had danced, they had remarked upon the extraordinary fragrance of the roses. She had raved about his cooking, she had sung a rousing "Happy Birthday," and she'd given him a book about himself and the parish of Mitford, which she had written and illustrated.

He was visibly moved and completely delighted. To have a book in which he saw himself walking down Main Street and standing on the church lawn in his vestments . . . Now he knew how Violet must feel.

He thought it immensely good of her not to comment on anything unusual in his appearance, though he was certain that he saw her staring a time or two, once with her mouth open.

He poured a final glass of champagne.

"This is like . . . like a date!" she said, flushed and happy.

"Which we never had, except for that movie where you ate all my Milk Duds."

"I detest dating!" she said. "I think it should be reserved for marriage."

"Amen!"

He served the poached pears he'd served the first time she came for dinner, drizzling hers with chocolate sauce.

"Dearest," she said, as they lolled on the study sofa, "there's something I've been wanting to say. . . ."

Here it comes, he thought, his heart sinking.

"You aren't looking well at all. You seem . . . a little green around the gills. I'm worried about you, Timothy."

"Aha." He had paid good money to look fifteen years younger, and wound up looking sick and infirm. He would never step foot in

Fancy Skinner's place again, not as long as he lived, so what if the round-trip to Memphis would take eighteen hours' hard driving?

"All that business about your retirement and the worry over Fernbank, and whatever this new, urgent project is for the mayor . . . I think it's time for a retreat."

His wife specialized, actually, in the domestic retreat. It was, to a worn-out clergyman, what retreads were to a tire. Once they'd had a picnic in Baxter Park, once a picnic overlooking the Land of Counterpane, and once she'd carried him off to the little yellow house where they had reclined on her king-size bed like two dissolute Romans, drinking lemonade and listening to the rain.

"Right," he said. "A retreat."

She peered at him again, her brow furrowed.

"Definitely!" she said, looking concerned.

§

While they partied in the study, Barnabas had stood up to the kitchen counter like a man and polished off what was left of the lamb. He also helped himself to two dinner rolls, half a stick of butter, a bowl of wild rice, and all the mint jelly he could lick off a spoon in the dishwasher.

At two in the morning, the rector felt a large paw on his shoulder. This was major, and no doubt about it.

He hastily pulled on his pants and a shirt, slipped his feet into his loafers, and thumped downstairs behind his desperate dog.

He barely got the leash on before Barnabas was out the back door and across to the hedge.

Barnabas sniffed his turf. Possums, raccoons, hedgehogs, squirrels, and cats had passed this way, not to mention the rector's least favorite of all creatures great and small, the mole. The place was a veritable smorgasbord of smells, apparently causing his dog to forget entirely why he had barreled outside in the middle of the night, dragging his master behind like a ball on a chain.

"Sometime in this century, pal?"

More sniffing.

Suddenly Barnabas had the urge to go around the house . . . then across the yard . . . then out to the sidewalk . . . then up the street.

"Not the monument!" he groaned.

Barnabas strained forward with the muscle and determination of a team of yoked oxen. They were going to the monument.

He trotted behind his dog, noting the peace of their village when no cars were on the street. There seemed an uncommon dignity in the glow of the streetlights tonight and the baskets brimming with flowers that hung from every lamppost.

They had a good life in Mitford, no doubt about it. Visitors were often amazed at its seeming charm and simplicity, wanting it for themselves, seeing in it, perhaps, the life they'd once had, or had missed entirely.

Yet there were Mitfords everywhere. He'd lived in them, preached in them, they were still out there, away from the fray, still containing something of innocence and dreaming, something of the past that other towns had freely let go, or allowed to be taken from them.

How much longer could the Esther Cunninghams of the world hold on? How much longer could common, decent, kind regard hold out against utter disregard?

Like the rest of us, he thought, the mayor may have her blind spots, but I'll take my chances with Esther any day.

He'd almost forgotten what he'd come out here for; he'd been walking as in a dream. Then, thanks be to God, his dog found a spot behind the hedge surrounding the monument.

He stood there as Barnabas did his business, and looked at the summer sky. Orion . . . the Three Sisters . . . the Bear . . .

He nearly missed seeing the car as it went around the monument and headed down Lilac Road.

Lincoln. New. Black. Quiet.

He felt alarmed, but couldn't figure why. The car seemed to remind him of something or someone. . . .

He had the strange thought that it didn't seem right for a car to be so quiet—it was oddly chilling.

§

"What's the scoop?" he asked Scott Murphy.

"Interesting. I can't figure it out exactly. When they come to see

Homeless on Wednesday night, they don't have much to say, but they seem to sense something special about being there, as if they're . . . waiting for something."

They are, he thought, suddenly moved. They are.

§

"I hate to tell you this," he said, glancing at his wife as they weeded the perennial bed next to her garage. The town festival was tomorrow, and all of Mitford was scurrying to look tidy and presentable. Certainly he was looking more presentable. The greenish cast to his skin had disappeared altogether.

A long silence ensued as he pulled knotgrass from among the foxgloves.

"Well? Spit it out, Timothy!"

"I did some simple arithmetic . . ."

"So?"

". . . and I was sixty-four yesterday."

"No!"

"Yes."

"I thought you were sixty-three! This means I'll be fifty-eight, not fifty-seven. Oh, *please!*"

Her moan might have ricocheted off the roof of the town museum two blocks away.

"The neighbors . . ." he said.

"We don't *have* any, remember? Since I moved to the rectory, we don't *have* any neighbors, which means I can wail as loud as I want to."

"Good thinking, Kavanagh."

Sixty-four! He felt like letting go with a lamentation of his own.

§

"Th' volts was down t' ten," said Harley, wiping his hands on a rag. "Hit was runnin' off the battery. Why don't you take it out and spin it around, I tuned it up some while I was at it."

"We thank you, Harley. This is terrific."

"Hit ought t' go like a scalded dog."

The rector opened the door and Barnabas jumped into the passenger seat, then he got in and backed his wife's Mazda out of the garage.

What a day! he thought as he drove up Main Street, glad to see the bustle of commerce. In a day of shopping malls on bypasses, not every town could boast of a lively business center.

He saw Dooley pedal out of The Local alleyway on his bicycle, wearing his helmet and hauling a full delivery basket. He honked the horn. Dooley grinned and waved.

There was Winnie, putting a tray of something sinful in the window of the Sweet Stuff, and he honked again but was gone before Winnie looked up.

As he approached the monument, he saw Uncle Billy and Miss Rose, stationed in their chrome dinette chairs on the lawn of the town museum, where everybody and his brother had gathered to put up tents, booths, flags, tables, umbrellas, hand-lettered signs, and the much-needed port-a-john, which this year, he observed, appeared to lean to the right instead of the left.

He honked and waved as Uncle Billy waved back and Miss Rose looked scornful.

How in the dickens he could have lived in this town for over fifteen years and still get a kick out of driving up Main Street was beyond him. He'd liked living in his little parish by the sea, too, but the main street hadn't been much to look at, and often, during the hurricane season, their few storefronts had stayed boarded up.

Count your blessings, his grandmother had told him. Count your blessings, his mother had often said.

He eased around the monument and headed west on Lilac Road.

Did anyone really count their blessings, anymore? There was, according to the world's dictum, no time to smell the roses, no time to count blessings. But how much time did it take to recognize that he was, in a sense, driving one around? Hadn't Harley Welch just saved them a hundred bucks, right in his own backyard?

Besides, if there were no time in Mitford, where would there ever be time?

"Ah, Barnabas," he said, reaching over to scratch his dog's ear.

Barnabas stared straight ahead, a behavior he'd always considered appropriate to riding in a car.

He turned on the radio and heard Mozart straining to come across the mountains from the tower in Asheville, and fiddled with the dial until he got a weather report. Sunshine all weekend. Hallelujah!

He realized he was grinning from ear to ear.

How often did he feel as if he didn't have a care in the world? Not often. He'd been equipped, after all, with a nature that could run to the melancholy if he didn't watch it.

"Serious-minded!" a neighbor had said of him as a child, putting on his glasses to get a better look at the tyke who stood before him with a large book under his skinny arm.

He thought of last night, of his vibrant and unstoppable wife sitting up in bed, reading to him, knowing how he loved this simple sacrifice of time and effort. He had put his head in her lap and reached down and held the warm calf of her leg, knowing with all that was in him how extraordinarily rich he was.

He had heard Dooley come in, racing up the stairs on the dot of his curfew, and afterward, the sound of his dog snoring in the hall. . . .

He thought of the old needlepoint sampler his grandmother had done, framed and hanging in the rectory kitchen. He had passed it so often over the years, he had quit seeing it. The patient stitching, embellished with faded cabbage roses, quoted a verse from the Sixtyeighth Psalm.

"Blessed be the Lord," it read, "who daily loadeth us with benefits."

"Loadeth!" he exclaimed aloud. "Daily!"

The car was running like a top, thanks to his live-in mechanic, but he didn't want to turn around and go home; he had a sudden taste for a view of the late-June countryside, maybe a little run out to Farmer, four miles away, then back to help Cynthia bake for the church booth tomorrow.

And while he did the run to Farmer, he would do a seemingly childish thing—he would count his blessings as far as he could.

Quite possibly the list could go on until Wednesday, for he knew a thing or two about blessings and how they were, even in the worst of times, inexhaustible.

It came to him that Patrick Henry Reardon had indirectly spoken of something like this. He had copied it into his sermon notebook only days ago.

"Suppose for a moment," Reardon had said, "that God began taking from us the many things for which we have failed to give thanks. Which of our limbs and faculties would be left? Would I still have my hands and my mind? And what about loved ones? If God were to take from me all those persons and things for which I have not given thanks, who or what would be left of me?"

What would be left of me, indeed? he wondered. The very thought struck him with a force he hadn't recognized when he copied it into his notebook.

He put his hand on his dog's head and hoarsely whispered the beginning of his list:

"Barnabas . . ."

§

He saw her standing at the corner of Main Street and Wisteria, looking toward the rectory. He had never seen her before in his life, but he knew exactly, precisely, who she was.

He felt himself loving her at once, as she held out her arms and smiled and started running toward him. He tried to run, also, to meet her, but found he moved as if through sand or deep water, and was dumbstruck, unable to call her name.

His wife was shaking him. "Wake up, dearest!"

"What . . . what . . . ?"

"You were dreaming."

He sat up with a pounding heart.

"We have to find Jessie," he said.

CHAPTER EIGHT

Political Barbecue

There was plenty of talk on the street. As early as seven-thirty on the morning of the festival, he couldn't walk from the south end to the north without picking up new funds of information.

Dora Pugh, who was setting flats of borage, chives, and rosemary outside the hardware door, asked if he'd seen the billboards on the highway. They must have been put up in the middle of the night, she said, because when she drove home yesterday, she certainly hadn't noticed Mack Stroupe's ugly mug plastered on three new boards, all the way from Hattie Cloer's market to the Shoe Barn.

"That," she snorted, "is three times more of that cracker than I ever wanted to see." Dora once lived in Georgia, where "cracker" had nothing to do with party snacks.

At the Sweet Stuff, Winnie Ivey hailed him in.

"I'm experimenting," she said, tucking a strand of graying hair under her bandanna. "My license says people can sit down, so I thought I should try fixin' things to where people don't have to stand at th' shelf."

The shelf along the wall had come down, replaced by posters of mountain scenery, and in the long-empty space in front of her display cases stood three tables and a dozen chairs.

"I'm tryin' to do all I can to bring in business. If I'm goin' to sell out, I want my ledgers lookin' good," she said.

"I'm proud of you, Winnie! And to think you've done all this by yourself!"

"I have to do whatever it takes, Father! Of course, it's just coffee and sweets, as usual, except now you get a chair to sit in—but I might add sandwiches next week. And soup in the winter. What do you think?"

"I think you should!"

She brightened. "It helps to have advice."

"Don't I know it!" Weren't his parishioners full of it?

"My husband, Johnny, used to know what to do about things, but he died so many years ago, I can hardly remember his face. Do you think that's bad?"

He could seldom recall his father's face. "No," he said, "it can happen like that. . . ."

"You know, sometimes I . . ." Winnie blushed.

"Sometimes you . . . ?"

"You wouldn't tell this?"

"You have my word."

"Sometimes I think of a man standin' beside me in th' kitchen back there, I don't know who it is because I can't exactly see his face, but it seems like he's tall and dark-headed, and I can tell he has a big heart." She paused, looking shy. "He bakes all th' cakes, and he's always laughin' and sayin' nice things, like how good my cream horns are, and how pretty I glazed the fruit tarts."

He nodded.

"He always has flour on his apron."

"He would."

"It would be nice. . . ." she said, looking at him.

"I know," he said, looking back.

"It might not be right to pray for such as that. . . ."

"I think it would be wrong if we didn't," he said.

§

Apparently, all of merchantdom was up and at it, a full two hours before the festival opened.

The Collar Button man was sweeping the sidewalk, with a sprinkler turned on the handkerchief-sized garden next to his store.

"Good morning, Father! How're you liking the jacket your wife selected for your birthday?"

"Immensely! It brings out the blue of her eyes. How's business?"

"Couldn't be better!" said the Collar Button man, going full tilt with his broom.

When he reached the Grill, he stopped and sniffed the balmy air. The smell of roasting pork drifted on the breeze from Mack Stroupe's campaign headquarters near the monument.

Then he squinted up at the sky.

Blue. Here and there, a few billowing clouds.

Perfect.

§

He slid into the booth with a mug of coffee

"Where's J.C?"

"Went upstairs to get film out of his refrigerator," said Mule.

"Film was all he had in his refrigerator 'til he married Adele. What's going on with you?"

"Feelin' like somethin' the cat covered up. I can't half sleep 'til Fancy gets to bed, and she was going like a circle saw 'til two o'clock this morning."

"Doing what?"

"Doin' hair."

"Who in the dickens would get their hair done at two o'clock in the morning?"

"You'd be surprised."

"That's true, I would."

"How's your new boarder?" asked the realtor.

"Working on my Buick. I pay for the parts, he insists on doing the labor. He was under the hood at seven o'clock this morning."

J.C. slung his briefcase into the corner and slid in.

"I looked out th' upstairs window and dadgum if th' street ain't *jumpin'*." The editor rubbed his hands together briskly. This was front-page stuff, everything from llamas and political barbecue to a clogging contest and tourists out the kazoo.

"Let me guess," said Velma, arriving at the rear booth in an unusually cheerful frame of mind. "Poached for th' preacher, scrambled for th' realtor—"

"Fried for th' editor," said J.C. "And don't be bringin' me any yogurt or all-bran."

Velma looked him over as if he were a boiled ham. "You're pickin' up weight again."

"I've picked up worse," said J.C.

Mule stirred his coffee. "Just dry toast with mine."

"No grits?" she asked, personally offended.

"Not today."

"What's the matter with Percy's grits?"

"Oh, well, all right. But no butter."

"Grits without butter?" What was wrong with these people?

"Lord, help," sighed Mule. "Just bring me whatever."

"I'll have mine all the way," said J.C., who had lately thrown caution to the wind. "Biscuits, grits, sausage, bacon, and give me a little mustard on the side."

"I'll have the usual," said Father Tim.

Mule looked approving. "That's what I need to do—figure out one thing and stick with it. Same thing every morning, and you don't have to mess with it again."

"Right," said the rector.

"Have you seen Mack's new boards?" asked J.C.

They hadn't.

"They rhyme like those Burma-Shave signs. First one says, *'If Mitford's economy is going to move'* . . . th' second one says, *'we've got to improve.'* Last one says, *'Mack for Mitford, Mack for Mayor.'*"

"Gag me with a forklift," said Mule.

"Esther Cunningham better get off her rear end, because like it or not, Mack Stroupe's eatin' her lunch. She's been lollin' around like this election was some kind of tea party. You're so all-fired thick with the mayor," J.C. said to the rector, "you ought to tell her the facts of life, and the fact is, she's lookin' dead in the water."

"Aha. I thought we agreed not to talk politics."

"Right," said Mule, whose escalating blood pressure had suddenly turned his face beet red.

J.C. looked bored. "So what else is new? Let's see, I was over at the town museum 'til midnight watchin' those turkeys get ready for the festival. Omer Cunningham was draping th' flag on Esther's booth and fell off the ladder and busted his foot."

"Busted his foot?" the rector blurted. "Good Lord! Can he fly?"

"Can he fly? I don't know as he could, with a busted foot."

Mule cackled. "He sure couldn't fly any crazier than when his foot's *not* busted."

"Toast!" said Velma, sliding two orders onto the table.

The rector felt his stomach wrench.

"Biscuits!" said Velma, handing off a plate to J.C.

"May I use your phone?" asked Father Tim.

"You can, if you stay out of Percy's way, you know where it's at."

He went to the red wall phone and dialed, knowing the number by heart. Hadn't he called it two dozen times in the last few days?

No answer.

He hung up and stood by the grill, dazed, his mouth as dry as cotton.

"I just busted th' yolk in one of y'r eggs," said Percy, who despised poaching.

So? Busted feet, busted yolks, busted plans.

He might possibly be looking at the worst day of his life.

§

His palms were damp, something he'd never appreciated in clergy. Also, his collar felt tight, even though he'd snapped the Velcro at the loosest point.

When he and Cynthia arrived on the lawn of the town museum at 9:35, they had to elbow their way to the Lord's Chapel booth, which was situated, this year, directly across from the llamas and the petting zoo.

"Excellent location!" said his wife, who was known to rely on animals as a drawing card.

They thumped down their cardboard box filled with the results of last night's bake-a-thon in the rectory kitchen. Three Lord's Chapel volunteers, dressed in aprons that said, *Have you hugged an Episcopalian today?* briskly set about unpacking the contents and displaying them in a case cooled by a generator humming at the rear of the tent.

Though the festival didn't officially open until ten o'clock, the yard of the Porter mansion–cum–town museum was jammed with villagers, tourists, and the contents of three buses from neighboring communities. The rear end of a church van from Tennessee displayed a sign, *Mitford or Bust.*

The Presbyterian brass band was already in full throttle on the museum porch, and the sixth grade of Mitford School was marching around the statue of Willard Porter, builder of the impressive Victorian home, with tambourines, drums, and maracas painted in their school colors.

Why was he surprised to see posters on every pole and tree, promoting Mack Stroupe's free barbecue at his campaign headquarters up the street?

His eyes searched the crowd for the mayor, who said she'd be under the elm tree this year, the one that had miraculously escaped the blight.

"I'll be back," he told Cynthia, who was giving him that concerned look. The way things were going, he'd need more than a domestic retreat, he'd need a set of pallbearers.

He saw Uncle Billy next to the lilac bushes, sitting in a hardback chair with a bottomless chair in front of him and a bucket of water at his feet.

"Stop in, Preacher! I'll be a-canin' chairs, don't you know, hit's a demonstration of th' old ways, and I've set out a few of m' birdhouses f'r sale."

"How's your arthur?" asked the rector, concerned.

"Well, sir, last night, I slapped it and said, 'Git on out of there, I ain't havin' nothin' t' do with you!' And m' hands are feelin' some better this mornin', don't you know." He wiggled a couple of fingers to prove his point.

"Where's Miss Rose?"

"She ain't a-comin' out this year, says she don't like s' many people ramblin' around on 'er property."

"Hold that green birdhouse for me, I'll be back!"

He spotted Esther and her husband, Ray, shaking hands by a booth draped with an American flag and a banner hand-lettered with the mayor's longtime political slogan.

"Mayor! Where's Omer?"

"Where's Omer? I thought you'd know where Omer is."

"What about his foot?"

"Broken in two places."

"Right, but what about . . . can he *fly?*"

She glared at him in a way that made Emma Newland look like a vestal virgin. "That's your business," she said, and turned back to the people she'd been shaking hands with.

He headed to the Lord's Chapel booth, his heart hammering. He was afraid to let his wife see his face, since she could obviously read it like a book—but where else could he go?

Dooley! Of course! A Taste of America!

He hung a hard left in the direction of Avis Packard's tent, cutting through the queue to the cotton candy truck, and ran slam into Omer Cunningham on a crutch.

"Good heavens! *Omer!*" He threw his arms around Esther Cunningham's strapping brother-in-law and could easily have kissed his ring, or even his plaster cast.

Heads turned. People stared. He wished he weren't wearing his collar.

Omer's big grin displayed teeth the size of keys on a spinet piano. "We're smokin'," he said, giving a thumbs-up to the rector, who, overcome with joyful relief, thumped down on a folding chair at the Baptists' display of tea towels, aprons, and oven mitts.

§

"Father!"

It was Andrew Gregory, the tall, handsome proprietor of Oxford Antiques, calling from his booth next to the statue of Willard Porter.

The rector could honestly say he felt a warm affection for the man who once courted Cynthia, escorting her hither and yon in his gray Mercedes, while Father Tim moped at the upstairs window of the rectory. Andrew might be six-four with a closetful of cashmere jackets, but hadn't the five-nine, less stylish country parson won Cynthia?

By jing!

He felt positively lighthearted as he stepped up to the booth and shook hands with the antique dealer, who looked elegant in a linen shirt and trousers.

"Great to see you, my friend!"

"How is it," asked Andrew, "that we seldom meet, though our doors are directly across the street from one another?"

"We've mused on that before," said the rector, "and always to no avail. I've missed you. How are you?"

"Off next week to Italy, to my mother's birthplace, a little town called Lucera."

"I've often visited Italy. . . ."

"You have?"

"In my imagination," confessed the rector.

Andrew smiled. "I'm afraid I've cultivated my paternal English side to the vast neglect of my Italian side. I'll do like you did a couple of years ago—go searching for my roots, sample the local wines, visit cousins."

"Good for the soul! You're selling your fine lemon oil, I see."

"Makes all the difference. Look at this eighteenth-century chest." One side of the late-Georgian walnut chest appeared dark and sullen. The other side shone, revealing the life of the wood.

"I'll take three bottles!" the rector announced.

"I've been wondering," said Andrew, as he bagged the lemon oil, "whether I might give you a price on the contents of Fernbank. If you're interested, I'd like to take a look before I chase off to the old country."

"Well! That's a thought. Let me run it by the vestry." He had certainly dragged his feet on emptying Miss Sadie's house in advance of the possible sale to Miami Development. Why had he tried to put the whole Fernbank issue out of his mind when it clearly needed to be handled—and pronto?

Walking away with his package under his arm, he also questioned why on earth he'd bought three bottles of lemon oil when he hardly had a stick of furniture to call his own. Living in partially furnished rectories since the age of twenty-eight had had its bright side, but it wasn't all it was cracked up to be.

"Father Tim!"

It was Margaret Ann Larkin with five-year old Amy, waving at him from the petting zoo.

He pushed through the crowd.

"Father, we've been looking all over for you. Amy wants to pet the animals, but she's afraid to do it. She wondered if . . . I know this is a strange request, but she wants you to do it for her."

"Aha."

Margaret Ann looked imploring. "She doesn't want me to do it."

Amy handed him a dollar. "You pet," she said soberly.

He knelt beside her, clutching his package. "You could walk inside the fence with me."

"You pet," she said.

He turned his lemon oil over to Margaret Ann and went through the gate, relinquishing the dollar to Jake Greer, a farmer from the valley.

"Pet the goat first," said Amy, looking through the fence.

"Please," instructed Margaret Ann.

"Please!" urged Amy.

He petted the goat, which trotted to the other side of the pen, clearly disgusted.

"Now pet the lamb, please."

He petted the lamb. What a black nose! What soulful eyes!

"Now pet the chickens."

A Dominecker rooster and two Leghorn hens squawked and scattered.

He turned and smiled at Amy. "Now what?"

"Pet the pony!"

He petted the pony, who nuzzled his arm and bared its teeth and flared its nostrils, giving him his money's worth. Having petted the entire assembly, including a small pig named Barney, he withdrew through the gate, laughing.

"That was . . . fun," he said, meaning it.

"Was you afraid?" asked Amy.

"Not a bit. I liked it."

"Was the lamb soft?"

"Very soft."

"Amy, honey, what do you say?"

Amy broke into a dazzling smile. "Thank you!" she said, patting him on the leg.

§

His wife peered at him again in that odd way. "You look like *you're* having a good time!"

"You mean you're not?" he asked.

"Not since Gene stepped in Esther's cake."

"No!"

"She came in and set the box behind the table, and when Gene came in, he stumbled over it . . ."

"Uh-oh."

". . . then fell on top of it."

"Good grief."

"Mashed flat," she said.

"Orange marmalade?"

"You got it."

"How's Gene?" he inquired, sounding like an undertaker.

"Unhurt but terrified."

"How's Esther?"

"Three guesses."

"That cake was worth some bucks for the Children's Home."

"I think we could still auction it."

"Mashed flat, we could auction it?"

"There was a top on the box when he fell on it. I mean, it's still Esther's orange marmalade cake—some people would be thrilled to eat it out of the box with a *spoon*."

"If you'll auction it, I'll start the bidding," he said, feeling expansive.

§

He had stopped to pass the time of day with the llamas, who looked at him peaceably through veils of sweeping lashes.

He'd bought a tea towel from the Baptists, a sack of tattered volumes from the Library Ladies, a cookbook from the Presbyterians, and was on his way to see Dooley Barlowe in action.

He paused to check the sky. As he started to look at his watch, he spied them through the queue for popcorn and ducked across.

Olivia kissed him on the cheek. Lace stood looking into the crowd.

He put his arm around Lace's shoulders and found them unyielding. "You ladies are looking lovely—a credit to the town!"

Lace nodded vaguely. "I got to go over yonder a minute."

"Go," said Olivia. "I'll meet you at the llamas in half an hour."

They sat on one of the town museum benches.

"Father, I've had time to think it through and I wanted to say I admire Dooley for the way he handled Lace's outburst. He might have . . . knocked her head off when she attacked him."

"He was asking for it."

"He did a fine job of delivering his apologies. He has character, your boy."

"So does Lace. But character often takes time to show itself. They've both come out of violence and neglect, a matched set. How are you holding up?"

"Better, I think. We're still visiting her mother every week, but it's never a happy visit—her mother is demanding and cold, and her health is deteriorating. Hoppy looked in on her; we're not encouraged."

"We keep you faithfully in our prayers. We're all flying by the seat of our pants." Who would have dreamed he'd be raising a boy? The challenge of it was breathtaking.

"I've read how Lindbergh often flew with the windshield iced over. It's rather like that, don't you think?"

"Indeed. Is she making any friends?"

"Mitford's children have been warned all their lives to avoid anyone from the Creek, so that is very much against her. Then she's smart and she's pretty. Some don't like that, either. They really don't know what to make of her."

"Lord bless you."

"And you, Father."

As they walked away from each other, he turned around and called, "Olivia! Philippians Four-thirteen, for Pete's sake!"

She threw up her hand, smiling at this reminder of the Scripture verse she claimed as a pivot for her life.

It was good to have a comrade in arms, he thought, trotting off to A Taste of America.

Avis Packard's booth was swamped with buyers, eager to tote home sacks of preserves, honey, pies, cakes, and bread from the valley kitchens, not to mention strawberries from California, corn from Georgia, and syrup from Vermont.

Avis stepped out of the booth for a break, while Tommy and Dooley bagged and made change. "I've about bit off more'n I can chew," said Avis, lighting up a Salem. "I've still got a load of new potatoes comin' from Georgia, and lookin' for a crate of asparagus from Florida. Thing is, I don't hardly see how a truck can get down th' street."

"I didn't know you smoked," said the rector, checking his watch.

Avis inhaled deeply. "I don't. I quit two or three years ago. I bummed this offa somebody."

The imported strawberries were selling at a pace, and Avis stepped to the booth and brought back a handful.

"Try one," he said, as proudly as if they'd come from his own patch. "You know how some taste more like straw than berry? Well, sir, these are the finest you'll ever put in your mouth. Juicy, sweet, full of sunshine. What you'd want to do is eat 'em right off th' stem, or slice 'em, marinate in a little sugar and brandy—you don't want to use th' cheap stuff—and serve with cream from the valley, whipped with a hint of fresh ginger."

Avis Packard was a regular poet laureate of grocery fare.

"Is that legal?" asked the rector.

He watched as Dooley passed a bag over the table to a customer. "Hope you like those strawberries!"

He was thrilled to see Dooley Barlowe excited about his work. His freckles, which he and Cynthia had earlier reported missing, seemed to be back with a vengeance.

Avis laughed. "Ain't he a deal?"

"Is he doing right by you?"

"That and then some!"

He noticed Jenny and her mother queuing up at A Taste of America, and saw Dooley glance up at them. Uh-oh. That look on Dooley's face . . .

Was this something he ought to discuss with him, man to man? The very thought made his heart pound.

Ben Sawyer hauled past, carrying a sack of tasseled corn in each arm. "That's a fine boy you got there, Preacher!"

He felt a foolish grin spread across his face, and didn't try to hold it back.

§

He noticed the crowd was starting to thin out, following the aroma of political barbecue.

In his mind, he saw it on the plate, thickly sliced and served with a dollop of hot sauce, nestled beside a mound of cole slaw and a half dozen hot, crisp hushpuppies. . . .

He shook himself and ate four raisins that had rolled around in his coat pocket since the last committee meeting on evangelism.

§

At eleven forty-five, Ray and Esther Cunningham strode up to the Lord's Chapel booth with all five of their beautiful daughters, who had populated half of Mitford with Sunday School teachers, deacons, police officers, garbage collectors, tax accountants, secretaries, retail clerks, and UPS drivers.

"Well?" said Esther. The rector thought she would have made an excellent Mafia don.

"Coming right up!" he exclaimed, checking his watch and looking pale.

Cynthia eyed him again. Mood swings, she thought. That seemed to be the key! Definitely a domestic retreat, and definitely soon.

And since the entire town seemed so demanding of her husband, definitely not in Mitford.

§

Nobody paid much attention to the airplane until it started smoking.

"Look!" somebody yelled. "That plane's on f'ar!"

He was sitting on the rock wall when Omer thumped down beside him. "Right on time!" said the mayor's brother-in-law. "All my flyin' buddies from here t' yonder have jumped on this." The rector thought somebody could have played "Moonlight Sonata" on Omer's ear-to-ear grin.

"OK, that's y'r basic Steerman, got a four-fifty horsepower engine in there. Luke Teeter's flyin' 'er, he's about as good as you can get, now watch this . . ."

The blue and orange airplane roared straight up into the fathomless blue sky, leaving a plume of smoke in its wake. Then it turned sharply and pitched downward at an angle.

"Wow!" somebody said, forgetting to close his mouth.

The plane did another climb into the blue.

Omer punched him in the ribs with an elbow. "She's got a tank in there pumpin' Corvis oil th'ough 'er exhaust system . . . ain't she a sight?"

"Looks like an *N*!" said a boy whose chocolate popsicle was melting down his arm.

The plane plummeted toward the rooftops again, smoke billowing from its exhaust.

"*M!*" shouted half the festivalgoers, as one.

Esther and Ray and their daughters were joined by assorted grandchildren, great-grandchildren, and in-laws, who formed an impenetrable mass in front of the church booth.

Gene Bolick limped over from the llamas as the perfect *I* appeared above them.

"*M . . . I!*" shouted the crowd.

"Lookit this!" said Omer, propping his crutch against the stone wall. "Man, oh, man!"

The bolt of blue and orange gunned straight up, leaving a vertical trail, then shut off the exhaust, veered right, and thundered across the top of the trail, forming a straight and unwavering line of smoke.

"*M . . . I . . . T!*"

The *M* was fading, the *I* was lingering, the *T* was perfect against the sapphire sky.

The crowd thickened again, racing back from Mack Stroupe's campaign headquarters, which was largely overhung by trees, racing back to the grounds of the town museum where the view was open, unobscured, and breathtaking, where something more than barbecue was going on.

"They won't be goin' back to Mack's place anytime soon," said Omer. "Ol' Mack's crowd has done eat an' run!"

"*F!*" they spelled in unison, and then, ". . . *O* . . . *R* . . . *D!*"

Even the tourists were cheering.

J. C. Hogan sank to the ground, rolled over on his back, pointed his Nikon at the sky, and fired off a roll of Tri-X. The *M* and the *I* were fading fast.

Uncle Billy hobbled up and spit into the bushes. "I bet them boys is glad this town ain't called Minneapolis."

"Now, look," said Omer, slapping his knee.

Slowly, but surely, the Steerman's exhaust trail wrote the next word. *T* . . . *A* . . . *K* . . . *E* . . . *S* . . . , the smoke said.

Cheers. Hoots. Whistles.

"Lord, my neck's about give out," said Uncle Billy.

"Mine's about broke," said a bystander.

C . . . *A* . . . *R* . . . *E* . . .

"Mitford takes care of its own!" shouted the villagers. The sixth grade trooped around the statue, beating on tambourines, shaking maracas, and chanting something they'd been taught since first grade.

> *Mitford takes care of its own, its own,*
> *Mitford takes care of its own!*

Over the village rooftops, the plane spelled out the rest of the message.

O . . . *F* . . . *I* . . . *T* . . . *S* . . . *O* . . . *W* . . . *N* . . .

TAKES soon faded into puffs of smoke that looked like stray summer clouds. *CARE OF* was on its way out, but *ITS OWN* stood proudly in the sky, seeming to linger.

"If that don't beat all!" exclaimed a woman from Tennessee, who had stood in one spot the entire time, holding a sleep-drugged baby on her hip.

Dogs barked and chickens squawked as people clapped and started drifting away.

Just then, a few festivalgoers saw them coming, the sun glinting on their wings.

They roared in from the east, in formation, two by two.

Red and yellow. Green and blue.

"Four little home-built Pitts specials," said Omer, as proudly as if he'd built them himself. "Two of 'em's from Fayetteville, got one out of Roanoke, and the other one's from Albany, New York. Not much power in y'r little ragwings, they're nice and light, about a hundred and eighty horses, and handle like a dream."

He looked at the sky as if it contained the most beautiful sight he had ever seen, and so did the rector.

"I was goin' to head th' formation, but a man can't fly with a busted foot."

The crowd started lying on the grass. They lay down along the rock wall. They climbed up on the statue of Willard Porter, transfixed, and a young father set a toddler on Willard's left knee.

People pulled chairs out of their booths and sat down, looking up. All commerce ceased.

The little yellow Pitts special rolled over and dived straight for the monument.

"Ahhhhhh!" said the crowd.

As the yellow plane straightened out and up, the blue plane nose-dived and rolled over.

"They're like little young 'uns a-playin'," said Uncle Billy, enthralled.

Miss Rose came out and stood on the back stoop in her frayed chenille robe and looked up, tears coursing down her cheeks for her long-dead brother, Captain Willard Porter, who had flown planes and been killed in the war in France and buried over there, with hardly anything sent home but his medals and a gold ring with the initials SEB and a few faded snapshots from his pockets.

The little planes romped and rolled and soared and glided, like so many bright crayons on a palette of blue, then vanished toward the west, the sun on their wings.

Here and there, a festivalgoer tried getting up from the grass or a chair or the wall, but couldn't. They felt mesmerized, intoxicated. "Blowed away!" someone said.

"OK, buddy, here you go," Omer whispered.

They heard a heavy-duty engine throbbing in the distance and knew at once this was serious business, this was what everyone had been waiting for without even knowing it.

The Cunningham daughters hugged their children, kissed their mother and daddy, wept unashamedly, and hooted and hollered like banshees, but not a soul looked their way, for the crowd was intent on not missing a lick, on seeing it all, and taking the whole thing, blow by blow, home to Johnson City and Elizabethton and Wesley and Holding and Aho and Farmer and Price and Todd and Hemingway and Morristown. . . .

"Got y'r high roller comin' in, now," said Omer. The rector could feel the mayor's brother-in-law shaking like a leaf from pure excitement. "You've had y'r basic smoke writin' and stunt flyin,' now here comes y'r banner towin'!"

A red Piper Super Cub blasted over the treetops from the direction of the highway, shaking drifts of clouds from its path, trembling the heavens in its wake, and towing a banner that streamed across the open sky:

ESTHER . . . RIGHT FOR MITFORD, RIGHT FOR MAYOR.

The Presbyterian brass band hammered down on their horns until the windows of the Porter mansion rattled and shook.

As the plane passed over, a wave of adrenaline shot through the festival grounds like so much electricity and, almost to a man, the crowd scrambled to its feet and shouted and cheered and whistled and whooped and applauded.

A few also waved and jumped up and down, and nearly all of them remembered what Esther had done, after all, putting the roof on old man Mueller's house, and turning the dilapidated wooden bridge over Mitford Creek into one that was safe and good to look at, and sending Ray in their RV to take old people to the grocery store, and jacking up Sophia's house and helping her kids, and making sure they had decent school buses to haul their own kids around in bad weather, and creating that thing at the hospital where you went and held and loved a new baby if its mama from the Creek was on drugs, and never one time raising taxes, and always being there when they had a problem, and actually listening when they talked, and . . .

. . . and taking care of them.

Some who had planned to vote for Mack Stroupe changed their minds, and came over and shook Esther's hand, and the brass band nearly busted a gut to be heard over the commotion.

Right! That was the ticket. Esther was *right* for Mitford. Mack Stroupe might be for change, but Esther would always be for the things that really counted.

Besides—and they'd tried to put it out of their minds time and time again—hadn't Mack Stroupe been known to beat his wife, who was quiet as a mouse and didn't deserve it, and hadn't he slithered over to that woman in Wesley for years, like a common, low-down snake in the grass?

"Law, do y'all vote in th' *summer*?" wondered a visitor. "We vote sometime in th' fall. I can't remember when, exactly, but I nearly always have to wear a coat to the polls."

Omer looked at the rector. The rector looked at Omer.

They shook hands.

It was done.

CHAPTER NINE

Life in the Fast Lane

"What I done was give you thirty more horses under y'r hood."

"Did I *need* thirty more horses?" He had to admit that stomping his gas pedal had been about as exciting as stepping on a fried pie. However . . .

Harley gave him a philosophical look, born from experience. "Rev'rend, I'd hate f'r you t' need 'em and not have 'em."

What could he say?

§

On Monday morning, he roared to the office, screeching to a halt at the intersection of Old Church Lane, where he let northbound traffic pass, then made a left turn, virtually catapulting into the parking lot.

Holy smoke! Had Harley dropped a Jag engine in his Buick?

Filled with curiosity, he got out and looked under the hood, but realized he wouldn't know a Jag engine from a Mazda alternator.

§

"Can you believe it?" asked Emma, tight-lipped.

He knew exactly what she was talking about. "Not really."

For a while, he thought they'd lost his secretary's vote to Esther Cunningham's competition. Last week, however, had turned the tide; she'd heard that Mack Stroupe had bought two little houses on the edge of town and jacked up the rent on a widow and a single mother.

"Sittin' in church like he owned th' place, is what I hear. Why th' roof didn't fall in on th' lot of you is beyond me."

"Umm."

"Church!" she snorted. "Is that some kind of new campaign trick, goin' to *church*?"

He believed that particular strategy had been used a time or two, but he didn't comment.

"The next thing you know, he'll be wantin' to *join*. If I were you, I'd run his hide up th' road to th' Presbyterians."

He laughed. "Emma, you're beautiful when you're mad."

She beamed. "Really?"

"Well . . ."

"So, what did he *do,* anyway? Did he kneel? Did he stand? Did he *sing*? Can you imagine a peckerwood like Mack Stroupe singin' those hymns from five hundred years ago, maybe a thousand? Lord, it was all *I* could do to sing th' dern things, which is *one* reason I went back to bein' a Baptist."

She booted her computer, furious.

"I heard Lucy was with him, wouldn't you know it, but that's the way they do, they trot their family out for all the world to see. Was she still blond? What was she wearin'? Esther Bolick said it was a sight the way the crowd ganged up at the museum watchin' the air show, and that barbecue sittin' down the street like so much chicken mash."

She peered intently at her screen.

"Well," she said, clicking her mouse, "has the cat got your tongue? Tell me somethin', *anything*! Were you floored when he showed up at Lord's Chapel, or what?"

"I was. Of course, there's always the possibility that he wants to turn over a new leaf. . . ."

"Right," she said, arching an eyebrow, "and Elvis is livin' at th' Wesley hotel."

§

As much as he liked mail, and the surprise it was capable of bringing, he let the pile sit on Emma's desk until she came back from lunch.

"No way! I can't believe it!" She held up an envelope, grinning proudly. "Albert Wilcox!"

She opened it. "Listen to this!

"'Dear one and all, it was a real treat to hear from you after so many years. My grandmother's prayer book that gave us such pain—and delight—sits on my desk as I write to you, waiting to be handed over to the museum in Seattle, which is near my home in Oak Harbor. . . .'"

She read the entire letter, which also contained a great deal of information about Albert's knee replacement, and his felicitations to the rector for having married.

"Have you ever? And all because of modern technology! OK, as soon as I open this other envelope, I've got a little surprise for you. Close your eyes."

He closed his eyes.

"Face the bookcase!" she said.

He faced the bookcase.

He heard fumbling and clicking. Then he heard Beethoven.

The opening strains of the Pastorale fairly lifted him out of his chair.

"OK! You can turn around!"

He didn't see anything unusual, but was swept away by the music, which seemed to come from nowhere, transforming the room.

"CD-ROM!" announced his resident computer expert, as if she'd just hung the moon.

§

He went home and jiggled Sassy and burped Sissy, as Puny collected an ocean of infant paraphernalia into something the size of a leaf bag.

After a quick trot through the hedge to say hello to his hardworking wife, he and Dooley changed into their old clothes. They were going to tear down Betty Craig's shed and stack the wood. He felt fit for anything.

"Let's see those muscles," he challenged Dooley, who flexed his arm. "Well done!" He wished he had some to show, himself, but thinking and preaching had never been ways to develop muscles.

What with a good job, plenty of sun, and a reasonable amount of home cooking, Dooley Barlowe was looking good. In fact, Dooley Barlowe was getting to be downright handsome, he mused, and tall into the bargain.

Dooley stood against the doorframe as the rector made a mark, then measured. Good heavens!

"I'll be et for a tater if you ain't growed a foot!" he exclaimed in Uncle Billy's vernacular.

Soon, he'd be looking up to the boy who had come to him in dirty overalls, searching for a place to "take a dump."

◈

They were greeted in the backyard by Russell Jacks and Dooley's young brother.

"I've leaned th' ladder ag'inst th' shed for you," said Russell.

"Half done, then!" The rector was happy to see his old sexton.

Poo Barlowe looked up at him. "Hey!"

"Hey, yourself!" he replied, tousling the boy's red hair. "Where were you on Saturday? We missed you at the town festival."

"Mama took me to buy some new clothes." The boy glanced down at his tennis shoes, hoping the rector would notice.

"Man alive! Look at those shoes! Made for leaping tall buildings, it appears."

Poo grinned.

"Want to help us pull that shed down?"

"It ain't hardly worth pullin' down," said Poo, "bein' ready t' fall down."

"Don't say ain't," commanded his older brother.

"Why not?"

"'Cause it ain't good English!" Realizing what he'd just said, Dooley colored furiously.

Father Tim laughed. He'd corrected Dooley's English for three long years. "You're sounding a lot like me, buddy. You might want to watch that."

Betty Craig ran down the back steps.

"Father! Law, this is good of you. I've been standin' at my kitchen window for years, lookin' at that old shed lean to the south. It's aggravated me to death."

"A good kick might be all it takes."

"Pauline's late comin' home, she called to say she'd be right here. Can I fix you and Dooley some lemonade? It's hot as August."

"We'll wait 'til our work is done."

"Let's get going," said Dooley.

Father Tim opened the toolbox and took out a clawhammer and put on his heavy work gloves. He'd never done this sort of thing before. He felt at once fierce and manly, and then again, completely uncertain how to begin.

"What're we going to do?" asked Dooley, pulling on his own pair of gloves.

He looked at the shed. Blast if it wasn't bigger than he'd thought. "We're going to start at the top," he said, as if he knew what he was talking about.

§

He had removed the rolled asphalt with a clawhammer, pulled off the roofboards, dismantled the rafters, torn off the sideboards with Dooley's help, then pulled nails from the corners of the rotten framework, and shoved what was left into the grass.

Running with sweat, he and Dooley had taken turns driving the rusty nails back and pulling them out of every stick and board so they could be used for winter firewood.

Dooley dropped the nails into a bucket.

"Wouldn't want t' be steppin' on one of them," said Russell, who was supervising.

They paused only briefly, to sit on the porch and devour a steaming portion of chicken pie, hot from Betty's oven, and guzzle a quart of tea that was sweet enough to send him to the emergency room.

Betty apologized. "Hot as it is, your supper ought to be somethin' cold, like chicken salad, but you men are workin' hard, and chicken salad won't stick to your ribs."

"Amen!"

"I want you to come and get your kindlin' off that pile all winter long, you hear?"

"I'll do it."

After they ate, he and Dooley and Poo carried and stacked and heaved and hauled, until it was nearly nine o'clock, and dark setting in.

"You've about killed me," grumbled Dooley.

"I've done sweated a bucket," said Poo.

"I'm give out jis' watchin'," sighed Russell.

As for himself, the rector felt oddly liberated. All that pulling up and yanking off and tearing down and pushing over had been good for him, somehow, creating an exhaustion completely different from the labors surrounding his life as a cleric.

And what better reward than to sit and look across the twilit yard at the mound of wood neatly stacked along the fence, with two boys beside him who had helped make it happen?

§

Dooley was inspecting Poo's new, if used, bicycle, Russell had shuffled off to bed, and Betty had gone in to watch TV. He sat alone with Pauline.

He didn't see any reason to beat around the bush. "We need to talk about Jessie."

There was a long silence.

"I can do it," she said.

"I need to know everything you can possibly tell me, and the name of the cousin who took her and where you think they might be, and the names of any of your cousin's relatives—everything."

He heard the absolute firmness in his voice and knew this was how it would have to be.

As she talked, he took notes on a piece of paper he had folded and put in his shirt pocket. Afterward, he sat back in the rocker.

"If we find Jessie, can you take care of her?"

"Yes!" she said, and now he heard the firmness in her own voice. "I think about it all the time, how I want to rent a little house and have a tree at Christmas. We never had a tree at Christmas . . . maybe once."

His mind went instantly to all that furniture collecting dust at Fernbank. He and Dooley would load up a truck and . . . But he was putting the cart before the horse.

"There's something we need to look at, Pauline."

"Is it about the drinking?"

"Yes."

"I don't crave it anymore."

"Alcohol is a tough call. Very tough. Do you want help?"

"No," she said. "I want to do this myself. With God's help."

"If you ever want or need help, you've got to have the guts to ask for it. For your sake, for the kids' sake. Can you do that?"

Betty switched the porch light on, and he saw Pauline's face as she turned and looked at him. "Yes," she said.

"Didn't want y'all to be setting out there in the dark," said Betty, going back to her room.

They were silent again. He heard Poo laughing, and faint snatches of music and applause from Betty's TV.

"There's something you need to know," she told him.

He waited.

"I won't make trouble, I won't try to make Dooley come and live with us. He's doing so well . . . you've done so much . . ."

"If he wants to, he can come and stay with us anytime he's home, but I want you to be the one who . . . the one who watches over him."

She was giving her boy away again. But this time, he fervently hoped and prayed, it was for all the right reasons.

§

He kissed her on the cheek as he came into the bedroom.

"Kavanagh . . ." he said, feeling spent.

"Hello, dearest," she said, looking worn.

After he showered, they crawled into bed on their respective sides and were snoring in tandem by ten o'clock.

⸭

"Emma, that program on your computer, that thing that helped you find Albert Wilcox . . ."

"What about it?"

"I'd like you to search for these names. I've written down the states I think they could be in."

"Hah!" she said, looking smug. "I knew you'd get to liking computers sooner or later."

⸭

Some days were like this. One phone call after another, nonstop.

"Father? Emil Kettner. We met when Buck Leeper—"

"Of course, Emil. Great to hear your voice." Emil Kettner owned the construction company that employed Buck Leeper as their star superintendent.

"I have good news for you, I think, if the timing works for Lord's Chapel."

"Shoot."

"The big job we thought we had fell through, and to tell the truth, I think it's for the best—as far as Buck's concerned. He needs a break, but he'd want to be working, all the same. I wondered if we could send him out to you for the attic job."

He was floored. This was the best news he'd had since . . .

"The way he described it, it sounds like six months, tops. I hate to send him on a job that small, I know you understand, but it's the kind of job he'd find . . . reviving, though he'd never admit it."

"We'd be thrilled to have Buck back in Mitford. We'll look after him, I promise."

"You looked after him before, and it worked wonders. There's been a real change in him, but he still works too hard, too fast, and too much. You won't hear many bosses complaining about that."

They laughed.

"The money's in place if we can keep on budget," said the rector.

"That's what Buck's all about, if you remember."

"I do! Well, I can't say enough for your timing, Emil. Our Sunday

School enrollment is mushrooming, I've had three baptisms this month, and the month's hardly begun. When can we expect to see Buck?"

"A week, maybe ten days. And we can't give him much support on this project, he'll be rounding up locals to do the job. How does that sound?"

"Terrific. The carved millwork in the Hope House chapel is locally done. We've got good people in the area."

"Well, then, Father, I'll be looking in on the project like I did last time. Until then."

"Emil. Thanks."

He'd asked for Buck Leeper to do the attic job, never really believing it could happen, only hoping.

And—bingo.

§

"Father? Buck Leeper."

"Buck!"

He heard Buck take a drag on his cigarette. "You talked to Emil."

"I did, and we're thrilled."

"You reckon I could get that cottage again?"

That dark, brooding cottage under the trees, where the finest construction superintendent on the East Coast had thrown furniture against the wall and smashed vodka bottles into the fireplace? He didn't think so.

"Let me look around. We'll take care of you."

"Thanks," Buck said, his voice sounding gruff.

And yet, there was something else in his voice, something just under the surface that the rector knew and understood. It was a kind of hope.

§

"Father. Ingrid Swenson."

Dadgum it, and just when he was having a great day.

"Ingrid."

"We're very close to getting everything in order. I'd like to personally make a proposal to you and your committee on the fifteenth. I'm sure the timing will be good for Lord's Chapel."

He didn't especially care for her almighty presumption about the timing.

"Let me get back to you," he said.

§

"Father, it's Esther." Esther Bolick didn't sound like herself. "This is th' most awful thing I ever got myself into. . . ."

"What do you mean?"

"I mean I've never heard such bawlin' and squallin' and snipin' and fussin' in my life! I'm about sick of workin' with women, and church women in particular!"

"Aha."

"Why I said I'd do it, I don't know. Th' *Bane*! Of all things to take on, and me sixty-seven my next birthday, can you believe it?" She sighed deeply. "I ought to be sent to Broughton."

"Don't beat yourself up."

"I don't have to, a whole gang of so-called church workers is thrilled to do it for me!"

"You want to come for a cup of coffee? Emma's home today. I'd love to hear more."

"I don't have time to come for a cup of coffee, I don't have time to pee, excuse me, and Gene hadn't had a hot meal in I don't know when!"

Esther Bolick sounded close to tears. "So even if I can't come for a cup of coffee, I wish you'd do your good deed for the day and pray for me. . . ."

"I will. I pray for you, anyway."

You *do*?"

"Of course. The Bane is a cornerstone event for Lord's Chapel, and you've taken on a big job. But you've got a big spirit, Esther, and you can do it. I know it's easy for me to say, but maybe you could stop looking at the big picture, which is always overwhelming, and just take it day by day."

"Day by day is th' problem! Nearly every day, somebody dumps something else in our garage, and mainly it's the worst old clothes and mildewed shoes you ever saw! Mitch Lewis backed his truck up to th' garage, *raked* out whatever it was in th' bed, and drove off. Gene said to me, he said, 'Esther, what's that mound of *stuff* layin' in th' garage?' We couldn't even *identify* it.

"We need *toaster ovens,* we need *framed prints* and *floor lamps* and *plant stands* and such! This sale's got a *reputation* to maintain, but so far, I never saw so much polyester in my *life,* it looks like we'll *never* get rid of polyester, they won't even take it at th' *landfill*!"

He wished he could offer some of the contents of Fernbank, but Miss Sadie hadn't wanted her possessions picked over. One thing was for certain, he wouldn't donate those mildewed loafers from the back of his closet. . . .

"You know the good stuff always comes in," he said, trying to sound upbeat. "It never fails."

"There's always a first time!" she said darkly.

"Let me ask you—are you praying about this, about the goods rolling in and your strength holding out?"

"I hope you don't think th' *Lord* would mess with the *Bane*?"

"I hope you don't think He wouldn't! Tell me again where the funds from the Bane will go."

"Mission fields, as you well know, including a few in our own backyard."

"Exactly! Some of the money will fly medical supplies to a village where people are dying of cholera. Do you think the Lord would mess with that?"

"Well . . ."

"Then there's the four-wheel drive ambulance they need in Landon," he said. "Remember the blizzard we had three years ago?"

"That's when I had to call an ambulance for Gene, who nearly killed himself shoveling snow! I shouted for joy when I saw it turn the corner. If it hadn't been for that ambulance . . ."

"That winter, two children died of burns because nobody could get a vehicle into the coves around Landon."

"I think I know where you're headed with this," she said.

"I don't believe He'll let Esther Bolick—or the Bane—fail."

"Maybe I could ask Hessie Mayhew to help me out, even if she is Presbyterian!" Esther was sounding more like herself.

"I believe it's going to be the best Bane yet. Now, about your volunteers—my guess is, they're moaning and groaning because they need strong leadership, which is why they elected you in the first place! Look," he said, "I have an idea. Why don't I pray for you? Right now."

"On the *phone?*"

"It's as good a place as any. Try taking a deep breath."

"Lately, it's all I can do to get a deep breath."

"I understand."

"You do?"

"I do."

"I didn't know men ever had trouble gettin' their breath."

"Are you sitting down?"

"Standin' up at the kitchen phone, which is where I've been ever since I let myself get roped into this."

"Could you get a chair?"

He heard her drag a kitchen chair from the table, and sit down.

"OK," she said, feeling brighter. "But don't go on and on 'til th' cows come home."

§

"Fernbank or bust!" cried Cynthia, huffing up Old Church Lane.

"It's only taken us a full year to do this."

"And it's all sitting right there, just as you left it."

He realized why he had put this off, over and over again. He had ducked into Fernbank a few times to check the roof leaks, and ducked out again as if pursued. To see those empty, silent rooms meant she was gone, utterly and eternally, and even now he could hardly bear the fact of it.

"This must be a hard time for Louella, the anniversary of—"

"I'll see her tomorrow," he said, doing some huffing of his own. "Let's have her down to dinner."

"I love that idea. Maybe sometime next week? Oh, for a taste of her fried chicken!"

"We'll have to settle for a taste of my meat loaf. . . ."

They were up to the brow of the hill and turning into the driveway, which was overhung by a thicket of grapevines gone wild. Though Fernbank hadn't been well groomed since the forties, it had still looked imposing and proud during Miss Sadie's lifetime. Now . . .

He saw the house, surrounded by a neglected lawn, and felt the dull beating of his heart.

"Let's buy it!" he croaked. Good Lord! What had he said?

She looked astounded. "Timothy, you don't need a domestic retreat, you need 911. How could you even *think* such a thing?"

And why couldn't he think such a thing? Didn't a man have a right to his own mind?

He felt suddenly peevish and disgruntled and wanted to turn around and run home, but he remembered Andrew Gregory was meeting them on the porch in ten minutes.

§

Andrew stood in the middle of the parlor and looked up.

That's what everyone did, thought the rector—they stared at the water stains like they were some kind of ominous cloud above their heads. Why couldn't people see the dentil molding, the millwork . . .

"Beautiful millwork!" said Andrew. "I've been here only once before, the day of the wedding reception. I was enchanted by the attention to detail. It's a privilege to see Fernbank again."

"Would you like to see it, stem to stern?"

"Stem to stern!" said Andrew, looking enthused.

§

Two hours later, they were close to a deal.

"The development firm has unfortunately asked for several of the finest pieces," said Andrew. He referred to notes that he had hastily jotted as they toured the house.

"Nonetheless, I'd be interested in the Federal loveseat in Miss Sadie's bedroom, the Georgian chest of drawers in her dressing room, the three leather trunks in the attic, the chaise in the storage room, which I believe is Louis XIV, the English china dresser, and all the beds in the house, which are exceedingly fine walnut . . . now, let's see . . . the six framed oils we discussed, which appear to be French . . . and the pine farm table in that wonderful kitchen! It must have been made by a local craftsman around the turn of the century."

"Anything else?" asked the rector, feeling like a traitor, a grave robber.

"In truth, I'd like the dining room suite, but it's Victorian, and I never fare well with Victorian. There are two chairs on the landing, however—I'm not certain of their origins, but they're charming. I'll have those chairs, into the bargain . . . and oh, yes, the contents of the linen drawers. I have a customer in Richmond who fancies brocade napery."

"Hardly used!" said Father Tim, knowing that Miss Sadie had certainly never trotted it out for him.

Cynthia roamed around, sounding like a squirrel in the attic, as he went through the miserable ordeal of dismantling someone's life, someone's history.

Miss Sadie's long letter, which was delivered to him after her death, gave very clear instructions: "Do not offer anything for view at a yard sale, or let people pick over the remains. I know you will understand."

Was Andrew picking over the remains? He didn't think so, he was being a four-square gentleman about the whole thing. Besides, something had to be done with the contents of twenty-one rooms and the detritus of nearly a century.

"How about the silver hollowware?" asked the rector. He felt like Avis Packard who, after selling and bagging a dozen ears of corn, was trying to get rid of last week's broccoli. "The, ah, flatware, perhaps?"

"Well, and why not?" agreed Andrew, looking jaunty. "Who cares if it's all monogrammed with *B,* I think I'll have it for my own!"

The rector drew a deep breath. This wasn't so hard.

"The rugs! How about the rugs?" After all, every cent he raised would go into the Hope House till. . . .

Andrew smiled gently. "I don't think Miss Sadie's father did his homework on the rugs." He jotted some more and offered a price that nearly floored the rector.

"Done!" he exclaimed.

Feeling vastly relieved, he shook Andrew's hand with undeniable vigor.

§

"While you and Andrew toured around like big shots, eyeing major pieces, I was burrowing into minor pieces. Look what I found!"

His wife's face was positively beaming.

"An easel! Hand-carved! Isn't it wonderful? And look at this—an ancient wooden box of watercolors, two whole compartments full! The cakes are dried and cracked, of course, but they'll spring back to life in no time at all, with—guess what?—water!"

He hadn't seen Christmas make her so jubilant.

"And look! A boxful of needlepoint chair covers, worked with roses and hydrangeas and pansies, in all my favorite colors! Perfect for our dining room! Oh, Timothy, how could we have neglected this treasure trove for a full year? It's as if we stayed away from a gold mine, content with digging ore!"

She held up a chair cover for him to admire.

"Now it's your turn to find something for yourself, like Miss Sadie asked you to do. She said 'Take anything you like,' those were her very words."

He stood frozen to the spot, suddenly feeling as if he'd burst into tears.

Cynthia quietly put the chair cover down, and came to him and held him.

§

He found it in the dimly lit attic.

Though the box appeared to be of no special consequence, he felt drawn to it, somehow, and knelt to remove the lid and unwrap the heavy object within.

The figure had the weight of a stone, but a certain lightness about its form, which rested on a sizeable chunk of marble.

Back at the rectory, he set the bronze angel on the living room mantel and stood looking at it.

It was enough. He wanted nothing more.

§

"Mule! What have you got in a little rental house, maybe two bedrooms, something bright and sunny, something spacious and open—and oh, yes, low-maintenance, in a nice part of Mitford, maybe with a fireplace and a washing machine, not too much money, and—"

"Hold it!" exclaimed Mule. "Are you kidding me? You're talkin' like a crazy person. Think about it. If I *had* anything like that, would it be *available*?"

He thought about it. "Guess not," he said.

§

Cynthia's interest was growing. "Let's invite Pauline and Poo!"

They sat in the kitchen, planning the dinner party while their own supper roasted in the oven.

"Terrific idea. Louella, Pauline, Dooley, Poo, Harley, you, and me. Meat loaf for seven!"

"Better make it for ten. Dooley has the appetite of a baseball team."

"Right! Ten, then."

"I'll make lemonade and tea and bake a cobbler," she said.

"Deal."

"In the meantime, dearest, I've planned our retreat."

"Really?"

"Really. Next week, I'm taking you away for two days."

"But Cynthia, I can't go away for two days. I have things to *do*."

"Darling, that's exactly why I'm taking you away!"

"But there's an important vestry meeting, and—"

"Poop on the vestry meeting. Since when does the rector have to attend every vestry meeting as if it were the Nicene Council?"

"Cynthia, Cynthia . . ."

"Timothy, Timothy. Let me remind you of all you've recently done—you've had three baptisms, a death at the hospital, you're working on that project with the bishop which keeps you talking on the phone like schoolgirls, you do two services every Sunday, Holy Eucharist every Wednesday, not to mention your weekly Bible class. *Plus*—"

"There's no way—"

"Plus your hospital visits every morning, and pulling together that huge thing for the mayor, and working on the benefit for the Children's Hospital, and tearing down Betty's shed—not to mention that on your birthday you made a wonderful evening for *me!*"

She took a deep breath. "*Plus*—"

Not that again. "But you see—"

"Plus you still think you haven't done enough."

What was enough? He'd never been able to figure it out.

"Well, dearest, I can see you have no intention of listening to reason, so . . . I shall be forced do what women have been forced to do for millennia."

She marched around the kitchen table and thumped down in his lap. Then she mussed what was left of his hair and kissed him on the top of his head. Next she gave him a lingering kiss on the mouth, and unsnapped his collar, and whispered in his ear.

He blushed. "OK," he said. "I'll do it."

§

While Cynthia scraped and stacked the dishes, he sat in the kitchen, awaiting his cue to wash, and read the *Muse*.

Violet was perched by the gloxinia, purring; Barnabas lay under the table, snoring.

Four Convicted in Wesley Drug Burst

He roared with laughter. This was one for his cousin Walter, all right! He got up and pulled the scissors from the kitchen drawer and clipped the story. Walter liked nothing better than a few choice headlines from the type fonts of J. C. Hogan.

"Who discovered America?" He heard Lace Turner's voice drifting up the stairs through the open basement door.

"Christopher Columbus!" said Harley.

"Who was America named for?"

"Amerigo Vespucci! Looks like it ought've been named f'r Mr. Columbus, don't it? But see, that's th' way of th' world, you discover somethin' and they don't even notice you f'r doin' it."

Cynthia whispered, "She's been coming over and teaching him for several nights, you've been too busy to notice."

"Who was th' king of England when North Carolina became a royal colony?" Lace Turner sounded emphatic.

"George th' Second!"

"When was th' French and Indian War?"

"Lord, Lace, as long as I've lived, ain't never a soul come up t' me and said, 'Harley, when was th' French and Injun war?'"

"Harley . . ."

"They ain't a bit of use f'r me t' know that, I done told you who discovered America."

"Who defeated George Washington at Great Meadows?"

"Th' dern French."

"Who was th' first state to urge independence from Great Britian?"

"North Carolina!" Harley's voice had a proud ring.

"See, you learn stuff real good, you just act like you don't."

"But you don't teach me nothin' worth knowin'. If we got t' do this aggravation, why don't you read me one of them riddles out of y'r number book?"

"OK, but listen good, Harley, this stuff is hard. You borrow five hundred dollars for one year. Th' rate is twenty percent per year. How much do you pay back by th' end of th' year?"

There was a long silence in the basement.

The rector put his arm around his wife, who had come to sit with him on the top basement step. They looked at each other, wordless.

"Six hundred dollars!" exclaimed Harley.

"Real good!"

"I done that in m' noggin."

"OK, here's another'n—"

"I ain't goin' t' do no more. You git on back home and worry y'r own head."

She pressed forward. "A recipe suggests two an' a half to three pounds of chicken t' serve four people. Karen bought nine-point-five pounds of chicken. Is this enough t' serve twelve people?"

"I told you I ain't goin' t' do it," said Harley. "Let Karen fig'r it out!"

The rector looked at Cynthia, who got up and fled the room, shaking with laughter.

He went to his study and took pen and paper from the desk drawer. Let's see, he thought, if the recipe calls for two and a half to three pounds of chicken to serve four people . . .

CHAPTER TEN

Those Who Are Able

He was changing shirts for a seven p.m. meeting when he heard
Harley's truck pull into the driveway. Almost immediately he heard
Harley's truck pull out of the driveway.

Harley must have forgotten something, he mused, buttoning a
cuff.

When he heard the truck roll into the driveway again, he looked
out his bathroom window and saw it backing toward the street. From
this vantage point, he could also see through the windshield.

Clearly, it wasn't Harley who was driving Harley's truck.

It was Dooley.

He stood at the bathroom window, buttoning the other cuff,
watching. In, out, in, out.

He didn't have five spare minutes to deal with it; he was already
cutting the time close since he was the speaker. He'd have to talk to
Dooley and Harley about this.

Dadgum it, he thought. He had a car-crazed boy living down the hall and a race-car mechanic in the basement. Was this a good combination? He didn't think so. . . .

§

Emma looked up from her computer, where she was keying in copy for the pew bulletin.

"I know I'm a Baptist and it's none of my business . . ."

You can take *that* to the bank, he thought.

" . . . but it seems to me that people who can't stand shouldn't have to."

"What do you mean?"

"I mean all those people you get in th' summer who don't know an Episcopal service from a hole in the ground, and think they have to do all th' stuff th' pew bulletin tells 'em to do. I mean, some of those people are old as the hills, and what does th' bulletin say? Stand, kneel, sit, stand, bow, stand, kneel, whatever! It's a workout."

"True."

"So why don't we do what they do at this Presbyterian church I heard about?"

"And what's that?" He noticed that his teeth were clenched.

"Put a little line at the bottom of the bulletin that says, 'Those who are *able,* please stand.'"

Who needed the assistance of a curate or a deacon when they had Emma Newland to think through the gritty issues facing the church today?

§

As he left the office for Mitford Blossoms, Andrew Gregory hailed him from his shop across the street.

"We go three months without laying eyes on each other," said the genteel Andrew, "and now—twice in a row!"

"I prefer this arrangement!"

"Before pushing off to Italy, I have something for your Bane and Blessing. I'll be back in only a month, but what with making room for the Fernbank pieces, I find I've got to move other pieces out. Would you mind having my contribution a dash early?"

"Mind? I should say not. Thrilled would be more like it." He could imagine Esther Bolick's face when she heard she was getting antiques from Andrew Gregory.

Talk about an answer to prayer. . . .

§

He climbed the hill, slightly out of breath, carrying the purple gloxinia, and stood for a moment gazing at the impressive structure they had named Hope House.

But for Sadie Baxter's generosity, this would be little more than the forlorn site of the original Lord's Chapel, which had long ago burned to the ground. Now that Miss Sadie was gone, he was the only living soul who knew what had happened the night of that terrible fire.

Ah, well. He could muddle on about the fire, or he could look at what had risen from the ashes. Wasn't that the gist of life, after all, making the everyday choice between fire and phoenix?

Louella sat by her sunny window, with its broad sill filled with gloxinias, begonias, philodendron, ivy, and a dozen other plants, including a bewildered amaryllis from Christmas.

Dressed to the nines, she opened her brown arms wide as he came in. "Law, honey! You lookin' like somebody on TV in that blue coat."

He leaned eagerly into her warm hug and returned it with one of his own.

"Have you got room for another gloxinia?"

"This make three gloxinias you done brought me!"

That's what he always took people; he couldn't help it.

"But I ain't never had purple, an' ain't it beautiful! You're good as gold an' that's th' truth!"

He set it on the windowsill and thumped down on the footstool by her chair. "How are you? Are they still treating you right?"

"Treatin' me *right*? They like to worry me to death treatin' me right. Have a stick of candy, eat a little ice cream wit' yo' apple pie, let me turn yo' bed down, slip on these socks to keep yo' feet toasty . . ." She shook her head and laughed in the dark chocolate voice that always made a difference in the singing at Lord's Chapel.

"You're rotten, then," he said, grinning.

"Rotten, honey, and no way 'round it. That little chaplain, too, ain't he a case with them dogs runnin' behind 'im ever' whichaway?"

"Are you still getting Taco every week?"

"Taco done got mange on 'is hip and they tryin' to fix it."

"You could have a cat or something 'til Taco gets fixed."

"A cat? You ain't never seen Louella messin' wit' a *cat*."

"Are you working in the new garden?"

"You ain't seen me messin' wit' a hoe, neither. Nossir, I done my duty, I sets right here, watches TV, and acts like somebody."

"Well, I've got a question," he said.

Louella, whose salt-and-pepper hair had turned snow-white in the past year, peered at him.

"Will you come to dinner at the rectory next Thursday? Say yes!"

"You talkin' 'bout dinner or supper?"

"Dinner!" he said. "Like in the evening." Louella, he remembered, called lunch "dinner," and the evening meal "supper."

"I doan hardly know 'bout goin' out at *night*," she said, looking perplexed. "What wit' my other knee needin' t' be operated on . . ."

"I'll hold on to you good and tight," he said, eager for her to accept.

"I doan know, honey. . . ."

"Please," he said.

"Let 'Amazin' Grace' be one of th' hymns this Sunday and I'll do it," she said, grinning. "We ain't sung that in a *month* of Sundays, an' a 'piscopal preacher *wrote* it!"

"Done!" he said, relieved and happy. He had always felt ten years old around Miss Sadie and Louella.

§

He took the stairs to the second floor to see Lida Willis.

He didn't have to tell her why he'd come.

Lida tapped her desk with a ballpoint pen, still looking stern. "She's doing well. Very well. We couldn't ask for better."

"Glad to hear it," he said, meaning it.

§

He found Pauline in the dining room, setting tables with the dishes Miss Sadie had paid to have monogrammed with HH. A lifelong miser where her own needs were concerned, she had spared no expense on Hope House.

"Pauline, you look . . . wonderful," he said.

"It's a new apron."

"I believe it's a new Pauline."

She laughed. He didn't think he'd heard her laugh before.

"I have a proposal."

She smiled at him, listening.

"Will you come to dinner next Thursday night and bring Poo? Dooley will be with us, and Harley and Louella."

He could see her pleasure in being asked and her hesitation in accepting.

"Please say yes," he requested. "It's just family, no airs to put on, and we'll all be wearing something comfortable."

"Yes, then. Yes! Thank you. . . ."

"Great!" he said. "Terrific!"

He'd heard people ask, "If you could have anyone, living or dead, come to dinner, who would it be?" Shakespeare's name usually came up at once; he'd also heard Mother Teresa, the Pope, St. Augustine, Thomas Jefferson, Pavarotti, Bach, Charles Schultz . . .

For his money, he couldn't think of anyone he'd rather be having for dinner than the very ones who were coming.

§

He found Scott Murphy at the kennels.

"That's Harry," said Scott, pointing to a doleful beagle. "He's new."

"Looks like an old bishop I once had."

"That's Taco over there."

"How's his mange?"

"You know everything!"

"I wish."

"I've been thinking," said the chaplain. "I'd like to get my crowd out of here, take them to—I don't know, a baseball game, a softball game, something out in the fresh air where they can hoot and holler and—"

"Eat hotdogs!"

"Right!"

"Great idea. I don't know who's playing around town these days. . . ."

"Maybe you and I could get up our own game? Sometime in August?"

"Well, sure! Before Dooley goes back to school."

"I'll start looking for players."

"Me, too," said the rector.

A softball game!

He felt like tossing his hat in the air. If he had a hat.

§

"Bingo!" said Emma, handing him the computer printout of names and addresses.

§

The vestry had said what he thought they'd say, virtually in unison: "Let's get on with it!"

Yes, they wanted Ingrid Swenson and her crew to come on the fifteenth. It was unspoken, but the message was clear—let's unload that white elephant before the roof caves in and we have to get a bank loan to pick up the tab.

He asked Ron Malcolm to call her immediately after the meeting.

§

There were quite a few R. Davises in the state of Florida, according to the printout, but Lakeland was the only town or city with a Rhody Davis. "Starts with a *L*," Russell Jacks had said of Rhody's dimly recalled whereabouts in Florida.

He was disappointed, but not surprised, that Rhody Davis had an unlisted phone number.

He called Stuart Cullen.

"Who do you know in Lakeland, Florida? Clergy, preferably."

"Let me get back to you."

By noon, he was talking to the rector at a church in Lakeland's inner city. It was an odd request, granted, but the rector said he'd find someone to do it.

The next morning, he got the report.

"Our junior warden drove by at nine o'clock in the morning, and a car was parked by the house. Same at three in the afternoon, and again at eight in the evening. Lights were on in the evening, but no other signs of anyone being around. Maybe this will help—there was a tricycle in the front yard. I used what clout my collar can summon, but no way to get the phone number."

"Ever make it up to our mountains?" asked Father Tim.

"No, but my wife and I have been wanting to. A few of my parish go every summer."

"We've got a guest room. Consider it yours when you come this way."

It was a long shot, but he knew what had to be done.

§

"I don't want t' worry you, Rev'rend, that's th' last thing I'd want t' do, but th' boy ragged me nearly t' death, an' I done like you'd want me to and told 'im no, then dern if I didn't leave m' key in th' ignition, an' since all he done was back it out and pull it in, I hope you won't lick 'im f'r it, hit's th' way a boy does at his age, hit's natural. . . ."

Harley looked devastated; the rector felt like a heel.

"Maybe you ought t' let me take 'im out to th' country an' put 'im behind th' wheel. In two years, he's goin' t' be runnin' up an' down th' road, anyhow, hit'd be good trainin'. I'd watch 'im like a hawk, Rev'rend, you couldn't git a better trainer than this ol' liquor hauler."

"I don't know, Harley. Let me think on it."

"What's it all about?" he asked his wife, sighing.

"Hormones!" she exclaimed.

§

Mitford, he noted, was becoming a veritable chatterbox of words and slogans wherever the eye landed.

The mayoral incumbent and her opponent had certainly done their part to litter the front lawns and telephone poles with signage, while the ECW had plastered hand-lettered signs in the churchyard and posters in every shop window.

Even the Library Ladies were putting in their two cents' worth.

14th annual Library Sale
10–4, July 28
Book It!

You Don't Want It? We Do!
34th Annual Bane and Blessing

MACK STROUPE:
Mack For Mitford,
Mack For Mayor

Esther Cunningham:
Right For Mitford
Right For Mayor

Clean Out Attics In Mitford
Help Dig Wells
In Africa!

Cunningham Cares.
Vote Esther Cunningham
For Mayor

YOUR BANE IS OUR BLESSING.
Lord's Chapel, October 4

Mack Stroupe:
I'll Make What's
Good Even Better

He thought he'd seen enough of Mack Stroupe's face to last a lifetime, since it was plastered nearly everywhere he looked. Worse than that, he was struggling with how he felt about seeing Mack's face in his congregation every Sunday morning.

§

When he dropped by her office at seven o'clock, the mayor was eating her customary sausage biscuit. It wasn't a pretty sight.

Three bites, max, and that sausage biscuit was out of here. But who was he to preach or pontificate? Hadn't he wolfed down a slab of cheesecake last night, looking over his shoulder like a chicken poacher lest his wife catch him in the act?

Oh, well, die young and make a good-looking corpse, his friend Tommy Noles always said.

"If Mack Stroupe's getting money under the table," he said, "isn't there some way—"

"What do you mean *if*? He *is* gettin' money under the table. I checked what it would cost to put up those billboards and—get this—four thousand bucks. I called th' barbecue place in Wesley that helps him commit his little Saturday afternoon crimes—six hundred smackers to run over here and set up and cook from eleven to three. Pitch in a new truck at twenty-five thousand, considering it's got a CD player and leather seats, and what do *you* think's goin' on?"

"Isn't he supposed to fill out a form that tells where his contributions come from? Somebody said that even the media can take a look at that form."

She wadded up the biscuit wrapper and lobbed it into the wastebasket. "You know what I always tell Ray? Preachers are the most innocent critters I've ever known! Do you think th' triflin' scum is goin' to *report* the money he's gettin' under th' table?"

"Maybe he's actually getting enough thousand-dollar contributions legally to pull all this together. It wouldn't hurt to ask."

She scratched a splotch on her neck and leaned toward him. "Who's going to ask?"

"Not me," he said, meaning it.

❧

The screen door of the Grill slapped behind him. "What's going on?" the rector asked Percy.

"All I lack of bein' dead is th' news gettin' out."

"What's the trouble?"

"Velma."

"Aha."

"Wants to drag me off on another cruise. I said we done been on a cruise, and if you've seen one, you've seen 'em all—drink somethin' with a little umbrella in it, dance th' hula, make a fool of yourself, and come home. I ain't goin' again. But she's nagged me 'til I'm blue in th' face."

" 'Til she's blue in the face."

"Whatever."

Velma, who had heard everything, walked over, looking disgusted.

"I hope you've told th' Father that th' cruise you took me on was paid for by our children, and I hope you mentioned that it's the only vacation I've had since I married you forty-three years ago, except for that run over to Wilkes County in th' car durin' which I threw up the entire time, bein' pregnant."

Velma took a deep breath and launched another volley. "And did you tell him about th' varicose veins I've got from stompin' around in this Grill since Teddy Roosevelt was president? Now you take the Father here, I'm sure he's carried *his* wife on *several* nice trips since *he* got married."

Velma tossed her order pad on the counter, stomped off to the toilet, and slammed the door.

Percy looked pained.

The rector looked pained.

If Velma only knew.

§

She would be let down, he thought, maybe even ticked off—and for good reason. After all, she had worked hard to plan something special.

"Listen to me, please," he said. "I can't go on our retreat."

She gazed at him, unwavering, knowing that he meant it.

"I've got to go and look for Jessie Barlowe."

"I'll go with you," she said.

He sat heavily on the side of the bed where she was propped against the pillows with a book. "It's in Florida, a long drive, and I don't know what we'll run into. I also need Pauline to come along. Since she's the birth mother and no papers were signed for Jessie to live with Rhody Davis, Pauline has custody. She can take Jessie legally."

"Would you need . . . police to go in with you? A social worker?"

"It's not required. Only if it looks like a bad situation."

"Does it look bad?"

"I don't know. There's no way to know."

"Do you think you should investigate further, I mean . . ."

"I feel we need to act on this now."

"Will we be back for our dinner next Thursday?"

"Yes," he said.

She leaned against him, and they sat together, silent for a time.

"We need to pray the prayer that never fails."

"Yes," he said again.

§

He pled Pauline's case with Lida Willis, who gave her dining room manager two days off.

"She'll make it up over Thanksgiving," said Lida. That was when families of Hope House residents would pour into Mitford, straining the reserves of the dining room.

He was vague with Dooley about what was going on and said nothing at all to Emma. He didn't want anyone getting their hopes up. As far as everyone was concerned, he was taking his wife on a small excursion, and Pauline was riding with them to South Carolina and visiting a great aunt. He regretted saying anything to anybody about Florida.

"Florida in July?" asked his secretary, aghast.

"Lord at th' salt they got down there!" said Harley. "Hit'll rust y'r fenders plumb off. Let me git m' stuff together and I'll give you a good wax job."

"You don't have to do that, Harley. Besides, we're leaving early in the morning."

"I'll git to it right now, Rev'rend, don't you worry 'bout a thing. And I'll sweep you out good, too."

It was all coming together so fast, it made his head swim.

"Look after Dooley," he told his resident mechanic as they loaded the car, "and hide your truck keys. Dooley will walk and feed Barnabas, Puny will be in tomorrow, help yourself to the pasta salad in the refrigerator, the car looks terrific, a thousand thanks, we'll bring you something."

Harley grinned. "Somethin' with Mickey on it, Rev'rend! I'd be much obliged."

§

Hot. He didn't remember being so hot in years, not since his parish by the sea.

And the colors in this part of the world—so vivid, so bright, so . . . different. In the mountains, in his high, green hills, he felt embraced, protected—consoled, somehow.

Here, it was all openness and blue sky and flat land and palm trees. He never ceased to be astonished by the palm tree, which was a staple of the biblical landscape. How did the same One who designed the mighty oak and the gentle mimosa come up with the totally fantastic concept of a palm tree? Extraordinary!

He chuckled.

"Why are you laughing, dearest?"

"I'm laughing at palm trees."

There went that puckered brow and concerned look again. Soon, he really would have to go on a retreat with his wife and act relaxed, so she'd stop looking at him like this.

§

"You're flying," announced Cynthia, craning her neck to see the speedometer.

Good Lord! Ninety! They'd be arriving in Lakeland in half the anticipated time.

He could feel the toll of the 670-mile one-way trip already grinding on him as they zoomed past Daytona and looped onto the Orlando exit.

The engine might be working in spades, and the wax job glittering like something off the showroom floor, but the air-conditioning performed only slightly better than a church fan at a tent meeting.

He hadn't noticed it at home where the elevation was a lofty five thousand feet, but here, where the sun blazed unhindered, they were all feeling the dismally weak effort of the a/c.

He peered into the rearview mirror, checking on Pauline. She had ridden for hours looking out the window.

He would let Cynthia drive when they got to the rest station in Providence, and once in Lakeland, they'd take a motel and rest before looking for Rhody Davis on Palm Court Way. In order to get Pauline back in time to keep Lida Willis satisfied, they would have only a few short hours to look for Jessie before they hauled back to Mitford on another ten-hour drive.

Maybe he'd been a fool to risk so much on this one grueling trip.

But if not now, when?

§

He parked the car under a tree by the sidewalk, where the early morning shade still held what fleeting cooler temperature had come in the night.

"That's Rhody's car in the driveway," said Pauline.

"Sit here," he said, "while I check this out. I'll leave the engine running, so you can stay cool."

"Cool!" said his wife. "Ha and double ha. Can't I come with you, Timothy?"

"No," he said.

He had worn his collar, but only after thinking it through. He always wore his collar, he reasoned—why should he not?

His eyes made a quick reconnaissance.

The small yard was nearly barren of grass. Plastic grocery bags were snared in the yucca plants bordering the unsheltered porch. The car was probably twenty years old, a huge thing, the hood almost completely bleached of its original color. A weather-beaten plastic tricycle lay by the steps. No curtains at the windows.

He rang the doorbell, but failed to hear a resulting blast inside, and knocked loudly on the frame of the screen door.

Hearing nothing, he knocked again, louder than before.

Already the perspiration was beginning a slow trickle under his shirt. He might have been a piece of flounder beneath a broiler, and it wasn't even nine a.m.

Had they come so far to find no one home?

He glanced at the bare windows again and saw her face pressed against the glass.

His heart pounded; he might have leaped for joy.

She looked at him soberly, and he looked at her, seeing the reddish blond hair damp against her cheeks, as if she'd been swimming. There was no doubt that this was five-year-old Jessie Barlowe; the resemblance to her brothers was startling.

Not knowing what else to do, he waved.

She lifted a small hand and waved back, eyeing him intently.

He gestured toward the door. "May I come in?" he said, mouthing the words.

She disappeared from the window, and he heard her running across a bare floor.

He knocked again.

This time, she appeared at the window on the left side of the door. She pressed her nose against the glass and stared at him. Perhaps she was in there alone, he thought with some alarm.

She vanished from the window.

Suddenly the door opened a few inches and she peered at him through the screen.

"Who is it?" she asked, frowning. She was barefoot and wearing a pair of filthy shorts. Her toenails were painted bright pink.

"It's Timothy Kavanagh."

"Rhody can't come!" she said, closing the door with force.

He was baking, he was frying, he was grilling.

He mopped his face with a handkerchief and looked toward the street, seeing only the rear end of his Buick sitting in the vanishing point of shade.

"Jessie!" he yelled, pounding again. "Jessie!"

He heard her running across the floor.

She opened the door again, this time wider. "Rhody can't come!" she said, looking stern.

He tried the screen door. It wasn't locked.

He opened it quickly and stepped across the threshold, feeling like a criminal, driven by his need.

The intense and suffocating heat of the small house hit him like a wall. And the smell. Good Lord! His stomach rolled.

He saw a nearly bare living room opening onto a dining area that was randomly filled with half-opened boxes and clothing scattered across the floor

"You ain't 'posed to come in," she said, backing away. "I ain't 'posed to talk to strangers."

"Where is Rhody?"

"Her foot's hurt, she done stepped on a nail." She wiped the sweat from her face with a dirty hand, and put her thumb in her mouth.

"Is she here?"

Jessie glanced down the hall.

"I'd like to talk with her, if I may."

"Rhody talks crazy."

"Can you take me to her?"

She looked at him with that sober expression, and turned and walked into the hall. "Come on!" she said.

The smell. What was it? It intensified as he followed her down the long, dark hallway to the bed where Rhody Davis lay in a nearly empty room. A baby crib stood by the window, containing a bare mattress and a rumpled sheet; a sea of garbage was strewn around the floor.

The woman was close to his own age, naked to the waist, a bulk of a woman with wispy hair and desperate eyes, and he saw instantly what created the odor. Her right foot, which was nearly black, had swollen grotesquely, and streaks of red advanced upward along her bloated leg. The abscesses in the foot were draining freely on the bed-clothes.

Her head rolled toward him on the pillow.

"Daddy? Daddy, is that you?" Sweat glistened on her body and poured onto the soaked sheets.

"Rhody—"

"You ain't got no business comin' here lookin' for Thelma."

"What—"

"Thelma's long gone, Daddy, long gone." She moaned and cursed and tossed her head and looked at him again, pleading. "Why'd you bring that dog in here? Git that dog out of here, it'll bite th' baby. . . ." She tried to raise herself, but fell back against the sodden pillow.

"Do you have a phone?" he asked Jessie. He was faint from the heat and the stench and the suffering.

Jessie sucked her thumb and pointed.

It was sitting on the floor by an empty saltine cracker box and a glass of spoiled milk. He tried to open the windows in the room, but found them nailed shut.

Then he dialed the number everyone was taught to dial and went through the agonizing process of giving the name, phone number, street address, and the particular brand of catastrophe.

"Gangrene," he said, knowing.

§

At the hospital, he got the payoff for wearing his collar. The emergency room doctor not only took time to examine Rhody Davis within an hour of their arrival, but was willing to talk about what he found.

"There was definitely a puncture to the sole of the foot. Blood poisoning resulted in a massive infection, and that led to gangrene."

"Bottom line?" asked the rector.

"There could be a need to amputate—we don't know yet. In the meantime, we're putting her on massive doses of antibiotics."

"What follows?"

"Based on what you've told me, our department of social services will plug her into the system."

"She'll be taken care of?" asked Cynthia.

The amiable doctor chuckled. "Our social services department loves to get their teeth into a tough case. This one looks like it fills that bill, hands down."

"I'll check on her," said Cynthia. "I'm his deacon."

§

He should have been exhausted, with one long trip behind him and another one ahead. But he wasn't exhausted, he was energized. They all were.

Cynthia chattered, fanning herself with one of the coloring books she'd been optimistic enough to bring. Pauline talked more freely, telling them Miss Pattie stories from Hope House, and holding Jessie on her lap.

Jessie alternately ate cookies, broke in a new box of crayons, and asked questions. What was that white thing around his neck? What was their dog's name? Where were they going? What was wrong with Rhody? Could they get some more french fries? Did they put her monkey in the trunk with her tricycle? Why didn't Cynthia paint her toenails? Why did the skin on Pauline's arm look funny? Could they stop so she could pee again?

Sitting behind the wheel on the first leg of the journey, he glanced often into the rearview mirror.

He saw Jessie touching her mother's face, though the concept of having a mother was not clear to her. "You're pretty," said the child.

"Thank you."

"You don't got no ear."

"It was . . . burned off."

"How'd you burn it off? Did you cry?"

"I'll tell you about it one day. That's why my arm looks funny. It was burned, too."

"Are we goin' back to get Rhody? Are you Rhody's friend?"

"I'm your mother."

Stick in there, he thought, feeling the pain as if part of it belonged to him. He looked at his wife. He knew when she was praying, because she often moved her lips, silently, like a child absorbed in the reading of a book.

As soon as they got around Daytona, they all played cow poker with enthusiasm, using truck-stop diners in place of the nearly nonexistent cows.

§

He felt as if he'd been hit by a truck, but thanks be to God, he hadn't.

They rolled into Mitford at midnight, dropped Pauline and Jessie at Betty Craig's, and went home and found Dooley's note that said he was spending the night at Tommy's. Crawling into bed on the stroke of one, he looked forward to sleeping in, until Cynthia told him she'd asked Pauline to leave Jessie with them on her way to work. Betty Craig was spending a rare day away from home with a sister, and did it make sense to leave Jessie with her elderly grandfather, who was a total stranger?

He slept until seven, when he heard Jessie come in, shrieking with either delight or fear upon encountering Barnabas. He woke again at eight, when he heard Puny, Sissy, Sassy, and the overloaded red wagon bound over the threshold and clatter down the hall like so much field artillery.

He burrowed under the covers, feeling the guilt of lying abed while the whole household erupted below him.

Someone was bounding up the stairs, and it definitely wasn't his wife.

"Wake up, Mr. Tim!"

Jessie Barlowe, freshly scrubbed, with her hair in a pony tail, trotted into the room. As he opened his eyes, she scrambled onto the bed and peered down at him.

"Time to put your collar on and get my tricycle out of your car!"

§

Actually, it was more like he'd gone a few rounds with Mike Tyson.

Standing helplessly by the coffeepot, he'd fallen prey to Puny's plea that he "watch" the twins while she did the floors upstairs. Cynthia and Jessie had gone next door, out of the fray, and here he was, drinking strong coffee in the study behind closed doors, as Sassy bolted back and forth from the bookcase to the desk, laughing hysterically, and Sissy lurched around the sofa with a string of quacking ducks, occasionally falling over and bawling. Barnabas crawled beneath the leather wing chair, trying desperately to hide.

"Ba!" said Sissy, abandoning the ducks and taking a fancy to him. "Ba!"

"Ba, yourself!" he said.

With the vacuum cleaner roaring above his head on bare hardwood, and Sissy banging his left knee with a rattle, he read Oswald Chambers.

"All your circumstances are in the hand of God," Chambers wrote, "so never think it strange concerning the circumstances you're in."

The fact that this piece of wisdom was the absolute gospel truth did not stop him from laughing out loud.

CHAPTER ELEVEN

Amazing Grace

Pauline and Jessie were sitting at the kitchen table as he cooked dinner.

They heard Dooley coming down the hall.

"It's Dooley," said Pauline, gently pushing Jessie toward her brother as he walked into the kitchen.

Dooley was suddenly pale under his summer tan.

"Jess?"

It had been three years, the rector thought, and for a five-year-old, three years is a long time.

"Jess?" Dooley said again, sinking to his knees on the kitchen floor.

Jessie looked at him soberly. Then, standing only a couple of feet away, she slowly lifted her hand and waved at her brother.

"Hey, Jess."

"Hey," she murmured, beginning to smile.

§

It came to him during the night.

At seven o'clock on Sunday morning he called Hope House,

knowing she would be sitting by the window, dressed for church and reading her Bible.

"Will you do it?" he asked

"Law, mercy . . . " she said, pondering.

"For Miss Sadie? For all of us?"

Louella took a deep breath. "I'll do it for Jesus!" she said.

§

Harley Welch was dressed in a dark blue jacket and pants, a dress shirt that Cynthia had plucked out of Bane contributions and washed and ironed, and a tie of his own. It was, in fact, his only tie, worn to his wife's funeral thirteen years ago, and never worn since.

"You look terrific!" exclaimed Cynthia.

"Yeah!" agreed Dooley.

"Here!" said the rector.

Harley took the box and opened what had been hastily purchased at a truck stop in South Carolina.

"Th' law, if it ain't a Mickey watch! I've always wanted a Mickey watch! Rev'rend, if you ain't th' beat!"

There went Harley's grin. . . .

Driving his crew to Lord's Chapel, he thought how it was Harley who was the beat. Harley Welch all rigged up for church and wearing a Mickey Mouse watch was still another amazing grace from an endlessly flowing fountain.

§

He stood in the pulpit and spoke the simple but profound words with which he always opened the sermon.

"In the name of the Father, and of the Son, and of the Holy Spirit, amen."

Then, he walked over and sat in the chair next to the chalice bearer, leaving the congregation wondering. This morning, someone else would preach the top part of the sermon—an English clergyman, long dead, and one of his own parishioners, very much alive.

In the middle of the nave, on the gospel side, Louella Baxter Marshall rose from her pew and, uttering a silent prayer of supplication, raised the palms of her hands heavenward and began to sing, alone and unaccompanied.

> *Amazing grace! how sweet the sound*
> *that saved a wretch like me!*
> *I once was lost but now am found*
> *was blind, but now I see.*

The power of her bronze voice lifted the hymn of the Reverend John Newton, a converted slave trader, to the rafters.

> *'Twas grace that taught my heart to fear,*
> *and grace my fears relieved;*
> *how precious did that grace appear*
> *the hour I first believed!*
>
> *The Lord has promised good to me,*
> *his word my hope secures;*
> *he will my shield and portion be*
> *as long as life endures.*

The words filled and somehow enlarged the nave, like yeast rising in a warm place. In more than one pew, hearts swelled with a message they had long known, but had somehow forgotten.

For those who had never known it at all, there was a yearning to know it, an urgent, beating desire to claim a shield and portion for their own lives, to be delivered out of loss into gain.

The rector's eyes roamed his congregation. This is for you, Dooley. And for you, Poo and Jessie, and for you, Pauline, whom the hound of heaven pursued and won. This is for you, Harley, and you, Lace Turner, and even for you, Cynthia, who was given to me so late, yet right on time. . . .

> *Through many dangers, toils, and snares,*
> *I have already come;*
> *'tis grace that brought me safe thus far,*
> *and grace will lead me home. . . .*

§

Today was the day. He was ready.

Ron Malcolm, who had priced Fernbank at three hundred and fifty thousand, suggested they accept an offer of no less than two ninety-five. Fernbank was not only an architecturally valuable structure, even with its flaws, but the acreage was sizable, chiefly flat, and eminently suited for development. At two hundred and ninety-five thousand, give or take a few dollars, it would be a smart buy as well as a smart sell.

The rector looked toward Fernbank as he walked to the Grill. He couldn't see the house, but he could see the upper portion of the fern-massed bank, and the great grove of trees.

A spa?

As hard as he tried, he couldn't even begin to imagine it.

§

"Softball?" said Percy. "Are you kiddin' me?"

"I am not kidding you. August tenth, be there or be square."

"Me'n Velma will do hotdogs, but I ain't runnin' around to any bases, I got enough bases to cover in th' food business."

"Fine. You're in. Expect twenty-five from Hope House, twenty or so players . . . and who knows how many in the bleachers?"

Percy scribbled on the back of an order pad. "That's a hundred and fifty beef dogs, max, plus all th' trimmin's, includin' Velma's chili—"

"Wrong!" said Velma. "I'm not standin' over a hot stove stirrin' chili another day of my life! I've decided to go with canned from here out."

"Canned chili?" Percy was unbelieving.

"And how long has it been since you peeled spuds for french fries? Years, that's how long. They come in here frozen as a rock, like they do everywhere else that people don't want to kill theirselves workin'."

"Yeah, but frozen fries is one thing, canned chili is another."

"To you, maybe. But not to me."

Velma stalked away. Percy sighed deeply.

The rector didn't say anything, but he knew darn well their conversation wasn't about chili.

It was about a cruise.

§

He turned into Happy Endings to see if the rare book search had yielded the John Buchan volume.

Hope Winchester shook her head. "Totally chimerical thus far."

"So be it," he said. "Oh. Know anybody who plays softball?"

⸙

Ingrid Swenson was, if possible, more deeply tanned than before. He didn't believe he'd ever seen so much gold jewelry on one person, as his wealthy seasonal parishioners tended to be fairly low-key while summering in Mitford.

She read from the offer-to-purchase document as if, being children, they couldn't read it for themselves. Every word seemed weighted with a kind of doom he couldn't explain, though he noted how happy, even ecstatic, his vestry appeared to be.

"Miami Development, as Buyer, hereby offers to purchase, and The Chapel of Our Lord and Savior, as Seller, upon acceptance of said offer, agrees to sell and convey—all of that plot, piece or parcel of land described below . . . "

While some appeared to savor every word as they would a first course leading to the entrée, he wanted to skip straight to the price and the conditions.

In the interim, they dealt with, and once again agreed upon, the pieces of personal property to be included in the contract.

"The purchase price," she said at last, looking around the table, "is one hundred and ninety-eight thousand dollars, and shall be paid as follows—twenty thousand in earnest money—"

"Excuse me," he said.

She glanced up.

"I don't think I heard the offer correctly."

"One hundred and ninety-eight thousand dollars." He noted the obvious edge of impatience in her voice.

"Thank you," he said, betraying an edge in his own.

⸙

Buddy Benfield made coffee, which they all trooped into the kitchen to pour for themselves. Ron brought Ingrid Swenson a china cup, not Styrofoam.

"You do realize," she said, smiling, "that the electrical system violates all state and local ordinances."

Had they realized that?

She withdrew a sheaf of papers from her briefcase. "Let's look at the numbers, which is always an informative place to look.

"The new roof, as you know, is coming in at around forty-five thousand. The plumbing as it stands is corroded cast-iron pipe, all of which must be removed and replaced with copper." She sipped her coffee. "Twenty thousand, minimum. Then, of course, there's the waste-lines replacement and the hookup to city water and sewage at a hundred thousand plus.

"As to the heating system, it is, as you're aware, an oil-fired furnace added several decades ago. Our inspection shows that the firebox is burned through." She sat back in her chair. "I'm sure I needn't remind you how lethal this can be. Estimates, then, for the installation of a forced warm-air system with new returns and ductwork is in excess of ten thousand."

Would this never end?

"Now, before we move to far brighter issues, let's revisit the electrical system."

There was a general shifting around in chairs, accompanied by discreet coughing.

"As you no doubt realize, Mr. Malcolm, Father—the attic has parallel wiring, which fails to pass inspection not merely because it is dangerous, but because it is . . . "—the agent for Miami Development Company gazed around the table—"illegal. Throughout the structure, there is exposed wiring not in conduit, all of which, to make a very long story conveniently shorter, is sufficient to have the structure condemned."

His heart pounded. Condemned.

Ron Malcolm sat forward in his chair. "Miss Swenson, have you stated your case?"

"Not completely, Mr. Malcolm. There are two remarks I'd like to make in closing. One is that the property improvements so far noted will cost the buyer in excess of two hundred and twenty thousand dollars. With that in mind, I believe you'll see the wisdom of selling your . . . distressed property . . . at the very fair price which we're offering.

"Now, to address the brighter side. What we propose to do will bring a vital new economy to Mitford. It will strengthen your tax base by, among other things, raising the value of every property in your village. Mr. Malcolm, I believe that you, for one, live on property contiguous to Fernbank. I don't have to tell you just how great an advantage this will be to your personal assets.

"Surely, all of you realize that nobody in Mitford could afford to take this uninhabitable property off your hands, and I know how grateful you must be to your own Mr. Stroupe for bringing our two parties together. Lacking the local means to reclaim this property, it would be tragic, would it not, to stand by helplessly while Fernbank, the very crown of your village, is torn down?"

The agony he felt was nearly unbearable. He wanted desperately to turn the clock back and have things as they were. He fought an urge to flee the smothering confines of this nightmarish meeting and run into the street.

"In closing, then," she said, looking into the faces of everyone assembled, "we're asking that you respond today, or within a maximum of seven days, to our offer—an offer that is as much designed for the good of Mitford as it is designed to accommodate the interests of Miami Development."

The rector stood, hearing the legs of his chair grate against the bare floor, against the overwhelmed silence of the vestry members.

"We will consider your offer for thirty days," he said evenly.

She paused, but was unruffled. "Thirty days, Father? I assume you understand that, in the volatile business of real estate, seven days is generous."

He saw his vestry's surprised alarm that he'd seized control of a sensitive issue. However, they silently reasoned, he'd been the liaison with Miss Sadie all these years. They probably wouldn't have the property at all if it weren't for the Father.

"And you do realize," Ingrid Swenson continued, "that our legal right to withdraw the offer in view of such a delay puts the sale of your property greatly at risk."

He said to her what she had said to him only weeks before. "Risk, Miss Swenson, has a certain adrenaline, after all."

§

She kissed his face tenderly—both cheeks, his forehead, his temples, the bridge of his nose. "There," she said, and trotted off to fetch him a glass of sherry.

He couldn't recall feeling so weary. Somehow, the road miles to Florida and back were still lurking in him, and the meeting . . . he felt as if it had delivered a blow to his very gut.

Ron Malcolm had argued that Miami Development was placing far too much emphasis on the flaws of the structure, and far too little on the valuable and outstanding piece of land that went with it. Though Ron made his case convincingly, even eloquently, Ingrid Swenson was not only unmoved, but in a big hurry to get out of there.

The rector couldn't dismiss some deeply intuitive sense that the whole thing was . . . he couldn't put his finger on what it was. But every time he denied his intuitions, trouble followed. He hadn't turned sixty-three—or was it sixty-four?—without learning a few things, and paying attention to his instincts was one of the precious few things he'd learned.

But how could he reasonably argue for holding on to a property that may, indeed, end up under the wrecking ball? His vestry hadn't said it in so many words, but they wanted the blasted thing behind them—their hands washed, and money in the till.

He put one of the old needlepoint pillows under his head and lay back on the study sofa. His dog sprawled on the rug beside him and licked his hand.

Dear God! If not for this consolation of home and all that now came with it, where or what would he be?

Wandering the waysides, a raving maniac. . . .

§

"Now that you've rested, dearest . . . "

He knew that look. He knew that look as well as his own face in the mirror.

She leaned her head to one side in the way he'd never been able to resist. "You have rested, haven't you?"

"Well . . . " He didn't know which way to step.

"So here's my idea. You know how formal the dining room is."

"Formal?" The dining room she'd painted that wild, heedless pumpkin color?

"I mean, with the carved walnut highboy from one of the Georges, and those stately chairs with the brocade cushions—"

"Spit it out, Kavanagh."

"I want to move the dining table into the kitchen."

"Are you mad?" he blurted.

"Only for Thursday night," she said, cool as a cucumber. "You see, Pauline and Harley aren't dining room people, and neither is Louella, they'd be stiff as boards in that setting. They know our kitchen, it's like home to them, it's . . . "

He couldn't believe his ears.

" . . . it's what we have to *do,*" she said, looking him in the eye. "Pumpkin walls notwithstanding, the dining room seems filled with the presence of . . . old bishops!"

He had definitely, absolutely heard it all.

§

Dooley Barlowe was nowhere to be found, and Harley's strengths lay in other areas of endeavor. It was fish or cut bait.

They turned the mahogany table on its side and, by careful engineering, managed to get it through the kitchen door without slashing the inlaid medallion in the center.

He was certain this was a dream; convinced of it, actually.

That there was hardly room to stand at the stove and cook, once the table was in and upright, was no surprise at all. Could he open the oven door?

"Perfect!" she said, obviously elated. "We'll just use that plaid damask cloth of your mother's."

"That old cloth is worn as thin as a moth's wing. Hardly suitable," he said, feeling distinctly grumpy.

"I love old tablecloths!" she exclaimed.

He sighed. "What don't you love?"

"Grits without butter. Dust balls on ceiling fans. Grumpy husbands."

"Aha," he said, going down on his hands and knees to put a matchbook under a table leg.

§

At breakfast the next morning, he found the much-larger table with the worn cloth looking wonderful in the light that streamed through the open windows. She had filled a basket with roses from the side garden and wrapped the basket with tendrils of ivy. Her cranberry-colored glasses, already set out for the evening meal, caught the light and poured ribbons of warm color across the damask.

Lovely! he mused, careful not to say it aloud.

§

Finding Jessie had been uncannily simple, he thought, walking to the office with Barnabas on his red leash. He had given thanks for this miracle over and over again. The chase, after all, might have led anywhere—or nowhere. But they'd gone straight to the door and knocked, and she had answered.

He would thank Emma Newland from his very heart, he would do something special for her, but what? Emma loved earrings, the bigger, the better. He would buy her a pair of earrings to end all earrings! No fit compensation for what she had done, but a token, nonetheless, of their appreciation for her inspired and creative thinking.

He pushed open the office door as Snickers rushed past him, snarled hideously into his own dog's face, barked at an octave that could puncture eardrums, and peed on the front step—seemingly all at once.

Barnabas dug in and barked back, grievously insulted and totally astounded. From her desk, Emma shouted over the uproar, "I wouldn't bring him in here if I were you!"

The rector saw that urging his dog over the threshold would result in a savage engagement with this desperately overwrought creature, an engagement in which someone, possibly even himself, could be injured.

Furious, he turned on his heel and stomped toward the Grill, dragging his even more furious dog behind.

He blew past the windows of the Irish Shop, as Minnie Lomax finished dressing a mannequin whose arms, years earlier, had been mistakenly carted off with the trash.

"Can't even get in my own office!" he snorted. "Earrings, indeed!"

"Not again," sighed Minnie, watching him disappear up the street.

❧

Passing the Collar Button, he was hailed by one of his parishioners, one who hadn't been even remotely amused by the announcement that he was going out to Canaan—or anywhere else.

"Father! You're looking well!"

Things were on an even keel again, thanks be to God. After all that uproar, most people seemed to have forgotten he was retiring, and it was business as usual.

He saw Dooley wheel out of the alley across the street and stop, looking both ways. As he glanced toward the monument, Jenny ran down the library steps, carrying a backpack. She saw Dooley and waved, and he pedaled toward her.

He didn't mean to stand there and watch, but he couldn't seem to turn away. Although Dooley's back was to him, he could see Jenny's face very clearly.

She was looking at The Local's summer help as if he had hung the moon.

❧

"It's big doin's," Mule was saying to J.C. as the rector slid into the booth.

"What is?" he asked.

"Th' real estate market in this town. There's Lord's Chapel with that fancy outfit tryin' to hook Fernbank, Edith Mallory's Shoe Barn just went on the block, and I hear major money's lookin' at Sweet Stuff."

"Whose major money?"

"I don't know, Winnie's trying to sell it herself to save the commission, so I don't have a clue who th' prospect is. Meantime, some realtor from Lord knows where is handlin' th' Shoe Barn, Ron Malcolm's brokerin' for Lord's Chapel, and as for yours truly, I can't get a lead, much less a listin'."

"Water, water everywhere, and not a drop to drink," said J.C., hammering down on a vegetable plate with a side of country-style steak.

"Speakin' of th' Shoe Barn, what ever became of that witch on a broom?" asked Mule.

The rector's stomach churned at the mention of Edith Mallory, who owned the large Shoe Barn property. Her focused, unrelenting pursuit of him before he married Cynthia was something he'd finally managed to put out of his mind.

"You're ruinin' his appetite," said Percy, pulling up a stool. Percy had fought his own battle with the woman, who also owned the roof under which they were sitting—she'd tried to jack up the rent and blow him off before his lease expired. That's when the rector discovered that the floor beams of the Grill were rotten and nearly ready to bring the whole building down. Bottom line, Percy walked off with a new lease—on his terms, not hers.

Percy grinned at the rector. "Boys howdy, you fixed her good, you put her high-and-mighty butt through th' *grinder.*"

"Watch your language," said Velma, passing with a tray of ham sandwiches.

"And she ain't been back, neither! No, sirree bob! Hadn't had th' guts to show her face in this town since th' night you whittled her down to size."

J.C. used his favorite epithet for Percy's lessor.

"So when are you closing the deal on Fernbank?" asked Mule.

"I don't know. We'll consider their offer for thirty days."

Mule gave him an astounded look. "You want to sit around for thirty days with that white elephant eatin' out of your pocket?"

He felt suddenly angry, impelled to get up and leave. Chill, he told himself, using advice learned from Dooley Barlowe.

"Do you play softball?" he asked the *Muse* editor, who was busy chewing a mouthful.

"Prezure fum dinnity monce."

"Right. So how about you?" he asked Mule. "Scott Murphy wants to get up a game for the residents at Hope House. August tenth. We need players."

"I ain't too bad a catcher."

"You're on," he said. "Percy, I wouldn't mind having a cheeseburger all the way. With fries!"

Percy scratched his head. "Man! In sixteen years, you prob'ly ordered a cheeseburger twice. And never all the way."

"Life is short," he said, still feeling ticked. "And put a strip of bacon on it."

§

"How's it coming, buddy?"

"I got Tommy and his dad and Avis. Ol' Avis says he can hit a ball off th' field and clean over our house."

"No kidding? What do you think about Harley? Think he could do it?"

"Harley, don't . . . doesn't have any teeth."

"What do teeth have to do with playing softball?"

Dooley grinned. "We could see if he wants to."

They were setting the table as Cynthia busied herself at the stove. He was leaving in five minutes to pick up Pauline and the kids, and run up the hill for Louella.

He liked setting the table with Dooley. Bit by bit, little by little, Dooley was coming into his own, something was easier in his spirit. Pauline had been part of it, and Poo, and now Jessie. Each brought with them a portion of the healing that was making Dooley whole. He watched the boy place the knife on the left side of the plate, look at it for a moment, then remove it and place it on the right. Good fellow! He saw, too, the smile playing at the corners of Dooley's mouth, as if he were thinking of something that pleased him.

Dooley looked up and caught the rector's gaze. "What are you staring at?"

"You. I'm looking at how you've grown, and taking into account the fine job you're doing for Avis—and feeling how good it is to have you home."

Dooley colored slightly. He thought for a moment, then said, "So let me drive your car this weekend."

Blast if it didn't fly out of his mouth. "Consider it done!"

§

"Low-fat meat loaf, hot from the oven!" he announced, setting the sizzling platter on the table.

Louella wrinkled her nose. "Low-fat? Pass it on by, honey, you can *skip* this chile!"

"Don't skip this 'un," said Harley.

"He was only kidding," Cynthia declared. "In truth, it contains everything our doctors ever warned us about."

He saw the light in Pauline's face, the softness of expression as she looked upon her scrubbed and freckled children. Thanks be to God! Three out of five. . . .

He sat down, feeling expansive, and shook out one of the linen napkins left behind, he was amused to recall, by an old bishop who once lived here.

He waited until all hands were clasped, linking them together in a circle.

"Our God and our Father, we thank You!" he began.

"Thank You, Jesus!" boomed Louella in happy accord.

"We thank You with full hearts for this family gathered here tonight, and ask Your mercy and blessings upon all those who hunger, not only for sustenance, but for the joy, the peace, and the one true salvation which You, through Your Son, freely offer. . . . "

They had just said "Amen!" when the doorbell rang.

"I'll get it! And for heaven's sake, don't wait for me. Who on earth . . . " Cynthia trotted down the hall to the door.

Father Tim passed the platter to Louella and was starting the potatoes around when he heard Cynthia coming back to the kitchen, a heavy tread in her wake.

"You'll never guess who's here!" said his wife.

Buck Leeper stepped awkwardly into the doorway. In the small, close kitchen, his considerable presence was arresting.

Good Lord! Finding Buck a place to stay had gone completely out of his head. It hadn't entered his mind again since he called Mule. He was mortified.

He stood up, nearly knocking his chair to the floor.

"Good timing, Buck! We'll set another plate, there's more than plenty. Good to see you!" He pumped Buck's large, callused hand. "You remember Louella, Miss Sadie's friend and companion. And Dooley, you remember Dooley."

Buck nodded. "Dooley . . . "

"Hey."

"And this is Harley Welch, Harley lives with us, and there's Pauline, Dooley's mother—as I recall, you brought her a rose when she was in the hospital."

Buck flushed and glanced at the floor.

Rats. He shouldn't have said that. "This is Dooley's brother Poo, and this is Jessie, his sister."

Poobaw grinned at Buck.

"I'm hungry!" said Jessie.

"This is Buck Leeper, everybody, the man who did such a splendid job at Hope House. Can you believe he was born just up the road from me in Mississippi? Keep the potatoes passing, Dooley, there's the gravy. Ah, I see we forgot to set out the butter for the rolls! Buck, I hope you're hungry, we've got enough for an army. Here, take this chair, we're glad to have you back in Mitford! Louella, have you got room over there? Dooley, scoot closer to your sister. . . . "

What a workout. He was exhausted.

"Please sit down, Mr. Leeper," said his smiling wife, taking over.

§

Dooley had taken Poo and Jessie to his room; Cynthia, Louella, and Pauline were making tea and coffee; and the men had gone into the study.

"What it was," said Harley, "Junior liked t' run on dirt better'n asphalt, which is why they called 'im th' Mud Dobber. One ol' boy said how th' law was tryin' t' jump Junior, said Junior cut out th'ough a cornfield in a '58 Pontiac with th' winders down, said he plowed th'ough about a ten-acre stand of corn 'til he come out th' other

side an' looked around an' 'is whole backseat was full of roastin'
ears."

Buck laughed the laugh that sounded, to the rector, like a kettle
boiling.

"Harley, you ought to tell Buck about your services as a mechanic.
There'll be a lot of vehicles on the Lord's Chapel job."

"Yes, sir, I work on most anything with wheels, but I don't touch
earth-movin' equipment. Course, I'm goin' t' be tied up pretty good,
I'm cleanin' out 'is missus's basement and garage, then startin' on th'
attic up yonder." Harley pointed to the ceiling. "Hit ain't been
touched since one of them old bishops lived here."

Pauline came to the door of the study. Jessie was right, thought
the rector, she's pretty.

"Excuse me . . . "

"Are you ready for us?" he asked.

She smiled. "Yes, sir. Cynthia said please come in."

Buck stood up from the wing chair, gazing at Pauline.

Father Tim saw that he appeared, for a moment, as eager and expectant as a boy.

&

"I couldn't do that," said Buck.

"Well, you see . . . the truth is, you have to. I looked for a place
for you to live and ran into a dead end, and, well, first thing you
know, I forgot to keep looking, and there you have it, you're stuck
with us—the sheets are clean and the toilet flushes."

Buck laughed. At least he was laughing. . . .

He showed Buck to the guest room at the top of the stairs, where
the superintendent's size somehow made the space much smaller.
Buck chewed a toothpick, and carefully scanned the room and its adjoining bath.

"I believe you'll be comfortable, and don't worry about a thing.
We'll have you out of here in no time, into a place of your own."

"If you're sure . . . "

"More than sure! Oh. By the way—do you play softball?"

Buck took the toothpick out of his mouth. "I've kicked more tail
on a softball field than I ever kicked on a construction site. Before I

hired on with Emil, I coached softball for a construction outfit in Tucson. The last couple of years I was there, we won every game, two seasons in a row."

Dooley suddenly appeared at the guest room door.

"I'm on his team," he said.

§

Buck offered to deliver Pauline and the children, while he took Louella to Hope House.

"I had a big time," said Louella, looking misty-eyed. "You and Miss Cynthia, you're family."

"Always will be," he said, meaning it.

At the door of Room Number One, he kissed her goodnight, loving the vaguely cinnamon smell of her cheek that had something of home in it.

§

Emma looked at him over her half-glasses.

"I guess you're hot about Snickers runnin' you off the other day."

"You might say that."

"How did I know you'd bring Barnabas to work? You never do, anymore. And besides, Snickers has never been here but twice, it seems like he *deserved* a turn. . . . "

"Ummm."

"Emily Hastings called, she said she has an axe to pick with you."

An axe to grind, a bone to pick, what difference did it make?

"Esther Bolick called, said things are looking up, Hessie Mayhew's th' biggest help since Santa's elves."

"Good."

"Hal Owen called, said it's time for Barnabas to get his shots."

"Right."

"Evie Adams called, guess what Miss Pattie's done now?"

"Can't guess," he said curtly, taking the cover off his Royal manual.

"She goes up and down the halls at Hope House, stealing the Jell-O off everybody's trays."

"That's a lot of Jell-O."

"Don't you care?"

"About what?"

"Stealing from old people."

"Miss Pattie is old people."

"So?"

He would like nothing better than to knock his secretary in the head. "So they have a staff of forty-plus at Hope House, I'm sure they can come up with some kind of curtailment of her behavior."

"Some kind of what?"

He didn't answer.

"How can you *use* that old thing?" she asked, glaring at his Royal manual.

He refused to respond.

There was a long silence as she peered at her computer monitor, and he rolled a sheet of paper into the carriage of his machine.

"So when are you going to give me some more names to find?" she inquired at last, trying to make up.

CHAPTER TWELVE

Waiting

"Will you do it?" he asked his wife.

"Of course I won't do it! It's not my job to do it."

"Deacons," he reminded her, "are supposed to do the dirty work."

"You amaze me, Timothy. You bury the dead, counsel the raving, and heedlessly pry into people's souls, yet when it comes to this . . ."

"I can't do it," he said.

"You have to do it."

Of course he had to do it. He knew that all along. He was only seeing how far he could get her to bend.

Not far.

§

"Dooley . . ."

He picked a piece of lint from his trousers. He stared at his right loafer, which appeared to have been licked by his dog, or possibly the twins, and after he had polished it only yesterday. . . .

"Yessir?"

Barnabas collapsed at his feet and yawned hugely, indicating his extreme boredom. Not a good sign.

"Well, Dooley . . . "

Dooley looked him squarely in the eye.

"It's about Jenny. I mean, it's not about Jenny, *exactly*. It's more indirectly than directly about Jenny, although we could leave her out of it altogether, actually. . . . "

"What about Jenny?"

"Like I said, it's not exactly about Jenny. It's more about . . . "

"About what?"

Had he seen this scenario in a movie? In a cartoon? He was old, he was retiring, he was out of here. He rose from the chair, then forced himself to sit again.

"It's about sex!" Good Lord, had he shouted?

"Sex?" Dooley's eyes were perfectly innocent. They might have been discussing Egyptology.

"Sex. Yes. You know." Hal Owen would have done this for him, Hal had raised a boy, why hadn't he thought of that before?

Dooley looked as if he might go to sleep on the footstool where he was sitting. "What about sex?"

"Well, for openers, what do you *know* about it? If you know anything at all, do you know what you *need* to know? And how do you *know* if you know what you need to know, that is to say, you can never be too *sure* that you know what you need to know, until—"

He actually felt a light spray as Dooley erupted with laughter in his very face. The boy grabbed his sides and threw back his head and hooted. Following that, he fell from the footstool onto the floor, where he rolled around in the fetal position, still clutching his sides and cackling like a hyena.

Father Tim had prayed for years to see Dooley Barlowe break down and really laugh. But this was ridiculous.

"When you're over your hysteria," he said, "we'll continue our discussion."

Not knowing what else to do, he examined his fingernails and tried to retain whatever dignity he'd come in here with.

§

"Good heavens, Timothy. You look awful! Is it done?"

"It's done."

"What did you tell him?"

"It's more like . . . what he told me."

"Really?" she said, amused. "And what did he tell you?"

"He knows it all."

"Most teenagers do. Figuratively speaking."

"And there's nothing to worry about, he's not even interested in *kissing* a girl."

Cynthia smiled patiently. "Right, darling," she said.

§

He wouldn't say a word to anybody about the two-thousand-dollar check Mack Stroupe had put in the collection plate on Sunday. He only hoped Emma would keep quiet about it.

On that score, at least, she was pretty dependable, though she'd been the one to tell him about the check. From the beginning, his instructions were, "Don't talk to me about the money, I don't need to know." As he'd often said, he didn't want to look into the faces of his parishioners and see dollar signs.

§

"Harley, ever played any softball?"

"No, sir, Rev'rend, I ain't been one t' play sports."

"Ah, well."

"I can run as good as th' next 'un, but hittin' and catchin' ain't my call."

The rector was peering into the tank of Harley's toilet, which had lately developed a tendency to run.

"I thank you f'r lookin' into my toilet, hit's bad t' keep me awake at night, settin' on th' other side of th' wall from m' head."

"It's old as Methuselah, but I think I can fix it."

"I want you t' let me fix somethin' f'r you, now, Rev'rend, I'm runnin' behind on that."

"Can't think of anything that needs it," he said, taking a wrench out of his tool kit.

"Maybe it's somethin' that don't need fixin', jis' tendin' to."

"Well, now." Wouldn't Dooley rather get his driving lesson from a bona fide race car mechanic than a preacher? He was sure Harley could make the lesson far more interesting, and even teach Dooley some professional safety tips from the track. Besides, even with the new torque in the Buick, Harley's truck would be a much more compelling vehicle to a fourteen-year-old boy.

"There is something you could do," he said, "if you're going to be around Saturday afternoon."

§

He could feel the bat in his hands. How many years had it been since he'd slammed a ball over the fence? Too many! He'd better get in shape, he thought, huffing up Old Church Lane in his running gear. Barnabas bounded along in front on the red leash.

Cooler today, but humid. Overcast skies, rain predicted. And didn't the garden need it? He'd worn a hood, just in case.

He wished he could get his wife to run with him, but no way. She was a slave to her drawing board, and lately looking the worse for it. The unofficial job of deacon, the job of organizing their jam-packed household, and the job of children's author/illustrator were wearing on her. And hadn't he helped put another portion on her already full plate by stowing Buck in the guest room?

He was frankly stumped about how to find housing for the superintendent, and with the attic job gearing up, Buck hardly had time to look around for himself. Maybe Scott Murphy would take in a boarder. . . .

He ran up to the low stone wall overlooking what he called the Land of Counterpane, and thumped down with Barnabas, panting.

There was the view that Louella and all the other residents farther along the hill could wake up and see every day of their lives. A feast for the eyes! He didn't get up here much, but when he did . . .

It was here, sitting on this wall, that he had known, at last, he *could* marry her, *must* marry her, and experienced the terrible anxiety of what it could mean to lose her. And it was here that he and Cynthia decided they both wanted to stay in Mitford when he retired.

Was he on time for the train? He looked at his watch. Another few minutes. Perhaps he would wait. Was life so all-fired urgent that he couldn't find five minutes to see a sight that always blessed and delighted him?

He was utterly alone in this place where, for all its singular beauty, few people ever came. It was set steeply above the village, it was off the beaten path, it was . . .

He heard the car below him, on the gravel road that ran along the side of the gorge and was seldom used except by a few local families.

He peered down and saw the black car pull to the shoulder of the road and stop. A man opened the driver's door and leaned out, looking around, then closed the door again. He was wearing a hat, a cap of some kind.

Mighty fine car to be out on Tucker's Mill Road, he thought, glancing again at his watch. Maybe the train would be early.

The pickup truck didn't move so slowly. He saw the plume of dust through the trees, then saw the blue truck screech to a stop beside the black car. A man jumped out, walked around the front of the truck, and stood for a moment by the car. It appeared that he was handed something through the car window.

The driver quickly got back in the truck, gunned the motor, and drove away, leaving a cloud of dust to settle over everything in its wake.

He watched as the car backed onto a narrow turnout, reversed direction, and rolled almost silently along Tucker's Mill.

By George, there was the train; he heard its horn faintly in the distance. Around the track it came, breaking through the trees by the red barn . . .

That scene he had just witnessed—had there been something strangely unsettling about it?

. . . then it huffed along the side of the open fields by the row of tiny houses and disappeared behind the trees.

He hadn't been able to tell from this vantage point what kind of car it was, but then, what difference did it make, anyway?

"Enough!" he said to his dog, and they bounded down the slope toward Baxter Park in the first drops of a misting rain.

§

Instead of turning into the park, he decided to run to the bottom of the hill and pop into Oxford Antiques. He'd inquire about Andrew and look for a present for Cynthia's birthday. He was barely getting in under the wire, considering that July 20 was two days hence.

Marcie Guthrie, Puny's mother-in-law and one of the mayor's five good-looking deluxe-size daughters, was reading a romance novel behind the cash register. "Father! Bring your dog in, but tell him to watch his tail!"

He tethered Barnabas to the leg of a heavy table. "Marcie, give me a few ideas for my wife's birthday, and I'll give you my eternal thanks."

"Well! Goodness! Let's see."

Cynthia was nearly as simple in her wants as he, thanks be to God. And she always seemed touchingly grateful when he gave her a gift.

"It must be something . . . wonderful," he said.

"I've got it!" she exclaimed. "The very thing! Come over here."

He trotted behind her to a gigantic walnut secretary with beveled glass doors. "There!" she said.

"Oh, no. That's far too large!"

"Not the secretary. The lap desk!"

Aha! Sitting next to the secretary on a Georgian buffet was a lap desk of exquisite proportions. That was it, all right, he knew it at once. A small lap desk with a pen drawer, a built-in inkstand, and a leather writing surface. Perfect!

He was afraid to ask.

"Four hundred and seventy-nine dollars!" she informed him. "It's not that old, just turn-of-the-century."

"Ummm."

"But for you, only four hundred. Andrew said whenever you come in to buy, to give you a special discount."

"Done!" he said, feeling a combination of vast relief, excitement over such a find, and momentary guilt for shelling out four hundred bucks. "I'll bring you a check in the morning. Will you wrap it?"

"Of course, and look at this little drawer. Lined with old Chinese tea paper, and here's one of the original pen nibs."

His guilt vanished at once.

"Have you heard about Andrew?" she asked.

"How is he, when is he coming home?"

"He doesn't know. It all sounds mysterious to me. He usually never stays away so long. But of course, it is his mama's hometown and he's probably visitin' cousins an' all. . . . "

"Probably. I seldom see him, but when he's not here, I miss him."

"He's called twice to see how business is. He sounds . . . different."

"Oh? How do you mean, different?"

"I mean, well, really *happy* or somethin'."

"Cousins can do that for you," he said, grinning. He suddenly realized he missed his own cousin, the only blood kin he had on the face of the earth. He'd call Walter tonight.

§

He put his hood up and sprinted along Main Street with his dog. May as well make one more stop, then head for home.

"Winnie?"

He parked Barnabas by the door and peered over the bakery counter.

"I'm comin'!" she said, breezing through the curtains that hid the bakery kitchen. "Father, I'm glad it's you!"

"I hear you got a bite!"

"Maybe a nibble, I don't know."

"What's the scoop?"

"Well, this real estate agency wants to know everything, so I sent 'em all the information, but nobody's turned up to see it yet."

"Terrific!" He didn't really think it was terrific, but what else could he say? "Who's the realtor?"

"Somebody named H. Tide Realty from—I forget, maybe Florida."

Florida again. "How do you feel about it?"

"After waitin' for somebody to be interested, when this finally happened, it kind of . . . "

"Kind of what?"

"Made me sick."

"I understand."

"You do?"

"Definitely."

She looked uncertain.

"You know we want you to stay. But if you decide to go, remember we'll stand behind that, too."

Winnie looked relieved. "Good! I don't know why, but I always feel better when I talk to you."

"Maybe it's the collar."

"Have a napoleon!" she urged, in her usual burst of generosity.

"Get thee behind me, absolutely not. But tell you what—I've got a houseful, so bag me a dozen donuts, Dooley will love that, and Harley, too, and let's see, a dozen oatmeal cookies . . . "

"Low-fat!" she said.

"Great. Now, what about that pie on the right? The one with the lattice top?"

"Cherry!"

"My favorite. Box it up!" Spending four hundred dollars had made him feel so good, he was trying to do it all over again.

§

Rhody Davis's leg was being amputated today.

He was praying for her this morning at first light, soon after reading Blaise Pascal. A young man who lived in the seventeenth century knew what Rhody Davis and several others on his current prayer list needed more than anything else.

"There is a God-shaped vacuum in the heart of every person," Pascal wrote. "And it can never be filled by any created thing. It can only be filled by God, made known through Jesus Christ."

Pascal had dazzled Europe with his sophisticated mathematical equations when he was only sixteen, and written about the God-shaped vacuum when he wasn't much older.

Nearly every day of his priesthood, Father Tim had seen what happened when people tried filling that vacuum with any created thing. Pauline had tried to fill it with alcohol. Rhody Davis had tried to fill it with someone else's child. . . .

He closed his eyes and prayed for all those who turn to the created thing, expecting much and receiving nothing.

§

The talk on the street was that Mack Stroupe was responsible for hooking the Fernbank sale, which would do wonders for Mitford's economy. Not only would such an enterprise draw people from other parts of the country, maybe even the world, but a major part of the staff would be locals. All that landscaping, all that maintenance, all that ocean of roofing and plumbing—and all that money flowing into Mitford pockets.

According to several reports, Fernbank was already sold, it was a done deal.

Mack Stroupe was looking good.

§

He called the mayor's office.

"She's not in," said the painfully shy Ernestine Ivory, who gave the mayor a hand two days a week.

"May I ask where she is?"

"Down at the school. She's doing a special program for the children."

"Children can't vote," he said.

"Yes, Father, that's true. But their parents can."

Bingo. "Tell her I called."

§

Harley nodded, looking sober.

"Don't let him talk you into anything you don't think is right . . . "

"Yes, sir."

" . . . or safe. Especially safe!"

"No, sir, I wouldn't."

The rector sighed and moved closer to Harley's oscillating fan.

"Now, don't you worry, Rev'rend. I'll watch after 'im like m' own young 'un."

"I know you will."

"Hit'll work some of th' juice out of 'im."

"Right."

"While I've got a educated man settin' here, I'd be beholden if you'd give me a little help with m' homework an' all."

"Your homework?"

"Lace has it in 'er head t' educate me, she's givin' me a test in a day or two."

"How do you feel about getting educated?"

"I've a good mind t' quit, but she's got 'er heart set on learnin' me somethin'. Lace has had a good bit of hard knocks, I don't want t' let 'er down."

"That's right. How can I help you?"

"Well, looky here. Sixty seventh-grade students toured th' Statue of Liberty in New York City. Two-thirds of 'em climbed to th' halfway point, and one-fourth of 'em was able t' climb all th' way to th' top. Now, th' remaining' group, they stayed down on th' base of th' pedestal, it says here. How many students didn't climb th' steps? I can't figger it t' save m' neck."

The rector mopped his brow. "Oh, boy."

"Here's another'n, this 'uns easier. The torch of th' Statue of Liberty is three hundred an' five foot from th' bottom of th' base. If th' pedestal on which th' statue rests is eighty-nine foot high, how high is th' base?"

"Let me go get a drink of water and I'll come back and see what I can do."

As he drank a glass of water at Harley's kitchen sink, he heard him muttering in the next room, "Elton washes winders at a office buildin'. Some offices has four winders and some has six . . . "

How did he get himself into these scrapes, anyway?

§

He kissed the nape of her neck, just under the ponytail she'd lately taken to sporting.

"Is there anything special you'd like to do for your birthday?" *Please, Lord, don't let her say a domestic retreat. I don't have time, she doesn't have time, it can't happen.*

She sighed. "We're both exhausted, dearest. Let's don't do any fancy dinners or tangos, let's get Chinese take-out from Wesley, lock our bedroom door, and just *be*."

And what would their teeming household think about such a thing? Oh, well.

"I can handle that," he said, drawing her close.

§

"Ron, was there ever any discussion with Miami Development about Fernbank's apple orchard? There are a hundred and sixty-two trees up there, and all are still bearing."

"She mentioned the orchard the first time she was here. They'd tear it out. That's where most of the cottages will be built."

A small point, but it stung him. Those trees had dropped their fruit into any hand that passed, for years. They had filled Mitford's freezers with pies and cobblers, and crowded endless pantry shelves with sauce and jelly.

An even smaller point, perhaps, but he noticed that Ron had said "*will* be built."

§

A new day-care program was getting under way at Lord's Chapel as Buck Leeper's crew began their invasion of the attic.

Given that the only access to the attic was through the trapdoor over the pulpit, merely getting into the attic was a project.

Under Buck's supervision, the crew removed stones from the east wall, cut through studs, sheeting, and insulation, installed a new header and a sill, and created a double-door entrance. Until the outside steps could be built, ladders and scaffolding permitted the crew to haul up endless feet of lumber for classroom partitions and a restroom.

It was all going forward exactly as he expected: his very hair, what was left of it, was filled with a fine dust, as were the pews and all that lay below. Kneelers got their share, so that when parishioners wearing black arose from prayer, the fronts of skirts and trousers displayed a clear mark of piety.

Anybody else, he thought, would have retired and left the attic project to the next poor fellow, but he had celebrated and preached beneath the vast, empty loft for sixteen years, dreaming of the day they could fill it with children.

Yes, there'd be the patter of little feet above the heads of the congregation, though measures would be taken to muffle the sound considerably. In any case, it was a sound he'd be glad to hear.

§

Puny met him at the front door with Sissy on one hip and Sassy on the other.

"Father, I jis' don't think I can keep bringin' th' girls to work with me, even though I know how much it means to you to have 'em here." She looked unusually distressed.

He took Sissy and walked down the hall behind his house help.

"Ba!" said the happy twin, bashing him on the head with a plastic frying pan. "Ba!"

"That's what she calls you, did you know that?"

"Really?"

"That's your name. When I show her your wedding picture at home, she always says Ba!"

He felt honored. Ba! He'd never had another name before, except Father.

He sat down at the kitchen table and took a twin on either knee, which he immediately geared to the jiggling mode. "I know it's hard for you trying to work with two little ones. . . . "

"I cain't hardly get my work done anymore, but I hated to put 'em out to day care, they'll only be babies once, and I didn't want . . . " Puny looked close to tears. "I didn't want to miss that!"

"Of course not! I know it's a strain for you, but we'll work with you on it. We're pleased with all you do, Puny. You're the best, and always have been."

Her face brightened. He loved the look of the red-haired, freckle-faced Puny Guthrie, who was like blood kin, the closest thing to a daughter he'd ever have. Besides, who else would clean the mildew off his shoes, wipe *behind* the picture frames, mend his shirts, bake cornbread deserving of a blue ribbon, and keep the clothes closets looking like racks at a department store? What she was able to do, even with two toddlers in tow, was more than anyone else *would* do, he was sure of it.

"The church day care will be open next week. Hang on, and if you'd like to put them in for a day or two to see how it goes, well . . . "

"Thank you, Father! You're a wonderful granpaw. Would you mind holdin' 'em a minute while I run up and bring th' laundry down?"

"Mama, Mama!" yelled Sassy.

"Ba!" sighed Sissy, snuggling against him.

He nuzzled the two heads of tousled hair and thought that, all things considered, he was a very fortunate man. He needed challenges in his life . . . But wait a minute, did he need that warm, wet feeling spreading over his left knee?

န

He had showered, she had bathed in a tubful of scented bubbles; she had laid out his clean robe, he had plumped up the pillows behind her head; they had devoured their chicken with almonds, shrimp with lobster sauce, and two spring rolls.

"What's your fortune?" she asked, looking discontented with her own.

"I will uncover a surprise and receive great recognition."

"Poop, darling, you're always receiving great recognition. Everyone loves you, it's like being married to the Pope. Here's mine. 'Prepare for victory ahead!' Who writes this stuff?"

"Now," he urged.

"OK!"

"Close your eyes."

"I love this part," she said, putting her hands over her eyes. "Don't you want me to guess?"

"Absolutely not. We're going straight to the punch line."

He fumbled the box out of the closet, which Marcie had wrapped in the signature brown paper of Oxford Antiques, and thumped it on the bed next to her.

"OK. You can look."

"A box! I love boxes!"

"Heave to, Kavanagh."

She tore the raffia bow off, and the paper, and pulled back the tape on top of the box.

He helped remove the writing desk and set it on her lap.

"Timothy!" she whispered, unbelieving.

"Happy birthday, my love."

No two ways about it, he had hit a home run.

§

They lay in bed, holding each other, the room warmed by the glow of her bedside lamp.

"You're wonderful," he said, meaning it.

She smiled. "But I'm old!"

"Old? You? Never!"

"Just look at these crow's feet. . . . "

"I don't see any crow's feet," he said, kissing her crow's feet.

§

"Father, this is Lottie Greer."

Lottie Greer—the spinster sister of Absalom Greer, the elderly revival preacher who had loved Sadie Baxter . . .

"It's Absalom." He heard the fear in her voice.

"What is it?"

"It's pneumonia. He wants you to pray."

"I will, Miss Lottie, and others with me. Shall I come?"

"He said to just pray. There's fluid in his lungs."

He told her he was available anytime, that she should let him know what he could do. Then he called Cynthia and the all-church prayer chain.

He had come to love Absalom Greer. The eloquent, unschooled preacher had been a force in his life and those of countless others, including Pauline and Lace. He was among the last of the old warriors who fearlessly confronted the issue of sin, preached repentence and salvation, and pulled no punches when it came to the Gospel of Jesus Christ.

Bottom line, the old man was his brother. He would go out on Sunday.

§

What was he waiting for?

The question was unspoken, but every time he ran into a member of the vestry, he felt the weight of it. Thirty days? For what? Ingrid Swenson didn't look like somebody who could be bluffed into coughing up two ninety-five after she offered one ninety-eight. But the point was, the property was fully worth two ninety-five, and in his opinion, Miami Development was trying to steal it. To be bluffed themselves was a humiliation not to be suffered lightly.

The answer was, he didn't know what he was waiting for. He only knew that selling Fernbank to Miami Development was something that didn't feel right. Maybe it would feel right later—then again, later could be too late.

He hated this, he hated it.

§

He tried to act nonchalant by puttering in the side garden as they backed out of the driveway. Dooley was lit up like downtown Holding at Christmas, and Harley was generating a few kilowatts himself.

He looked up and waved, and they waved back.

Four-thirty. Dooley had left work a half hour early, and they had promised to be back at the rectory around six.

He looked through the hedge to the little yellow house. A window box needed fixing, the bolt had come loose and the box was hanging whomper-jawed under the studio window.

Too bad that little house didn't get more use. But one day . . .

He'd better get cracking and have Buck look it over, tell them what to do, help them get started with the additions and renovations. If there was ever a perfect opportunity to get top-drawer input, Buck Leeper was providing it.

He turned to go inside, then stopped and looked at the yellow house again.

By jing!

§

"But he'll never be there when you're there, because when you're working, he'll be working."

"That great big man in work boots and chinos stomping around and picking his teeth? In my *house*? Goodness, Timothy . . ."

"His company will pay the rent."

"Do you really think it would be all right?"

"Of course it would be all right. With Buck living there, he'd get to know exactly what we need and how to pull it off, and we wouldn't have to hire an architect, he can draw it up—*and* hire the crew."

She wrinkled her brow. "I don't know. . . . "

"It's a great opportunity."

"Consider it done, then," she said, quoting her priest.

§

At a quarter 'til six, he was standing at the front door, searching the street. Then he walked out and sat on the top step of the front porch.

"Come out with me," he called to Cynthia.

She came and sat with him and took his hand.

"I've been thinking," she said.

"Uh-oh."

"I want to play in that softball game."

"You do?"

"Yes. I can hit a ball. I can run. I can—"

"You can whistle."

She put her fingers to her mouth and blew out the windows.

"You're good, Kavanagh."

"So hire me."

"You're the only female."

"So far," she said. "I hear Adele Hogan wants to play."

"The police officer? J.C.'s wife?"

"She's the baddest softball player you ever want to see. At least, that's what she said."

"J.C. didn't mention that."

"He probably thought it was a guy's game."

"Well," he said, "it was. . . . "

§

At seven o'clock, he was ready to make a search of Farmer, which he and Harley had judged a perfect location for the driving lesson.

But maybe he should call the hospital first. He went to the study to find his cordless.

Cynthia wasn't worried at all. "Give them another fifteen minutes. It's a beautiful summer evening. . . . "

"Yes, but Harley knew the curfew, he wouldn't do this. I'm calling the police."

Barnabas let out a loud series of barks. As the rector raced up the front hall, he saw Harley standing on the porch. He looked like he'd gone a few rounds with a grizzly.

"Now, Rev'rend, I wouldn't want you t' worry. . . . "

He pushed open the screen door. "Where's Dooley? What happened?"

"Th' last thing I'd want t' do is cause you an' th' missus t' worry. . . . "

"Tell me, Harley."

"No, sir, worry's not what I'd ever want to' bring in y'r house. . . . "

"Dadgum it, Harley, I am worried, and will be 'til you tell me what the dickens went on."

"Well, sir, y'r boy's fine."

"Thank God."

"We crashed m' truck."

"No!"

"We did."

"Who did?"

"Now, I don't want you t' worry. . . . "

"Harley . . . "

"Y'r boy did."

"Good Lord!"

"But hit 'us my fault."

"You're sure he wasn't hurt? Where is he?"

"No, sir, he won't hurt, but m' truck was."

"How bad?"

"Tore up th' front an' all."

"Any damage to your engine?"

"Good as new."

"How'd you get home?"

"You mean after we hauled it out'n th' ditch?"

"Yes."

"You mean after we hauled it out'n th' ditch an' had t' help th' farmer chase 'is cow back to th' pasture?"

"What about a cow?"

"That's what come high-tailin' 'cross th' road an' made th' boy hit 'is brakes an' land in th' ditch."

"I see."

The rector glanced toward the driveway and saw Dooley peering at him around a bush.

"I'd sure hate f'r you t' worry. . . . "

Ha. Worry had just become his middle name—at least until Dooley Barlowe went back to school where somebody else could do the worrying.

CHAPTER THIRTEEN

The Fields Are White

He unlocked the office and went in, feeling an odd foreboding as he raised the windows and turned on the fan. Today's temperature was nearly what they'd had in Florida.

He heard the bathroom door creak on its hinges and wheeled around. Edith Mallory was standing there in something like a bathrobe.

"Edith . . . "

She smiled and moved toward him, smelling of the dark cigarettes she smoked, untying the sash. . . .

"Timothy!"

He opened his eyes and looked into the face of his anxious wife. "Thank God!" he said, sitting up.

"These dreams you've been having . . . it's scary. What was it this time?"

"I can't remember," he lied. Bathed with perspiration, he reached to the bedside table and turned the fan on high.

"That's better," she said. "Are you all right?"

"Yes. Sorry I woke you."

"Don't be. I remember the times I used to wake in the night with bad dreams and there was no one to turn to."

She switched off her bedside lamp and rolled over to him and held his hand.

Soon she was sleeping again, but he was not.

This wasn't the first dream he'd had of Edith Mallory. He distinctly remembered the one in which he was locked with her in the parish hall coat closet, pounding on the door for help.

While he was in Ireland a couple of years ago, her husband, Pat, had died of a heart attack. When the rector returned home, she had tried every strategy imaginable to seduce and dominate him. Always seeking to entice, always looking at him in a way that made him want to run for the hills, once detaining him overnight at Clear Day, her house on the highest ridge above Mitford.

He recalled the visit to Children's Hospital, where she gave $15,000 as imperiously as if it were a quarter million, and afterward being trapped in the backseat of her car while she stroked his leg. He had demanded that Ed Coffey, her chauffeur, stop the car, and had jumped from the Lincoln while it was still rolling.

After the miserable wrestling match over the Grill, which she had thumpingly lost, she had gone to Spain and, as far as he knew, hadn't returned—nor had she sent her annual contribution to Lord's Chapel. Fine. So be it. It was money he didn't want, though the finance chairman was certainly anxious about it.

He'd been able to put her out of his mind until someone at the Grill had brought up her name.

Suddenly he was feeling the old contamination he'd felt for years as her eyes roved over him in the pulpit. . . .

Blast.

He rolled on his side and tried to imagine the breeze from the fan was an island trade wind somewhere in the Indian Ocean.

§

"My wife's house is nonsmoking. Will that be a problem?" Buck Leeper was known for sucking down two packs of unfiltered Lucky Strikes a day.

"No problem. I've cut back, anyhow."

They walked into Cynthia's kitchen, where a faint breeze stirred through the open windows.

"The house is small, but—"

"There's something I've been wanting to tell you," said the superintendent.

There was a brief silence while Buck looked at his work boots, then directly at Father Tim.

"I appreciate what you did for me."

The rector nodded, silent.

"I could have killed you, slingin' th' furniture around like that."

He remembered Buck's drunken violence at Tanner Cottage during the construction of Hope House. Unable to flee, he had sat, praying, as Buck's torrential anger poured forth for hours.

"Sorry," Buck said, hoarse with feeling.

"Don't even think about it." He hadn't expected an apology for that long-ago night, but it felt better to have it, somehow. He knew instinctively that Buck didn't want to say anything more.

"Well . . . you can see how cramped the house is. Built for one, really."

"What are you lookin' to do?"

"We'd like to knock out this rear wall and add a large studio with a bank of windows, maybe French doors leading to a patio, perhaps connecting with a two-car garage and extra storage. I know you can help us figure it out.

"Also, we thought it would be good to have a fireplace at that end, possibly of native stone, with bookshelves on either side. Oh, and hardwood floors, of course, with another bathroom adjoining the studio. The only bathroom is upstairs, which reminds me . . . "

This was exciting. His blood was up for it.

" . . . we're thinking of widening the stairway, if possible, and building storage closets on the landing, but I'm getting ahead of myself. Since we're in the kitchen, what would you think about a cooking island, and bay windows looking out to the hedge?"

Buck took the toothpick from his mouth and stared around the small room. "You want to live in it a year from now?"

"Right!"

"You'll have to haul ass," he said.

❦

Mack Struope
Already Working For
Improved Economy

"I'm not going to wait til I'm elected to work hard for Mitford," says mahoral candidate MackStrouope at his downtown campaign headquarters. "I'm already working hard to bring in new growth and development.

"For example, I recommended the fine property of Sweet Stuff Bakery to one real estate company, and was able to get another realtor to look at Fernbank. When the Fernbank deal goes through, it will put big dollars in everybody's pockets.

"I'm not one to say if it ain't broke, don't fix it. I say let's make a good thing better."

Strouple is running against mayoral incumbent, Esther Cunninghanm, who has seen eight terms in local office, with three of those terms unopposed.

Stroupe's free Saturday barbecues will be held until election week at his campaign headquarters on Main Street.

ThisSaturdzy will feature the live country music of everybody's favorit, the Wesley Washtub Band. All are invited.

He hadn't missed Mack's terminology, *"when* the Fernbank deal goes through . . . "

Part of Miss Sadie's letter had been running through his mind like a chanted refrain.

"I leave Fernbank to supply any requirements of Hope House," she had written. "Do with it what you will, but please treat it kindly."

Treat it kindly.

Was selling it for half its worth treating it kindly? All her adult life, Sadie Baxter had done without, so that her mother's and father's money could be invested wisely. Hadn't her penury and smart management provided a five-million-dollar budget for Hope House, and a home for forty people who needed one?

Who was he to swallow down an arrogant offer that robbed the coffers of a deserving institution?

But then, what was the alternative?

Back and forth, back and forth—always the same questions, and never any answers. At least, not as far as he was concerned.

He couldn't deal with this any longer.

He got up from the sofa and knelt by his desk in the quiet study.

"Lord, Miss Sadie's house belongs to You, she told me that several times. You know I've got a real problem here."

He paused. "Actually, You've got it, because I'm giving it to You right now, free and clear. I'll do my part, just show me what it is. In Jesus' name, amen."

§

"Poached, whole wheat, no grits," he told Velma, as he walked to the rear booth and slid in.

"J.C., I've got a story idea for you."

"Don't give me any small-town, feel-good stuff," snapped the editor. "I've had enough of that to choke a horse."

"I hear political candidates have to fill out a form that discloses the amount of a campaign contribution and who made it. I'm also told that anyone, including media, can ask to see that form."

He could tell J.C. was getting the message, and didn't particularly like it, either. "So why don't you get Mack to show it to you?" asked the editor.

"So why don't *you*?" asked the rector.

§

"Father?"

It was Lottie Greer. Years of experience told him all he needed to know.

"I'm on my way," he said.

§

He parked behind a long line of cars and pickup trucks on the country road, and walked to Greer's Store.

Men were congregated on the porch, dressed in overalls and work clothes; many were smoking, and all talked in undertones.

They nodded to him as he came up the steps. He heard the faint singing inside.

"How is he?" he asked an elderly man sitting on a bench.

"Bad off, Preacher."

He opened the fragile screen door that had slapped behind him on happier occasions, and entered the store that resembled a room in a Rembrandt canvas. The aged floors and burnished wood, the low wattage in the bulbs, the fading afternoon light through the windows—it was beautiful; saintly, somehow, more a church than a store. But then, hadn't Absalom Greer preached the gospel in this place for nearly seventy years?

Several women sat around the cold summer stove, talking in low voices. One sang softly with the chorus inside. "*. . . that calls me from a world of care, and bids me at my Father's throne, make all my wants and wishes known . . .* "

Three men in ill-fitting dark suits met him at the door of the rooms where Absalom lived with his sister, Lottie. All were clutching Bibles, and all spoke or nodded as if they knew him.

Lottie Greer sat in the chair by the fireplace, where she always implored him to sit when he visited.

"Miss Lottie . . . "

She looked up, gaunt and shockingly frail, her cane across her knees. "He said yesterday he wanted to see you, Father. He asked to die at home, the old way."

He put his hand on her shoulder.

"He's lingered on," she murmured, lowering her head. "It's been hard."

"Yes," he said. "I understand." And he did. His mother had lingered, fighting the good fight.

Seven or eight men were gathered outside Absalom's open bedroom door, and quietly, but forcefully, singing the old hymn the rector had known since a child.

"He wanted us to sing his favorites," said one of the men with a Bible. "Join in, if you take a notion. Th' doctor's with 'im right now, looks like he's in an' out of knowin' where he's at."

"Lena, get the Father something," said Lottie.

"I've just poured him a glass of tea, Miss Lottie. I hope you like it sweet," she said, placing the icy glass in his hand.

"Oh, I do. Thank you."

"And some cake, you'll want some cake," she said, eager to please.

"Thank you, not now."

"You help yourself, then, anytime," she said, pointing to the kitchen table, which was laden with food. "It's to eat, not throw out." She colored slightly, and made a faint curtsy. "I hope you'll try my pineapple upside down, it's over by the sink."

"Sing up!" said one of the chorus. "Brother Greer likes it loud."

"Jesus, lover of my soul . . ." they began, limning the words of Charles Wesley.

He joined in.

> *. . . Let me to Thy bosom fly,*
> *While the nearer waters roll,*
> *While the tempest still is high:*
> *Hide me, O my Savior hide,*
> *Till the storm of life is past;*
> *Safe into the haven guide,*
> *O receive my soul at last.*
>
> *Other refuge have I none;*
> *Hangs my helpless soul on Thee;*
> *Leave, O leave me not alone,*
> *Still support and comfort me . . .*

He felt as if he were a child again, in his mother's Mississippi Baptist church, where his own grandfather once preached. A kind of joy was rising in him, but how could it not? Absalom Greer would soon pass safely into the haven. . . .

Someone who appeared to be the doctor stepped out of Absalom's room. "Go in, Father," he said. "He's asked for you."

The bed on the other side of the spartan room seemed far away. It was as if he treaded water to reach it.

He heard the dense rattle in Absalom's chest.

"Brother Timothy, is that you?" The old man kept his filmy blue eyes fixed on the ceiling.

"It is."

"I've been lookin' for you."

Over the years, he'd seen it—as death drew near, the skin had a way of connecting with the bones, of fusing into a kind of cold marble that was at once terrible and beautiful.

"The Lord's given me a truth for you," said Absalom. It was as if each word were delicately formed, so it would move through the maze of the rattle and come forth whole and lucid.

Father Tim bent closer. "I'm listening, my Brother."

"The fields are white. . . . "

Jesus had said it to the disciples. . . .

Then Absalom turned his head and looked past him, his face growing suffused with a kind of joy. "Glory, glory . . . there they are . . . I knew they'd come again. . . . "

The rector's heart raced with feeling—he knew instinctively that Absalom Greer was seeing the angels, the angels he'd once seen as a young boy, swarming around his mother and baby sister in the next room.

The old preacher lifted his trembling hands above the coverlet, issuing a last pastoral command.

The men stopped singing. The talking in the kitchen ceased.

Lottie came into the room, leaning on her cane. "Is it his angels?" she whispered.

"I believe so," he said.

§

He took the back roads, wanting to see pastures and open fields, wanting a span of silence between dying and living.

Perhaps Sadie Baxter had been among the first to greet Absalom, to bestow some heavenly welcome upon one to whom God would surely say, "Well done, good and faithful servant."

He would miss Absalom Greer. It had been a privilege to know him. He was the last of a breed, willing, like Saint Paul, to be "a fool for Christ."

In the fields, Queen of the Meadow towered over goldenrod and fleabane, over milkweed and wild blue aster. Beautiful, but dry. They needed rain. He wished he had his dog with him, licking up the windows to a fare-thee-well.

He made a turn onto the state highway and spoke it aloud: "The fields are white. . . . "

"Lift up your eyes, and look on the fields," Jesus had said to his disciples, "for they are white already to harvest."

The standing fields were the legions who hadn't filled their God-vacuum with the One who was born to fill it; the standing fields were those who waited for someone to reach out and speak the truth, and tell them how they might be saved.

He had received Absalom's message as a reminder, and did not take it lightly.

He glanced at the gas gauge. Nearly empty.

There was a little grocery store and service station up the road. He'd once stopped there for a pack of Nabs and a Cheerwine.

It came up sooner than he expected. He wheeled in and parked beside the building, then got the key from the store owner and walked around and unlocked the restroom. First things first.

Coming out of the restroom, he saw the black Lincoln pull off the road and ease past the gas pumps.

He stepped back instinctively, and watched Ed Coffey get out of the Lincoln and go into the station.

Ed Coffey. Edith Mallory's chauffeur. The one who was driving when he leaped from the moving car in the Shoe Barn parking lot, the one who'd driven him home after the gruesome, rain-drenched night at Clear Day.

Ed wasn't wearing his uniform. The rector didn't think he'd ever seen Ed out of uniform since Pat Mallory died.

He stood by the building, wondering why he didn't step forward and speak to the man, a Mitford native who had always seemed a decent fellow, though clearly snared by the lure of Mallory money. Hadn't Ed looked at him a couple of times as if to say, I don't want to do this, I know better, but it's too late?

Ed left the station with a bulging paper sack in his arm, which he put in the trunk. Then he got in the car and quietly pulled onto the road, headed south.

A new Lincoln, clearly, not the old model Edith had kept around after Pat's death. And this one had dark windows. He despised dark windows in a car. . . .

So Edith was back in Mitford. He could probably expect to see her at Lord's Chapel. Edith on the gospel side, Mack Stroupe on the epistle side.

What happened when clergy looked into their congregations, only to see a growing number of people whose motives they distrusted, and whose spirits made their own feel anxious and uneasy?

§

He noticed that a new battery of yard signs had gone up, along with the general clutter.

We're stickin' with Esther
BILL AND ARLENE

We're stickin' with Esther
Ralph And Fay Lewis

OUR BANE WILL
BE YOUR BLESSING
Best Sale Ever!
Oct. 4, from 10 a.m.
After Work Supper
6:00 p.m.

MACK MEANS
MONEY IN
MITFORD POCKETS.
$Mack for Mayor$

VOTE YOUR VALUES
Esther for Mayor

Play Ball!
Come one, come all
Baxter Field, August 10
HOTDOGS $1

§

"Seventy-five bucks from the glove factory, a thousand from Lee-land Mining Company—which should be no surprise, that's his fourth cousin. Five hundred from the canning plant, who'd also like to see some more development in these parts, ten bucks from Lew Boyd's cousin, fifteen from Henry Watts, blah, blah, blah—exactly what you'd expect." J.C. looked pleased with himself. "You can get off your high horse, buddyroe."

Why pursue it? "So, tell me, have you seen Ed Coffey around lately?"

"Ed Coffey? If he's around, so's your old girlfriend."

He felt as if he'd been dashed with cold water. "You might rephrase that," he said.

"You're plenty touchy," snapped the editor.

"I learned it from you," he replied.

§

Lace Turner was visiting Harley and had come up to the kitchen to have a piece of cake with Cynthia. He was taking the pitcher of tea out of the refrigerator when they heard a light knock at the door.

Jenny stood outside, peering through the screen. "Hello! Is Doo-ley home?"

Barnabas skidded into the kitchen, barking.

"He ain't here!" Lace said.

"Why, Lace!" said Cynthia. "He *is* here. Won't you come in, Jenny?"

"No ma'am. I just brought Dooley this."

Cynthia opened the screen door and took the parcel. "We're having cake, it's chocolate—"

"No, ma'am, I can't. Thank you." She ran down the steps and across the yard.

Cynthia looked at Lace. "Why did you lie?"

"I didn't know he was here."

"But you did. You saw him come in ten minutes ago. So, that's two lies." His wife never pulled punches.

Lace shrugged.

"I'm not going to preach you a sermon," said Cynthia, "but I want you to know something. I'm disappointed that you'd lie to her and to me. You're better than that."

Lace stared at the half-eaten cake on her plate. "I hate that girl."

"Why?"

"She thinks she's so smart, so pretty, so . . . *fine.*" Lace spit the word.

"Lace, look at me, please." Lace looked at her. "You're smart. You're pretty. You're—"

"I ain't! I ain't nothin'!" She stood up from the table, weeping, and ran down the basement stairs.

"So," said his wife, looking grim. "She's crying—it's what Olivia's been hoping for."

"That's good news," he said, putting his arm around her shoulders.

She smiled weakly. "Yes, but sometimes even good news feels bad."

§

Esther Bolick picked up on the first ring.

"So, Esther, how's it coming?"

"You'll never believe it—we got an armoire from Marie Sanders!"

If he had anything to do with it, Esther would have two armoires. "How's Hessie working out for you?"

"A saint, Hessie's a saint. She's heading up the After Work Sale, includin' th' supper."

"Wow."

"Did you know Hessie and I are wearin' beepers? I feel like Dick Tracy."

"I've heard everything."

"Course, th' polyester and double-knit is still pourin' in."

"Find me an orange leisure suit with stitched lapels, I'll pay big money."

"Too late, Mule Skinner already spoke for it."

"Oh, well."

"But the quality's picking up, we just got a Hoover vacuum cleaner and a whole set of Hummel figurines. Oh, and a mink jacket, th' hole's where you can't even see it."

"How's Gene?"

"Suing for divorce."

"It could be worse," he said.

Esther laughed heartily. How he loved hearing a Bane chairperson laugh. A minor miracle!

He was putting the receiver on the hook when it came to him out of left field.

Land of Counterpane. Black car, blue pickup.

Surely not . . .

And the black car that had eased around the monument at two in the morning, so quiet he scarcely heard the engine . . .

But that was weeks ago. That was the evening of his birthday, which was well over a month back, maybe five or six weeks. If Edith was around, why hadn't anyone seen her?

Was Ed Coffey steering clear of Mitford, buying their groceries at country stores, keeping to the back roads, going ununiformed to attract less attention?

He'd drive by Clear Day and see what was going on, but there wasn't any way to spot the house, since it sat a half mile beyond a locked electronic gate. That gate had been locked even on evenings when Edith invited the vestry to meet at her house. Guests were required to punch a password into a black box at the entrance.

There was a churning sensation in his stomach.

Not knowing what else to do, he went into the office bathroom and stuck his finger for a glucometer check. In his opinion, the glucometer was a decided improvement over peeing on a strip to check his sugar.

One twenty-four. Not bad.

§

He made a call from the office, still knowing the number by heart, and went home and got his old gardening hat from the closet shelf.

Rifling through the chest of drawers, he found the sunglasses he seldom wore because someone said they made him look like a housefly.

He put on the hat and glasses as he went down the stairs, thinking he'd check himself out in the kitchen mirror.

"Lord God!" shrieked Puny, standing frozen at the foot of the stairs. "You like to scared me to death!"

Hearing their mother's alarm, both babies set up an earsplitting wail in the kitchen.

He tried bouncing their car seats, squeaking a rubber duck, making a face, and barking like a dog, but they were inconsolable, and he was out of there.

§

"This Cessna 152 don't make as much noise as m' little ragwing," shouted Omer.

The rector was holding up pretty well, all things considered. He had skipped lunch, knowing he'd be airborne, had driven twenty-five miles to the airstrip, and here he was, skimming above the treetops with the mayor's brother-in-law in a borrowed plane, wearing a decrepit garden hat and shades.

Father Roland, who occasionally wrote from the wilds of Canada, was totally wrong to think he was having all the fun, celebrating the Eucharist in crude forest huts and being chased by a bull moose. Mitford had its grand adventures, too. You just had to go looking for—

"Holy smoke, Omer!"

Omer flashed his piano-key grin at the rector, who was only momentarily hanging upside down.

"That's what you call a one-G maneuver."

"No more, thanks!" His face had been green twice in only a few weeks.

"OK, I'll fly steady," yelled his pilot. "How low d'you think you'll want to go?"

"Low enough to see what's going on."

"I can take you down to two hundred feet, how's that?"

He swallowed hard. "Fine."

"You sure don't look like yourself in that getup," Omer shouted.

"Good!" he shouted back.

§

They saw the ridge looming ahead, the ridge from which Clear Day could see forever, but could not be seen.

"Here she comes!" Omer said. Father Tim pulled the brim of the hat farther down and adjusted the glasses.

What could have been a small landing strip emerged from the trees. It was the shake roof that covered the much-talked-about eight thousand square feet of living space, with its vast expanse of driveway and parking area to the left.

Bingo.

A blue pickup truck was parked next to a black car. And there, on the uncovered terrace, standing by the striped umbrellas, were two people.

"Circle back!" he shouted to his pilot.

He wanted to be dead sure.

Omer circled back and buzzed the house. The man and woman on the terrace looked up angrily as he looked down.

Then the blue Cessna roared over the quaking treetops and across the gorge.

Omer glanced at him and winked.

Edith Mallory was not touring Spain or France or Malaysia or any of her other haunts, and neither was she living in her sprawling home in Florida.

She was living in Mitford, at Clear Day, and masterminding the political career of Mack Stroupe.

CHAPTER FOURTEEN

Play Ball

On the morning of the game at Baxter Field, Velma Mosely had a change of heart and started chopping onions.

This, she told herself, would absolutely, positively be her last pot of homemade chili.

§

"Listen up!"

Buck Leeper looked ten feet tall as he stood in the dugout before the Mitford Reds.

"We're not here to fool around," said the team manager, "we're here to win. Got it?"

"Got it!" said his players, who were wearing red-dyed T-shirts and ball caps advertising The Local.

It was twenty minutes before game time, and the rector felt his adrenaline pumping like oil through a Texas derrick.

"Father, you're th' team captain, and I'm lookin' to you to be th' coach on th' field. Keep 'em pepped up and give 'em advice when they need it—your job is to call the shots." Buck looked him in the eye. "I know you can do it."

Could he do it? He had prayed about this softball game as if it were life or death, instead of good, clean fun on a Saturday afternoon. Surely the three practice games, which had gone pretty well, would count for something.

Buck took a Lucky Strike out of his shirt pocket and paced in front of them. "Dooley, you're my first batter. I've watched you get ready for today's game, and you're always hustlin', always quick on your feet. I want you to wait on the pitch that's yours, got it?"

"Got it," said Dooley.

"We want you on that base."

"Yes, sir."

"Adele, you're plenty quick and sure-handed, you'll play first base. I'm hittin' you in th' second slot. When Dooley gets on, advance th' runner at any cost. We've got to get somebody in scoring position."

Adele socked her right fist into her glove.

Buck laughed his water-boiling-in-a-kettle laugh. "We want those turkeys to play with their backs to the wall. Right?"

"Right!" said his team.

"Avis, you're my first power hitter. I want you to slam it clear to Wesley. Father, you're my cleanup batter—stay strong and quick, and remember to keep your shoulders straight."

Buck might have been commandeering a crew of backhoe operators in a thirty-foot excavation.

"Mrs. Kavanagh—"

"Cynthia," she said.

"Cynthia, you're battin' in my number five spot. I want you to dig in and crush that ball. As the catcher, I want you to call our pitches—look at how they're standin', check out their feet. Bottom line, be alert at all times."

"You got it, Coach."

Buck completed the lineup with Hal Owen as second baseman and Mule Skinner, Jena Ivey, Pauline Barlowe, and Lew Boyd in the outfield.

"I've been watchin' th' other team," said Buck, "and we're better than they are. We can do the job. I want you to give it a hundred percent, understand? Not eighty-five, not ninety-five—a *hundred.*"

He looked at every earnest face, rolling the unlit cigarette between his fingers. "Father, you want to pray?"

"He wants to!" said Dooley.

After the prayer, they scrambled to their feet and trooped past the concession stand. At that moment, the rector was certain he experienced a brief out-of-body reverie. He saw their team charging out on the field, and there he was in the middle of the fray, wearing, for Pete's sake, his green Pentecost vestments.

§

"Man!" exclaimed Dooley.

The stands were full, people were sitting on the grass, and the smell of hotdogs and chili wafted through the humid summer air.

Tommy's dad, who was the plate umpire, looked at the coin he'd just flipped. The Mitford Reds were the home team.

The rector scanned the crowd, just as he always did at Lord's Chapel.

The residents of Hope House were lined up in wheelchairs and seated on the front bleachers, looking expectant.

There was Mack Stroupe, standing with one foot on a bleacher and a cigarette in his mouth, and over to the right, Harley and Lace. He spotted Fancy Skinner and Uncle Billy and Miss Rose and Coot and Omer, and about midway up, Tommy, who had hurt his leg and couldn't play. He noted that quite a few sported a strawberry sucker stuck in their jaw, evidence that the mayor had doled out her customary campaign favors.

From the front row, where she sat with Russell Jacks and Betty Craig, Jessie waved to the field with both hands.

"Ladies and gentlemen," announced town councilman, Linder Hayes, "it is my immense privilege to introduce Esther Cunningham, our beloved mayor, who for sixteen years and eight great terms in office has diligently helped Mitford take care of its own! Your Honor, you are hereby officially invited to . . . *throw out the first ball.*"

"Burn it in, Esther!" somebody yelled.

The other umpire ran a ball to the mayor, who stood proudly in the dignitaries section, cheek by jowl with the county sheriff.

At this, the *Muse* editor bounded from the concession stand to the bleachers and skidded to a stop about a yard from the mayor. He dropped to his knees and pointed the Nikon upward.

"Dadgum it," hissed the mayor, "don't shoot from down there, it gives me three double chins!"

"And behind the plate," boomed Linder Hayes, "our esteemed police chief and vigilant overseer of law and order, Mr. Rodney Underwood!"

Applause. Hoots. Whistles. Rodney adjusted his holster belt and waved to the crowd with a gloved hand.

"Hey, Esther, smoke it in there!"

The mayor threw back her head, circled her arm like a prop on a P-51, and let the ball fly.

"*Stee-rike* one!" said the umpire.

"Oh, *please,*" said Cynthia, who was perspiring from infield practice.

"What is it?" whispered the rector.

"I have to use the port-a-john."

"It's your nerves," declared her husband, who appeared to know.

"Take the field!" yelled Buck.

The players sprinted to their positions. Then, the home-plate ump took a deep breath, pointed at the pitcher, and shouted what they'd all been waiting to hear.

"*Play ball!*"

§

The Reds' batboy, Poo Barlowe, passed his brother a bat which he had personally inscribed with the name *Dools* and a zigzag flash of lightning. He had rendered this personal I.D. with a red ballpoint pen, bearing down hard and repeatedly until it appeared etched into the wood.

Dooley took a couple of warm-up swings, then stepped into the batter's box. He gripped the bat, positioned his feet, and waited for the pitch.

A high, looping pitch barely missed the strike zone.

"Ball one!"

The second pitch came in chest-high, as Dooley tightened his grip, took a hefty swing, and connected. *Crack!* It was the first ball hitting the bat for the newly formed Mitford Reds; the sound seemed to reverberate into the stands.

"Go, buddy!"

Dooley streaked to first base, his long legs eating the distance, and blew past it to second as the crowd cheered. He slid into second a heartbeat ahead of the ball that socked into Scott Murphy's glove.

"Ride 'em, cowboy!" warbled Miss Pattie, who believed herself to be at a rodeo.

The game was definitely off to a good start.

§

"Mama!"

Fancy Skinner waved to her mother, who was shading her eyes and peering into the stands. "I'm up here!"

Fancy was wearing shocking pink tights and a matching tunic, and stood out so vividly from the crowd that her mother recognized her at once and made the climb to the fifth row, carrying a knitting bag with the beginnings of an afghan.

"I declare," said Fancy, "I hardly knew that was you, don't you just love bein' blond, didn't I tell you it would be more fun? I mean, look at you, out at a softball game instead of sittin' home watchin' th' Wheel or whatever. And oh, my lord, what're you wearin', I can't believe it, a Dale Jarrett T-shirt, aren't you th' cat's pajamas, you look a hundred years younger!

"Next, you might want to lose some weight, if you don't mind my sayin' so, around forty pounds seems right to me, it would take a strain off your heart. Lord have mercy, would you look at that, he backed th' right fielder clean to th' fence. *Hey, ump, open your eyes, I thought only horses went to sleep standin' up!*

"Oh, shoot, I forgot about your hearin' aid bein' so sensitive, was that me that made it go off? It sounds like a burglar alarm, I thought th' old one was better, here, have some gun, it's sugarless. Look! There he is, there's Mule, mama, see? Th' one in the grass over yonder, idn't he cute, *Mule, honey, we're up here, look up here, sweetie,* oh mercy, the ball like to knocked his head off. *Pay attention to what you're doin', Mule!*

"Mama, you want a hotdog? I'll get us one at th' end of fifth innin', Velma made th' chili. I didn't say it's chilly, I said Velma— mama, are you sure that hearin' aid works right, it seems like th' old one did better, and look at what you paid for it, an arm and a leg, you want relish? I can't hardly eat relish, it gives me sour stomach.

"How in th' world you can knit and watch a ballgame is beyond me, I have to concentrate. See there, that's th' preacher Mule hangs out with at the Grill, th' one I gave a mask to th' day you got a perm, you remember, I can't tell whether he tries to hit a ball or club it to death. That's his wife on third base, I think she bleaches with a cap, I never heard of a preacher's wife playin' softball, times sure have changed, our preacher's wife leads th' choir and volunteers at th' hospital.

"*Go get 'em, Avis! Hit it outta there!* I wonder why Avis idn't married, I think he likes summer squash better than women, but it's important to really like your work. Lord, he sent that ball to th' moon! Look, Mama, right over yonder, see that man eyeballin' you? So what if he's younger, that's th' goin' thing these days, I told you blondes have more fun. Whoa, did you see that, he winked at you, well, maybe he got somethin' in his eye. *Hey, ump, pitcher's off th' plate, how thick are your glasses?*

"That red-headed kid, that's Dooley, he's sort of th' preacher's boy, he's a real slugger and he can run, too. Was that a spitball, Mama, did it look like a spitball to you? *Spitball! Spitball!* Who is that umpire, anyway, he's blind as a bat and deaf as a tater, oops, I better go down an' get in line, did you say you want relish?"

§

Ben Isaac Berman, whose family had brought him to Hope House all the way from Decatur, Illinois, was liking this ball game better than anything he'd done since coming to Mitford in July.

He liked the fresh air, the shouting, the tumult—even the heat was a *makhyeh*—though he didn't like the way his hotdog had landed in his lap, requiring two Hope House attendants to clean it up. What he couldn't figure was how chili had somehow made its way into one of his pants cuffs.

He felt like a *shlimazel* for not having better control of his limbs. But then, there was Miss Pattie sitting right next to him, who couldn't control a thought in her head, God forbid it should happen to him.

He also liked the game because it reminded him of his boyhood, which was as vivid in his recall as if he had lived it last week.

Take that boy at second base, that red-haired kid who could run like the wind. That was the kind of kid he'd been, that was the kind of kid he still was, deep down where nobody else had ever seen or ever would, not even his wife, blessed be her memory. Even he forgot about the kid living inside him, until he came out to a game like this and smelled the mountain air and heard the crack of the bat—that was when he began to feel his own legs churning, flying around to the bases and tearing up the dirt as he slid into home. . . .

§

At the bottom of the seventh inning, the score was 10–10.

"It's our bat and we've got three outs," said the rector. "We don't want any extra innings, so let's finish now and go home winners."

His shirt was sticking to him. He felt like he'd been rode hard and put up wet, as Tommy Noles used to say.

He watched as Mule Skinner stepped up to bat.

The ball came in high.

"Ball one!"

Mule swung at the next pitch and cracked it over second base into center field. The rector was amazed at Mule's speed as he sprinted to first. This game would be fodder for the Grill regulars 'til kingdom come.

After Jena Ivey made the first out of the inning, it was Pauline Barlowe's turn to bat.

She looked confident, he thought. In fact, she'd made a pretty good showing all afternoon, but had a tendency to waffle, to be strong one minute and lose it the next.

She took a couple of pitches, and slammed a hit to second base. Dadgum, a double play! But the second baseman kicked the ball, and all runners were safe.

The bases were loaded.

"Time out!" yelled Buck, striding onto the field.

"OK, Pitch," he said to Lew Boyd, "you've been a defensive star all day, I want you to use that bat and get the big hit. Or give me a fly ball to the outfield to advance the runners."

"I'm gonna give you premium unleaded on this 'un."

The first pitch came down the middle.

"Strike one!"

Lew hit the next pitch into right field, where the outfielder nailed it and threw it to third. The runners held.

Two outs.

Dooley hurried into the batter's box and scratched the loose dirt to get a strong foothold.

Buck yelled, "You've got to get on base. Can you do it?"

"I can do it!"

Poobaw Barlowe squeezed his eyes shut and prayed, *Jesus, God, and ever'body . . .*

The rector was holding his breath. Dooley had been on base every time he came to bat today. He saw the determined look on the boy's face as he waited for the pitch.

Realizing her feet were swelling, Fancy Skinner removed her high heel shoes and put them in her mother's knitting bag.

Coot Hendrick hoped to the good Lord he would not lose the twenty-five dollars he had bet on the Reds. He had borrowed it out of the sugar bowl, leaving only a few packages of NutraSweet and three dimes. He squirmed with anxiety. His mama might be old, but she could still whip his head.

Crack!

Dooley connected on a line shot into the outfield, which was hit so sharply that Father Tim stopped Mule at third.

"Way to go, buddy, way to do it, great job!" he yelled.

Dooley punched his fist into the air and pumped it, as the crowd hooted and cheered.

With two outs and the bases loaded, it was Adele Hogan's turn at bat.

"OK, Adele, let's get 'em, let's go, you can do it!" For tomorrow's services, he would sound like a bullfrog with laryngitis.

"Ball one!"

The second ball came in on the outside.

"Ball two!"

She swung at the next pitch.

"Strike one!"

The stands were going crazy. "Hey, ump," somebody yelled. "Wake up, you're missin' a great game!"

The ball came down the middle.

"Strike two!"

Two balls, two strikes. Adele stooped down, grabbed some dirt and rubbed it in her hands, then took the bat and gripped it hard. The rector thought he could see white knuckles as she rocked slightly on her feet and watched the pitch.

She caught the ball on the inside of her bat, away from the heavy part, sending it into short left center field.

Nobody called for the ball.

The outfielders all moved at once, collided, and stumbled over each other as the ball fell in. Adele Hogan ran for her life and reached first base as Mule scored.

The game was over.

The crowd was wild.

The score was 11–10.

Ray Cunningham huffed to the field with the mayor's ball and asked Adele to sign it. Unable to restrain himself, he pounded her on the back and gave her a big hug, wondering how in the world J. C. Hogan had ever gotten so lucky.

Ben Isaac Berman pulled himself up on his aluminum walker and waved to the red-haired kid on the field. He squinted into the sun, almost certain that the boy waved back.

The *Muse* editor, who had been sitting under a shade tree, panted to first base and cranked off a roll of Tri-X. All the frames featured his wife, who, as far as he was concerned, looked dynamite even with sweat running down her face. He wondered something that had never occurred to him before; he wondered how he'd ever gotten so lucky, and decided he would tell her that very thing—tonight.

Well, maybe tomorrow.

Soon, anyway.

CHAPTER FIFTEEN

Day into Night

"You know how I respect your judgment, I don't fight you on much."

"That's true, you don't."

Ron Malcolm had come to the rectory, and they'd taken refuge behind the closed door of the study.

His senior warden looked pained, but firm. "The time to sit on this thing is over. We've got to make a decision, and the only decision to make is to sell it to Miami Development. You know why, I know why. We can't afford to do otherwise."

Father Tim sat back in the chair. He was exhausted from the ordeal of it, from the conflict between hard-nosed reality and his own intuitions, however vague. He had prayed, he had stalled, he had wrestled, he had hoped—all the avenues open to most mortals—and like it or not, there was nothing else he could do.

"All right," he said.

At the front door, they shook hands on what had been agreed, and Ron went down the walk to his car.

The rector stood there, looking through the screen into the dusk. Treat it kindly. . . .

"Now, Miss Sadie," he said aloud, "don't be wagging your cane at me. I did the best I could."

§

He was running late for the meeting, having just fled one at First Baptist, and stopped at the water fountain in the parish hall corridor.

Around the bend to the right, he heard footsteps on the tile floor, and someone talking.

"The old woman was lucky to die a natural death, the furnace in that dump could have blown her head off."

Ingrid Swenson. Then he heard the murmured assent of her nail-biting crony, and their mutual laughter as they passed through the door into the parish hall.

§

The voices around the table droned on. He tried to pay attention, but couldn't. It was all done but the signing of the contract. There was hardly any reason for him to be here.

His gaze roamed the assembly. Buddy Benfield was grinning from ear to ear. Ron Malcolm was facing down Ingrid Swenson in a last contest of wills concerning the crumbling pavement of the Fernbank driveway. Mamie Gordon, who had a new job at the Collar Button, was looking anxiously at her watch. Sandra Harris was trying to figure how she could pop outside for a smoke. Clarence Daly was trooping in with a tray of cups and a pot of coffee.

The phone rang in the parish kitchen, but no one moved to answer it.

Sandra drummed her nails on the table, impatient. "We look forward to seeing Fernbank turned into a spa," she said to Ingrid, "but I hope you don't try to push body wraps and mud, I don't think anybody around here would go for that."

The phone continued to ring.

"So," said Ron, "even though our attorneys have gone over the contract thoroughly, let's take one last look before we sign, to the advantage of all concerned."

"I can't imagine what purpose that will serve."

Ron smiled. "Won't take but a couple of minutes."

The phone persisted.

"Here you go," said Clarence, setting cups before Ingrid and her associate. "Fresh out of th' pot."

"Oh, for Pete's *sake*," said Sandra, "why doesn't somebody answer the phone?"

Nobody moved.

"Who would let a phone ring like that, anyway?" Scowling, she marched to the kitchen.

Ron glanced at Ingrid. "I've struck through and initialed your clause about the driveway repairs being a responsibility of Lord's Chapel."

She gave him a cold look and pushed the coffee away.

"Father! It's Andrew Gregory on the phone!"

"Tell him—"

"He's calling all the way from Italy. Says it's *important*!"

"Excuse me," he said, leaving the table.

Sandra handed him the receiver with a look of rekindled interest in the morning's proceedings. The most exotic call she'd ever had was from Billings, Montana.

"Andrew?"

"Father, Emma told me I could find you in the parish hall. Sorry to disturb you, but something . . . terribly important has just happened. Is the Fernbank property still available?"

"Well . . . " For about five minutes, maximum.

"I'd like to make an offer. I'll wire earnest money at once."

Had he heard right? Was he dreaming this?

"Two hundred and ninety-five thousand, Father." Andrew took a deep breath. "As is."

He felt a sudden, intense warmth throughout his body, as if he were melting in a spring thaw.

"Andrew?"

"Yes?"

"Consider it done!"

§

He didn't think he'd ever confess to anyone, not even his wife, how thrilled he'd been to see the look on Ingrid Swenson's face.

No. *Ecstatic* was the word. He'd been forced to restrain himself from leaping into the air, clicking his heels together, and whooping.

Upon being told that Fernbank would in fact be sold, but not to Miami Development, Ingrid Swenson had used language that, as far as he knew, had never been spoken on the grounds of Lord's Chapel. Mamie Gordon had actually put her hands over her ears, her mouth forming a perfect O.

When he saw Andrew, he would kiss his ring, the very cuff of his trousers! He would sweep his chimney, wash his windows, put him at the head of the Christmas parade in Tommy Ledbetter's yellow Mustang convertible . . . the possibilities for thanking Andrew Gregory were unlimited.

Hallelujah!

"I'm jealous," said his wife, rejoicing with him.

"Whatever for?"

"You weren't this happy on our wedding day!"

"How quickly you forget. Let's dance!"

"But there's no music."

"No problem!" he said, doing a jig step. "I'll hum!"

§

Happy Endings was having a twenty-percent-off sale on any book title starting with A, to commemorate August.

"What about Jane Austen, can I get twenty percent off?" asked Hessie Mayhew, who didn't have time to read a book in the first place.

"Sorry, no authors starting with A, just book titles," said Hope Winchester.

He staggered to the counter with *A Guide to Fragrance in the Garden, Andersonville: Men and Myth* (Walter's Christmas present), *A Reunion of Trees, A Grief Observed, Alone* by Admiral Byrd, *Anchor Book of Latin Quotations,* and *A Child's Garden of Verses.*

"A very perspicacious selection!" said Hope.

"Thank you. My wife will not be thrilled, however, as we have no place to put them."

"As long as you have any floor space at all, you have room for books! Just make two stacks of books the same height, place them three or four feet apart, lay a board across them, and repeat. Violà! Bookshelves!"

"I'll be darned."

He nearly always learned something new on Main Street.

§

The nave of Lord's Chapel became a deep chiaroscuro shadow as dusk settled over Mitford. Candles burned on the sills of the stained-glass windows to light the way of the remnant who came for the evening worship on Thursday, scheduled unexpectedly by the rector.

Winnie Ivey had donated tarts and cookies for a bit of refreshment afterward, and the rector's wife had made pitchers of lemonade from scratch, not frozen. Hearing of this, Uncle Billy and Miss Rose Watson, not much used to being out after dark, arrived in good spirits.

Esther Bolick, weary in every bone, trudged down the aisle with Gene to what had long ago become their pew on the gospel side. Several Bane volunteers, already feeling the numbing effects of pulling together the largest fund-raiser in the diocese, slipped in quietly, glad for the peace, for the sweetness of every shadow, and for the familiar, mingled smells of incense and flowers, lemon wax and burning wick.

Most of the vestry turned out, some with the lingering apprehension that they'd robbed Mitford of a thriving new business, others completely satisfied with a job well done.

Hope Winchester, invited by the rector and deeply relieved that the A sale was successful, stood inside the door and looked around awkwardly. She found it daunting to be here, since she hadn't been raised in church, but Father Tim was one of their good customers and never pushy about God, so she figured she had nothing to lose.

She slid into the rear pew, in case she needed to make a quick exit, and lowered her head at once. It was a perfect time to think about the S sale, coming in September, and how they ought to feature *Sea of Grass* by Conrad Richter, which nobody ever seemed to know about, but certainly should.

The *Muse* editor and his wife, Adele, slid into the rear pew across the aisle, and wondered what they would do when everybody got down on their knees. They both had Baptist backgrounds and felt deeply that kneeling in public, even if it was in church, was too in-your-face, like those people who prayed loud enough for everybody in the temple to hear.

Sophia Burton, who had seen the rector on the street that morning, had been glad to come and bring Liza, glad to get away from the little house with the TV set she knew she should turn off sometimes, but couldn't, glad to get away from thinking about her job at the canning plant, and the supervisor who made her do things nobody else had to do. Not wanting her own church, which was First Baptist, to think she was defecting, she had invited a member of her Sunday School class so it would look more like a social outing than something religious.

Farther forward on the gospel side, Lace Turner sat with Olivia and Hoppy Harper, and Nurse Kennedy, who had been at the hospital long before Dr. Harper arrived and was known to be the glue that held the place together.

And there, noted the rector, as he stood waiting at the rear of the nave, were his own, Cynthia and Dooley, and next to them, Pauline and Jessie and Poo and . . . amazing! Buck Leeper.

The rector might have come to the church alone and given thanks on his knees in the empty nave. But he'd delighted in inviting one and all to a service that would express his own private thanksgiving—for the outcome of Fernbank, for Jessie, for this life, for so much.

He came briskly down the aisle in his robe, and, in front of the steps to the altar, turned eagerly to face his people.

"Grace to you and peace from God our Father and from the Lord Jesus Christ!" he quoted from Philippians.

"I will bless the Lord who gives me counsel," he said with the psalmist, "my heart teaches me, night after night. I have set the Lord always before me; because He is at my right hand, I shall not fall."

He spoke the ancient words of the sheep farmer, Amos: "Seek Him who made the Pleiades and Orion, and turns deep darkness into the morning, and darkens the day into night; who calls for the waters of the sea and pours them out upon the surface of the earth: the Lord is His name!"

There it was, the smile he was seeking from his wife. And lo, not one but two, because Dooley was giving him a grin into the bargain.

"Dear friends in Christ, here in the presence of Almighty God, let us kneel in silence, and with patient and obedient hearts confess our sins, so that we may obtain forgiveness by His infinite goodness and mercy."

Here it comes, thought Adele Hogan, who, astonishing herself, slid off the worn oak pew onto the kneeler.

Hope Winchester couldn't do it; she was as frozen as a mullet, and felt her heart pounding like she'd drunk a gallon of coffee. Her mouth felt dry, too. Maybe she'd leave, who would notice anyway, with their heads bowed, but the thing was, there was always somebody who probably wasn't keeping his eyes closed, and would see her dart away like a convict. . . .

"Most merciful God," Esther Bolick prayed aloud and in unison with the others from the Book of Common Prayer, "we confess that we have sinned against You in thought, word, and deed . . . "

She felt the words enter her aching bones like balm.

" . . . by what we have done," prayed Gene, "and by what we have left undone."

"We have not loved You with our whole heart," intoned Uncle Billy Watson, squinting through a magnifying glass to see the words in the prayer book, "we have not loved our neighbors as ourselves."

He found the words of the prayer beautiful. They made him feel hopeful and closer to the Lord, and maybe it was true that he hadn't always done right by his neighbors, but he would try to do better, he would start before he hit the street this very night. He quickly offered a silent thanks that somebody would be driving them home afterward, since it was pitch-dark out there, and still hot as a depot stove into the bargain.

"We are truly sorry and we humbly repent," prayed Pauline Barlowe, unable to keep the tears back, not wanting to look at the big, powerful man beside her. Though plainly reluctant to be there, he nonetheless held the hand of her daughter, who was sucking her thumb and gazing at the motion of the ceiling fans.

"For the sake of Your Son Jesus Christ, have mercy on us and forgive us," prayed Cynthia Kavanagh, amazed all over again at how she'd come to be kneeling in this place, and hoping that the stress she'd recently seen in her husband was past, and that this service would mark the beginning of renewal and refreshment.

" . . . that we may delight in Your will, and walk in Your ways," prayed Sophia Burton, wishing with all her heart that she could do that very thing every day of her life, really do it and not just pray it— but then, maybe she could, she was beginning to feel like she could . . . maybe.

" . . . to the glory of Your Name!" prayed the rector, feeling his spirit moved toward all who had gathered in this place.

"Amen!" they said in unison.

§

It wasn't that it didn't trouble him; in fact, it made him a little crazy whenever the thought crossed his mind. But what could he do? What could he prove?

He couldn't talk about it around town—it would seem like the worst sort of rumor-mongering and political meddling; he certainly wouldn't mention it at the Grill, and didn't think it wise to tell his wife, either. The new Violet book was wearing on her, and why clutter her mind with what appeared to be a very nasty piece of business?

Omer had sworn he'd keep quiet, at least for the time being. What could talk like that do, after all, except give his sister-in-law a stroke? And who could prove anything, anyway?

The rector took some comfort in the fact that election day was more than a couple of months away. Surely by that time Mack would show his hand, somebody would stumble, something . . .

§

The attic job was the current local recreation for those who had nothing better to do. Uncle Billy shambled down the street on his cane and gave all manner of directions to the crew, occasionally sharing the lunches they carried in bags from home or raced to the highway to pick up from Hardee's. So far, he had wheedled french fries from two stonecutters and a joiner.

Coot Hendrick pulled his rusted pickup truck to the curb every morning around eleven, scooted over to the passenger side, rolled the window down, and watched the whole show in the privacy and comfort of his vehicle. While the crew mixed mortar, sawed lumber, and in general tore up large expanses of grass and two perennial beds, he ate Nabs, shucked peanuts, and drank Cheerwine until three o'clock. He then drove to Lew Boyd's Esso, where he played checkers until five, after which he went home to his elderly mother and fixed her supper, usually a small cake of cornbread accompanied by a bowl of lettuce and onions, which he wilted with a blast of sizzling bacon grease and cider vinegar.

Beneath the attic, yet another church project was going at a trot.

While the preschool crowd gave new life to the old verger's quarters, the kindergarten had stationed itself in the largest of the Sunday School rooms, where all manner of shrieking, cackling, giggling, and wailing could be heard emanating from its walls.

The rector loved walking into a room that was completely alien to the adult world—filled with fat plastic tricycles and huge vinyl balls that could be knocked around without smashing the windows. He especially liked the rocking horses, which, upon each visit, were going at a frantic pace with astonished babies hanging on for dear life.

Sissy and Sassy had taken to the fray like fish to water. After a full day of howling for their mother, they had settled down to a new life and hardly noticed the guilt-stricken Puny when he went with her to see them at lunchtime.

"Sassy, it's Mama, come to Mama, *please!*" Sassy turned her head and chewed on a string of rubber clowns, recently chewed by a toddler who had poured a cup of juice on his head.

Sissy pulled up on a wooden table and tottered toward him at full throttle. "Ba!" she shouted. "Ba!"

"Ba, yourself!" He fell to his knees and held out his arms. "Come to granpaw, you little punkinhead!"

"I didn't know he was a granpaw," said Marsha Hunt, who was in charge of the mayhem.

Puny looked suddenly cheerful. "Oh, yes!" she declared. "And it's the best thing that ever happened to him!"

§

After the eleven o'clock, Mack Stroupe positioned himself a couple of yards to the left of the rector and pumped hands enthusiastically as the crowd flowed through the door. Anyone driving by, thought Father Tim, wouldn't have known which was the priest if one of them hadn't worn vestments.

As she tallied the collection on Monday morning, Emma couldn't wait to tell him:

Mack Stroupe had dropped a thousand bucks in the plate.

§

Rain. Torrents of rain. Rain that washed driveways, devastated what was left of the gardens, and hammered its way through roofs all over Mitford. The little yellow house had its first known leak, which Buck fixed by climbing around on the slate in a late afternoon downpour.

The rector drove up to check the leak problem at Fernbank and arrived in the nick of time. The turkey roaster and other assorted pots and pans were only moments before overflowing. He dutifully dumped each potful down the toilet, giving Fernbank a free flush, an economy which Miss Sadie had often employed.

He had tried to be completely candid with Andrew in a subsequent phone conversation, giving him the hair-raising truth about everything from roof to furnace. Oddly, Andrew had seemed jubilant about the whole prospect.

The wire for the earnest money had arrived at the bank and was deposited, the papers were being drawn up, and all was on go. Andrew would return to Mitford in a few weeks, anxious to begin work on the house before winter.

Father Tim stood in the vast, empty kitchen, looking out to sheets of rain lashing the windows. Even on a day like this, he hadn't felt so good about Fernbank in a very long time.

§

Everywhere he went, he made known that he was on the incumbent's side—without, he hoped, seeming preachy. Local politics was a fine line to walk for anybody, much less clergy.

What else could he do?

"You've already *done*!" said Cynthia. "An air show with banners and barrel rolls!"

"Yesterday's barrel rolls can't compete with today's barbecue."

"You've got a point there," she said.

He watched as his wife furrowed her brow, looking thoughtful. Maybe *she'd* be able to come up with something.

§

"Tell me how things are, Betty."

He'd gone to sit on the porch with Betty Craig, who heaved a sigh at his question.

"Well, Father, Jessie wets the bed and has awful bad dreams."

"I'm sorry, but not surprised."

"And poor Pauline, she's just tryin' ever' whichaway to be a good mama, but I don't think anybody ever showed her how."

"I'm hoping preschool will help Jessie. I doubt if she's been with other children very much."

"She came home cryin' her heart out yesterday, sayin' she didn't want to go back. But of course she seemed all right about it this morning when I took her to day care at Lord's Chapel. I take her, you know, because Pauline goes to work so early."

"Can you handle all this crowd in your house?"

"Oh, yes! It's good to have a crowd, but I don't think we could stuff another one in, unless they set on their fist and lean back on their thumb. You won't be . . . sendin' any more?"

"I believe Pauline will be looking for a little house soon."

Betty was quiet, rocking. "You know, Mr. Leeper's coming around."

"What do you think of that?" he asked, trusting her judgment.

"Oh, I like Mr. Leeper, and he's good to th' children, too. But with her tryin' to stay off alcohol . . . and I hear he's still drinkin' some . . . I don't know if it's the best thing."

He'd thought the same, but hadn't wanted to admit it to himself.

§

"I'd like to see," he said, feeling shy as a schoolboy.

"Are you sure?" she asked.

"Of course! I've been wanting to do it for weeks."

They trooped through the hedge to her workroom, where she showed him the growing stack of large watercolor illustrations for *Violet Goes Back to School.* He sat on her minuscule love seat and she displayed the results of her labors, revealing at the same time a shyness of her own.

He was dazzled by his wife's gift. It knocked his socks off. "It's wonderful, absolutely wonderful. The best yet!"

"Thank you! That means so much."

"And Violet—in this one, she looks so, what shall I say? Happy!"

"Yes! You see, Violet likes going to school."

"Aha."

"Which reminds me—I've been wanting to tell you something, dearest."

"Tell me," he said, loving the earnest look of her in a bandanna and denim jumper.

"I'll be traveling for several weeks after the book is released, going to schools and libraries. I know how you feel about that."

He hated it, actually. He remembered how pathetically lost he felt when she traveled a couple of times last year. Worse, he'd gotten the most bizarre notions—that she might miss the bridge and drive into the river, or be mugged in the school parking lot, or that her crankcase was leaking oil. And what if she were stranded on the side of the road? Did she realize that people had been murdered doing that very thing?

He said what he always said. "Do you have to?"

And she said what she always said. "Yes."

§

Ron removed his cap and jacket and shook the rain onto the rug at the office door.

"Feast or famine," he said. "Drought or flood."

"Are you talking about life or the weather?" queried Father Tim.

"Life *and* the weather," said Ron. "We're currently seeing a flood of real estate activity."

"Now what?" He was sick of real estate activity.

"We've got a prospective buyer for the rectory."

His blood chilled. "Already?"

Ron sat on the visitor's bench. "They're very interested, and said they'd like to see it next week."

"Who is they?" Why did he feel so defensive, even angry?

"H. Tide. Out of Orlando."

"That's who's looking at Sweet Stuff." And if that's who's looking at Sweet Stuff, then Mack Stroupe was involved. Hadn't Mack taken credit in the newspaper article for sending Winnie a realtor who was, in fact, H. Tide?

He'd never been able to bear the brunt of bad news in his head, in his intellect; he felt it instead in his body—in his chest, in his stomach, in his throat.

"Sorry," said Ron, seeing the look on his face. "If they want it right away, we'll do all we can to help you find whatever situation you need. Ideally, we'll try to work something out that lets you stay in the rectory 'til you retire."

"You'll *try* to work something out?"

"Well . . . " Ron looked embarrassed and uneasy.

"Keep me posted," he said, hearing the cold anger in his voice. He hadn't meant to sound that way, but he couldn't help it, couldn't mask it.

He felt strangely frightened and alone.

§

Walking home, he concluded that he wouldn't mention this to Cynthia, not until he had to. After all, nothing was written in stone.

Here was yet another circumstance he'd be withholding from his wife, and he knew instinctively this wasn't a good tactic—the most fundamental counseling book would tell him that.

Disrupting the household . . . where would they go? Buck had a crew starting next door in September, in only a couple of weeks, and Cynthia would be moving her drawing board and library into his study. He had never liked change, and here he was, facing the biggest change of his life, combined with a possible change of address at the most inconvenient time imaginable.

His retirement had all looked so smooth, so easy, so . . . reviving when he made the decision last year. Now it looked as if he could be set out on the sidewalk like so much rubbish.

But he was being hasty. Premature. He was overreacting.

He sucked in a draught of fresh air and turned the corner onto Wisteria. He dreaded facing Cynthia Kavanagh, who could look in his eyes and know instantly that something was wrong.

For two cents, he'd get in the car and drive.

And keep going.

CHAPTER SIXTEEN

Bookends

Going at a clip toward the Grill, they met Uncle Billy tottering home-ward from the construction site at Lord's Chapel.

"I'll be et f'r a tater if y'r boy ain't growed a foot!"

Dooley cackled, looking at his feet. "Where's it at?"

The rector noted that Dooley was slipping back into the vernacu-lar, which, frankly, he had rather missed. Any wild departure from the King's English, of course, would be remedied just ten days hence. Blast, he hated the thought of driving Dooley to Virginia and de-positing him in that place, even if it was helping him learn and grow and expand his horizons.

Percy turned from the grill and beamed. "Lookit th' big ball player. You ought t' be traded to th' Yankees and that's a fact."

"Dodgers," said Dooley, laughing again.

The rector had seen more laughter in his boy this summer than ever before. And why not? He had a steady paycheck, a girl who was crazy about him, a best friend, a family that was pulling itself to-gether, and, generally, a swarm of people who loved him. Not to mention, of course, an education that was annually the cost of a new car—with leather and airbags.

"Hey, buddyroe," said J.C., cracking one of his biennial grins.

"Hey," said Dooley, sliding into the rear booth. This was his first time hanging with these old guys, and he wasn't too sure about it. He could have been scarfing down a pizza with Tommy over on the highway.

"Hey, slugger!" said Mule. "Let's see that arm!"

Dooley flexed the muscle in his upper right arm, and everybody helped themselves to squeezing it.

"A rock," said J.C., approving.

Mule nodded soberly.

"Killer!" said the rector.

J.C. pulled out a handkerchief and mopped his face. "I'll treat!"

"There it is again," said Mule. "The feelin' I'm goin' deaf as a doorknob."

"I mean I'll treat Dooley, not th' whole bloomin' booth."

"You better have some deep pockets if you're feeding Dooley Barlowe," said Father Tim, as proud as if the boy had an appetite for Aristotle.

"I'll have a large Coke, large fries, and two hotdogs all th' way," announced the editor's guest.

"All th' way?" Mule raised his eyebrows. "I thought you had a girlfriend, you don't want to be eatin' onions."

"Don't listen to these turkeys," said J.C., "they tried to run my . . . my, ah . . . thing with Adele and like to ruined my life. Anything you want to know about women, you ask me."

Mule nearly fell out of the booth laughing.

"What's goin' on over here?" asked Velma, who couldn't bear to hear laughter unless she knew what it was about.

"You don't want to know," said Father Tim.

"I certainly do want to know!" She put her hands on her hips and squinted at them over her glasses.

"Oh, shoot," said Mule. "Can't a bunch of men have a little joke without women wantin' to know what it's about?"

"No," said Velma. "So what's it about?"

"We're teachin' Dooley about the opposite sex," said Mule.

"Oh, Lord, help!" Velma looked thoroughly disgusted.

"I wish y'all would quit," said Dooley. "I don't need to know anything about girls, I already know it."

"See?" said Velma. "Now, let 'im alone. Dooley, if you ever want to know anything about th' opposite sex, you come and ask me or Percy, you hear? We'll tell you th' blessed truth."

"Dadgum!" Mule covered his face with his hands. "He'll be glad to get back to school after listenin' to this mess. . . . "

"Right!" said Dooley.

§

Ron Malcolm called to say that he'd be at the rectory Wednesday at noon, with the people from H. Tide.

Father Tim decided he'd be in the piney woods, as far from that miserable experience as he could get.

When he finally got the nerve to tell Cynthia, she looked at him blankly.

"Why are they showing it now if they're not going to sell it until we move?"

"The truth is, if they get the right offer and the buyer's anxious to move in, they'll sell it now and find us something. . . . "

He could tell she didn't believe her ears. "Find us something . . . ?"

He looked away. "The real estate scene in Mitford, as you know, is historically sluggish. The vestry feels they can't afford to pass up the offer, if it's right. People have known for two or three years that it would be on the market, and nobody's spoken up for it."

"The real estate market is historically sluggish because development in Mitford goes at a snail's pace." She turned away, and he saw a muscle moving in her cheek. "It's almost enough to make me vote for Mack Stroupe."

"I can't believe you said that."

"I was only kidding, for Pete's sake, you don't have to bite my head off."

"I didn't bite your head off."

"You most certainly did. And furthermore, your nerves stay ab-

solutely frazzled these days. You tote every barge and lift every bale in
Mitford, with nothing left over for yourself. And now you tell me we
could be run out of our home, thanks to a parish you have faithfully
served for sixteen years? If that's the way your vestry thinks, Timothy,
then I would ask you to do me the favor of lining them up, one by
one, and enjoining them to bend over. I will then go down the row
and give every distinguished member exactly what they deserve,
which is, need I say it, a good, swift kick!"

She turned and left the study, and he heard her charging up the
stairs. Their bedroom door, which was rarely closed, slammed.

He felt as if he'd been dashed with ice water. All the feelings he'd
lately had, the heaviness on his chest, the pounding of blood in his
temples, the wrenching in his stomach . . . all rushed in again, except
worse.

He sat at the kitchen table, stricken. They'd never before had
words like that. They were both overworked, overstressed, and who
wanted to be told they might be dumped on the street?

He was grieved that this was even a consideration by his own
church officers.

Also, he was humiliated for Ron Malcolm, one of the finest men
he'd ever known, and a personal friend into the bargain. Ron Malcolm was behaving like . . . like Ed Coffey, doing whatever it took,
and all because of money.

Money!

He was glad he didn't have enough money to matter, glad he'd
given most of it away in this fleeting life. Dear God, to see what some
people would do for a dollar was enough to make him call his broker
and have the whole lot transferred to the coffers of Children's Hospital.

What was the amount, anyway, that was left of his mother's estate?
A hundred and forty thousand or so, which he'd been growing for
years. Even though he'd dipped into it heavily every time the Children's Hospital had a need, smart investing had maintained most of
the original two hundred thousand.

Actually, it hadn't been smart investing, it had been safe investing.
He was as timid as a hare when it came to flinging assets around. He

wished he'd asked Miss Sadie her investing strategies. There were a thousand things he'd thought of asking after she died, and now it was too late to find out how she'd come up with more than a million bucks for Dooley, even after spending five million on Hope House.

Should he go upstairs and talk to Cynthia? What would he say?

He couldn't remember feeling so weary, so . . . He searched for the word that would express how he felt, but couldn't find it.

He didn't have the energy to say he was sorry. Actually, he didn't know if he was sorry. What had he said, after all? He couldn't remember, but it all had something to do with Mack Stroupe.

Blast Mack Stroupe to the lowest regions of the earth. He was sick of Mack Stroupe.

§

So what if he shouldn't have a napoleon? Hadn't he waited more than a decade to eat a measly cheeseburger the other day?

He was no ascetic living in the desert, he was a busy, active clergyman in need of proper nourishment.

He did the glucometer check and marched to Winnie Ivey's, blowing past several people who greeted him, but to whom he merely lifted a hand. They stared after him, dumbfounded. They'd never seen the local priest scowling like that. It was completely unlike him.

The bell on the Sweet Stuff door jingled, which turned the heads of four customers sitting at a table. It was fifth- and sixth-grade teachers from Mitford School, having tea. He could tell at once they wanted to talk, and he turned to leave.

"Father?" said Winnie, coming through the curtains behind the bake cases. "Can you stay a minute?"

Good heavens, Winnie Ivey looked as glum and pressed to the wall as he felt. What was wrong with people these days?

She set out another pot of hot water for the teachers, who were peering at him oddly, and caught his sleeve. "I need to talk to you about something," she said, whispering.

They went to the kitchen, which, as always, smelled like a child's version of paradise—cinnamon, rising dough, baking cookies. Somebody should put the aroma in an aerosol container. It was so soothing that he immediately felt more relaxed.

"You look terrible," she said.

"Oh, well." If Winnie Ivey didn't tell him so, Emma Newland certainly would, or, for that matter, any number of others.

"Father, the most awful thing . . . "

If it wasn't one awful thing these days, it was two.

"That real estate company wants to buy my business."

"They do?"

"And I can't get a minute's peace about selling it. After runnin' ads and prayin' my head off, here's my big chance and I feel awful about it."

"If you've prayed and there's no peace about a decision, then wait. That's one rule I stick with."

"But they want to buy it right away."

"Will they give you your asking price?"

"Not exactly. Mr. Skinner believes it's worth seventy-five thousand, but I'm asking sixty, and they want to give me forty-five."

"Forty-five thousand for twenty years' work," he said, musing. "That's not much more than two thousand a year."

"Oh," she said, stricken.

He was feeling worse by the minute. Any longing for a napoleon had flown out the window.

"I'd really like your advice, Father, I trust what you say."

He didn't like being anyone's Providence, but she'd asked for help and he'd give her his best shot. He said what he was becoming known for saying in all real estate matters these days.

"Tell them you'd like to think about it for thirty days."

She looked alarmed. "I don't believe they'd like that."

"They probably wouldn't. That's true."

"And I might not get another offer."

"That's true, too. However, consider this: You're the only game in town. There's not another business currently for sale on Main Street, and this is highly desirable property. I think you're holding the ace."

She hugged herself, furrowing her brow and thinking. "Well, I *might* do that. But . . . it's risky."

He wouldn't tell her that risk had a certain adrenaline.

§

Didn't he have a bishop? An advocate? He wasn't hanging out there in space, all alone. Stuart Cullen would go to bat for him. That's what bishops were for, wasn't it?

But Stuart wasn't in the office and wouldn't be in for two long weeks, as his wife, according to Stuart's secretary, had forced the bishop to go away to—she wasn't sure where, but she thought it was southern France, or at least someplace where they spoke another language and wore bikinis on the beach.

ⴼ

Dooley, whose job had ended day before yesterday, showed up at the church office with a letter in his hand.

He sat on the visitor's bench and examined his tennis shoes, whistled, jiggled his leg, and stared into space while the rector opened it and read:

My dearest husband,

I regret that I snapped at you this morning. You snapped, I snapped. And for what? As you left, looking hurt, I wanted to run after you and hold you, but I could not move. I stood upstairs on the landing and moped at the window like a schoolgirl, watching as you went along the sidewalk.

I saw you stop for a moment and look around, as if you wanted to turn back. You seemed forlorn, and I was overcome with sorrow for anything I might ever do to give you pain. My darling Timothy, who means all the world to me—forgive me.

It was the slightest thing between us, something that would hardly matter to anyone else, I think. We are both so sensitive, so alike in that region of the heart which fears rejection and resists chastisement.

As I looked down upon you, I received your hurt as my own, and so have had a double measure all these hours.

Hurry home, dearest husband!

Come and kiss me and let us hold one another in that way which God has set aside for us. You are precious to me, more than breath.

Ever thine,
Cynthia
(still your bookend?)

PS *I know it is a pitiable gesture, but I shall roast something savoury for your supper and make your favorite oven-browned potatoes.*

Truce?

Dooley looked at the ceiling, got up, peered out the window, sat down again, then found some gum on the sole of his left shoe and painstakingly peeled it off. "You an' Cynthia had a fuss?"

"Yes."

"I understand."

"You do?" He was thrilled to hear those words out of Dooley Barlowe. *I understand.* A mature thing for anyone, much less a fourteen-year-old boy, to utter.

"Jenny and I had a fuss. She blamed me for somethin' I didn't do."

"Aha."

"She said I paid too much attention to Lace Turner the other day."

"No kidding. . . ."

"I didn't."

"I'm sure."

"Lace wanted to talk about American history, is all, and I talked back." He shrugged.

"Right. What did you talk about—I mean, concerning American history?"

"About going west in a wagon train. I'd like to do that. Lace said she'd like to." His freckles were showing. "That's all."

"I'm amazed every day," said the rector, "how people can misunderstand each other about the simplest things."

"Lace is writing a story about going west on a wagon train from Springfield, Illinois, where the Donner party started out. In her story, the leader gets killed and a woman has to lead the train."

"Wow."

"She got A's for her stories last year."

"Well done."

"She quit wearin' that stupid hat."

"I noticed."

"So, look, I don't have all day. Are you goin' to write Cynthia back?"

"You bet."

"I've got to go see Poo and Jessie. You goin' to type or write by hand?"

"Type. I'll hurry."

He took the cover off the Royal manual and rolled in a sheet of paper.

Bookend—
 dooley has delivered your letter and is waiting for me to respond.
ii have suffered, you have suffered.
 Enough!
You are dear to me beyond measure. That God allowed us to have thiis union at all stuns me daily/
 "Bright star, would I were stedfast as thou art—"
love, timothy—who, barely two years ago, you may recall, vowed to cherish you always, no matter what
 Truce.
ps. ii will gladly wash the dishes and barnabas will dry.

      ❦

He had to do something for Esther.

More billboards on the highway wouldn't cut it. Esther's campaign needed one-on-one, it needed looking into people's eyes and talking about her record. It needed . . . a coffee in someone's home.

But not in his home. No, indeed. For a priest to dip his spoon into mayoral coffee was not politically correct. He would have to talk someone else into doing it.

Esther Bolick laughed in his face. "Are you kidding me?" she said. He should have known better than to call Esther. What a dumb notion; he felt like an idiot. So why did he pick up the phone and call Hessie?

"You must have the wrong number," said Hessie Mayhew, and hung up.

He called the president of ECW, thinking she might be interested in having the mayor do a program at the next monthly meeting.

"She did a program last year," said Erlene Douglas, "and we never repeat a speaker unless it's the bishop or a bigwig."

"Put a sign in your window," he implored Percy, "one of those that says, 'We're stickin' with Esther.'"

"No way," said Percy. "I run a business. I'm not campaignin' for anybody. Let 'em tough it out whichever way they can."

"Olivia," he said in his best pulpit voice, "I was wondering if . . ."

But Olivia, Hoppy, and Lace were going to the coast for the last couple of days before school started, which, except for their honeymoon, would be the first vacation her husband had had in ten years.

He sat staring at his office bookshelves, drumming his fingers on the desk. Maybe Esther could visit the police station and hand around donuts one morning. Better still, what about giving out balloons at Hattie Cloer's market on the highway? He was running on fumes with this thing.

He called Esther's office, noting that she sounded depressed.

"I don't know," she said, sighing heavily. "Who needs this aggravation? Th' low-down egg sucker has been campaignin' practically since Easter, it's more politics than I can stomach."

"But you can't give up now!"

"Who says I can't?" demanded the mayor.

§

"Mr. Tim!"

On his livermush delivery to Betty Craig's, Jessie met him at the door, carrying a coloring book. "Look!" she said, holding it up for his close inspection.

"Outstanding!" he said squatting down.

"Them's camels. Camels stores water in their humps."

"Right. Amazing!"

"Can I sit on your lap?"

"Absolutely."

He set the bag of livermush down and sought out the slipcovered armchair in the living room. Jessie crawled into his lap and clung to him, sucking her thumb.

"I thought you were going to try and quit sucking your thumb," he said, cradling her in his arm.

"Betty put pepper on it, but I washed it off."

He didn't know much about thumb-sucking, but he knew the cure. It was the thing that cured every other ill in this world, and of which there was far too little in general supply.

§

After talking with Pauline, he put another list, however brief, on Emma's desk.

But this time, Emma found nothing. Nothing at all.

§

The realtors from Orlando had made an offer. A hundred and five thousand, cash. Which was, to a penny, the asking price.

He hadn't heard of anybody meeting an asking price lately.

When he spoke to Ron about it, he felt as if his jaws were frozen, or partially wired shut. "When do they want occupancy?"

"October fifteenth."

"Who's buying it?"

"They didn't specify. Whoever it is may be renting it."

"I'd like you to wait on this."

"They made it clear they don't want to drag their feet. They were ready to shell out the cash today, but I won't sign anything of course, 'til I run all this by the vestry."

"I'm going to ask you to do something."

"You know I want to help, Father."

Did he know that? "I want you to wait on this for ten days. Don't do anything for ten days." He didn't think his now-customary thirty days would wash, but he had to have some time to adjust to this. The thought of the deal being done immediately made him feel trapped, helpless.

Ron pulled at his chin. "They've already said they want me to get back to them by the end of the week. If we make them wait, they could withdraw the offer."

"Look. If you think we feel good about being swept out of our house like this, you've got another think coming. I've got to tell you that I don't appreciate it, and if you have in mind some early retirement plan I don't know about, then let's lay the cards on the table."

His heart wasn't pounding, his brow wasn't perspiring. He was as cool as a cucumber.

Ron tried to smile, but couldn't. "Early retirement? Father, we'd keep you forever, if you'd let us. Retirement wasn't our idea, it was yours."

"And it's my idea to have ten days to digest all this. Sixteen years in this parish has earned me ten days." Period.

He wasn't taking no for an answer, and Ron knew it.

§

"Father! Stop! Wait!"

It was Winnie Ivey in her apron, running up Main Street behind him.

"I saw you pass, but I was on th' phone. Oh, you won't believe this! You won't believe it!"

"I'll believe it!" he said, laughing at her excitement.

"I won that cruise! I won it! A cruise to a whole bunch of islands!"

"Hallelujah!" he said, taking her hands as she jumped up and down. Her bandanna slipped back from her forehead, and graying curls sprung loose.

"I've never won anything, not even a stuffed animal in a shootin' gallery!"

"First time for everything!" he said, rejoicing with her.

"Golden Band said I could go anytime, starting in October! They were the nicest people, they said my entry was just perfect, they said it hit th' nail on th' head! I thank you for helpin' me with it, Father, stop by for a napoleon anytime! Well, gosh, I better get back, I've got two customers havin' donuts and coffee."

He watched her dash down the street, thinking he might see her leap off the pavement and fly.

§

In two short days, Harley had hauled away three barrows of trash from Cynthia's garage, washed and waxed her car, mowed the grass at both houses, removed the dead and dying stems of the hosta, and weeded the flower beds.

"Harley, you'd better slow down," said the rector, taking a turn at the weeding himself.

"No, sir, I ain't goin' to, I'm glad t' be workin', it's th' best fix I've been in and I thank th' Lord 'n Master f'r it."

Right there, he thought, was another consideration. Any interim living arrangement the vestry might provide may not accommodate Harley Welch.

Father Tim squatted by the perennial bed and watched the dappled light play over the grass. He and Cynthia had prayed the prayer that never fails, and besides that, what else could they do?

He pondered the sudden, unexpected idea he'd had this morning as he ran. It had come to him out of the blue and slowed him to a walk. Of course, he'd never done anything like that before. But was that any reason not to do it now? Cynthia would know the answer.

The rotten thing about this new development with the rectory was that every time he turned around these days, he was standing under an ax waiting to fall. Thirty days here, ten days there, it seemed endless.

There was an upside, however. Going out to Canaan didn't look so ominous anymore. It looked like a blasted good way to introduce a little peace into his life.

§

He thought they might have to talk about it until the wee hours. But it was coming together very quickly.

"I think we should do it," he told his wife.

"I think we should, too," she said, looking intrigued.

She reached out to him, put her warm palm to his cheek, and smiled. "It would solve everything," she said.

CHAPTER SEVENTEEN

Deep Blue Sea

The following morning, he reached the office earlier than usual and found a message on his machine.

"Father? Ron here. I talked with H. Tide and they want to do the deal now—or never." Ron cleared his throat. "Ah, also, they're saying they don't want to rent to us, they'd like to take possession by October fifteenth."

There was a moment of uneven breathing. "Don't worry about a thing, Father, we'll take care of you."

Wilma Malcolm's voice sounded in the background. "The Randall house!"

"Wilma heard the Randall house is available, and I'm sure we could work something out. Well, listen, we're headed to see the grandkids for a couple of days, I'll get back to you." The machine clicked, whirred, and clicked again.

He sat at his desk, frozen.

In all his years as a priest. . . .

He didn't move for what seemed a long time.

Then he got up, hit the erase button on the machine, and walked out the door.

§

He went home to oversee Dooley's packing for the trip to Virginia in the morning.

He didn't know how he could face anybody right now, much less Dooley Barlowe. Would he break down and bawl like a baby? Or worse, reach for some heavy object and slam it through a window?

He made an effort to remember how Ron had stood by him the night they faced down Edith Mallory. It had happened a few years ago at Clear Day.

After confronting her with the rotten floor beams that they discovered under the Grill, Edith was persuaded to repair the damage and extend Percy's lease for five years, at a fraction of the rent hike she'd originally hit him with—the rent hike that had, in fact, been designed to put the Grill out of business.

Edith Mallory hated his guts, no two ways about it. She had revealed her rage toward him that night in a way he didn't care to recall.

He and Ron had left Clear Day, triumphant and ecstatic, brothers in a victory that had less to do with winning than with maintaining something central to the core and spirit of the village. While the sense of connectedness was vanishing in small towns everywhere, he and Ron had fought for something vital, and won.

Before he let this thing with the rectory eat him alive, he'd better forgive Ron Malcolm. By God's grace, maybe he could actually do it. So what if he might have to start all over again every five minutes?

The point was to start.

"You home?" yelled Dooley from the landing.

"I'm home. Give me a half hour." He stopped in the kitchen to drink a glass of ice water.

Cynthia was shopping in Wesley, and Lace, who was leaving for the beach tomorrow, was baking cookies in Harley's kitchen. The fragrance drifted up the stairs like a sylph.

He went to his bedroom with Barnabas at his heels and sat in the wing chair, taking a few deep breaths to quiet the turmoil that had moved from his head and invaded his heart.

He and Cynthia had already prayed the prayer that never fails regarding the rectory, but he felt the need to pray it again.

Barnabas laid his head on his master's foot.

"Ah, fella," he sighed, nudging his good dog's neck with the toe of his loafer.

§

The sound came through the open bedroom windows—a terrible screeching noise, a loud thud, the high-pitched yelping of a dog. Dooley was shouting.

He bolted to the front window and looked down on Wisteria Lane.

Good God! Barnabas lay in the street with Dooley bending over him.

He didn't remember racing down the stairs, but seemed to be instantly in the street with Dooley, crouching over Barnabas, hearing the horrific sound that welled up from his own gut like a long moan.

Blood ran from his dog's chest, staining the asphalt, and he reached out. . . .

"Don't touch 'im!" shouted Dooley. "He'll bite. We got t' muzzle 'im! Git Lace! Git Lace!"

The rector was on his feet and running for the house, calling, shouting. "And git me some towels!" yelled Dooley. "He's got a flail chest, I got t' have towels!"

His heart was pounding into his throat. Dear God, don't take my dog, don't take this good creature, have mercy!

Lace flew through the door. "Help Dooley!" he said, running toward the guest bathroom, where he picked up an armload of towels, then turned and sprinted up the hall and down the steps and into the street in a nightmarish eternity of slow motion.

"Give me that thing on your head," Dooley told Lace, "and help me hold 'im! We got to muzzle 'im or he'll bite, look, do it this way, hold 'im right here."

Father Tim could hardly bear the look of his dog, suffering, whimpering, thrashing on the asphalt, as fresh blood poured from the wound in his chest.

Dooley tied the bandanna around the dog's nose and mouth, and knotted it. "Okay," he said, taking off his T-shirt. "Don't look, you can see 'is lungs workin' in there." He pressed the balled-up shirt partially into the gaping wound; immediately, the dark stain of blood seeped into the white cotton.

"Give me a towel," Dooley said, clenching his jaw. He took the towel and wrapped the heaving chest, making a bandage. "Another one," said Dooley, working quickly. "And git me a blanket, we got t' git 'im to Doc Owen. He could die."

The rector ran into the house, praying, sweat streaming from him, and opened the storage closet in the hall. No blankets. The armoire! *He could die.*

Christ, have mercy. He dashed up the stairs and flung open the door of the armoire and grabbed two blankets and ran down again, breathless, swept out of himself with fear.

Cynthia, come home . . . *he could die.*

"Spread 'em down right there," Dooley told the rector. "Help 'im," he said to Lace.

They spread the blankets, one on top of the other, next to Barnabas, as a car slowed down and stopped. "Can we help?" someone called.

"You can pray!" shouted Lace, waving the car around them.

Together, they managed to move Barnabas onto the blankets. "Careful," said Dooley, "careful. He's in awful pain, and his leg's broke, too, but they ain't nothin' I can do about it now, we got to hurry. Where's Harley?"

"He walked t' town," said Lace, her face white.

"Git his keys, they're hangin' on th' nail. Back 'is truck out here, we'll put Barnabas in th' back, an' you'n me'll ride with 'im."

She raced to the house as Dooley, naked to the waist, crouched over Barnabas and put his hand on the dog's head. "It's OK, boy, it's OK, you're goin' t' be fine."

"Thank You, Jesus, for Your presence in this," the rector prayed. "Give us your healing hands. . . . "

They heard Lace gun the truck motor and back out of the driveway. She hauled up beside them and screeched to a stop, the motor running.

"Let down th' tailgate," said Dooley. Lace jumped out of the truck and let it down.

"Grab this corner of th' blanket with me," he said to Lace. "Dad, you haul up that end. Take it easy. Easy!"

The dog's weight seemed enormous as they lifted him into the truck bed. "OK, boy, we're layin' you down, now."

Lace and Dooley climbed up with Barnabas and gently positioned the whimpering dog in the center of the bed. Then Dooley slammed the tailgate and looked at the rector.

"Hurry," he said.

§

They blew past Harley, who was walking home on Main Street. He turned to look after them, bewildered.

In twenty-five minutes, Barnabas was on the table at Meadowgate, and Hal Owen and Blake Eddistoe were at work. "You'd better not come in," said Dooley, closing the door to the surgery.

The rector sat with Lace in the small waiting room. A fan droned overhead. The front door stood open to a yard where four chickens scratched in the grass.

His legs had turned to rubber when he got out of the truck a few minutes ago. He had driven like the wind, praying without ceasing, making the half-hour run in twenty minutes. Twice, he glanced behind him, through the window of the cab, to see Dooley give him the high sign.

Lace looked firm. "I believe he's goin' to make it."

"I believe that with you," he said, taking her hand. "You were wonderful."

"I like your dog," she said.

§

Barnabas would stay at Meadowgate for a couple of weeks, recovering. The leg would mend; it was a clean break. But the chest wound, apparently caused by the violent assault of the chassis when the vehicle ran over him, would take longer, and could even open the door to pneumonia.

Bottom line, it would be a while before Barnabas would go jogging with his master.

The rector went into the surgery, where Hal had made a comfortable bed on the floor, and looked at Barnabas sleeping, his chest swaddled in bandages, his left leg stiff in the splint. He watched for his breathing, then knelt and put his hand on his forepaws, which were curled together peacefully.

He wept, tasting the salt in his mouth.

Afterward, they sat in Hal's office, drinking Marge Owen's iced tea, trying to reconstruct the chain of events.

He supposed he had fallen asleep in the chair in the bedroom, with Barnabas lying at his feet. When Barnabas heard Dooley go downstairs, he followed, and at the moment Dooley opened the front door to look for Tommy, Barnabas saw a squirrel on the lawn.

"I didn't even know he was standin' there," said Dooley, "and then he was through the door so fast I couldn't have stopped him." Dooley, sitting bare-chested in his jeans and tennis shoes, dropped his head.

"Don't blame yourself," said Father Tim. "A dog is a dog. He saw the squirrel and did what dogs do. It could have happened with me just as easily."

"Right," said Hal. "The issue isn't that you opened the door, it's that you saved his life."

"I agree," said Lace, her amber eyes intense.

"I don't want to go back to school," said Dooley. "I want to stay here and look after Barn."

Hal leaned against the wall, lighting his pipe. "You can trust me to do that, pal. I'll even give you a report once a week. How's that?"

"No kidding? You will?"

"You bet. Leave me your new phone number at school. Just write it on the wall over there, everybody else does."

"What I don't understand," said Lace, "is why the person who hit 'im didn't stop."

Dooley shrugged. "It happened so fast. . . . I saw Barnabas run after the squirrel, and then the car . . . I don't know what kind of car it was. Maybe brown, I think it was brown."

Father Tim phoned Cynthia, who was frantic. A neighbor across the street told her Barnabas had been hurt and the preacher had taken him to the hospital. Harley reported he'd seen his truck roaring up Main Street, but didn't have any idea what was going on.

"He's going to be fine, Timothy," said Hal. "I'll watch him carefully for any signs of pneumonia. You know we love Barnabas like family. We won't let him suffer."

Marge nodded. "It's true, Tim. And Blake and Rebecca and I will also look after him."

Still, he felt like a heel for leaving his dog.

Blake Eddistoe walked into the yard with them and shook hands with Dooley. "Well done," he said.

At the truck, Dooley suddenly turned and said, "You ought to let me drive."

When it came to persistence, the kid was a regular Churchill. He tossed him the keys.

Dooley's eyes grew bigger. "You mean it?"

"All the way to the highway."

Dooley, now wearing one of Hal's shirts, opened the driver's door. "Get in," he said to Lace. "You can ride in th' middle."

He was glad the Meadowgate road to the highway seemed a little longer than he remembered, glad for the boy's sake. He wished the road could go all the way to Canada before it reached the highway.

§

He was home and in the shower before it hit him.

Today, for the first time, Dooley Barlowe had called him "Dad."

§

Driving to Virginia, part of Miss Sadie's letter ran through his mind.

> . . . *the money is his when he reaches the age of twenty-one. (I am old-fashioned and believe that eighteen is far too young to receive an inheritance.)*
>
> *I have put one and a quarter million dollars where it will grow,*

*and have made provisions to complete his preparatory education.
When he is eighteen, the income from the trust will help send him
through college.*

*I am depending on you never to mention this to him until he is old
enough to bear it with dignity. I am also depending on you to stick
with him, Father, through thick and thin, just as you've done all along.*

The question of sticking with Dooley had been answered nearly
four years ago; he was in for the long haul. The question of when the
boy might bear such information with dignity was another matter.

In truth, if he'd ever seen dignity, he'd seen it yesterday in the
street. Dooley had acted with the utmost precision, wisdom, and
grace.

Even so, something cautioned him about speaking of the inheri-
tance. Soon before they reached the school, he knew the answer, and
the answer was, "Wait."

"Buddy?"

"Yes, sir?"

"When you come home at Christmas, I'll loan you the keys to the
Buick."

Ah, the bright hope that leapt into the boy's face. . . .

"There's only one problem."

The bright hope dimmed.

"You'll have to do your driving on back roads, and I'll have to ride
in the backseat."

Dooley munched one of the cookies Lace had sent along. "OK,"
he said, grinning, "but try and hunker down so nobody can see you."

§

He rang Buddy Benfield to ask when the contract would be
signed. "Whenever Ron gets back," said the junior warden, clearly
uncomfortable to be talking to a man who would soon be evicted.

"Timothy."

His wife was sitting on the back stoop, having her morning coffee
and looking determined about something.

"I want you to call Father Douglas to lead the service for you on
Sunday."

"Whatever for?" he asked.

"Because you're exhausted."

She didn't argue, she didn't nag. She just stated the fact, and looked at him with her cornflower-blue eyes, meaning business.

"All right," he said.

She was clearly surprised. "I suppose I should quit while I'm ahead . . . "

"Probably."

" . . . but I'd also like you to plan to sleep late on Sunday morning. None of that padding around in your slippers at five a.m., like a Christmas elf."

"Keep talking," he said.

"You mean you'll actually *do* it?"

"Whatever you say," he assured her. "Just don't ask me to go to any beaches wearing a bikini."

❦

What had Velma done to herself? She was sporting some gaudy garland of colored paper around her neck, and earrings that appeared to be small bananas. He wouldn't say so, but it looked like she'd dressed herself out of Emma Newland's closet.

"What's that?" he asked.

"A lei. Didn't you hear?"

"Hear what?"

"She's goin' on that cruise with Winnie!" said Percy, looking relieved. "Sailin' over th' deep blue sea to five ports, an' eatin' eight meals a day, includin' a midnight buffet!"

"No kidding! That's perfect! Fantastic!"

Velma put her hands over her head and wiggled her hips, which wasn't a pretty sight.

"Course, I don't know if they do the hula in St. Thomas."

"I don't think they do," said the rector. "I believe that's more of a limbo kind of place."

"Stand still," said J.C. "I'll take your picture." He raised the Nikon and banged off four shots of Velma standing at the cash register. "Won't be front page, but I think I can work it in next to 'Home Gardenin' Tips.'"

Coot Hendrick put in his two cents' worth from the counter. "You ought to have waited and took a snap of Winnie standin' next to Velma."

"You got to jump on news where you find it," said J.C. "I'm headin' to th' booth, I'm starved!"

"*You're* starved?" said Coot. "I've done had to eat a table leg to keep my strength." He despaired that Velma would ever get back to work and bring his regular order of Breakfast Number One with a fountain Pepsi.

§

Mule looked worried. "How's Barnabas?"

"If pneumonia doesn't set in, he'll be fine, thanks for asking. It was bad. Dooley saved his life."

"Fancy says to tell you she's sorry about what happened."

"Adele says the same."

"Thanks. I'll go out and see him tomorrow."

"Fancy said to ask why you haven't been around, said to call her anytime, she'll work you in." Mule eyed the rector's head as if searching for chicken mites. "Lookin' a little scraggly around the collar."

So be it. He didn't care if he looked like John the Baptist on a bad day, he was never setting foot—

"Th' Randall place is empty, they moved to California to be with their kids," said Mule, dispensing a round of late-breaking real estate news. "Winnie's buyer is breathin' on her pretty heavy, and Shoe Barn sold this week."

"Who to?" asked J.C., spooning yogurt onto half a cling peach.

"Who else? H. Tide."

The editor looked disgusted. "What are they tryin' to do, anyway, make Mitford a colony of Orlando?"

"I've been wondering," said the rector, "what H. Tide stands for."

"Beats me," said Mule. "Maybe High Tide. Or Henry Tide, somethin' like that. Did I hear your deacons got an offer on your house?"

"They're not deacons, they're vestry. And it's not my house."

"They'll sell it out from under you, I reckon, if they get the right price."

"Who knows?" he asked, appearing casual.

"Lookit," said J.C., pulling the *Muse* out of his briefcase. "Hot off th' press, get your own copy on th' street." He turned a couple of pages, folded the paper face out, and laid it on the table.

An entire page of small-space ads . . .

We're stickin' with Esther. Love, Esther and Gene Bolick

We're stickin' with Esther. Hope you do the same.
Tucker, Ginny, and Sue

We're stickin with Esther. She's the best. Sophia and Liza Burton

We're stickin' with Esther. Vote your conscience! The Simpson family

We're stickin' with Esther. She does what it talks about
in Psalm 72:12. A supporter

The rector slapped the table. "This is terrific! Terrific! How much do the ads cost?"

"Forty bucks," said J.C., pleased with himself.

"Where did Sophia get forty bucks?"

J.C. looked uncomfortable. "Don't ask."

"She doesn't have forty bucks."

"So? She wanted to stick up for Esther but didn't have the money. Big deal, I gave 'er the ad free, but if you tell anybody I said that . . . "

Mule gave J.C. a thumbs-up. "I don't care what people say about you, buddyroe, you're all right."

"Look here." J.C. pointed to a couple of the ads.

We're stickin' with Esther. Minnie Lomax, The Irish Woolen Shop

We're stickin' with Esther. Dora Pugh, Mitford Hardware

"Two businesses that aren't afraid to show their politics in front of God an' everybody!" said the editor, approving.

The rector drew a deep breath. Maybe this cloud had a silver lining, after all. He'd certainly drop by and congratulate Minnie and Dora. "You get around town," he said to J.C. "From where you stand, how's the election looking?"

"From where I stand?" J.C. scowled and pushed the yogurt away.

"I'd say that once this edition gets out to th' readers, it'll be runnin' about fifty-fifty."

Something or somebody would have to tip the numbers in Esther's favor, or Edith Mallory would have her claws all over Mitford. This was September fifth, and the election would be hitting the fan less than two months hence. Surely on Sunday he could offer a special prayer, or dedicate the communion service to those who unflaggingly devote themselves to the nobler welfare of the community. And speaking of Psalms, didn't the reading for Sunday say that "the mouth of them that speak lies shall be stopped"?

Ah, well. He remembered that he wouldn't be in the pulpit on Sunday, he'd be sleeping 'til noon, according to his wife's plan, and waking up strong, renewed, and altogether carefree.

"Here," he said, giving J.C. two tens and a twenty. "Run one for me next week and sign it, 'A Friend.'"

§

They stopped at The Local on their way to Meadowgate, to pick up a brisket for Marge Owen. While Cynthia paid their monthly bill, he inspected the contents of the butcher's case.

"Father!" It was Winnie Ivey, carrying a ten-pound bag of flour.

"I'm glad I ran into you, I've made a decision! I decided to go on th' cruise with Velma and not do anything about sellin' 'til I get back. I told the real estate people to wait, just like you said, and I feel like a different person!"

She flushed. "Can you believe I did that?"

"I can! Well done!"

"They didn't like it, they tried to push me, they said I might not get another chance. But then, guess what?"

"What?"

"They offered me another three thousand, but I said no, I'm goin' to wait, and that's that. Besides, thank th' Lord, I'm up seven percent over this time last year!"

"You don't mean it!"

"I do!" He thought Winnie Ivey looked ten years younger, all of which made him feel immeasurably better into the bargain.

"You know what?"

"What?" he asked.

"I'm gettin' to where I don't hardly want to go to Tennessee n'more. Joe said he thought he could get me a job at Graceland, but to tell th' truth, Father, I never cared much for rock an' roll."

§

He didn't have to be George Burns to know that timing was everything.

According to Buddy Benfield, the Malcolms would be getting back to Mitford around eleven o'clock.

He was waiting in front of their house when they pulled into the driveway.

§

Saturday night, and he was looking at a clean slate. No services tomorrow, no arriving early to unlock the church. . . .

Thank God he could rest in the morning. Why did he never know he needed refreshment 'til somebody hit him over the head with a two-by-four?

He ached all over with a weariness he felt even in his teeth.

Yet, how could he lie here like a hog in slop, when there was so much to be thankful for? He ought to be up and shouting and clicking his heels.

"How does it feel?" asked his beaming wife, sitting in bed against a stack of pillows.

"Wonderful. Amazing. *Powerful!*"

"Exactly how I felt!"

"I should have done something like this years ago," he said.

"Maybe. But God's timing is perfect."

"Do you really think we should go ahead with . . . ?"

She nodded. "I think so. It's a nuisance now, but it will pay off down the road."

"Maybe a breezeway someday."

"Maybe. But I'd miss popping back and forth through the hedge, wouldn't you?"

"Ah, the hedge. Where I first laid eyes on my attractive new neighbor."

She laughed happily. "Your doom was sealed."

He sat up and took her in his arms and brushed her cheek with his. "Thank you," he murmured.

"For what?"

"For being the woman you are, for putting up with me, for looking after me."

"You mean you don't think I'm a bossy dame?"

"Sometimes."

"You know what tomorrow is," she said.

"I do. Two years."

"Two *long* years?"

"Not so long," he said, kissing her ear. "But alas, I haven't had a chance to buy—"

"Don't buy me anything," she said, leaning against him. "Don't give me anything you have to wrap."

"You can count on it," he said, feeling the softness of her shoulders, the blue satin gown. . . .

She pulled away, laughing. "Maybe we should try to get some sleep, darling. It's been a long day, a whole string of long days, and besides, now that you're a home owner, you need to save your strength for all those little chores that crop up—like fixing the foundation where it's crumbling, and mending the leak over Dooley's room."

"Aha. The vestry won't be having that done anymore, will they?"

"That's right," she said, kissing him goodnight. "It's just you and me."

"And Harley," he said, brightening.

She turned out the light and rolled on her side, and for a time, he listened for her light, whiffling snore.

He missed his dog and prayed for him, thankful he was mending. He wondered about Dooley, and thought they should call him at school tomorrow, though it might be a trifle soon.

What's more, he was concerned that Father Douglas would leave out The Peace—which he was known, on occasion and for no good reason, to do.

And how would he fix the foundation, anyway? He supposed Harley would know, but what if he didn't? Probably a little mortar; and some new stones where the old had crumbled and fallen out. . . .

He rolled on his back and looked at the ceiling—his ceiling, their ceiling, the first ceiling he had ever owned, as soon as the papers were signed. Now she had a house and he had a house. Bookends. After the work on hers was finished, they would live there and rent this. "To someone with children!" Cynthia hoped.

He had liked handing Ron the check for a hundred and five thousand dollars, though it had taken his breath away to write it. . . .

"Timothy?" she said.

"Yes?"

"You're thinking."

"Right."

"Stop it at once, dearest."

He chuckled. "OK," he said.

He knew the truth, now, of what Stuart Cullen had written to him several years ago:

> *Martha has come in to tell me it is bedtime. I cannot express how wonderful it is to be sometimes told, rather than always doing the telling. . . . There she is again, my friend, and believe me, my wife does not enjoy reminding me twice. That she monitors my energy is a good thing. Otherwise, I would spill it all for Him and have nothing left with which to get out of bed in the mornings. . . .*

He reached for her, and she turned to him, eagerly, smiling in the darkness.

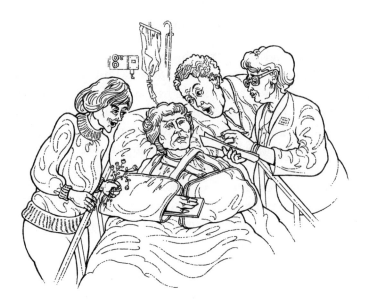

CHAPTER EIGHTEEN

A Cup of Kindness

An early October hurricane gathered its forces in the Caribbean, roared north along the eastern seaboard, and veered inland off Cape Hatteras. In a few short hours, it reached the mountains at the western end of the state, where it pounded Mitford with alarming force.

Rain lashed Lord's Chapel in gusting sheets, rattled the latched shutters of the bell tower, blew the tarps off lumber stacked on the construction site, and crashed a wheelbarrow into a rose bed.

The tin roof of Omer Cunningham's shed, formerly a hangar for his antique ragwing, was hurled toward Luther Green's pasture, where the sight of it, gleaming and rattling and banging through the air, made the cows bawl with trepidation.

Coot Hendrick's flock of three Rhode Island Reds took cover on the back porch after nearly drowning in a pothole in the yard, and Lew Boyd, who was pumping a tank of premium unleaded into an out-of-town Mustang, reported that his hat was whipped off his head and flung into a boxwood at the town monument, nearly a block away.

Phone lines went out; a mudslide slalomed down a deforested

ridge near Farmer, burying a Dodge van; and a metal Coca-Cola sign from Hattie Cloer's market on the highway landed in Hessie Mayhew's porch swing.

At the edge of the village, Old Man Mueller sat in his kitchen, trying to repair the mantel clock his wife asked him to fix several years before her death. He happened to glance out the window in time to see his ancient barn collapse to the ground. He noted that it swayed slightly before it fell, and when it fell, it went fast.

"Hot ding!" he muttered aloud, glad to be spared the aggravation of taking it down himself. "Now," he said to the furious roar outside, "if you'd stack th' boards, I'd be much obliged."

§

The villagers emerged into the sunshine that followed, dazzled by the spectacular beauty of the storm's aftermath, which seemed in direct proportion to its violence.

The mountain ridges appeared etched in glass, set against clear, perfectly blue skies from horizon to horizon.

At Fernbank, a bumper crop of crisp, tart cooking apples lay on the orchard floor, ready to be gathered into local sacks. The storm had done the picking, and not a single ladder would be needed for the job.

"You see," said Jena Ivey, "there's always two sides to everything!" Jena had closed Mitford Blossoms to run up to Fernbank and gather apples, having promised to bake pies for the Bane just three days hence.

"But," said another apple gatherer, "the autumn color won't be worth two cents. The storm took all the leaves!"

"Whatever," sighed Jena, who thought some people were mighty hard to please.

§

Balmy. Like spring. It was that glad fifth season called Indian summer, which came only on the rarest occasions.

He was doing his duties, he was going his rounds, he was poking his nose into everybody's business. How else could a priest know what was happening?

He rang the Bolicks. "Esther? How's it going?"

"I'd kill Gene Bolick if I could catch him, that's how it's goin'!"

"What now?"

"Haven't I been bakin' since the bloomin' Boer War, tryin' to get ready for Friday? And didn't I tell him, I said, 'Gene, don't you mess with these cookies, there's three hundred cookies I just baked, and I'm puttin' 'em in these two-gallon freezer bags this minute, so you'll keep your paws off.' Well, I zipped up those bags and stacked 'em in th' freezer and first thing you know, I came home last night and *who* was sittin' at the table with his head stuck in one of those two-gallon bags, goin' at it like a fox in a henhouse? I ask you!"

"You don't mean it!"

"Frozen hard as bricks and him hammerin' down on those cookies like they'd just come out of th' oven."

"Aha."

"It's a desperate man who'll do a trick like that."

"I agree. But try to forgive him," he said, knowing that Gene Bolick had not had a cookie to call his own since this whole event began brewing several months ago.

He rang off, assuring her that he'd do his part on Friday, down in the trenches with the rest of the troops.

§

He flipped quickly through the *Muse,* looking for another batch of *Stickin'* ads.

"Looks like Esther's pullin' ahead," said J.C., totally convinced that his small-space ad idea had done the trick. It was generally agreed that the full page of Mack Stroupe's face had been a dire mistake by the other camp. It was one thing to look at Mack's mug on a billboard, but somehow seeing it right under your nose had been a definite turnoff, according to the buzz around town.

Along with a growing number of others, the rector was beginning to feel upbeat about the outcome of the election just one month away. The wife of a deacon at First Baptist had planned a preelection Stickin' With Esther tea, and the mayor would also be riding down Main Street in a fire truck during a parade for Fire Awareness Day.

Things were definitely looking up.

❧

Coming into the kitchen to make a pot of tea, he noted that Violet had descended from her penthouse atop the refrigerator and was curled up on his dog's bed under the table.

Thank God Barnabas was coming home on Saturday, the day after the Bane. Hal had kept him at Meadowgate nearly a month, just in case.

He'd still have the splint on for a couple of weeks, but the chest wrap had come off. The job of healing could be finished up neatly by close confinement for five or six months, with no running, chasing, or stick-fetching.

"There's certainly a lot of hilarity going on in my house," said Cynthia. She stood at the kitchen door, her head cocked to one side.

"What do you mean?"

She listened intently, as if to the music of the spheres. "Somebody's laughing!"

"What's wrong with laughter?"

She didn't answer, but came and stood by the stove, her brow furrowed, as he put the kettle on.

"Elton used six blocks t' build a model of a staircase that has three steps . . ." Harley's voice drifted up to the kitchen.

"Poor Harley," said Cynthia. "I hope he makes an A this time."

"That B-minus cut him to the quick."

"I think Lace is too hard on him."

"And you're too soft! Delivering his breakfast downstairs on a *tray*, for Pete's sake."

"You're jealous because I don't deliver yours, much less on a tray, but then, dear fellow, you have never, ever once cleaned out and organized my attic so that it looks better than my studio!"

"True."

"Nor have you ever hauled the detritus from said cleanup to the Bane, and brought me back a form which makes it all tax deductible." She turned and went quickly to the door.

"Good Lord, Timothy! Listen!"

He heard a woman's hysterical laughter coming from the little house next door.

They went out to the back stoop. The high-pitched laughter continued, followed by a crash that sounded like breaking glass.

"What on earth?" she asked. Her alarm was evident.

"I'll go and see." He didn't want to go and see; he didn't want anything out of the ordinary to be going on next door.

He darted through the hedge and up the dark steps to the screen door. He looked into Cynthia's kitchen and saw Pauline Barlowe standing at the sink. She was throwing up.

"Pauline," he said.

She retched into the sink again, then turned and stared toward the door, her eyes swollen, wiping her mouth.

"What?" she said. Her voice was cold, coarse; the stench of warm bile and alcohol permeated the room.

He opened the door and went in. "What's going on?" He tried to keep his voice free of anger, tried to make it a simple question, but failed.

"Ask y'r big high an' mighty in there what's goin' on, and if you find out, let me know, that's what *I've* been tryin' to do, is figure out what's goin' on."

She laughed suddenly and sank to the floor, leaning against the cabinets.

He walked down the hall and into the living room, where Buck Leeper sat in a Queen Anne chair, asleep and snoring, an empty vodka bottle on the lamp table and a glass on the floor at his feet.

§

He cleaned the kitchen and swept up a broken glass on the back stoop, while Pauline sat in a chair with her head in her hands. He sensed that she was crying, though she made no sound. Then he turned off the downstairs lights, except for the lamp in the living room and the light in the hallway. Buck didn't stir and he didn't wake him. He would deal with this tomorrow.

He drove Pauline home and they sat in the car in front of the house where her father, son, and daughter were sleeping.

The hilarity and weeping had passed; she was silent as a stone, her face turned away from him.

"We need to talk," he said.

She nodded.

"Sunday afternoon, if you can."

She nodded again. "I'm so sorry," she whispered.

He got out of the car and opened her door and helped her up the sidewalk. The temperature had dropped considerably and she was shivering in a sleeveless dress. "Will you wake anyone?"

"Don't worry," she said, still avoiding his gaze. "I won't let nobody see me like this."

§

When he came in from the garage, Cynthia met him in the hallway.

"It's Esther!" she said. "She had an accident, and they say it looks bad. They want you to come to the hospital at once!"

Esther! He raced to the bathroom, splashed water on his face, took his jacket off the hook in the kitchen, and once again backed the Buick out of the garage, tires screeching.

There were many ways to lose an election. He prayed to God this wasn't one of them.

§

"What happened?" he asked Nurse Kennedy in the hospital corridor.

"She fell off a ladder, broke her left wrist, broke the right elbow, and . . ." Nurse Kennedy shook her head.

"And what?"

"Fractured her jaw. Dr. Harper is wiring her mouth shut as we speak."

"Good Lord!"

"But she'll be fine."

"Be *fine*? How could anybody be fine with two broken limbs and her mouth wired shut?"

"It happens, Father." Nurse Kennedy sighed and continued down the hall.

He wound his way along the corridor to the waiting room, where Gene Bolick sat on a Danish modern sofa in shock.

"Where's Ray?" he asked Gene. Why wasn't Ray Cunningham here? Didn't he know his wife had had a terrible accident?

"Ray who?" queried Gene, looking stupefied.

"Esther's husband!"

"I'm Esther's husband," said Gene, as plainly as he knew how.

"You mean . . . you mean, the mayor didn't fall off a ladder?"

"I don't know about th' mayor, but Esther sure did, and it busted her up pretty bad." He appeared disconsolate.

"Good heavens, Gene, I'm sorry. Terribly sorry." He sat beside his parishioner on the sofa. "How is she?"

"Not so good, if you ask me. She was down at th' parish hall on a ladder, puttin' up signs—you know, *Kitchen Goods, Clothing Items,* such as that, and went to step down and . . ." Gene lifted his hands. "And crashed."

"Where is everybody?" Usually, when someone was rushed to the hospital in Mitford, a whole gaggle of friends and family showed up to pray, make a run on the vending machines, and rip recipes from outdated issues of *Southern Living.*

"They're down at th' parish hall, I reckon, where they've been for th' last forty-eight hours."

"I'll get the prayer chain going," said the rector. He sped along the hall to the phone, where he called his wife to put the chain in motion. "How bad is it?" asked Cynthia.

"There's a break in both arms, and they're wiring her jaws shut."

She gasped. "Good heavens!"

"I'll be here for a while."

"Poor Esther. How awful. Please tell Gene I'm sorry, I'll go see Esther tomorrow, and I'll call the chain right now. Love you, dearest."

"Love you. Keep my place warm."

Hurrying down the hall, he stopped briefly at a vending machine for a pack of Nabs and a Sprite.

§

He'd just finished praying with Gene for Esther to be knit back together as good as new when Hessie Mayhew rushed into the waiting room. He looked at his watch. Eleven o'clock. Hardly anyone in this town stayed up 'til eleven o'clock.

"How is she?" asked Hessie.

"Doped up," said Gene.

"I've got to see her," insisted the Bane co-chair. Given her wide eyes and frazzled hair, Hessie looked as if she'd been plugged into an electrical outlet.

"You can't see 'er," said Gene. "Just me an' th' Father can go in."

"Do you realize that at seven in the morning, the Food Committee's gettin' together at my house to bake twelve two-layer orange marmalades, and we don't even have th' *recipe*?"

Gene slapped his forehead. "Oh, Lord help!"

"I'm sure it's written down somewhere," suggested the rector.

"Nope, it's not," said Gene.

"That's right. It's not." Hessie pursed her lips. "If I've told her once, I've told her a thousand times to write her recipes down, *especially* the orange marmalade, for heaven's sake."

"It's in her head," said Gene, defending his wife.

"Well," announced the co-chair, looking determined, "we'll have to find a way to get it out!"

§

He arrived at the office the next morning, feeling the exhaustion of half a night at the hospital.

At two a.m., he'd left Esther resting, one arm in a cast, the other in a cast and a sling, and unable to speak a word even if she wanted to. Gene slept by her bed on a hospital cot.

How on earth anybody was going to get a cake recipe out of Esther Bolick was beyond him. In any case, Hessie had postponed the baking session until Thursday afternoon, which meant the cakes would be squeaking in under the wire—if at all.

"We *have* to have Esther's orange marmalades," she had said flatly. "People *expect* Esther's marmalades. At twenty dollars per cake times twelve, that's two hundred and forty dollars, which is nothing to sneeze at."

He yawned and sat wearily at his desk.

He was rubbing his eyes as Buck Leeper opened the door and walked in, taking off his hard hat.

"Good morning," said the rector.

Buck stood in the doorway, uneasy. "I need to talk."

"Sit down."

"I can't stay. I came to tell you I'm . . ." Buck looked at the floor, then met the rector's gaze. "I'm sorry. That was bad, what happened. I took a drink, I offered her one, and it went from there."

"Did you know she's an alcoholic? An addict?"

"Yes." Buck's voice was hoarse. "I got to tell you, I talked her into it, I shouldn't have done it, I'm sick to my gut about it."

"There's help, Buck."

The superintendent scraped his work boot on the floor, looking down. "No. I can beat this, I've been beatin' it, this is th' first time in . . . in a while. I wanted to tell you I'm movin' out, one of the crew knows a house for sale, but thinks they'll rent."

"Before we talk about that, let's name the problem. It has a name. It's your alcoholism. Your addiction."

Buck stiffened and turned away, but didn't walk to the door.

"How long have you been drinking, seriously drinking?"

"I was thirteen when my old man started pourin' it down my gullet. The first time, he made me drink 'til I puked." He faced the rector. "Bourbon. Sour mash. He liked it when I got to where I could drink him under the table, not many people could. When he died, I swore I'd never touch th' stuff again."

"But you did, and now you're suffering on your own account as well as Pauline's. Do you care for Pauline?"

"Yeah. I care for her."

"Why?"

"I respect what she's been able to do, to come back like that, out of her hell, and find faith. God, I hate what I did."

"You did it together. It takes two."

"And her kids. They're great kids. Who deserves kids like that? Nobody, not even people who have it all together, who never took a drink! I thought that maybe I could . . . maybe we could . . ."

"You can."

"No." His voice was hard. "It's too late for me."

"What if you had somebody in this thing with you, somebody who'd stick closer than a brother, somebody who'd go to bat for you, help you through it—help you over it?"

"Oh, Jesus Christ!" Buck said with disgust, moving toward the door.

"That's who I had in mind, actually."

Buck's face colored. "That crap don't work for me."

"How long have you hauled the pain of your dead brother in your gut? And how much longer do you want to haul it? Stop, friend. Stop and look at this thing that cheats you out of all that's valuable, all that's precious."

The superintendent turned and stared out the window, his back to the rector.

"You can't beat this alone, Buck. You've tried for years and it never worked. Bottom line, we're not created to go it alone, we're made to hammer out our lives with God as our defender. Going it alone may work for a while, but it never has and never will go the mile."

Buck shrugged his shoulders, still looking out the window. "Pauline knows about God and she couldn't make it."

"No, but she's going to. In any case, we don't come to God to attain perfection, we come to be saved."

"You remember my grandaddy was a preacher. There's no way I could be good enough to get saved or whatever you call it. No way."

"It isn't about being good enough."

Buck turned to him, furious. "So what is it about, for Christ's sake?"

"It's about letting Him into our lives in a personal way. You can do that with a simple prayer you can repeat with me. When we let Him in, He guarantees that we become new creatures."

"New creatures?" Buck laughed bitterly. "Who wants to be a new creature when you can't even get the old one to work?"

"New creatures make mistakes, too, they stumble around and fall in a ditch. But once the commitment is made with the heart, He takes it from there."

"It always sounded like a lot of bull to me."

Father Tim got up and stood beside his desk. "I could tell you all day what you'd gain by making that commitment—but look at it another way: What do you have to lose?"

For a time, the only sound was the ticking of the clock on the bookshelf.

"Listen," said Buck, "I'll be out of the house in a couple of days."

He moved suddenly to the door and opened it, then went down the walk to his truck, not looking back.

"The fields are white . . ."

"Buck!" said the rector. "Wait . . ."

But he didn't wait.

§

"They want to buy me out and let me run it," said Winnie, looking anxious. "What do you think?"

If he ever had to mess with another real estate deal . . .

"What do *you* think?" he asked.

"It sounds like a good idea. I mean, I do the work and get a regular paycheck, and they have all th' headaches." She sighed. "That might be refreshin'."

"Weren't you going to wait 'til after the cruise to make a decision?"

"They want an answer right away. Soon." She wrung her hands. "At once!"

He didn't feel he had the credentials to counsel Winnie on what amounted to the next few years of her life. "What's God saying to you about all this?"

"I still have that stuck feelin', like I don't know which way to turn."

Definitely not a good sign, but what more could he say?

§

"Your hair . . ." said Emma.

"What about it?" he snapped.

"Dearest," said Cynthia, "about your hair . . ."

"Don't touch it!" he said. So what if he had hacked on it himself? At least it wasn't draping over his collar like so much seaweed.

"Man!" exclaimed Mule, eyeing him with interest.

"You don't *like* it?" he asked. "I never say anything about *your* hair, I never even *notice* your hair, why you can't do the same for *me* is beyond all *imagining*—"

"Gee whiz," said Mule, looking perplexed. "I was just goin' to ask where you got that blue shirt."

§

When he walked into Esther's hospital room on Thursday morning, her bed was surrounded by Bane volunteers. One of them held a notepad at the ready, and he felt a definite tension in the air.

They didn't even look up as he came in.

Hessie leaned over Esther, speaking as if the patient's hearing had been severely impaired by the fall.

"Esther!" she shouted. "You've got to cooperate! The doctor said he'd give us twenty minutes and not a second more!"

"Ummaummhhhh," said Esther, desperately trying to speak through clamped jaws.

"Why couldn't she write something?" asked Vanita Bentley. "I see two fingers sticking out of her cast."

"Uhnuhhh," said Esther.

"You can't write with two fingers. Have you ever tried writing with two fingers?"

"Oh, Lord," said Vanita. "Then *you* think of something! We've got to hurry!"

"We need an alphabet board!" Hessie declared.

"Who has time to go lookin' for an alphabet board? Where would we find one, anyway?"

"Make one!" instructed the co-chair. "Write down the alphabet on your notepad and let her point 'til she spells it out."

"Ummuhuhnuh," said Esther.

"She can't move her arm to point!"

"So? We can move the notepad!"

Esther raised the forefinger of her right hand.

"One finger. *One!* Right, Esther? If it's yes, blink once, if it's no, blink twice."

"She blinked once, so it's yes. *One!* One what, Esther? Cup? Teaspoon? Vanita, are you writin' this down?"

"Two blinks," said Marge Crowder. "So, it's not a cup and it's not a teaspoon."

"Butter!" said somebody. "Is it one stick of butter?"

"She blinked twice, that's no. Try again. One *teaspoon*? Oh, thank God! Vanita, one teaspoon."

"Right. But one teaspoon of what? Salt?"

"Oh, please, you wouldn't use a teaspoon of *salt* in a *cake!*"

"Excuse me for living," said Vanita.

"Maybe cinnamon? Look! One blink. One teaspoon of cinnamon!"

"Hallelujah!" they chorused.

Esther wagged her finger.

"One, two, three, four, five . . ." someone counted.

"Five what?" asked Vanita. "Cups? No. Teaspoons? No. *Table-spoons?*"

"One blink, it's tablespoons! *Five tablespoons!*"

"Oh, mercy, I'm glad I took my heart pill this morning," said Hessie. "Is it of butter? I just have a feelin' it's butter. Look! One blink!"

"Five tablespoons of butter!" shouted the crowd, in unison.

"OK, in cakes, you'd have to have baking powder. How much baking powder, Esther?"

Esther held up one finger.

"One teaspoon?"

"Uhnuhhh," said Esther, looking desperate.

"One *tablespoon?*" asked Vanita.

"You wouldn't use a *tablespoon* of baking powder in a cake!" sniffed Marge Crowder.

"Look," said Vanita, "I'm helpin' y'all just to be nice. My husband personally thinks I am a great cook, but I don't do cakes, OK, so if you'd like somebody else to take these notes, just step right up and help yourself, thank you!"

"You're doin' great, honey, keep goin'," said Hessie.

"Look at that!" exclaimed Vanita. "She's got one finger out straight and the other one bent back! Is that one and a half? It *is,* she blinked once! I declare, that is the cleverest thing I ever saw. OK, one and a half teaspoons of bakin' powder!"

Everyone applauded.

"This is a killer," said Vanita, fanning herself with the notebook. "Don't you think we could sell two-layer triple chocolates just as easy?"

"Ummunnuhhh," said Esther, her eyes burning with disapproval.

Hessie snorted. "This could take 'til kingdom come. How much time have we got left?"

"Ten minutes, maybe eleven!"

"Eleven minutes? Are you kidding me? We'll never finish this in eleven minutes."

"I think she told me she uses buttermilk in this recipe," said Marge Crowder. "Esther," she shouted, "how much buttermilk?"

Esther made the finger and a half gesture.

"One and a half cups, right? Great! Now we're cookin'!"

More applause.

"OK," commanded the co-chair, "what have we got so far?"

Vanita, being excessively near-sighted, held the notepad up for close inspection. "One teaspoon of cinnamon, five tablespoons of butter, one and a half teaspoons of baking powder, and one and a half cups of buttermilk."

"I've got to sit down," said the head of the Food Committee, pressing her temples.

"It looks like Esther's droppin' off to sleep, oh, Lord, Esther, honey, don't go to sleep, you can sleep tonight!"

"Could somebody ask th' nurse for a stress tab?" wondered Vanita. "Do you think they'd mind, I've written checks to th' hospital fund for nine years, goin' on ten!"

"By the way," asked Marge Crowder, "is this recipe for one layer or two?"

He decided to step into the hall for a breath of fresh air.

§

Hammer and tong. That's how one Bane worker said they went at it on Friday.

The weather was glorious, the parish hall was full to overflowing with both goods and people, the lawn was adorned with three white tents, sheltering from any possible bad weather everything from fine antiques and children's toys to hot meals and homemade desserts. Three tour buses stood parked at the curb, signaling the penultimate event of the year.

Parkers filled the two church lots first, then sent traffic up the hill to satellite hospital parking, and down a side street to the Methodists. A stream of cars and pickups also flowed into lots behind the Collar Button, the Irish Woolen Shop, and the Sweet Stuff Bakery.

Mitford Blossoms kicked in ten parking spaces while several Main Street residents, including Evie Adams, earned good money renting their private driveways.

For the Bane workers, it was down in the trenches, and no two ways about it.

For eleven hours running, the rector made change, sorted through plunder for eager customers, dished up chili and spaghetti, boxed cakes, bagged cookies, carried trash bags to Gene Bolick's pickup, made coffee, hauled ice, picked up debris, found Band-Aids and patched a skinned knee, demonstrated a Hoover vacuum cleaner, took several cash contributions for the dig-a-well fund, told the story of the stained-glass windows, and mopped up a spilled soft drink in the parish hall corridor.

Uncle Billy came to supervise, armed with three new jokes collected especially for the occasion.

After five o'clock, vans from area companies and organizations hauled in and out like clockwork, carrying employees who proceeded to eat heartily and shop heavily.

By eight o'clock, the cleaning crew came on with a vengeance, and at eight-fifteen, a small but faithful remnant, despite weariness in every bone, arrived at the hospital, where they gathered around Esther Bolick's bed and sang, "For she's a jolly good fellow."

The marmalades, they reported, had been among the first items to go, with some anonymous donor kicking in sixty bucks—thereby bringing the total to three hundred dollars, or ten feet of well-digging.

It had been the most successful Bane in anyone's memory, and had raised the phenomenal sum of twenty-two thousand dollars. This total not only defeated the Bane's previous record by several thousand, it clearly put every other church fund-raiser, possibly in the entire world, to utter vexation and shame.

§

Pauline came to his office in the afternoon and sat on the visitor's bench, looking proud and strong.

"I'm goin' to AA," she said, "and I'm not seein' Buck anymore. That's the best I can do, Father, and I want to do it, and I'm askin' God to give me strength to do it." She looked at him earnestly. "Will you pray that I can?"

It was the longest speech he'd ever heard her make.

He walked home with Pauline, loving the crisp air, the blue skies.

"Whenever you think you'd like to move into your own place, I'll give you a hand, and so will Harley."

"Thank you. But I don't deserve—"

"Pauline, you've given me one of the richest gifts of this life—the chance to know Dooley Barlowe. I don't deserve that. So, let's not talk about deserving, OK?"

She looked at him and smiled. And then she laughed.

"Mr. Tim!" Jessie ran up the hall and grabbed him around the legs. "I ain't suckin' my thumb n'more. Looky there!" She held her thumb aloft and he inspected it closely.

"Buck got me to quit," she said, grinning up at him. "He give me a baby doll with hair to comb, you want to see it?"

"I do!" he said.

Jessie darted into the living room and returned with the doll. "See how 'er hair's th' color of mine, Buck said he looked at a whole *bunch* of baby dolls 'til he found this 'un. You want to hold it? Her name's Mollie, she don't wet or nothin'." She took him by the hand. "Come and sit down if you're goin' to hold 'er. Buck holds 'er a lot, but he cain't come n'more, Pauline said he cain't."

Jessie popped her thumb in her mouth, then took it out again.

Pauline glanced at the rector and shrugged and turned away, but he'd seen the sorrow in her eyes.

§

Bane is a Blessing
To Thousands

Last Friday, Lord's Chapel gave their annual Bane and Blessing sale, which netted the record-braking sum of $22,000.

According to Bane co-chair Hessie Mayhew, major funding will be provided to dig wells in east Africa, and buy an ambulance for a hospital in Landon county. Other recipients of Bane funds include mission fields in Bosnia, Croatia, Ruwanda, Harlan County, Kentucky, and food banks throughout our local area.

Mrs. Mayhew said that special thanks are due to co-chai, Esther Bolck, who demanded the best from all voluntears and got it.

A list of voluntears is printed on the back page of today's edition. As Mrs. Bolik is sadly laid up in the hospital with two broken arms and a fractured jaw, you may send a card to room 107, but please, no visits until next Wednesday, doctor's orders. She is allergic to lilies, which kill her sinuses, but likes everything else.

A photograph of a large, fake check for twenty-two thousand dollars was included in the story.

"Who *wrote* this?" asked Father Tim.

"I've hired help," said J.C., looking expansive. "Vanita Bentley!"

"Who keyed it in?"

"I did, Vanita only does longhand. She'll be writin' a special 'Around Town' column every week from here out."

"Congratulations!" said the rector. So what if the *Muse* would never win a Pulitzer? It wasn't like it was *The New York Times,* for Pete's sake.

§

"*Buon giorno,* Father! Andrew Gregory, home at last!"

"Andrew! By George, you've been missed!"

Andrew laughed. The rector didn't think he'd ever heard his friend sounding quite so . . .

"Fernbank has been my fervent contemplation since we last talked," said Andrew. "I'm eager to go up and have a look. How's it faring?"

"Well, for one thing, you have an orchard full of apples, and the roof is holding its own."

"Splendid! Can you let me in to have a look around?"

"Absolutely. What's good for you? How about . . . fifteen minutes?"

"Perfect!" said Andrew, sounding . . . how *was* Andrew sounding, anyway? Was it carefree? Boyish? Relaxed?

Come to think of it, who wouldn't be relaxed after three months of visiting cousins in Italy?

§

When Father Tim arrived at Fernbank, Andrew's gray Mercedes was already parked in the drive, and Andrew stood waiting on the porch with a man and woman.

As he trotted up the steps, he couldn't help but notice that the woman was exceedingly attractive, nearly as tall as the tall Andrew, and with a striking figure. He blinked into the dazzling warmth of her smile, hardly noticing the dark-haired man standing with them.

"Father!"

"Welcome home, my friend!"

They embraced, and Andrew kissed the rector, European-style, on both cheeks.

"Father, first I'd like to introduce you to Anna, my cousin . . ."

Good heavens, this was a *cousin*?

". . . and my wife," said the beaming Andrew.

CHAPTER NINETEEN

Fernbank

Surprised, if not stunned, by joy, the rector could scarcely speak. "Congratulations!" he blurted. "*Mazel tov!* Ah, *felicitaziones!*"

Andrew pumped his hand. "Well done, Father! And this is Anna's brother, Antonio Nocelli."

"Call me Tony!" said Antonio, embracing the rector and kissing him on either cheek. "I have heard much about you, Father."

"While I have heard nothing at all about you and Anna!"

Anna laughed, throwing her head back. "Let me say, Father, that Andrew is our *fourth* cousin, so you must not alarm."

"Yes, for heaven's sake, don't alarm!" said Andrew, chuckling.

Anna shrugged and smiled. "My English? Not perfect."

"Whose is?" asked the rector. "Well, shall we go in? Would you like to take them in while I wait outside?"

"Heavens, no, you must come in, also," said Andrew. The rector thought he'd never seen his friend so tanned, so boyish, so eager.

"Here's the key, then. Fernbank will be yours soon enough, why don't you unlock the door?"

"I am very excited," Anna told her husband.

Tony agreed. "We could not sleep for thinking of the house Andrew has taken into his heart."

Andrew swung the double doors open, and they walked in. There was a moment of hushed silence.

"Ahh, *bella . . ."* said Tony. *"Molto bella!"*

Anna opened her arms to the room. "It is beautiful! Just as you said!"

"A bit damp, my dear, but—"

"But, *amore mio,* sunlight can fix!"

"Anna believes sunlight can fix everything," Andrew told the rector, pleased.

They strolled through the house, savoring each room.

Anna touched the walls, the banisters, the furnishings, often murmuring, "Fernbank . . ."

In the ballroom, he told the story of the painted ceiling and two other Italians, a father and son, who had come all the way to Mitford to paint it, living with Miss Sadie's family for nearly three years.

As angels soared above them among rose-tinted clouds, he felt oddly proud, like a father proud of a child, eagerly savoring the cries of delight.

Someone to love Fernbank! Thanks be to God!

§

Indian summer had drawn on, offering a final moment of glad weather.

They sat on Miss Sadie's frail porch furniture, which the rector had dusted off. Andrew and Anna took the wicker love seat.

"Now!" said Andrew. "We will tell you everything."

Father Tim laughed. "Easy. I can't handle much more excitement."

"Tony and Anna owned a wonderful little restaurant in Lucera, only a few steps from my *penzione.* The food was outstanding, perhaps the best I've had in my travels around the Mediterranean. I began to go there every day for lunch."

"Soon," said Anna, looking boldly at Andrew, "he came also for dinner."

"Tony cooked, Anna served, we discovered we were cousins, and, well . . ." Andrew smiled, suddenly speechless.

"Shy," said the rector, nodding to the others.

Anna made a wickedly funny face. "He is not shy, Father, he is English!" She put her arms stiffly by her sides, pretending to be a board. "But that is outside! Inside, he is Italian, tender as fresh *ravioli*! If not this, I could not marry him and come so far from home!" She laughed with pleasure, and brushed Andrew's cheek with her hand.

"The building that contained the restaurant was being rezoned," said Andrew, "and Mrs. Nocelli died last year . . ."

Anna and Tony crossed themselves.

"The cousins had moved away, some to Rome, others to Verona; the vineyard had sold out of the family, so there were almost no ties left. Yet, when I asked Anna to marry me, I feared she wouldn't leave Italy."

Anna patted her husband's knee. "Timing is good, Father."

"Don't I know it?"

Andrew smiled easily. "The Nocellis are an old wine-making family in Lucera. We were married by their priest of many years. Fortunately, I was able to squeak in under the wire because of my Catholic boyhood."

"Your children," said the rector, "do they know?"

"Oh, yes. They came to Lucera for the wedding. They are very happy for us."

"Any children for you, Anna?"

"I never had children, Father, and my husband was killed ten years behind by a crazy person in a fast car."

"And so at Fernbank," Andrew said, "Anna and Tony and I will have our home and open a very small restaurant."

"Very small!" exclaimed Anna.

"And very good!" said Tony, giving a thumbs-up. The rector thought Tony was nearly as good-looking—and good-natured—as his sister.

Unable to sit still another moment, Andrew rose and made a proclamation. "We will call the restaurant Lucera, in honor of their lovely village and my mother's girlhood home—and the wine for the restaurant will come from one of the many old vineyards which have produced there since the tenth century."

"*Brava,* Lucera!" said Tony. "*Brava,* Mitford!"

"Good heavens!" The rector felt the wonder of it. "An Italian restaurant in Mitford, wine from old vineyards, and handsome people to live in this grand house! Miss Sadie would be dazzled. We shall all be dazzled!"

Anna stood, nearly dancing with expectation. "I am longing to visit the apples!"

"In those shoes, my dear?" asked Andrew.

"I shall take them off at once!" she said, and did so.

§

As he walked up Wisteria toward the rectory, he looked at his house in the growing darkness, trying to find the sense of ownership he expected to feel. Oh, well, he thought, that will come when the pipes burst in a hard winter and I'm the one to pick up the tab.

He patted his coat pocket. In it was a check for fifteen thousand dollars, given him at this evening's vestry meeting.

Ron Malcolm had presented it with some ceremony. "Father, we priced the house to allow for a little negotiation. H. Tide wanted it so badly, they didn't try to negotiate, so you paid top price. We all feel that ninety thousand is fair to you and to us, and . . . we thank you for your business!"

Warm applause all around.

He was feeling positively over the top. A two-story residence of native stone, all paid for, and fifteen thousand bucks in his pocket. Not bad for an old guy.

He whistled a few bars from the Pastorale as he ran up the front steps to tell his wife the good news.

§

He didn't know where Buck had moved, and though he saw the superintendent on the job site, nothing was mentioned of his new whereabouts.

Buck had left the yellow house spotless. This, however, hardly mattered, since the late-starting conversion would be getting under

way next week. It would be all sawdust and sawhorses for longer than
he cared to think, and Buck would probably leave it in someone else's
hands as soon as the attic job was finished.

He didn't want to lose Buck Leeper. In some way he couldn't explain, Buck was part of Mitford now.

§

"Timothy!"

"Stuart! I was just thinking of you."

"Good, I hope?"

"I wouldn't go that far," said the rector, chuckling. "What's up,
old friend?"

"*Old* friend. How odd you'd say that. I'm feeling a hundred and
four."

"Whatever for? You've just been where people wear bikinis."

Stuart groaned. "Yes, and where I held my stomach in for two
long weeks."

"Holding your stomach in is no vacation," said the rector.

"Look, I'm over on the highway, headed to a meeting in South
Carolina. Can we meet for coffee?"

"Coffee. Hmmm. How about the Grill? It's close to lunchtime.
I'll treat."

"Terrific. Main Street, as I recall?"

"North of The Local, green awning, name on the window.
When?"

"Five minutes," said the bishop, sounding brighter.

§

"This," he said, introducing his still-youthful seminary friend, "is
my bishop, the Right Reverend Stuart Cullen."

"Right Reverend . . ." said Percy, pondering. "I guess you wouldn't
hardly talk about it if you was th' Wrong Reverend."

"Percy!" said Velma.

"Oh, for heaven's sake, don't listen to Timothy, call me Stuart."
Stuart shook hands all around, and the rector watched him charm the
entire assembly.

"Hold it right there!" J.C. hunkered over his Nikon and cranked off six shots in rapid succession.

"I ain't never seen a pope," said Coot Hendrick, wide-eyed.

"Not a pope, a bishop," said Mule.

Percy looked puzzled. "I thought you said he was a reverend."

"Call me Stuart and get it over with," pleaded the bishop, hastening to a booth with Father Tim.

$

Stuart poured cream in his coffee. "By the way, someone told me that Abraham's route to Canaan now requires four visas."

"Not surprising, since it's a six-hundred-mile trip. I wouldn't mind seeing the real thing one day. I was just remembering from a study we did in seminary that Canaan is the birthplace of the word *Bible.*"

"Not to mention the birthplace of our alphabet. So, how would you like a stint on the Outer Banks at some point? I fancy it might be your Plain of Jezreel, at the very least."

"Tell me more."

"Wonderful parish, small Carpenter Gothic church, historic cemetery, gorgeous setting . . ."

"Keep talking."

"There's a rector down there who'd like nothing better than a mountain church. I have just the church, and Bill Harvey, who's the bishop in that diocese, thinks we might work out a trade—you could go down as an interim . . . the summer after you retire."

"I'll mention it to Cynthia. Let me know more. So when are *you* going out to Canaan, my friend?"

"I knew you'd ask, but I don't know. I'm still terrified, just as you were."

"How did I get smarter than you?"

"You're older," said Stuart, grinning. "Much older."

"Remember Edith Mallory?"

"The vulture who tried to get her talons in your hide."

"We have an election coming up, and I feel certain she's been funneling big money to the opposition."

"Who's the opposition?" asked Stuart, taking a bite of his grilled cheese sandwich.

"Not known as the sort who'd be good for this town."

"If I know where you're going with this, the best policy is hands off."

"I agree. Especially since I have no proof."

"Poisonous business. But you know the antidote."

"Prayer."

"Exactly. How's your Search Committee coming along? I haven't had a report recently."

"I'm pretty much out of the loop," said the rector, "but they seem excited. We surveyed the parish, and the consensus is for a young priest with children."

"They can save all of us some heartache by asking the candidates a central question."

"Which is?"

"'Do you believe Jesus is God?'"

"Right. I've talked about that with the committee. Sad state of affairs when we have to point such a question at candidates who took the ordination vows . . ."

The bishop sighed. "Paul said in the second epistle to the good chap you were named after, 'The time is coming when people will not put up with sound doctrine . . . they will accumulate for themselves teachers to suit their own desires, and will turn from the truth and wander away to myths.' Ah, Timothy . . ."

"Eat up, my friend. You've got a long haul ahead of you. Why aren't you flying?"

"I'm driving because I need time to think, I need some time alone."

"A man has to get in a car and hurtle down the interstate to get time alone? Ah, Stuart . . ."

Stuart chuckled. "Two weeks at the beach doesn't solve everything."

"Especially not when you're holding your stomach in," said the rector.

§

"I've done it," Winnie announced.

He couldn't tell whether she was going to laugh or cry.

"Would you take this copy of the contract home and look it over?" she asked. "I had a lawyer look it over, but I don't know how good he is, maybe if you're not too busy, you could do it, I should have asked you before. Course I guess it's too late now, since it's mailed, but still, if you would . . ."

"I don't know what help I can be, but yes, I'll look it over." Dadgum it, why didn't he just go study for a broker's license? He seemed to be spending as much time in real estate as in the priesthood.

"They've about ragged me to death, Father. I guess I'll stay on and run it." She looked white as a sheet, he thought.

"I'm thrilled to hear you'll stay in Mitford. Your business is thriving, you have a legion of friends here—"

"But my family's up there—a brother and sister and two nieces and a nephew."

"I know. But aren't we family? Don't we love you?" Shame on him, trying to win her heart from her own blood kin.

"I'll be glad to go on that cruise next week," she said, not looking glad about anything.

§

Lace was sitting at the kitchen table doing her history homework when Dooley called from school. Father Tim answered the wall phone by the sink. "Rectory . . ."

"I'm on my way to study hall."

"Hey, buddy!"

"Hey, yourself," said Dooley. "What's going on?"

"Not much. What about you?"

"We're having our fall mixer tomorrow night. Man!"

"Man, what?"

"Four busloads of girls are coming, maybe five."

"Man!" He agreed that seemed to say it all.

"How's Barn?"

"Looking good. Eating well. Sleeping a lot."

"I sort of miss him."

"He misses you more. So, what kind of mixer is it?"

"We're having a band, it's gong to be in the field house. I helped decorate."

"Aha."

"We hung a lot of sheets with wires and turned it into a huge tent. It's neat, you should see it."

"When are we coming up for a visit?"

"I'll let you know. I gotta go."

"Want to say a quick hello to Lace? She's here."

"Sure."

He handed the phone to Lace. "Dr. Barlowe."

Her smile, which he had seldom seen, was so spontaneous and unguarded, he blushed and left the room.

§

They were sitting at the table having a cup of tea as Lace organized her books and papers to go home.

"What's interesting in school these days?" Cynthia wanted to know.

"I just found out about palindromes, I'm always lookin' for 'em," she said.

"Like Bob, right?"

"Right. Words that're the same spelled forwards or backwards. Like that," she said, pointing to the contract he'd left lying on the table, "isn't a palindrome, it says H. Tide readin' forwards, and Edith if you read it backwards. But guess what, you can also make a palindrome with whole sentences, like 'Poor Dan is in a droop.'"

"Neat!" said Cynthia.

"See you later," she said, going to the basement door. "'Bye, Harley! Read your book I left on the sink!"

"What did you leave on the sink?" inquired the rector, filled with curiosity.

"Silas Marner."

"Aha. Well, come back, Lace."

"Anytime," said Cynthia.

"OK!"

He pulled the contract toward him.

EdiT .H

His blood pounded in his temples. Edith? Could H. Tide be owned by Edith Mallory?

Is that why H. Tide wanted the rectory so urgently? Edith knew he and Cynthia would be living in the yellow house. Did she want to control the house next door to him in some morbid, devious way?

"What is it, Timothy?"

"Nothing. Just thinking." He took the contract into the study and sat at his desk, looking out the window at the deepening shadows of Baxter Park.

Mack Stroupe. H. Tide. Edith Mallory.

If what Lace just prompted him to think was true, Edith was now trying to get her hands on another piece of Main Street property. The way she had treated Percy wasn't something he'd like to see happen to anyone else, especially Winnie. And what might Edith be trying to gouge from Winnie, who was selling her business without the aid of a realtor?

He glanced at the contract—it was right up there with cave-wall hieroglyphs—and called his attorney cousin, Walter. "You've reached Walter and Katherine, please leave a message at the sound of the beep. We'll return your call with haste."

Wasn't a signed contract legal and binding?

He paced the floor.

Edith Mallory had always held a lot of real estate. But why would she sell the Shoe Barn to her own company? He didn't understand this. Was he making too much of a name spelled backward?

Then again, why had Mack Stroupe swaggered around town, boasting of his influence on H. Tide's buying missions?

Another thing. Could Miami Development have anything to do with all this? Or was that merely a fluke?

He didn't know what the deal was, but he knew something was much worse than he had originally believed.

He knew it because the feeling in the pit of his stomach told him so.

§

Walter rang back.

"Cousin! What transpires in the hinterlands?"

"More than you want to know. Legal question."

"Shoot," said his cousin and lifelong best friend.

After talking with Walter, he rang an old acquaintance who worked at the state capitol. So what if it was nine-thirty in the evening and he hadn't seen Dewey Morgan in twelve years? Maybe Dewey didn't even work at the state capitol anymore.

"No problem," said Dewey, who'd received quite a bureaucratic leg up in the intervening years. "I'll call you tomorrow."

"As quickly as possible, if you'd be so kind. And if you're ever in Mitford, our guest room is yours."

"I may take you up on it. Arlene has always wanted to see Mitford."

If all the people he'd invited to use the guest room ever cashed in their invitations . . .

§

At ten o'clock, the phone rang at the church office.

"Tim? Dewey. I looked up the name of the undisclosed partner in H. Tide of Orlando, right? And also Miami Development. It says here Edith A. Mallory—both companies. Hope that's what you're looking for."

"Oh, yes," he said. "Exactly!"

He'd been looking for it, all right, but he hated finding it.

§

He pushed through the curtains to the bakery kitchen without announcing himself from the other side.

"Winnie, I've got to tell you something."

"What is it, Father? Sit down, you don't look so good."

"H. Tide is owned by someone who may not treat you very well, I won't go into the details. The truth is, you probably don't want to sell to these people and be under their management."

"Oh, no!"

"You'd be in the hands of Percy's landlord. I think you should talk to Percy."

"But I've already signed the contract and sent it off."

"And I've just talked with my cousin who's an attorney. Please.

Talk with Percy about his landlord. And if you don't like what you hear, we need to move fast."

She wiped her hands and straightened her bandanna. "Whatever you say, Father."

§

"Don't get 'is blood pressure up 'til we've served th' lunch crowd," said Velma.

She turned to Winnie. "I'm takin' three pairs of shorts, not short short, just medium, three tops, and two sleeveless dresses with my white sweater. Are you takin' a formal for Captain's Night?"

"Oh, law," said Winnie, looking addled, "I don't even have time to think about it, I don't know what I'm takin', I don't have a formal."

"Well, be sure and take a pair of shoes with rubber soles so you don't slip around on deck." Velma had been on a cruise sponsored by her children, and knew what was what.

"Velma," urged the rector, "we need to move quickly. May I ask Percy just one question? How high can his blood pressure shoot if we ask just one question?"

"Oh, all right, but don't go on and on."

Coot Hendrick banged a spoon against his water glass. Ever since Velma got invited on that cruise, she hadn't once refilled his coffee cup unless he asked for it outright.

The rector motioned to the proprietor. "Percy, give us a second, if you can."

Percy stepped away from the grill, slapping a towel over his shoulder, and came to the counter.

Why was he always putting himself in the middle of some unpleasant circumstance? Had he become the worst thing a clergyman could possibly become—a meddler?

"Percy, now, take it easy. Don't get upset. I just need you to tell Winnie about . . ."

"About what?"

"Your landlord."

The color surged into Percy's face. Two hundred and forty volts, minimum.

"Just a sentence or two," he said lamely.

§

He marched down to Sweet Stuff with Winnie, who called H. Tide to say she was withdrawing the contract. She held the phone out for him to hear the general babble that erupted on the other end.

According to Walter, until the contract had been delivered back to the seller by the buyer, either by hand or U.S. mail, it was unenforceable.

When she hung up, he went to a table out front and thumped down in a chair. His own blood pressure wasn't exactly one-twenty over eighty.

"Earl Grey!" he said to Winnie. "Straight up, and make it a double."

Once again, the candy had been snatched from Edith Mallory's hand. She'd lost Fernbank. She'd lost the rectory. And now she'd lost a prime property on Main Street.

In truth, the only property she'd been able to buy was one she already owned.

He was certain she'd make every effort not to lose Mack Stroupe.

Winnie served his tea, looking buoyant. "Lord help, I feel like a truck's just rolled off of me. Now I'm right back where I started—and glad to be there!"

"I have a verse for you, Winnie, from the prophet Jeremiah. 'The Lord is good to those whose hope is in Him, to the one who seeks Him; His compassions never fail. They are new every morning; great is His faithfulness.'"

"Have a piece of chocolate cake!" said Winnie, beaming. "Or would you like a low-fat cookie?"

§

Esther Bolick was at home and mending, Barnabas was gaining strength, the yellow house was full of sawing and sanding, Cynthia's book was finished, and Winnie and Velma had sent postcards back to Mitford.

Percy taped Velma's to the cash register.

Dear Everybody, Wish you were here, you wouldn't believe the colors of the fish, their like neon. Winnie is sunburnt. If you include the ice

cream sundae party and early bird breakfast on deck, you can eat 11 times a day. I am keeping it to 9 or 10. Ha ha.
Velma

Winnie had left a sign in her window:

Gone cruisin.' Back on October 30

Percy trotted down the street and taped her postcard next to the sign.

Hi, folks, sorry I can't be here to serve you, but I am in the Caribbean soaking up some sun. The Golden Band people had a fruit basket in our cabin and champagne which gave Velma a rash. Gosh, its beautiful down here, some places there are pigs in the road, though. Well, you keep it in the road til I get back, I will have you a big surprise in the bake case. Winnie

§

"Father? Scott Murphy!"
He could hear it in Scott's voice. "When? Who?" he asked.
"Last night! Two men who've been showing up every Wednesday, one with his kids. They said they wanted to know more about God's plan for their lives, and we talked, and they prayed and it was a wondrous thing, marvelous. Homeless is beside himself. He thinks that next summer we may be able to do what Absalom Greer did, have weekly services on the creek bank."
"You must tell me every detail," said the rector. "Want to run together tomorrow morning?"
"Six-thirty, starting from my place?"
"You got it."
Scott laughed, exultant. "Eat your Wheaties," he said.

§

Andrew rang to find out if Buck Leeper might be available for the renovation of Fernbank. "I don't think so, but I'll ask him," he said.
"I'll also be looking for a good nursery. I'd like to replace some of the shrubs and trees."

"I know a splendid nursery, though their trees are fairly small."

"At my age, Father, one doesn't permit oneself two things—young wine and small trees."

The rector laughed.

"I'd give credit to the fellow who said that, but I can't remember who it was—another distinguishing mark of advancing years."

"Come, come, Andrew. You're looking like a lad, thanks to your beautiful bride! I'm smitten with Anna, as everyone else will be. Thanks for bringing Anna and Tony to Mitford. I know they'll make a wonderful difference."

"Thank you, Father, we're anxious to get started on the hill. Anna would like to have a couple of rooms finished by Christmas, though it could take a year to do the whole job properly, given our weather."

"Let me step down to the church and see what's up. If Buck is interested, I'll have him ring you."

He left the office, zipping his jacket, eager to be in the cold, snapping air, and on a construction site where the real stuff of life was going on.

"Early December, I'm out of here," said Buck, stomping the mud off his work boots. "Your house is in good hands and I'll keep in touch, I'll check on it."

"Well, you see, there's another job for you up the hill at Fernbank. I know Andrew Gregory would be a fine person to work with, and certainly Miss Sadie would be thrilled, she was so pleased with what you did at Hope House—"

"I've laid out long enough," Buck said curtly.

Father Tim pressed on. "I believe if you stayed in Mitford, there'd be plenty of work for you. You could grow your own business."

"No way. There's nothing here for me."

He thought of Jessie and the doll . . .

"Well, then," he said, feeling a kind of despair.

§

"I brought you somethin'!" said Velma.

"Me? You brought *me* something?"

"Lookit," said Velma, taking a tissue-wrapped item from a bag.

She held up a shirt with orange, red, and green monkeys leaping around in palm trees.

"Aha. Well. That's mighty generous . . ."

"You helped Winnie win th' contest, and I got to go free, so . . ."

"I'll wear it!" he said, getting up for the idea.

"Have you seen what Winnie brought home?" asked Percy.

"Can't imagine."

"And don't you tell 'im, either," said Velma. "He gets to find that out for hisself. Go on down there and look and I'll start your order. But hop to it."

Tanned people returning from exotic places seemed to bring new energy home with them. He fairly skipped to the bake shop.

He inhaled deeply as he went in. The very gates of heaven! "Winnie!" he bellowed.

She came through the curtains. Or was that Winnie?

"Winnie?" he said, taking off his glasses. He fogged them and wiped them with his handkerchief. "Is that you?"

"Course it's me!" she said. Winnie was looking ten years younger, maybe twenty, and tanned to the gills.

"Velma said you brought something back."

"Come on," she said, laughing. "I'll show you."

He passed through the curtains and there, standing beside the ovens, was a tall, very large fellow with full, dark hair and twinkling eyes, wearing an apron dusted with flour.

"This is *him*!" crowed Winnie, looking radiant.

"Him?"

"You know, the one I always dreamed about standin' beside me in th' kitchen. Father Kavanagh, this is Thomas Kendall from Topeka, Kansas."

"What . . . where . . . ?"

"I met him on th' ship!"

"In the kitchen, actually," said Thomas, extending a large hand and grinning from ear to ear. "I'm a pastry chef, Father."

"You stole the ship's pastry chef? Winnie!"

They all laughed. "No," said Winnie, "it was his last week on the job, he was going back to Kansas and decided he'd come home with me first. He's stayin' with Velma and Percy."

No doubt about it, he was dumbfounded. First Andrew, now Winnie . . .

"He likes my cream horns," she said, suddenly shy.

"Who doesn't?"

Thomas put his arm around Winnie and looked down at her, obviously proud. "I'm mighty glad to be in Mitford," he said simply.

"By jing, we're mighty glad to have you," replied the rector, meaning it.

§

Esther Cunningham released a special news story to the *Mitford Muse,* which ran the morning before the election.

"When I'm re-elected," she was quoted as saying, "I'll give you something we've all been waiting for—new Christmas decorations!" The single ropes of lights up and down Main Street had caused squawking and grumbling for over a decade. So what if this solution had been forced by economic considerations, when it made the town look like a commuter landing strip?

"Stick with the platform that sticks by the people," said the mayor, "and I'll give you angels on Main Street!"

§

He was among the first at the polls on Tuesday morning. He didn't have to wonder about Mule's and Percy's vote, but he was plenty skeptical about J.C.'s. Had J.C. avoided looking him in the eye when they saw each other in front of Town Hall?

His eyes scanned the crowd.

The Perkinses, they were big Esther fans. And there were Ron and Wilma . . . surely the Malcolms were voting for Esther. Based on the crowd standing near the door, he figured eight or nine out of ten were good, solid, dependable *Stickin'* votes.

So what was there to worry about?

Mack's last hoorah had been another billboard, which definitely hadn't gone over well, as far as the rector could determine.

"Did you see th' pores in his face?" asked Emma, who appeared completely disgusted. They looked like craters on th' moon. If I never set eyes on Mack Stroupe again, it'll be too soon!"

From the corner of his eye, he watched her boot the computer and check her E-mail from an old schoolmate in Atlanta, a prayer chain in Uruguay, and a church in northern England. Emma Newland in cyberspace. He wouldn't have believed he'd live to see the day.

He walked up the street after lunch, leaning into a bitter wind. As Esther Bolick still wasn't going out, he hoped Gene had seen to turning in her proxy vote.

"Good crowd?" he asked at the polls.

"Oh, yes, Father. Real good. Bigger than in a long while."

He adjusted his *Stickin'* button and stood outside, greeting voters, for as long as he could bear the knifing wind.

He hoped his bishop didn't drive by.

§

"You and Cynthia come on over and bring that little fella who lives in your basement," said the mayor.

"Harley."

"Right. I'd like to get him workin' on our RV. Anyway, we're havin' a big rib feast while they count th' votes, Ray's cookin'."

"What time?" he asked, thrilled that his carefully watched food exchange would actually permit such an indulgence.

"Th' polls close at seven-thirty, be at my office at seven thirty-five."

"Done!" he said. He could just see the red splotches breaking out on the mayor.

§

Uncle Billy and Miss Rose were there when he arrived with Cynthia and Harley. Cynthia zoomed over to help Ray finish setting up the food table.

"I've done got a joke t' tell you, Preacher."

"Shoot!" he said. "And tell Harley, while you're at it."

Miss Rose sniffed and stomped away.

"Rose don't like this 'un," said Uncle Billy. "Well, sir, a feller died who had lived a mighty sinful life, don't you know. Th' minute he got down t' hell, he commenced t' bossin' around th' imps an' all, a-sayin' do this, do that, and jump to it. Well, sir, he got so dominatin' that th' little devils reported 'im to th' head devil who called th' feller in, said, 'How come you act like you own this place?'

"Feller said, 'I do own it, my wife give it to me when I was livin'.'"

Harley bent over and slapped his leg, cackling. Father Tim laughed happily. Oh, the delight of an Uncle Billy joke.

"Seein' as you like that 'un, I'll tell you 'uns another'n after we've eat."

"I'll keep up with you," promised the rector.

Aha, there was a fellow clergyman, heedlessly exposing his political views. Bill Sprouse of First Baptist bowled over with his dog, Sparky, on a leash. "Sparky and I were out walking, Esther hailed us in."

"You stuck with Esther at the polls, I devoutly hope."

"Is the Pope a Catholic?"

"You bet," said the rector, shaking his colleague's hand. "Reverend Sprouse, Harley Welch."

"Pleased to meet you, Harley. I heard you're mighty good with automobiles. Here lately, my car's been actin' funny, don't know what th' trouble is, makes a real peculiar sound. Kind of like *ooahooojigjigooump*. Like that."

Harley nodded, listening intently. "Might be y'r fan belt."

Ray Cunningham strode up, wiping his hands on a tea towel. "Got you boys some ribs laid on back there, I want you to eat up. Harley, be sure and get with me before you leave. I got a awful knock in my RV engine."

"What time do you think we'll know somethin'?" wondered Bill Sprouse.

"Oh, 'bout nine," said Ray, who, after eight elections, considered himself heavily clued in.

The rector backed away from Sparky, who seemed intent on raising his leg on his loafer.

"For th' Lord's sake, Sparky!" the preacher hastily picked up his dog, whereupon Sparky draped himself over his master's arm, looking doleful.

"Esther's got Ernestine Ivory up at th' polls where the countin's goin' on," said Ray. "She'll run down here when it's all over, shoutin' th' good news. Well, come on, boys, and don't hold back, I been standin' over a hot stove all day."

Omer rolled in, flashing a fugue in G major. "Ninth term comin' up!" he said to his sister-in-law, giving her a good pounding on the back.

§

Uncle Billy yawned hugely. "Hit's way after m' bedtime," he said as the clock struck nine. Miss Rose, who even in her sleep looked fierce, was snoring in a blue armchair transported years ago from the mayor's family room. In her hands, Miss Rose clutched several tightly sealed baggies of take-outs.

"Won't be long," announced Ray. "Doll, does Ernestine have the cell phone? She ought to at least be callin' in with a status report."

The phone rang as if on cue, making several people jump.

"Speak of th' devil," said Bill Sprouse, who often did.

The mayor bounded across the room to her desk. "Hello? Ernestine? Right. Right."

Every eye in the room was on Esther Cunningham, as the color drained slowly from her face.

"You don't mean that, Ernestine," she said in a low voice.

Everybody looked at everybody else, wondering, aghast.

Esther slowly hung up the phone.

"Mack Stroupe," she said, unbelieving, "is th' mayor of Mitford."

CHAPTER TWENTY

New Every Morning

In the stunned silence that followed the announcement of Mack Stroupe's win, Ernestine Ivory delivered yet another confounding report:

He had won by one vote.

Esther Cunningham's various red splotches congregated as a single flame as she dialed the Board of Elections bigwig at home and demanded a recount on the following Thursday.

No problem, he said.

Feeling Ray's supper turned to stone in their alarmed digestive systems, and not knowing what else to say or do, nearly everyone fled for home.

Looking ashen, Uncle Billy shook Miss Rose awake. "Esther's lost," he said.

"Esther's *boss?*" shouted Miss Rose. "She's always been boss, and always will be, so what's the commotion?"

§

As the Lord's Chapel bells tolled seven a.m., he left home with Barnabas and turned north on Main Street. Following Hal's orders, they could now cover a couple of blocks of their running route, but only at normal walking speed.

As they passed Sweet Stuff, he saw Thomas, attired in an apron and baker's hat, putting a tray of something illegal in the window. The big, dark-haired fellow looked up and smiled, waving.

This was only the second time he'd laid eyes on Thomas Kendall, yet it seemed as if the jovial baker had always been there. His face was utterly comfortable and familiar.

"Father!"

He was hoofing past the office building and closing in on the Grill when he turned around and saw Winnie. She waved furiously. "Can you come back a minute?"

Barnabas yanked the leash from his hand and galloped toward Winnie, who always smelled like something good to eat. Before she could duck, he lunged up to give her face a proper licking.

"Oh, no!" she whooped.

"The Lord is good to those whose hope is in Him," bellowed the rector, "His compassions never fail!"

Barnabas sprawled on the sidewalk, obedient. He could, not, however, resist licking the powdered sugar off Winnie's shoes.

"They are new every morning! Great is his faithfulness!"

Barnabas sighed, desisted, and rolled over on his back.

"Amen!" shouted Winnie. "You said my verse!"

"What's up with you on this glorious day?"

"Can you come in a minute, Father? We were going to call you today, we have somethin' special to tell you." He thought she might begin jumping up and down.

They trooped into the bakery, as Thomas came through the curtains with yet another tray from the kitchen.

"Good morning, Father! Top of the day! It's baclava!" The rector felt his knees grow weak as Thomas displayed the tray of honey-drenched morsels under his very nose; Barnabas salivated.

"Please have one," urged Winnie. "I never made baclava in my life, but Thomas is an expert."

Thomas decided they should all thump down and have a diamond-shaped piece of the flaky baclava. This moment's indiscretion would cramp his food exchanges for a week, mused the rector. How could he be such a reckless gambler when he appeared so altogether conservative?

"Guess what?" said Winnie, unable to wait any longer.

"I can't guess," he replied, although, in truth, he thought he might be able to.

"Thomas isn't going back to Kansas City."

"Aha."

"Not to live, anyway."

"Father," said Thomas, "I'd like to ask you for Winnie's hand in marriage."

"Aha!" Was Thomas Kendall a man of character? Would he be good for Winnie? He'd simply have to trust his instincts, which, as far as he could tell, had no reservations at all.

"He's th' one, Father," Winnie said with conviction. "God sent him."

"Well, then!"

The men laughed, then stood and embraced, slapping each other on the back. The rector pulled out a handkerchief and blew his nose.

"Oh, for gosh sake!" said Winnie, dabbing her eyes with the hem of her apron.

"I'll be gladder than glad to give you her hand in marriage, Thomas, but Winnie, what about your brother? Shouldn't he have the say in this?"

Winnie beamed. "Joe told us to ask you. He said whatever you say is fine with him." She looked proudly at the gentle man beside her.

"Would you perform the ceremony, Father? Sometime in early January? I need to run back to Kansas to see my mother and pack up a few boxes. I've lived on and off a cruise ship for fifteen years, so I haven't accumulated much." Thomas's large hand covered Winnie's.

"Velma will be matron of honor," Winnie said, barely able to contain her joy.

The rector took Winnie's other hand.

"May the Lord bless you both!" he said, meaning it.

§

"Hello, Father Kavanagh here—"

"Town Hall, tomorrow at four o'clock," said Esther Cunningham darkly. "I told th' Lord I'd give up sausage biscuits. *Pray!*"

"I *am* praying!" he exclaimed.

§

"Timothy?" Cynthia looked thoughtful. "About your hair . . ."

Not again.

"You could drive to Charlotte."

"Not in this lifetime."

"You could forgive Fancy Skinner, and—"

"I have forgiven Fancy Skinner, which has nothing to do with the fact that I will never set foot in her chair again."

She eyed him. "That's one way to put it."

"Never," he said, eyeing her back.

§

He was there at three forty-five, as was nearly everyone else, as far as he could see. Even Esther Bolick turned up, with Gene, who looked worried.

Mack Stroupe stood near the door, shaking hands as if the event were in his honor. He frequently stepped outside to smoke, where he flipped the butts into the pansy bed.

Esther Cunningham steamed in with Ray, their five beautiful daughters, and a mixture of grandchildren and great-grandchildren, including Sissy and Sassy, who had come in tow with Puny, straight from day care. He lifted Sissy into his arms and sat next to Puny in the block of seats occupied by the Cunningham contingent.

"This is the most aggravation in th' world," announced his house help. "I had to let your toilets go to come over here and mess with this foolishness."

"You can let my toilets go anytime," he said, jiggling Sissy.

She glared at Mack Stroupe, who was laughing his loud, whinnying laugh and talking with a band of supporters. "If I wadn't a Christian, I'd march over there an' scratch his eyes out!" She examined her nails, as if she might really consider doing such a thing.

Joe Joe Guthrie, Puny's husband and the Cunninghams' grandson, slipped in next to them. "What do you think, Father?"

Joe Joe looked at him the way so many had looked at him over the years, as if he could prophesy exactly how things would turn out. It was not one of the ways he enjoyed being looked at.

§

The recounting was labored, taking nearly three hours. People milled around, going in and out, smoking, muttering, laughing. Some of those accustomed to an early dinner drove over to the highway, wolfed down a pizza, and returned smelling of pepperoni.

Others stayed glued to their seats, counting every vote with the three Board of Elections officials. Sassy fell asleep, while Sissy tore around the hall as if on wheels.

At a little before seven, he moved across the aisle to sit with the Bolicks. "The end is near," said Gene, looking worn.

The votes were running neck and neck. Mack or Esther would pull ahead in the counting, and then the other would catch up and move ahead.

As the stack of ballots slowly dwindled, the laughing and muttering, hooting and yelping died down.

Something had better happen here pretty quick, he thought, as the last three ballots were held up and counted.

"Ladies and gentlemen!" exclaimed the Board of Elections official, "according to the recount, which ya'll have witnessed here with your own eyes . . . it's a tie."

A communal gasp resounded through the hall, followed by murmurs and shouts.

"What we do . . ." the elections official said, trying to speak over the hubbub. The hubbub escalated wildly.

He pounded the mayor's podium with the gavel. "According to th' by-laws, what we do in such a case is . . . we flip a coin."

The rector leaned forward in his chair. Flip a coin? You determine the well-being of a whole town by flipping a coin?

"God help us," said Esther Bolick.

He saw that Esther Cunningham had turned deathly pale. Where were the fiery splotches, the indomitable spirit? Come on, Esther . . .

He prayed the prayer that never fails.

"Ladies first," said the elections official. "Heads . . . or tails?"

Breathless silence.

Esther Cunningham stood and peered into the crowd as if she were about to deliver the Gettysburg Address.

"Heads!" she said in a voice that thundered beyond the back row and bounced off the wall.

The elections official looked toward the door. "Mr. Stroupe?"

Mack Stroupe shrugged.

The official put his hand into his pocket and brought it out again, looking embarrassed. "Ah, anybody got a nickel or a dime?"

Someone rushed to give him a quarter, as the other two officials drew near, ready to verify the outcome.

He took a deep breath, cleared his throat, and bowed slightly over the coin. Then, working his mouth silently as if uttering an official oath, he flipped it.

§

Around Town
—by Vanita Bentley

Last night, in the parish hole of Lord's Chapel, Bane and Blessing co-chairs Esther Bolick and Hessie Mayhe, were feted at a supper in their honor.

Along with nearly eighty voluntears, some from other Mitford churches, Bolck and Mayhew raised $22,000 and were praised for their "heroic endeavor" by Father Timothy Kavanagh.

"Hero simply means someone who models the ideal" said Rev. Kavanagh, "and these voluntears have done this for all of us.

"Also, a hero can be someone who saves lives in a valiant way and these voluntears have almost certainly done that, as well."

The reverend said Bane proceeds have been used for food

and medical supplys to Zaiear, pure well water in several east African villages, and a ambulance for Landon, where two children died last yr for lack of medical ade.

"The Bane has always been a blessing to others," he said. "But this year, thanks to the outstanding organizational skills of two women and their willingness to serve as unto the Lord, we may all celebrate a special triumph for His kingdom."

Bolk and Mayew were presented with plaques and other voluntears were each given a bag of goodies by local merchants.

Mrs. Bvolk whose jaws were wired shut due an accident reported here previously got to request a special dinner of mashed potatoes and gravey to celebrate being able to eat real food again.

§

If time does, indeed, fly, it was the season when it became a Concorde jet, as far as the rector was concerned.

Following the annual All-Church Thanksgiving Feast, which, thankfully, was held this year at First Baptist, events went into overdrive.

Cynthia drove Dooley back to school on St. Andrew's Day, while the rector prepared the sermon for the first Sunday of Advent and began the serious business of trying to juggle the innumerable Advent activities, not the least of which was Lessons and Carols, to be performed this year on a grand scale with the addition of a visiting choir and an organist from Cambridge, England, all of whom would stay over in parish homes for five days and participate in the Advent Walk on December 15, after which everyone would come to the rectory for a light supper in front of the fire.

"Light supper, heavy dessert," said Cynthia, paging frantically through their cookbooks.

He panted just thinking about it all, and so did his wife, who was making something for everyone on her list, and running behind.

"Whatever you do," she told him at least three times, "don't look in *there*." Upon saying this, she would point to the armoire, which he always stayed as far away from as possible.

Then, of course, there was the annual trek into the woods at the north end of the Fernbank property, to hew down a Fraser fir with the Youth Group, which would become the Jesse tree in front of the altar, followed by a visit to the Sunday School to discuss the meaning of the ornaments the children would be making for the tree, and the courtesy call on the Christmas pageant rehearsal, which this year, much to the shock of the parents and the dismay of at least two teachers, would be done in modern dress, inspired by the recent success of the movie *Hamlet* in which Hamlet had worn blue jeans with what appeared to be a golf shirt.

"What will we do with all these *wings*?" wailed a teacher who had voted for traditional costumes, and lost.

He made himself scarce whenever the wrangling over the pageant issue erupted, and gave himself to the more rewarding annual task of negotiating with Jena Ivey for forty-five white poinsettias and the cartload of boxwood, balsam, fir, and gypsophila to be used on Christmas Eve for the greening of the church.

"Why can't you do the negotiating?" he once asked a member of the Altar Guild.

"Because she likes you better and you get a better price," he was told. This notion of improved economics had engraved the mission in stone and caused it to belong, forever, to him.

He had to remember to order the Belgian chocolates for the nurses at the hospital, and meet with the organist and choir director to thrash through the music for the Christmas Eve services, and put in his two cents' worth about the furniture being ordered for the new upstairs Sunday School rooms, and call Dooley's schoolmate's parents to see if they'd bring him to Mitford on their way to Holding, and check to see if anybody was going to visit Homeless Hobbes and sing carols with him this year, and go through what Andrew Gregory didn't want at Fernbank and help Harley haul it to Pauline's tiny house behind the post office so it would look like a home in time for . . .

"We've done it again," proclaimed his wife, shaking her head.

They gazed at each other, spent and pale.

"Next year," she said, relieved, "it will be different."

Next year, he would not be running around like a chicken with its head cut off, because next year, he would not have a parish.

Suddenly his eyes misted, just thinking about it.

Less than twelve months hence, his parishioners would be standing around him in the parish hall, singing "For he's a jolly good fellow," and giving him money, and a plaque of some sort, and tins of mixed nuts.

§

After the wedding, Winnie and Thomas planned to move into her cottage by the creek, while Scott Murphy would move his wok and precious few other possessions into Winnie's present quarters, once the home of Olivia Harper's socialite mother.

"Musical chairs!" said Cynthia.

§

It was the season of good news and glad tidings, in every way. Joe Ivey was moving back to Mitford.

"Hallelujah!" Father Tim said.

Winnie looked pleased as punch. "He said people kept askin' if Elvis was really dead, and he just couldn't take it anymore. He'll barber in that little room behind th' Sweet Stuff kitchen."

"Baking and barbering!" said the jubilant rector. "I like it!" A little off the sides and a fruit tart to go.

§

"Look!" said Jessie. "A baby in a box."

She stood on tiptoes, holding her doll, and gazed into the crèche that had belonged to his grandmother.

He realized she didn't know about the Babe, and wondered how his life could be so sheltered that he should be surprised.

He glanced at his watch and picked her up and stood looking down upon the crèche with her. Standing there in the lamplit study, he told her about the Babe and why He came, as she sucked her thumb and patted his shoulder and listened intently.

Four days before Christmas, and he was running ragged like the rest of crazed humanity. He resisted glancing at his watch again, and set her down gently as the front doorbell gave a blast.

If that wasn't a fruitcake from the ECW, he'd eat his hat. Or, more likely, it was the annual oranges from Walter.

"I came to say . . . so long." Buck Leeper stood in the stinging cold, bareheaded.

He had dreaded this moment. "Come in, Buck!"

"I can't, I'm on my way to Mississippi, I just—"

"Buck!" Jessie came trotting down the hall and grabbed the superintendent around the legs, as Barnabas raced in from the kitchen, barking.

"Please," said the rector, standing back for Buck to come in. "We're keeping Jessie while Pauline shops for pots and pans. Come on back, we'll scare up something hot for the road."

"Well," Buck said, awkward, then stooped and picked Jessie up in his arms.

They walked down the hall and into the study, where a fire simmered on the hearth. Buck stood in the doorway as if in a trance, taking in the tree ablaze with tiny lights and the train running around its base.

Suddenly the rector saw the room with new eyes, also—the freshly pungent garlands over the mantel and the candles burning on his desk, reflected in the window. He had been passing in and out of this room for days, scarcely noticing, enjoying it with his head instead of his heart.

Buck abruptly set Jessie down and squatted beside her on one knee. "Look, you have a good Christmas," he said, speaking with some difficulty.

Her eyes filled with tears. "Buck, please don't go off nowhere!"

"I've got to," he said.

She threw her arms around his neck, sobbing. "Me an' Poo wanted you to live with us!"

Buck held her close and covered his eyes with his hand.

"Don't cry," said Jessie, clinging to him and patting his shoulder. "Please don't cry, Buck."

He stood and wiped his eyes on the sleeve of his jacket. "Thanks for . . . everything. Your job is in good hands. I'll let myself out."

Buck stalked out of the study and up the hall, closing the front door behind him. The rector had been oddly frozen in place, unable to move; Jessie stood at the study door, crying, holding her doll.

The clock ticked, the train whistled and clacked, the fire hissed.

He walked over to her with a heavy heart and touched her shoulder.

She looked up at him, stricken. "Buck shouldn't of done that," she said.

§

Seven-thirty a.m., and he'd already gone through yesterday's mail, typed two letters, and been to see Louella.

Surely he could take ten minutes . . .

He walked to the end of the corridor and opened the door without knocking, just as he'd always done.

"Oh, rats, I might have known that was you," said Esther Cunningham, using both hands to hide something on her desk.

"What's the deal? What're you hiding? Aha! A sausage biscuit!"

"It's no such thing, it's a *ham* biscuit!"

"Sausage, ham, what's the difference?"

"I specifically spoke to th' Lord about *sausage*," she said, her eyes snapping, "so lay off."

"Esther, Esther."

He sat down and put his feet up on the Danish modern coffee table, grinning.

She grinned in return, gave him a thumbs-up, then threw back her head and roared with laughter.

Ah, but it was good to hear the mayor laughing again.

§

As a bachelor, he had wondered every year what to do on Christmas eve. With both a five o'clock and a midnight service, he struggled to figure out when or what to eat, whether to open a few presents after he returned home at nearly one a.m. on Christmas morning, or wait and do the whole thing on Christmas afternoon while he was still exhausted from the night before.

Now it was all put into perspective and, like his bishop who loved being told what to do for a change, he listened eagerly to his wife.

"We're having a sit-down dinner at two o'clock on Christmas Eve, and we'll open one present each before we go to the midnight service. We will open our presents from Dooley on Christmas morning, because he can't wait around 'til us old people get the stiffness out of our joints, and after brunch at precisely one o'clock, we'll open the whole shebang."

She put her hands on her hips and continued to dish out the battle plan.

"For brunch, of course, we'll invite Harley upstairs. The menu will include roasted chicken and oyster pie, which I'll do while you squeeze the juice and bake the asparagus puffs."

All she needed was a few military epaulets.

"After that, Dooley will go to Pauline's and spend the night, and our Christmas dinner will be served in front of the fire, and we shall both wear our robes and slippers!"

She took a deep breath and smiled like a schoolgirl. "How's that?"

How was that? It was better than good, it was wonderful, it was fabulous. He gave her a grunting bear hug and made her laugh, which was a sound he courted from his overworked wife these days.

§

He reached up to the closet shelf for the camera and touched the box of his mother's things—the handkerchiefs, her wedding ring, an evening purse, buttons . . .

He stood there, not seeing the box with his eyes, but in his memory. It was covered with wallpaper from their dining room in Holly Springs a half century, an eon, ago. Cream colored roses with pale green leaves . . .

He would not take it down, but it had somehow released memories of his mother's Christmases, and the scent of chickory coffee and steaming puddings and cookies baking on great sheets; his friends from seminary gathering 'round her table; and the guest room with its swirl of gifts and carefully selected surprises, tied with the signature white satin ribbon.

He stood there, still touching the box, recalling what C. S. Lewis had said. It was something which, long ago, had expressed his own feelings so clearly.

"With my mother's death," Lewis wrote, "all settled happiness, all that was tranquil and reliable, disappeared from my life. There was to be much fun, many pleasures, many stabs of Joy; but no more of the old security. It was sea and islands now; the great continent had sunk like Atlantis. . . ."

"Mother . . ." he whispered into the darkened warmth of the closet. "I remember. . . ."

§

He wasn't surprised that he hadn't seen Mack Stroupe again at Lord's Chapel. It appeared that even his hotdog stand was closed—perhaps for the holidays, he thought.

He didn't want to consider whether he'd ever see Edith Mallory again.

§

"I do this every year!" said Cynthia, looking alarmed.

"Do what?"

"Forget the cream for tomorrow's oyster pie. And of course no one will be open tomorrow."

It was that lovely lull between the five o'clock and midnight services of Christmas Eve, and he was sitting by the fire in a state of contentment that he hadn't felt in some time. Tonight, after the simplicity of the five o'clock, which was always held without the choir and the lush profusion of garlands and greenery, would come the swelling rush of voices and organ, and the breathtaking spectacle of the nave bedecked, as if by grace, with balsam, fir, and the flickering lights of candles.

He roused himself as from a dream. "I'll run out and find some. I think Hattie Cloer is open 'til eight."

"I'm so sorry."

"Don't be. You cook, I fetch. I get a much better deal." He took her face in his hands and kissed her on the forehead, then went to the kitchen peg for his jacket.

"Man! What's that terrific smell?" He sniffed the air, homing in on the oven.

"Esther's orange marmalade cake! Vanita Bentley gave me a bootleg copy of her recipe. She ran off dozens on her husband's Xerox."

"Where's your conscience, Kavanagh?"

"Don't worry, this is legal. I called Esther and she gave me permission to use it. Have at it! she said."

"Oh, well," he sighed, feeling diabetic and out of the loop.

"You can have the tiniest sliver, dearest. I'm sure your food exchange will allow it."

If she only knew. "Harley!" he called down the basement stairs. "Want to run to the highway?"

"Yessir, Rev'rend, I do, I'm about t' gag on this book about that feller hoardin' 'is gold."

He heard Dooley and Barnabas clambering down from above. "Where're you going?" asked Dooley.

"To the store. Want to come?"

"Sure. Can I drive?"

"Well . . ."

"You said I could when I came home for Christmas."

"Right. Consider it done, then!" Perfect timing! It was just getting dark, and hardly a soul would be out on a cold Yuletide eve.

Harley came up the stairs, wearing a fleece-lined jacket that he'd found, good as new, at the Bane. "I was hopin' f'r a excuse t' lay that book down. It ain't even got a picture in it!"

Barnabas stood in the fray, wagging his tail and hoping to be invited, as the doorbell gave a sharp blast.

"I'll get it!" said the rector, hurrying along the hall.

It was Buck Leeper, standing in the pale glow of the porch light.

"I got as far as Alabama and turned around," he said. "I'm willing to do whatever it takes."

CHAPTER TWENTY-ONE

Lion and Lamb

Buck was shaking as they went into the study. Though the rector knew it wasn't from the cold, he asked him to sit by the fire.

There was a long silence as Buck waited for the trembling to pass; he sat with his head down, looking at the floor. The rector remembered the times of his own trembling, when his very teeth chattered as from ague.

"Does Pauline know you're back in Mitford?"

"No. I came for . . . I came for this." He looked up. "I didn't want to come back."

"I know."

"It was sucking the life out of me all the way. I was driving into Huntsville when I knew I couldn't keep going . . ."

He was shaking again, and closed his eyes. Father Tim could see a muscle flexing in his jaw.

"God a'mighty," said Buck.

Father Tim looked at him, praying. The man who had controlled some of the biggest construction jobs in the Southeast and some of the most powerful machinery in the business couldn't, at this moment, control the shaking.

"I pulled into an Arby's parkin' lot and sat in the car and tried to pray. The only thing that came was somethin' I'd heard all those years in my grandaddy's church." Buck looked into the fire. "I said, Thy will be done."

"That's the prayer that never fails."

The clock ticked.

"He can be for your life what the foundation is for a building."

Buck met his gaze. "I want to do whatever it takes, Father."

"In the beginning, it takes only a simple prayer. Some think it's too simple, but if you pray it with your heart, it can change everything. Will you pray it with me?"

"I don't know if I can live up to . . . whatever."

"You can't, of course. No one can be completely good. The point is to surrender it all to him, all the garbage, all the possibilities. All."

"What will happen when . . . I pray this prayer?"

"You mean what will happen now, tonight, in this room?"

"Yes."

"Something extraordinary could happen. Or it could be so subtle, so gradual, you'll never know the exact moment He comes in."

"Right," said Buck, whispering.

The rector held out his hand to a man he'd come to love, and they stood before the fire and bowed their heads.

"Thank You, God, for loving me . . ."

"Thank You, God . . ." Buck hesitated and went on, "for loving me."

". . . and for sending Your Son to die for my sins. I sincerely repent of my sins, and receive Christ as my personal savior."

The superintendent repeated the words slowly, carefully.

"Now, as Your child, I turn my entire life over to You."

". . . as Your child," said Buck, weeping quietly, "I turn my entire life over to You."

"Amen."

"Amen."

He didn't know how long they stood before the fire, embracing as brothers—two men from Mississippi; two men who had never known the kindness of earthly fathers; two men who had determined to put their lives into the hands of yet another Father, one believing—and one hoping—that He was kindness, Itself.

§

In the kitchen, Cynthia said, "You won't believe this! Look!"

She pointed under the kitchen table, where Barnabas and Violet were sleeping together. The white cat was curled against the black mass of the dog's fur, against his chest, against the healing wound.

Father Tim sank to his knees, astounded, peering under the table with unbelieving eyes.

"It's a miracle," Cynthia told Buck. "They've been mortal enemies for years. You can't imagine how he's chased her, and how she's despised him."

Barnabas opened one eye and peered at the rector, then closed it.

"The lion shall lie down with the lamb!" crowed Cynthia.

"Merry Christmas, one and all!" whooped the rector.

"Merry Christmas!" exclaimed his wife.

"Right," said Buck. "You, too."

"I thought you'd never get finished." Dooley came up the basement steps with Harley. "Hey, Buck, I thought you'd left for Mississippi. How's it goin'?"

"Real good, what are you up to?"

Dooley pulled a pair of gloves out of his jacket pocket. "I'm drivin' to the store! Let's bust out of here, I'm ready."

"Settin' on high idle, is what he is," said Harley.

They trooped to the garage and pushed the button that opened the automatic door. It rose slowly, like a stage curtain, on a scene that stopped them in their tracks.

"Snow!" Dooley shouted.

It was swirling down in large, thick flakes and already lay like a frosting of sugar on the silent lawn.

"Maybe you'd better let me drive," said the rector.

"I can drive in snow! Besides, I won't go fast, I'll go really slow."

"I don't reckon they's any cows out plunderin' around in this, Rev'rend."

Buck and Harley climbed into the backseat, and he slid in beside Dooley. "This isn't Harley's truck, buddy, so there's no clutch. Remember to keep your left foot—"

"I know how," said Dooley.

As they turned right on Main Street, there they were, on every lamppost—angels formed of sparkling lights, keeping watch over the snow-covered streets.

"By jing," said Harley, "hit's another world!"

"Glorious!" said the rector. The Buick seemed to be floating through a wonderland, lighter than air. He turned the radio to his favorite music station. *Hark the herald angels . . .*

"Buck, where are you staying?"

"I'll bunk in with one of my crew for a couple days, then head back. Emil's got me on a big job in Texas startin' January."

"Why don't you bunk in with us? Harley, would you let Buck use your sofa bed? Cynthia's using the guest room as a gift-wrapping station."

"Hit'd be a treat. I sleep s' far down th' hall, I don't reckon I'd keep you awake with m' snorin'."

"And you'll have brunch with us tomorrow, if that suits."

"I'd like that," said Buck. "Thank you."

Dooley braked at the corner. "Let's ride by Mama's, want to?"

"I'll go anywhere you 'uns say," declared Harley.

"We'll just ride by and honk th' horn," said Dooley, "then let's ride by some more places before we go to the store, OK?"

The rector grinned. "Whatever you say, buddy. You're driving."

Dooley turned left at the corner and made a right into the alley. Pauline's small house, nestled into a grove of laurels, was a cheerful sight, with the lights of a tree sparkling behind its front windows and the snow swirling like moths around the porch light.

Dooley hammered on the horn, and the rector cranked his window down as Pauline, Poo, and Jessie appeared at the door.

"Look, Mama, I'm drivin'!"

"Dooley! Father! Can you come in?" She peered at the rear window, but was unable to see anyone in the darkened backseat.

"We're on a mission to the store, but we'll see you tomorrow. Merry Christmas! Stay warm!"

"Merry Christmas, Mama, Jessie, Poo! See you tomorrow!"

"Merry Christmas! We're bakin' the ham you sent, Father, be careful, Dooley!"

"Merry Christmas, Mr. Tim!"

Sammy and Kenny, thought the rector. He hoped he would live to see the day . . .

Dooley put the Buick in low gear and glided off.

"Burn rubber!" yelled Poo.

At the end of the alley, Buck leaned forward, urgent. "Father, I can't . . . I'd like to go back and see Pauline and the kids. Do you think it would be all right?"

Dooley spoke at once. "I think it would."

"Go," said the rector.

In the side mirror, he saw Buck running along the alley, running toward the light that spilled onto the snow from the house in the laurels.

§

"The last time we had snow at Christmas, we burned the furniture, remember that?" he asked, as Dooley turned onto Main Street. It was, in fact, the blizzard the media had called the Storm of the Century.

Dooley cackled. "We were bustin' up that ol' chair and throwin' it in th' fireplace, and fryin' baloney . . ."

"Those were the good old days," sighed the rector, who certainly hadn't thought so at the time.

Dashing through the snow . . .

He was losing track of time, happy out here in this strange and magical land where hardly a soul marred the snow with footprints, where Dooley sang along with the radio, and Harley looked as wide-eyed as a child. . . .

And there was Fernbank, ablaze with lights through the leafless winter trees, crowning the hill with some marvelous presence he'd never seen before. He wanted suddenly to see it up close, feel its warmth, discover whether it was real, after all, or a fanciful dream come to please him at Christmas.

"Want to run by Jenny's?" he asked. "It's on the way to the store."

"Nope," said Dooley. "Let's go by Lace's."

"Excellent! Then we can run over to Fernbank while we're at it."

"And by Tommy's! He'll hate my guts."

"Anywhere you want to run, Harley?"

"No, sir, I've done run to where I want t' go, hit's right here with you 'uns."

They should have brought presents—fruitcakes, candy, tangerines! He was wanting to hand something out, give something away, make someone's face light up . . .

Bells on bobtail ring, making spirits bright, what fun it is to ride and sing a sleighing song tonight! Hey! . . .

They honked the horn in the Harper driveway and shouted their season's greetings, then drove up the long, winding lane to Fernbank, where he would have been contented merely to sit in the car and look at its lighted rooms with a candle in every window.

They circled around to the front steps and honked, as Andrew and Anna came to the door and opened it and waved, calling out felicitations of their own. "Don't mention this to Rodney Underwood!" he said to the couple on the porch.

Andrew laughed. "Our lips are sealed! *Joyeux noël!*"

"*Ciao!*" cried Anna. "Come soon again!"

They eased down the Fernbank drive and saw the town lying at the foot of the steep hill like a make-believe village under a tree. There was the huge fir at Town Hall with its ropes of colored lights, and the glittering ribbon of Main Street, and the shining houses.

An English writer, coincidentally named Mitford, had said it so well, he could recite it like a schoolboy.

She had called her village "a world of our own, close-packed and insulated like . . . bees in a hive or sheep in a fold or nuns in a convent or sailors in a ship, where we know everyone, and are authorized to hope that everyone feels an interest in us."

Go tell it on the mountain, over the hills and everywhere . . .

After a stop by Tommy's and then by Hattie Cloer's, they headed home.

"Harley, want to have a cup of tea with us before tonight's service?"

"No, sir, Rev'rend, I'm tryin' t' fool with a batch of fudge brownies to bring upstairs tomorrow."

Temptation on every side, and no hope for it.

"Say, Dad, want to watch a video before church? Tommy loaned me his VCR. It's a baseball movie, you'll like it."

If there were a tax on joy on this night of nights, he'd be dead broke.

"Consider it done!" he said.

He sat clutching the pint of cream in a bag, feeling they'd gone forth and captured some valuable trophy or prize, as they rode slowly between the ranks of angels on high and turned onto their trackless street.

About the Author

Jan Karon, who lives in Blowing Rock, North Carolina, was an award-winning advertising executive before following her dream of writing books. She is the author of three previous Mitford novels, *At Home in Mitford*, *A Light in the Window*, and *These High, Green Hills,* all available from Penguin. *At Home in Minford* was named an ABBY Honor Book by the American Booksellers Association.

More from Mitford

All the Mitford books, read by the author, are available on audio-cassette from Penguin Audiobooks.

If you would like a free copy of *More from Mitford*, an entertaining newsletter about Mitford, written by Jan Karon, and/or a newly revised reading-group guide to the Mitford books, please send your request to:

Penguin Marketing Dept. CC
More from Mitford
375 Hudson St.
New York, NY 10014